The Devil of Light

A Cass Elliot Crime Novel

Gae-Lynn Woods

Dead Head Press

Copyright

For Martyn, for that very expensive cup of coffee.

Why do the wicked have it so good, live to a ripe old age and get rich?

Job 21:7

PROLOGUE

THE MOON VANISHED AS the first raindrop plunked into a bucket, rippling its dark surface. Hitch looked heavenward and sucked a last drag, the lines in his face etched deeper in the ember's glow. Crushing the cigarette against his boot, he shoved the butt into a pocket, pausing beneath wide limbs as the next flush of drops chattered across the river's surface and left smoking dimples in the dusty clearing. A lone cloud whisked its bulk beyond the moon's face, releasing the starlight and carrying its payload of tiny missiles deeper into the forest. He tugged his work gloves on and snapped lids on buckets, enjoying the creak of heavy rope against the still night.

He'd first killed for the old man in the autumn. Fresh from prison, he was toying with but unable to fully grasp the idea of living a clean life. He honored no particular religion, but somehow knew that God had created each man for a purpose. And try as he might, he couldn't find a purpose for which he was better suited than killing. Oddly enough, he'd been popped for armed robbery – not one of his God-given talents, obviously – but never for the lives he had taken. Spat out of the justice system and grateful to breathe free again, he drifted from town to town using false identities and traded manual labor for cash, careful to avoid any place small enough that a strange face would attract attention, sampling the taste of a life without death.

He'd come across the old man in the feed store outside of Arcadia while loading another man's order of hay. Although neither spoke, each recognized in the other something he needed, and in himself, something he was willing to give in return. Hitchhiking back into town, he was unsurprised when the old man pulled alongside him on the highway.

To his credit, the old man had spoken little, stating only that he had an opening for a crew boss on one of his cattle ranches. Pay wasn't much, but the man who took the job would have a roof to himself and access to a

1

vehicle. If things worked out, the old man added, more lucrative work would find him.

He'd listened, nose full of the pickup's ancient vinyl scent and the sweet smell of cherry tobacco, watching the tight jaw bristling with white five o'clock shadow as it bunched around the pipe clenched between thin lips. With a glance away from the road, the old man had asked for his name. He'd looked out the window and remembered his outstretched thumb, a dry smile on his lips.

"Hitch," he stated, setting the old man to laughing.

"Good," came the reply, chortle dying away. "I need a man who don't gab like some woman." The old man slipped a shiny cell phone from his shirt pocket and passed it across the cab. "It's clean. Set with my number. Once you're with me, you won't come into town. My wife'll do what shopping you need." He sucked on the empty pipe as they pulled up to a dingy motel. "Put your notice in at the feed store. Two weeks. I'll expect to hear from you then."

Hitch paused, hand on the door. "What should I call you?"

The old man grinned, long teeth gleaming faint green in the blue light stuttering from the motel's sign. "Sir."

"Yes, sir. Two weeks."

He shut the pickup's door, watched the old man drive away and felt as if he'd made a pact with the devil. The thought was oddly exhilarating for a man who had been thinking of going straight. Hunching his shoulders against a sudden chill, he slid the phone into his jeans pocket and headed inside.

But that had been months ago. Good to his word, the old man had set him up with legitimate work as crew boss, and with illegitimate work as need dictated. Hitch possessed special skills that the old man had sensed and used; cautiously at first, and now, it seemed, with more confidence. His eyes followed the strong length of trunk upward to a thick branch, pleased that his improvised pulley system was working. The first time, last autumn, he had still been dithering over that mythical clean life, and truth be told, his stretch in Huntsville had left him out of practice. He completed the task with a measure more mess and less productivity than he would have liked – he'd discovered long ago that a job poorly completed left its mark on the soul – but he followed the old man's instructions as closely as possible.

Hitch had dressed and dumped the corpse where instructed, taking with him one small bucket and a newspaper wrapped package.

The old man was disappointed with the bucket's weight but had cackled with pleasure at the sight of the wetback's foot nestled in the previous day's sports section. Patting Hitch on the back, he had told him where to find payment for this unusual job and instructed him to consider what he would do differently given the same set of instructions.

And so he had. He was back in the same small clearing in the early spring, but this time with the tools to make his work much easier.

Hitch gazed up again at the clear sky and was tempted to smoke another cigarette, but shook off the urge. He removed his leather work gloves and replaced them with heavy latex before he took the drill apart and wrapped it in a towel to be cleaned later. The buckets were warm and heavy as he lifted them into the passenger side floor of the old truck. Hitch climbed behind the wheel and with a low growl from the engine, slowly reversed the pickup beneath the motionless form suspended between heaven and earth, catching the young body just at the shoulders. When he glanced in the rearview mirror at the dead man's legs, bound together and pointing toward the stars, his soul sang with satisfaction. Death was his purpose, and no one was better at it than him.

CHAPTER 1

Saturday

DETECTIVE MITCH STONE WAS out cold, head mashed into the window, lip raised in a snarl where his face had slid from its original position. Drool snaked down the glass, shimmering in the glow from the dashboard lights. His partner glanced at his reflection in the dark windshield and twisted in the driver's seat, irritation flaring as she searched for a comfortable position. Mitch was sixteen years her senior but he looked younger than forty-one, his blonde hair still fair, body respectably muscled with little effort on his part, the few lines on his face only adding to his charm. *Perhaps*, she thought, *he looks so good because he can slip into a dead sleep no matter the situation.*

Cass Elliot drew a deep breath and slowly released it. Her irritation wasn't directed at Mitch. She'd been lost in a black funk during the hours they'd spent on the road today. Wondering again why Sheriff Hoffner had bothered to hire and promote her, the first woman detective in Forney County, only to look right through her even when she was standing in front of him. As Mitch settled against the passenger door and began to snore, her thoughts had whirled farther back in time, searching the events of that night long ago, seeking clues to the identity of the man who had changed the course of her life. She was sucked again into an ugly pit of anger and helplessness. The dreams had been worse lately; they jolted her awake with the phantom sensation of fire streaking across her breast and a scream frozen in her throat.

She glanced in the rearview mirror and caught the fury in the flat line of her mouth and the contraction of her brow. Again she breathed deeply, forced the tension from her body and felt exhaustion ooze in to fill the void. When she checked her reflection again, her violet eyes were still weary and her creamy skin too pale, but the imprint of anger and fear on her features was gone. Cass looked at her sleeping partner and snorted in reluctant amusement, resisting the urge to lower his window. Instead, she raised Queen's "Fat Bottomed Girls" into audible range on the radio.

One blue eye stuttered open. "Are we home yet?"

"Almost." Her stomach gurgled. "Is Darla there?"

Mitch straightened his long form, gently rocking his head from side to side and swiping at his chin. Stifling a yawn, he checked his watch. "She should be by now. Probably have Zeus with her. Which one of your brothers is cooking?"

"Bruce. Harry'll be there and *want* to cook, but Bruce will have control. He always does in the Elliot kitchen. Harry has the girls this weekend so he'll be wrapped up with them anyway. If Daddy's home, he'll stay out of their way." She grinned, a movement that brought mischievousness to her delicate features. "We're pretty dysfunctional, aren't we?"

"When you add up all six brothers, yeah, you're more Munsters than Brady Bunch," he teased. "So, how do you feel about today?"

"My butt is numb."

"It's a long road from Arcadia, Texas to El Dorado, Arkansas, I'll give you that."

"We still have no motive or suspects." She released the steering wheel and twisted her thick coppery hair into a loose knot at the base of her neck. "We're not any closer to closing his case," she said as she glanced at the file resting on the console between them, "this Humberto Gonzalez. We know so little about him, about what he was doing in Arcadia, what happened to his foot."

"It's not easy to hack a foot off. Somebody wanted it for something. And why was Humberto wearing a woman's jogging suit? Think he was a cross-dresser?"

"If he was, he didn't know how to pick his clothes. That jogging suit was at least one size too small. I wonder," she said, braking gently for three deer grazing on the tender spring grass by the road, "if that pink outfit might be a signature."

Mitch laughed.

"What's so funny?"

"Come on, Cass. No self-respecting serial killer would dress his victims like that. The press would have a field day – the Pink Assassin, the Pepto Pervert, the Crimson Killer. Wait, I like that one –"

"Good point," she chuckled. "Besides, why would a serial killer bother with Arcadia? Nothing ever happens around here."

CHAPTER 2

"WELL, F- ME." MARK Grove stood in the middle of the road. The sky above was littered with faintly glowing stars. Darkness was deep on the countryside and the trees flanking the road were visible only as a shadowy mass against the blackness of the night. He looked to the east, then to the west, gazing down the satiny ribbon of blacktop. It was empty. Saturday night in the middle of nowhere meant the county roads would be quiet until curfew time. He turned back to the car and took in his mirror image.

Matt Grove looked from the car to the body on the side of the road, scratching his scraggly beard. "Dude. That was almost a dollar for the cuss bucket."

"How bad is it?"

"Fender's dented. I might be able to pop it out, but not until we get home."

"Shoot," Mark said, running a hand along his stubbly cheek and envying his brother's decision to grow a beard. "I guess we'd better take the body home."

Matt's mouth dropped open. "What for?"

"How else are we gonna convince Momma this wasn't our fault?"

"Hey man, you were driving."

"You were in the car. That's guilt by association. And she's already mad because we're late."

"That's your fault. If you'd kept your phone charged –"

"And if you'd *brought* your damn phone we wouldn't be having this conversation, would we, dickweed? Get the extension cord."

Matt slunk away to open the hatch. The car was an old but well maintained Chevy Vega, a good starter car for most sixteen year olds, but maybe not for these two. These were the Grove boys. Six feet five inches tall and finally gaining some control over their very long limbs. They were murder on the basketball court and the track field, and now it seemed they

7

were murder on the road.

"What are we tying it up for?"

"Do you know how to tell if a deer's alive?"

"Good point. By the way, that's a dollar for the cuss bucket. Might be two. Don't know about dickweed."

"What *is* your obsession with the cuss bucket? Mom's not even around."

"The more you put in, the sooner I eat all the pizza the all-you-can-eat buffet will let me."

"It's alive," Mark said, rubbing his shirtsleeve across his forehead as they finished hog-tying the deer.

"How do you know that, Einstein?"

"It snorted. Or farted."

"Great."

"Lift on three."

Grunting with the effort, they heaved the unconscious deer into the back of the Vega. The car moaned with the added weight, creaking as they shoved the lifeless body deeper into the hatch area. Breathing heavily, they leaned against the car.

"You get us into some serious messes."

"Hey man, it could have been you. The coin just flipped my way, and –"

"What's that?" Matt asked, pointing into the woods. A light bobbed faintly in the distance.

"Not a flashlight."

"More like a torch."

They exchanged grins and trotted for the tree line, watching for a fence but finding none. The boys spotted a reddish glow and pushed underbrush aside to change direction, marking their trail. They moved forward another fifty yards and the smell of campfire underpinned with a slight tang hung in the air. The torchlight had vanished, either by virtue of distance or because it had been extinguished.

"Ouch! Damn honey locusts. I hate those things."

"That's another dollar," Matt said.

"Shut up."

They came to the edge of a clearing and hovered outside the perimeter, watching for movement. It was a crude circle no more than twenty feet across, a natural break in the woods rather than an area hacked open by man. The remains of a fire glowed inside a protective circle of small stones. Larger stones provided seating around the fire pit and the boys moved forward eagerly.

The seating stones were still warm and the stench hung heavier here. The underlying tang they had smelled in the woods had blossomed into a stinging odor.

"Nasty."

"What did they cook?"

"Something with feathers on it," Mark said, pointing to white down that clung to the stones ringing the fire.

"Think they would've plucked it first." Matt stepped into the woods and twisted a branch from a bush. He poked at the ash. "They couldn't have eaten it. Too foul." He honked with laughter. "No pun intended, of course."

"Lame, dickhead. If they didn't eat it, what'd they cook it for?"

Matt shrugged, using the stick to scoot a small bone to the edge of the pit. "They leave anything?"

The two scavenged around the fire and made a quick survey of the surrounding woods, Matt returning to pick up the cooled bone. He turned it over in his hand as Mark wrinkled his nose. "Gross. Put it down."

"Nope. It's a talisman."

"No it's not."

"It is if I say it is." Matt shoved the bone in his jeans pocket and wandered around the clearing, eyes focused on the ground.

Mark scratched his chin, torn over the possibility that the bone *could* be a talisman, and then grabbed the stick and scooted a larger object out of the ashes. Using the hem of his shirt, he plucked it from the stones and bounced it between his hands until it cooled. "Mine's bigger than yours," he said, shoving his find into his brother's line of sight before tucking it in his pocket, where it bulged.

"In your dreams, nimnod, we're twins."

"Let's go. I'm hungry."

They wove back through the woods, arguing over how best to inform their mother about the accident. As they cleared the tree line, Mark stopped in his tracks. "Dude."

"What?"

Mark pointed at the car, where a pair of angry eyes glared through the side window. "It's awake."

CHAPTER 3

CASS PULLED THE TRUCK to a stop in front of the Elliot home, headlights fixed on the rambling building. The front porch had started to sag again, and she made a mental note to remind Bruce to fix it. It was long past suppertime and through the open cab windows they heard peals of laughter coming from the backyard. The house across the road was dark save for the porch light. A solitary figure marched back and forth in the yard, steps high and precise, arm raised in a salute at the neighbors.

"Herman?" Mitch asked.

Cass rolled her eyes and nodded.

"What's he protecting?"

"Lord knows. He's been stalking like that for months now. Seems to sleep during the day and play guard at night. Bruce calls him Herman the German," she answered as she stepped stiffly from the cab and stretched her lean form to work out the travel kinks. A lanky greyhound bounded around the house and went airborne, thunking squarely into her chest.

"Hey, big boy," Cass gasped, slipping Zeus a treat over Mitch's protests that the dog was getting fat. He crunched his contraband snack and wiggled around the truck to greet Mitch before loping toward the backyard.

The smell of charcoal and barbeque floated on the evening air and Cass rounded the house to see her brother Bruce in front of the grill, flipping two steaks. "Medium all right?" he asked.

Cass stopped to hug Darla Stone.

"You gave up a date with one of those McGee boys for unpaid overtime? I had to do some serious work on him, Cass. He was terrified to ask you out," the petite woman said.

"I appreciate it. Really, I do. But his IQ, Darla. It must be single digits."

"Honey, it's pretty slim pickins around here. He's cute and he's breathing, two things in his favor." Darla's eyebrows lowered over her brown eyes. "Are you still upset about the last guy I set you up with?"

"Are you serious? He abandoned me at a gas station."

"You drew your gun on him, Cass. What did you expect?"

She rolled her eyes. "I didn't draw on *him*. He stopped at a station where a robbery was in progress. What was I supposed to do?"

"You scared him to death when you yanked that revolver from your ankle holster. It was your night off. He had no idea you'd be carrying."

"He's from Texas and afraid of a woman with a gun?" Cass sniffed. "He drove off and *left* me. Patrol had to bring me home. What a wimp."

Darla smothered a grin. "Well, keep your eyes open and your gun holstered. Mr. Right will come along." She ran long fingers through her dark hair. "How was today?"

"Very long. Mitch drove most of it. I imagine he's wiped out."

"Any luck?"

"Some," she answered, and her gaze drifted to the garden. The first tender shoots of the weeds that would engulf it had emerged, wrapped in a gauzy layer of smoke from the grill. Memories of her mother, her face serene in the midst of her beloved flowers and vegetables flicked like a slideshow through Cass's mind and brought the familiar ache of longing for things to have happened differently. She sighed inwardly and released thoughts of what might have been, pulling her eyes back to Darla. "We've got a name and some information about his family but I don't think we'll catch his killer. Too much time has passed."

"Mitch was just as pessimistic when he first made detective. I think he's finally realized that life is a very funny thing, and you never know where a lead will come from." She paused to look for her husband, lips curving into a soft smile. "What is that man doing?"

Mitch was hunched over the grill with Bruce and Harry Elliot, eyeballing the steaks and offering advice. The three men were strikingly different – Bruce, fourth of the seven Elliot children, dark and brooding with a thick, solid build; Harry, two years older than Bruce and with a fair complexion and wiry form like their father; and Mitch, his long, athletic body topped with dirty blond hair. He was no blood relation to the Elliot clan, but was their oldest brother Jack's best friend since childhood. Through that long bond he had wed himself to the family, living its triumphs and tragedies with as much passion as each of them. Bruce stepped away from the grill and brandished a long set of tongs, holding a small piece of steak until it cooled, and then presented the prize to Zeus.

Cass spoke in a low voice. "Wasn't Harry supposed to have the girls tonight?"

"Your sister-in-law has been yanking his chain all day, poor man. He was seriously frustrated when I got here. Abe calmed him down."

"Daddy's sober?"

"And apparently talking some sense."

"Harry hoped the divorce could be amicable."

"Fat chance. Carly's a Drama Queen," Darla replied as she pushed up from the picnic table. "This one's gonna take some blood and tears, you mark my words."

Cass followed Darla to the grill and briefly hugged Bruce's solid form before wrapping her arms around Harry. She stood on her tiptoes to whisper, "Sorry about the girls."

He kissed the top of her head and reached for the screen door, standing aside as their father came down the steps with glasses of iced tea. Although Abe Elliot's hair had been as cottony as Harry's at one time, it had darkened to a light brown and finally started turning a distinguished white as he aged. Cass eyed her father, a repentant but recidivist drunk, and confirmed Darla's assessment that he was indeed sober. The tightness in her chest eased.

"Baked potatoes smell done to me, Harry. You'd better ask Bruce if you can have a look," Abe grinned.

"Oh honored brother," Harry sang. "Might I enter the kitchen of Elliot and brave the oven?"

Bruce waved the tongs. "Don't forget the sour cream."

Abe hugged his daughter and then slid in next to Darla at the picnic table. Bruce joined them, squeezing mustard over a hot dog. "How'd it go?"

Mitch shook his head. "Irritating. Oh man, Bruce, this smells good."

Cass snorted. "We ate lunch early. He's bound to be starving."

"Did you get an ID?" Harry called, darting down the porch steps while juggling baked potatoes in his bare hands.

"We think so," Mitch answered, holding his plate out. "The man's son filed the missing persons report. The age and characteristics are right – the skeleton had a broken leg from sometime in his youth and the report says that the father broke his leg when he was sixteen or seventeen."

"Did you talk to the son?" Darla asked.

"Nope. He's missing, too."

"Strange."

"Everything was strange." Mitch reached for the sour cream. "This sheriff is temporary. The full-time sheriff had a heart attack and they pulled this guy in from another county to help out. He happened to find the missing persons report when he was digging through the sheriff's desk, and he made the match to the bulletin about our skeleton."

"Did you talk to anybody?" Abe asked.

Cass snuck pieces of fat under the table to Zeus. "The sheriff took us to the address on the report, but the house was empty. The old lady next door owns it. She said a family of Mexicans was renting it, and the father left sometime last autumn. She didn't realize he was missing, just figured he'd gone to visit relatives or something."

"What about the son?"

"She said he left one weekend and didn't come back. The rest of the family seemed upset, but wouldn't talk about it. The old lady went to visit a friend last week, and when she got back, the house was empty."

"That didn't worry her?" Darla asked.

"Didn't seem like she was worried, did it Mitch?"

He shook his head, wiping butter from his chin. "She keeps the rest of the rent, the deposit and she'll have new renters before month end."

"Who were these people?" Abe asked.

"Sounds like illegals."

"What happens now?" Bruce asked, reaching for another hot dog, grinning at his sister's expression and flexing a rock-solid biceps. "I'm a growing boy, need my nutrition."

"We keep working the skeleton," Mitch answered. "He's got a name now, Humberto Gonzalez."

Bruce sniffed deeply and frowned at Harry. "You put the cake in the oven?"

"Yeah."

"Set the timer?"

"Oops."

"It'll burn, idiot, and the icing has to be ready when the cake comes out." Bruce trotted for the house. "This is why *I* control the kitchen."

CHAPTER 4

GOOBER'S BREATH CAUGHT IN his throat as the lawn mower sputtered to a stop in the middle of Possum Creek Bridge. This was a lonely stretch of road, infrequently traveled. Rare farmhouses rested at the end of rutted dirt tracks masquerading as driveways, and the heavy forest obscured the welcome warmth of electric light. Goober hated the dark. Monsters did their dirty work in the dark. They hid in the dark, beneath beds and in closets, under bridges and behind trees, lunging when your guard was down. Cries for help went unanswered in the dark. Alone was worse in the dark.

It was no surprise that he was afraid of the dark, or of being alone, for Goober's origins were a mystery. He'd been found one morning nearly forty years ago, nestled in the gnarled roots of the ancient hanging tree on the courthouse lawn, sleeping peacefully next to the town drunk. A scandal of magnificent proportions ensued. *Who was this child? Where had he come from? And* where *were his parents?* The grapevine drums were beaten, gossip smoke signals went up, and the newspaper and radio made repeated announcements encouraging his parents to come forward. But no one came to claim the gentle-natured toddler whose passion for chocolate covered peanuts earned him his nickname. An elderly widow had taken the boy in, and so his life as Arcadia's child began.

Goober wasn't retarded, but he was slow at formal education. He never learned to read or write beyond a fourth grade level and he dropped out of school when he was sixteen, picking up odd jobs and developing a talent for gardening. When the widow died, she left Goober her small trailer and enough money to get by. For years he'd ridden a decrepit tandem bicycle, happily pedaling Forney County's highways and byways. At some point, a generous soul had given Goober a red riding lawn mower with no blades. And at exactly that point, Goober entered the glorious world of combustible engines, whose maintenance requirements outstripped his abilities. Which brought him to his precarious position on the bridge this evening.

His eyes darted into the murky shadows surrounding Possum Creek as he twisted the mower's key. Her engine whirred but refused to turn over, and as her groans faded into a desperate click, Goober was flooded with a sudden urge to pee.

Reluctantly, he lifted his long frame from the mower, his imagination running wild. He'd heard rumors of ghosts roaming the woods, the spirits of slaughtered cowboys and Indians seeking revenge for past wrongs. Standing stock-still with his stomach churning, Goober waited. When only the night noises reached him, he gathered his courage, dried his sweaty palms on his overalls and unhooked the small can bungeed to a platform behind the seat. Unlocking the mower's gas cap, he prepared to tip the can up when starlight shimmered across the fuel tank's gaping maw. He paused, and the memory of stopping at the filling station this morning streaked across his brain. Confused, he frowned at the mower, forgetting his fear as he struggled to understand why she wouldn't start.

A sudden clanking rang across the still night and drove Goober into a squat. His heart pounded as he clutched the gas can against his chest and scuttled behind the mower, breath coming in shallow gasps. He tried to listen past the blood thrumming in his ears but the evening remained stubbornly closed, refusing to reveal its secrets. Rattled but reassured that the noise had stopped, Goober rose on shaking legs and relocked the tank before returning the can to its platform. One hand on her seat, he examined the mower with a mixture of dread and affection. His source of freedom had failed him and Goober's childlike mind cranked through his options. Slowly, he realized that he had no choice but to walk to town, through the terrifying night.

He tried to swallow, but found that his tongue was stuck to the roof of his mouth. Lifting his baseball cap to run a hand over his thinning hair, Goober turned resolutely away from the mower and sought the city's glow arcing over the black forest. He firmed the cap back on his head and hummed a jumpy tune, walking steadily toward Arcadia, eyes fixed on the strip of road before him.

The blossoming of an unnatural radiance off to his left spooked him. A bright fire danced among the tall pine trees and the vague silhouette of a distant building engulfed in flames captivated him. A devilish ghost danced between Goober and the flickering light, startling him from his trance. Heart pounding, bladder releasing a warm torrent, he turned and fled from Possum Creek, too terrified to scream.

In the blushing night air, a monster slunk to the edge of the road, taking in the man pelting toward town. He moved to the lawn mower, his amber eyes narrowing. Turning to the fleeing man with a look of recognition, Hitch took two steps forward and then stopped, head cocked to one side, seeming to consider the situation. Reluctantly, the monster left the road and melted back between the trees.

CHAPTER 5

EVELYN GROVE'S ARMS WERE wrapped tight across her chest, her dark eyes blazing as rumpled Officer Ernest Munk climbed from his pickup. He suppressed a grin and wrapped her small frame in a huge hug, resting his chin on the top of her head. Her gentle curves were a fragile contrast to his bulky form, her features delicate and still smooth, his rough with too much sorrow and the long-ago marks of chicken pox. His sister pulled back, gently patting his stomach.

"Gaby's feeding you too well," she teased.

"I never thought the restaurant would survive, but she's a great cook. And Robert says you've got some deer meat out here. Anything Gabrielle can use in her kitchen?" He winked over her head at his gangly nephews, fighting a stab of jealousy at his sister's luck with children. The boys would grow into strong, handsome men while his own child –. Munk stopped the thought. The boys were watching their mother for signs of forgiveness or, failing that, belief. Given Evelyn's notorious hardheadedness, his own self-pity could wait.

She pushed away from his hug. "Did Robert tell you what happened?"

"Nope. He couldn't stop laughing."

She thrust her chin at the boys. "Tell your Uncle Ernie what you've done."

One of them looked at the ground, digging the toe of his sneaker into the grass. The other heaved a huge sigh. "He was driving," Matt said, pointing to his brother. "Not doing anything funny, just driving along FM 419. A deer ran across the road and hit the car."

Evelyn popped her hands onto her hips. "Have you ever heard anything so ridiculous?"

"It does happen," Munk conceded. "They usually make a suicide run in front of the car and cause all sorts of damage, but sometimes they get the timing better and hit the side instead. Knocks 'em out and leaves a dent, but the car and the deer normally survive."

The boys were visibly relieved to have their story supported by a source as reliable as Uncle Ernie. Evelyn turned to watch her husband cross the driveway. "Robert, Ernie says that a deer will hit the side of a car. I guess they could be telling the truth."

Robert Grove stuck out his hand to Munk. "Thanks for coming. I thought she was gonna skin both boys." He looked at his wife, a smile playing across his lips. "Everything's all right now?"

"Absolutely not," she said. "Who's going to fix that dent?"

"We will, Momma," Mark answered, eyes alight.

"Not if I want it done right," Evelyn snapped, "and I do. Iced tea?" she asked Munk.

"Yes, please," he answered, watching her march toward the house. He and Robert exchanged glances.

"She does get worked up," Robert said.

"Always has," Munk said with a grin. He turned to the twins. "You two all right?"

The boys relaxed, relief on their faces. "Thanks for saving us."

"No problem." His faced turned sheepish. "I don't see y'all often enough, and I know I do this every time, but who's who?"

"I'm Mark," one answered. He pointed to his brother. "Matt's got the beard."

Munk shook his head. "I figured I'd be able to tell you apart after you grew out of your baby fat, or maybe when you hit your teenage years, but when the doctors said you were identical twins, they meant it."

"How've you been, Ernie? We haven't seen you in the longest time," Robert said as they walked toward the car.

"Busy. Especially this week."

"We heard about the skeleton. Is that what you're working on?"

Munk was unsurprised that the news had traveled the county so fast. "A couple of the detectives were checking out a lead to his identity today."

"What happened?"

"He was shot twice in the head and his foot was chopped off. It looks like the body was moved, so we don't know where he was killed."

"Was it true," Robert began, eyes darting to his boys, "that he had on women's clothes?"

Munk nodded. "The whole thing is kind of weird. We only found the body because a patrol officer saw smoke and found a trash fire that had gotten out of the barrel. He was smart enough to call the fire department and then search the area. That's when he found the skeleton. But he tried to stomp out the flames and caught his uniform on fire." Matt and Mark giggled and Munk bit back a grin, turning toward the damaged car. "He's definitely not the brightest bulb on the Christmas tree."

Floodlights from the house lit the scene. The deer lay quietly where the boys had pulled it from the car, large eyes watchful. "Electrical cord?" Munk asked.

Mark blushed. "That's all we had with us."

"Sure is a pretty little thing," Munk said. "If it's not hurt too badly, the game warden said to turn it loose." He bent and deftly rolled the deer from side to side. "His eyes are clear, and I don't see any blood. One of you help me untie him."

Matt looked to Mark. "I rode in back with it. It's your turn."

Munk motioned for Mark to join him. "Put your knees on its ribs, hold its hooves and watch those antlers." Munk quickly unwound the electrical cord. "On three, let him go."

The men jumped up and watched the deer stagger to its feet. It shook its head and snorted, eyeing them as it staggered around the yard, stretching its bruised muscles. Evelyn returned with a tray of iced tea, stopping to watch the deer regain its balance and in a swift leap, jump the fence to the pasture and disappear into the night.

"My goodness, that thing was bigger than I thought," she said, holding the tray out.

Robert and Munk took their glasses and squatted down next to the car, discussing the merits of trying to pop the dent out with a suction cup, or bang it out with a mallet from underneath the car.

"Where were you?" Munk asked the boys.

"In the dead middle of 419," Mark answered. "Wasn't anybody around out there to stop, or we would've called you to come look at the deer out there."

"What about your phones?"

Evelyn snorted. "I don't know why we pay for those things."

Matt sighed. "I left mine at home, and Mark's battery ran out. But there was somebody out there."

"Yeah," Matt said. "They were in the woods and cooked a chicken with the feathers on it. Stunk like crazy."

Munk frowned. "How did you know it was a chicken?"

"White feathers around a fire pit. I guess it could've been a cow bird or a heron, but we just figured it was a chicken."

"Did they leave the carcass?"

The boys exchanged a glance. "Not that we saw, but there were bones in the ashes." Matt dug in his pocket and pulled the small bone out for his uncle to examine. Munk turned it over in his hand, holding it up to the light from the house to examine its shape. Seeing his uncle's interest, Mark pulled the rounded bone from his pocket, and Munk struggled to contain his shock.

"Can you find that pit again?" he asked.

"Sure. Why?"

"I'd just like to take a look at it."

Robert kept his gaze away from the boys. "Problem?"

Munk shook his head. "Just seems a little strange. I need the boys to show me where this pit is."

"Tonight?" Evelyn exclaimed, checking her watch. "They've been out all day at a track meet. And it's getting late. They haven't had any supper yet."

"Come on Mom," Mark said, a whine in his voice. "It won't take long. We know right where it is. And if we take the car we can come straight home."

Evelyn's lips tightened into a thin line. "You've had enough fun with that car for tonight. Uncle Ernie can drive." She glanced at her brother. "Don't keep them out late," she ordered before pivoting on her heel to stride back to the house.

CHAPTER 6

THE OLD MAN LOWERED the glasses from his forehead and jabbed at several numbers on the keypad before raising the phone to an ear thickened with age.

"Yes, sir?" Hitch answered.

"Evening. Everything go all right?"

"Yes, sir."

"That's one more drug-runner that's out of business in Forney County."

"Yes, sir. But someone was there."

The old man clamped down on his unlit pipe, teeth clacking against the stem. "Who?"

"That retarded man who rides the lawn mower. He must've called it in. The fire department arrived before the hot house was completely destroyed. I'm not sure how much he saw." Hitch hesitated. "Should I take care of him, sir?"

"Not yet," the old man answered, sucking on his pipe and considering Goober. "Let's see what comes of it."

CHAPTER 7

CASS TOSSED HER BOOT into the corner and unbuttoned her shirt. The pipes groaned softly at a shower somewhere in the house, and the comfort that comes from being at home settled into her. They had sat outside until the candles burned low and the sky deepened to a velvety black, the men sucking on cheap cigars and the women fanning smoke from their faces. Abe had looked as content as Cass could remember, delighted with having three of his seven children at home and two of their best friends laughing in his backyard. He'd sat on the top step to the house, leaning against the screen door's frame. As the cigar ash grew long and the night closed in, he fell asleep. His bullfrog-like snores had brought Zeus growling from beneath the picnic table and Mitch and Darla said their goodnights, leaving Bruce and Harry to help Abe inside.

She caught her reflection in the dresser mirror, surprised at the glimpse of her mother she saw there; the same creamy skin and intense violet eyes. Cass's hair was a riot of red that changed with the light, where Nell's had been a flowing chestnut. She leaned close to the mirror to check for lines, stopping short as her shirt fell open to reveal a thin tail of scar. Lifting a finger, Cass followed its cool, smooth spiral over the exposed skin until it dipped into her bra. From there it meandered beneath her breast's curve, looping and swirling up its underside, stopping just short of her areole. An image of the face always appeared with thought of the scar. It had taken weeks of searching the features embedded in her fuzzy memory before she'd realized that the wobbling jowls, heavy brow and deep-set eyes hovering over her that awful night had belonged to a mask fashioned to look like Richard Nixon. The sight of the scar usually evoked a potent fuel of fear and rage that drove her toward a single consuming goal: killing the man who hid behind the mask. But she was too tired tonight to give the emotions their head, and her thoughts turned instead to the question of what might have been if only she had only stayed in College Station that weekend. If only she had gone to a different bar. If only – she jumped as her cell phone rang and glanced at the screen. "Hey," she answered.

"You're not in bed, are you?" Mitch asked.

"I was working on it. What's up?"

"Just got a call from Munk. He's out on FM 419 looking for foot bones. I'm about to drop off Darla and Zeus, then head back that way. Meet you out there?"

Unconsciously, Cass closed the shirt gaping at her neck. "Humberto Gonzalez's foot?"

"Has to be. Listen, after today's trip, feel free to take a pass. I'll fill you in on Monday."

"I'll be there," she said quickly, snugging the phone between her ear and shoulder and buttoning her shirt. "Got a location?"

"Just look for the ME's van on the side of the road."

Cass heard gravel beneath Mitch's tires and knew that he was home. "Hurry up," she said. "I've got a funny feeling about this one."

But she was talking to dead air.

———————

CASS QUIETLY TOOK THE camera from Forney County's Medical Examiner, John Grey, feeling small next to his six feet eight inches. Grey was a praying mantis of a man, long and thin almost to the point of emaciation, skin pale as that of the cadavers that crossed his autopsy table. His dark hair rose in a thick shock above his narrow face, matching the bushy eyebrows that hung over his serious eyes. She nudged him aside and took several shots of the clearing. Portable floodlights illuminated the ash hanging in the night air like a morbid fog. A man with unruly golden hair squatted next to the fire pit, seemingly mesmerized. He sneezed into his facemask and looked up at Grey, his startling green eyes widening at the sight of Cass.

"Hello, my dear," he said, pushing himself upright, adjusting his safari vest and khaki trousers. Both were studded with pockets. "Who is this beautiful creature?"

"Bernie," Grey began, stifling a smile, "this is Detective Cass Elliot. Cass, may I introduce Bernie Winterbottom? He's a friend of mine from

England, a forensic anthropologist."

Bernie dipped his head in a slight bow. "Bernard Aloysius Nelson Winterbottom, Esquire." Cass pushed a loose strand of hair from her cheek and raised an eyebrow. "A bit of a mouthful, I'm afraid. Ever so pleased to meet you, Miss Elliot. May I call you Cass? You are the antithesis of your namesake, if I do say so myself."

"Not many people make that connection anymore, Mr. Winterbottom," she said, warming to the disheveled stranger.

"Disgraceful, that. Mama Cass was one of the finest voices of her time. Quite a range." His eyes grew misty and Cass listened harder as his British accent thickened. "She was at her best when she wasn't held back by Michelle, but her voice was powerful enough that she might have sung over John and Denny, which would have ruined The Mamas and The Papas." Bernie sighed. "Mama Cass died in London, did you know that?"

"Yes, sir, I did. Technically, I wasn't named after Mama Cass. My oldest brother named me after the Cassandra from Greek mythology."

"The prophetess that no one heeded. She was quite accurate, as I recall, even foretelling the destruction of Troy. The world would be a different place if the Trojans had listened to her warnings. It was a bloody death our Cassandra endured. A jealous wife with a sword, I believe." He smiled. "I am quite pleased to make your acquaintance. Grey didn't mention that Arcadia is home to such lovely women as yourself." Bernie turned to the tall medical examiner. "In answer to your earlier question, yes, it's possible that this foot belongs to your elderly skeleton."

"Any cut marks?" Grey asked.

Bernie squatted again, absently stirring the ash in the fire pit, holding a length of bone between his fingers. "Difficult to determine out here. I've found charred meat and the bones from at least one bird. I'll need to clean and sort the bones. If this is a foot, it was not placed into the fire whole. And it smells of paraffin."

Bernie held the fragment up to Grey, who bent his long frame in half to give it a delicate sniff. Cass did the same and through the stench of burning feathers and flesh still hanging in the air, could pick out the scent of an accelerant.

"Is that kerosene?" she asked.

Grey shrugged. "The new forensics guy can figure it out. What's his name?"

"Dunno. He's on his way?"

"No. Munk called him, but he's out at a fire over near Possum Creek."

"House fire?"

"Not sure. He told Munk to bring in the bones, secure this scene and he'll be out in the morning to process it. Munk went to take his brother-in-law and nephews home. He should be back shortly."

"His nephews found this place?" she asked, circling the clearing.

"They don't have any idea what they've found. Most of the footprints you see are theirs."

"That's a shame. There might've been something we could use." Cass blew air out in a frustrated stream. "Okay, I'll take a few more shots and be done with it."

"Good. You can help us sift the ash. Bernie, would you grab the mesh and buckets behind you?"

"This is good fun, Cass," Bernie said eagerly, reaching for the equipment they had carried from Grey's van. She tucked the camera into its case and joined him by the pit. "We do quite a bit of sifting on dig sites. It's rewarding when you come across a bone fragment or an artifact such as a coin. Very rewarding indeed. You'll need a face mask, and you may want goggles for all this ash." Bernie pulled several delicate brushes from a pocket on his vest and demonstrated how to use a trowel to lift ash and spread it over a mesh screen, shifting gently back and forth to separate the ash from any solid fragments.

"What brought you to Arcadia, Mr. Winterbottom? Vacation?" Cass asked.

He held a small bone up to the light. "Human," he announced before placing it in a paper bag. "Please, call me Bernie. I'm involved in an exchange program with Texas A&M University. There's an archaeology dig at the George C. Davis site near Alto."

"The Indian mounds?"

"That's the one."

"I thought they were done down there."

"As I understand it, this new project originated when a developer filed plans for an apartment complex on what is suspected to be part of the Davis site. The state contacted A&M to request a survey and initial results indicate that there is a burial ground of some note in the area." Bernie stopped to pluck a bone from his screen, examine it briefly, and place it in another bag. "Where was I? Oh yes. It seems the developer has filed a petition to block the dig, citing older research indicating that the site is not historically significant. So, we wait for the bureaucracy to sort itself out." He scooped another trowel of ash. "After seeing the data collected so far and walking the site myself, I'm convinced there are Indian burial mounds at the George C. Davis location. It will be most unfortunate if the developer is allowed to block the dig." Cass handed Bernie a bone. He examined it and placed it into a bag. "We may be archaic in many ways compared to the states, but Britain takes the protection of her historical treasures seriously."

Grey snorted. "When are the Elgin Marbles going home to Greece?"

"Ahh yes," Bernie agreed, smiling beneath his facemask. "We also have a fondness for protecting the treasures of others. Particularly after we've gone to so much trouble to liberate them from their original owners."

Brush rustled nearby and a light bobbed into the clearing. "Man, it's a dust storm out here," Mitch coughed, waving a hand in front of his face. "Munk is right behind me. You need help?"

Grey uncurled his long form from its squatting position, like a bug pushing from its cocoon. He ran a gloved hand across his bushy hair, sending a fine white mist soaring into the air. "We're about done. Bernie?"

He nodded, face buried in a paper bag. "Probably just one foot here."

"Has to belong to Humberto Gonzalez," Mitch commented.

"Is that his name?" Grey asked.

"Yeah. We think he's an illegal who was living up in El Dorado. But we've got no idea who killed him or why they cut his foot off."

"Or if the foot even belongs to him. Let the science do its job, Mitch," Grey said.

"You got any one-footed corpses in the morgue?"

"Nope."

"I haven't seen many guys hobbling around town on one foot, so it's gotta be Gonzalez's. But it's creepy that someone would cut it off and then burn it six months after they killed him."

"Maybe they needed to get rid of it. We did find the body last week," Cass said.

"Yeah, but why burn it? They could've tossed the foot in the river or left it in the woods for the hogs to eat. Burning's like some voodoo thing." Mitch turned at the sound of coughing coming from the trees behind him. "Hey Munk, what made you think these were human bones?"

He pushed into the clearing and sneezed, the angle of the halogen lights shadowing the chicken pox scars on his face, making him look more haggard than usual. "I broke a toe in college and saw my foot on the x-ray. As much as that little booger hurt, I'd know a toe bone anywhere. That one," he said, pointing at a fragment resting on a stone, "is a metatarsal. And when Mark pulled that rounded bone out of his pocket, I knew it wasn't from a bird." Munk stopped, taking in Bernie's disheveled appearance, his glance darting to Grey before he stuck his hand out in greeting. "Good evening, sir. I'm Ernest Munk. My nephews found this site."

"Sorry," said Grey. "This is Bernie Winterbottom, a friend of mine from England. He's an anthropologist working on the Indian Mounds project down in Alto. I thought he might be able to help us figure out if these bones are the foot that belongs to our skeleton. Bernie, this is Detective Mitch Stone, Cass's partner, and Officer Ernest Munk."

"Pleased to meet you all. Excellent call on the metatarsal, Officer Munk, and the rounded bone is the talus," Bernie answered. "There are definitely bones from a human foot mixed with the hollow bones from at least one bird. From the feathers on the rocks, we believe it's a chicken. Regardless, it looks as if the bird was intact when it was put into the fire."

"Call me Munk. Everybody else does. Somebody tossed in a whole bird?"

"Given the way it has burned, yes."

"I'm telling you, man," Mitch shivered, "this is some freaky voodoo ritual."

Munk ignored him. "Flesh?"

"Yes. On the bones and in the pit," Bernie answered, brushing ash from his safari outfit and all but disappearing into the cloud that billowed around him. "We'll know more after everything has been cleaned and sorted. We kept the ash in case your forensic man wants it. I believe an accelerant of some sort was used."

"Whose land is this?" Cass asked.

"The game warden said it was forestry land," Munk grunted as he lifted a bucket.

"Munk," Mitch yawned, breaking down a spotlight, "how about if we tape this area off and work it on Monday?"

"I talked to Kado earlier –"

"That's an uncommon name," Cass interrupted.

"Tom Kado. He wants it done ASAP. He said that if this is a human foot, we should treat the site as a crime scene. From what I've heard, he's a stickler for the science," he groused. "Things were a lot easier when Comfrey was in charge of forensics." He paused, hands resting on a recently sealed bucket. "I started this, so I'll be here to help." A smile teased at his lips. "Gaby's catering the Elm Creek Cemetery Homecoming. If I'm not on duty she'll have me in an apron serving rice and beans."

Grey turned to Bernie. "I'll open the ME's office if you can come in. I'd like to see how you determine if this foot is from our elderly skeleton."

Bernie snapped a pocket closed on his jacket. "Lovely. I'll be there."

"Fine," Mitch pouted, dismantling another light. "I reckon I can finish some paperwork."

"Courthouse at eight?" Cass said. "I'll bring the donuts."

Mitch sniffed. "From The Palace?"

Munk stiffened. "From The Donut Hole."

"Oh come on. The Palace beats the pants off The Donut Hole."

"The Palace doesn't use enough glaze, and their donuts just aren't as… substantial."

"You mean The Donut Hole uses more grease." Mitch glanced at Munk's stout form. "Gaby might be happier if you ate donuts from The Palace. Keep you light on your feet, man. Ready to dish up rice and beans at a moment's notice."

"Invoking Gabrielle's name, Mitch. That's low." He rubbed his protruding stomach before hoisting two buckets of ash and turning toward the woods and his waiting pickup. "Whatever Cass wants is fine with me."

Bernie watched Munk leave, a curious expression on his face. "Pastry problems?"

Cass pulled him aside. "Arcadia has two donut shops. Always has. Old families run them and people are generally loyal to one or the other."

"Loyal to a bakery?"

"Donut disagreements have divided families. But Mitch is right. The Palace makes a better donut. They're not heavy, just sweet enough. You'll see tomorrow." She turned back to Mitch. "Will you quit whining if I get donuts at The Palace?"

"I'll be downright full of sunshine if you bring donuts from The Palace." Cass snorted. "I'll wear my shades."

CHAPTER 8

Sunday

"I FORGOT TO ASK last night. Did you find out who the skeleton is?" Munk asked as he joined them in the dull conference room, his round face still puffy with sleep. Cass glanced around the room and realized that they were all a little fuzzy around the edges from their late night. Bernie was again dressed in a khaki safari outfit, his wavy golden hair flattened against one side of his head from sleep. His green eyes blinked slowly as he examined the donut he held. Grey wore a dark blue fleece over his scrubs and a pair of yacht-sized tennis shoes. He balanced his head in one long, thin hand and stifled a yawn before taking another bite. Mitch was dressed in his customary starched button-down shirt and jeans, and his blue eyes were slowly coming to life as he sipped his coffee. Cass reached for the pot and poured Munk a cup, watching as he eyed the box of donuts.

Mitch swallowed a bite. "Go on. You know you want one. His name is Humberto Gonzalez. He disappeared about the time we think our John Doe was killed."

Munk eased into a creaky plastic chair between Bernie and Grey, who nudged the donuts toward him. "Did the family know who might have killed him?"

"This is where it gets weird." Mitch sipped a cup of coffee and talked them through their visit to Arkansas on Saturday.

"The old man disappeared last autumn, the son reported the father missing in early spring, and now the son and the rest of the family are missing?" Grey asked, slowly licking chocolate glaze from his fingers. Mitch nodded, stuffing the last bite in his mouth and wiping his fingers. "Is anyone worried about that?"

"I don't think so. Least ways, the temporary sheriff ain't worried. He seemed green to me," Mitch looked to Cass, who nodded in agreement, "and I imagine he's just riding this until the regular sheriff is back on duty."

"Let me put it another way," Grey said, tracing a crack in the table's faded top. "Are *you* worried about it?"

"Why would I worry about people going missing in another state?"

"Because the last one who did ended up murdered and skeletonized in your state and, more importantly, your county."

Mitch scratched the back of his neck. "I'm not sure what we can do with it. No one has reported the family missing. They might've just up and moved somewhere. You know, rented a new house or something."

"Possible. But it doesn't smell right, and these people need to know that a member of their family is dead."

"Good point. I'll talk to Sheriff Hoffner about it. What's on for today?"

"I'd like to begin on last night's bones," Bernie answered.

"That works for me," Grey said.

Mitch glanced at his watch and then stretched. "I'm gonna take a ride out to Possum Creek, see what this Kado guy is up to."

Cass frowned. "He went back out? What burned?"

"He's *still* out there. Worked all night. I talked to Sheriff Hoffner this morning, and he said it was a hot house."

"Like for plants?" She cocked her head to one side. "What happened?"

"The fire department got an anonymous call from Goober."

Cass chuckled. "He gave his name?"

"Of course. He was freaked out about a devil in the forest."

"A what?"

"Sheriff Hoffner said Goober wanted to report a devil made out of light. But there's no telling what he really saw."

Cass paused, brow furrowed. "What's in this hot house?"

"Pot."

"So that's why Kado's still there."

"Hoffner said it looked like a professional operation."

"If it burned," Cass asked, "what kind of forensics can he get?"

"The fire boys saved part of the building. This guy's been dusting pots for prints all night. We've got to teach him to move faster. Old Comfrey would've been done by now. Munk, you want to come with me?"

He nodded, wiping donut glaze from his chin. Mitch raised an eyebrow and Munk shrugged, reaching for the nearly empty box. "I need a few more before I can commit."

"Fair enough." Mitch turned to Cass. "What about you?"

She lifted the coffee pot. "I'll deal with Humberto Gonzalez's paperwork."

"You hate that stuff."

"Almost as much as you do. So you can buy lunch."

CHAPTER 9

LENNY SCARBOROUGH TAPPED THE syringe and placed the glass vial in the pocket of his overalls. He reached through the loading chute's weathered planks, deftly pinched together the heavy hide and inoculated Cleopatra with an antibiotic. She'd been limping for the past few days and he'd spotted the beginnings of foot rot, a dangerous condition for a cow. He'd rounded the cattle up this morning to medicate those who were showing signs of the disease. Extracting the needle, he rubbed the injection site and ran an appraising eye over his lead cow, her coat gleaming in the misty morning light. She was a Black Angus, full-blooded and full of herself, if you asked the other cows. Top of the pecking order, Cleopatra was first to the feeding trough, first at the pond and first into the loading chute when Lenny had treatments to dish out.

Fondling her ears, he slipped her a feed cube as a reward for good behavior and released the heavy headlock. She trundled through, trotting for the far gate and fresh hay. He watched to see if she would avoid the unconscious form in the corral's cool grass. The damage inflicted by the sharp hooves of a twelve-hundred pound animal would've been a sight to behold, but a part of him relaxed when Cleopatra grunted once and swung wide of the body resting near the long arms of the hay dolly attached to the old farm pickup. Bruises were one thing, but severe injuries from a cow would require a doctor; that kind of intrusion into his life Lenny did not need.

The next cow in line rushed forward and he clamped the headlock around her neck to begin his examination. He sang as he worked, low voice reciting the hymns his little Methodist church used in worship. Life had been good to Lenny, and such was his faith in himself and his Lord that he only smiled briefly at the strangled sound of movement behind him. A few quiet gasps later, the corral settled back into stillness and Lenny returned to his work, so absorbed in the care of his cattle and the praise of his Lord that he was momentarily startled by the creak of the rusty pickup's door. A derisive laugh escaped him, and he shook his head once, reluctantly impressed at this display of dogged determination.

The engine hiccupped to life, roaring as a foot was applied to the accelerator, but still Lenny did not turn from his task. He was thumping an air bubble from the syringe when the engine's rattling changed and his senses prickled, searching for the oddity in this otherwise mundane sound. As the engine screamed and mud flew from beneath the spinning tires, the hair on the nape of his neck rose, and he turned as the tires gained purchase. The sharp point of the hay dolly's long spike plunged into his chest, lifting him from his feet and pinning him against the loading chute's weathered planks. Warmth spread down his chest and between his legs. His eyes met those reflected in the pickup's rearview mirror and he was shocked at the exhausted fury burning in them. As his heart thumped its last weary beat, Lenny Scarborough's face reflected his amazement that something so weak and worthless could've at last gotten the better of him.

CHAPTER 10

CASS GLANCED AT HER watch and stretched. Almost ten thirty, and she was nearly done with Humberto Gonzalez's paperwork. She pushed back from her desk in the squad room and glanced at the group of officers who were pouring a cup of coffee before heading out. An older detective with a build as solid as a bull was pinning a photograph of an elderly woman to a bulletin board, carefully arranging the other photos so that each face was clearly visible. He turned and caught sight of Cass, smiling as he strode to her desk.

"Good work on the skeleton," Carlos Martinez said, running a hand across his close-cropped steely hair.

"You heard?"

"Mitch left me a message. Humberto Gonzalez. I'll go back out to the Mexican churches tonight and to the road crews tomorrow."

"You think the illegals will talk?"

"It's worth a shot. Last week, all I had was a vague description. Now I've got a name."

"Is there anything I can do to help?"

Carlos snapped his fingers. "Do you know David Cronus?"

"At the big Baptist church off the square?"

"First Baptist. He runs the outreach program for illegals. Different churches pool their resources to get food and clothes to the community, and Deacon Cronus heads it up. If you've got time, call him and see if he'll spread Humberto Gonzalez's name around. I'd call but an old lady has gone missing."

"Who?"

"Iris Glenthorne. Know her?"

"I don't think so. What happened?"

"She missed her bridge game last night and Judge Shackleford's wife is worried about her," Carlos answered, glancing at the bulletin board. Iris

Glenthorne sported a full head of white hair, and her emerald eyes sparkled within the wrinkled folds of a smiling face. She was surrounded by shots of other missing people, mostly children, but several who were close to her age, as well. "At least it's not another missing teenager, although we're getting quite a collection of the disappeared on that board."

Cass saw the older detective's face harden as someone trotted into the squad room and brushed past the officers at the coffee bar. She leaned forward to see who had disturbed him. The newcomer's eyes were bloodshot and his dark hair dusted with ash. As he drew nearer, she caught a whiff of the acrid stench of smoke. Pausing, he glanced from Cass to Carlos and back again. Her stomach flipped as his eyes met hers. They were a unique shade of gray tinged with green, and made her think of clouds before a storm. His skin was tanned, his cheekbones high and pronounced. Cass Elliot was no stranger to appreciative glances from men, but they usually generated little interest from her. Now, as his glance flicked almost imperceptibly over her body, she was flooded with warmth. She blinked in surprise before shutting down the unwelcome sensation.

He pulled his eyes from hers and stuck his hand out toward Carlos. "Don't think we've met. I'm Tom Kado."

Carlos shook his hand and introduced himself. "You took old Comfrey's place in forensics."

"Yeah," Kado sighed. "I did."

Carlos crossed his bulging arms over his massive chest. Kado held up his hand in a placatory gesture. "No offense. I've heard he was a nice guy, but his lab and procedures were a mess."

"We never had any problem with his 'lab' or his 'procedures'. Neither did the courts." Carlos replied, a chill in his voice. "We'll see how things go with you."

A frown knit Kado's brow as he watched Carlos grab his holster and leave the room without looking back. "Guess I've pissed him off, too."

"You rubbing people the wrong way?"

Kado dug his knuckles into his weary eyes. "I don't mean to, but I've been getting some hassle about how long it takes to process a crime scene. The old guy, Comfrey, he might've been fast, but he was a joke."

Cass raised an eyebrow.

"Seriously. The lab equipment isn't bad, but files are missing documentation, some files are completely missing, and I've got decades of cold case DNA to load into the system." He hesitated, searching her face. "A *good* forensics program can make your job easier. It can help you do a better job. But forensic analysis takes time."

"Then you might think about how you phrase things, Mr. Kado."

"You're probably right." He rubbed his eyes again, smearing soot across his high, sharp cheekbones, and attempted a smile. "People call me Kado. You must be Detective Elliot."

"It's Cass. Where are you from?"

"Oklahoma." He hesitated. "Have I pissed you off, too?"

"I liked old Comfrey as much as the rest of the guys, but I never felt comfortable with the way he handled a scene. It seemed too loose to me. I'm the new girl on the block, so there wasn't much I could say."

"How new?"

She straightened her shoulders. "I worked patrol in Dallas for two years and did another eighteen months here. I was promoted to detective six months ago."

He examined her unlined face. "Impressive."

"Call me motivated."

"So maybe we can find a way to work together?"

She nodded slowly, fighting the tickle in her belly. "I imagine we can."

He stretched, checked his watch, and flashed a grin that revealed deep dimples. "Any chance we can start now?"

Cass laughed. "You need an extra pair of hands?"

"I'm a one man band, so yeah, I'll appreciate any help I can get." He pulled his cell phone out of his pocket. "I've sent one of the guys from patrol, an Officer Truman, out to the fire pit those boys found last night. Do you know him?"

"Scott Truman's young. Why'd you pick him?"

"He's had some recent experience with the drug business. Sheriff Hoffner said he worked undercover at a local high school for a while."

"Yeah, at Elysian Fields. They had no idea he was a cop. I heard the building that burned last night housed a marijuana operation."

"A big one. I wanted someone young like Truman because I can train him right. I need to get out there and see how he's doing. Want to ride along?"

Her phone rang. "Hey Mitch… Lenny Scarborough? Did dispatch send an ambulance?… I'll go out and let you know what's up… You're still buying lunch." Cass hung up and turned to Kado, a thoughtful look on her face. "Guess my ride out to the fire pit will have to wait."

"What's up?"

"Some sort of domestic dispute."

"That's surprising?"

"Maybe. Lenny Scarborough is the last man I'd expect to beat his wife." She stood from her desk and headed for the squad room door.

"From what I've seen, Texas women are pretty tough," Kado called after her. "Maybe Mrs. Scarborough was beating on *him*."

———————

TOM KADO DRANK IN Detective Cass Elliot's fluid movements as she wove between the desks to get to the squad room's door, and wondered what was wrong with him. He crossed the empty room to the coffee bar and poured himself a cup.

She was gorgeous. Stunning, actually. And a bright intelligence brought light to those strangely colored eyes. They were such a deep blue they looked purple. When Cass had stood from her desk, he'd realized that they were almost the same height.

Kado shook his head and scolded himself as he strode toward the evidence room. God knew he was in no shape to handle a relationship and in reality, he didn't even want one. Caroline had only been dead a year. Barely a year. Kado's nostrils still flared at the phantom scent of the death that had oozed from her pores as cancer had eaten her alive. He still saw her in crowds and had to stop himself from calling out to her, had to endure the rush of hope every time he spotted a petite woman with shiny, straight black hair. She was slowly leaving him, occupying his dreams less frequently these days. But he couldn't stand the thought of losing her completely, of not loving her. Of violating her memory by noticing other women.

Unlocking the evidence room door, Kado tried to push Cass from his mind. *Cass Elliot is a colleague, somebody you work with, pure and simple*, he told himself as he settled behind his computer and typed in a password. *Besides, a woman with those looks probably has men waiting in line. She's out of your league and,* he reminded himself, *you're not in the game anyway.*

CHAPTER 11

CASS PULLED TO A stop in front of the large white frame house and frowned at the scene. An ambulance was parked in a small pasture and paramedics were tending to someone on the ground near a truck on the far side of the barn. Cows stood quietly in a fenced enclosure in front of the barn, and another group milled around several long feeding troughs in a separate lot. Two cars stood in front of the house and a police cruiser was parked behind them. A police officer was near the fence that circled the pasture, bent in two as his stomach emptied its contents. An older woman waited beside him, her hand on his back. Lush clover was shin high and sparkled with dew. Cass headed toward the barn and the woman met her inside the fence, face flushed. "Who are you?" she demanded.

"Detective Cass Elliot, ma'am. We received a call about a domestic disturbance. Do you live here?"

"No, I don't. I'm Edith Lovil, I live down the road a piece," she said, hand fluttering near her face like a wounded bird. Her complexion was sickly, eyes straining in their sockets, lips pressed tightly together. "I stopped to see if Angie wanted some eggs this morning. I keep chickens." She ran a trembling hand through her hair and barked a laugh. "You don't want to know about that. Best thing is to show you. Come with me."

Edith moved with long strides toward the house and Cass hurried to keep pace with the older woman. "Ma'am, did you call the police?"

"Yes, I did. I found Angie and Lenny out there," she answered, jerking her head toward the barn, "and came back to the house to call the ambulance. That's when I found this," she said, sweeping open a screen door at the top of steps.

Cass stepped into the kitchen behind Edith, following the woman's downward glance at a collection of four-by-six color photographs scattered across the floor. Most were upside down, innocuous white rectangles against pristine linoleum. She squatted, counted seventeen photos, and squinted at the nearest shot. It showed an angled expanse of pale colors against a darker background. She looked more closely and realized that the pale colors represented two sets of legs, one set folded behind and into the other. One pair were muscled and matted with dark hair, the other frail and covered with a translucent gray down. She lifted her eyes slowly from the bottom of the photograph where the sharp jut of anklebones could be seen, following the bend of knees to the top of the image where a side view of a flabby buttock was fully visible. Behind it, its fullness cut off in the photograph, was a hairy hip where the muscled legs ended. A length of dark, engorged flesh bridged the distance between the buttock and the hip. Cass caught her breath and glanced at the next photo to see a freckled arm reaching around a corpulent belly and a fair hand grasping a short, fat penis framed by the gaping fly of a pair of faded blue jeans. Testicles had been pulled up and were resting at the base of the zipper, and in a random flash that bore no relation to the shock she felt, she considered it reckless for the owner to allow his balls to be placed in such a position. Dimpled fingers circling the enlarged organ were in sharp contrast to the dark, thick matt of pubic hair that curled around the pale skin and drifted over the sagging gut.

She leaned forward to look at a third photograph, a knot forming in her stomach. A lithe torso stretched away from the camera, ending in a burlap sack covering a head. A single lock of blonde hair had slipped from beneath the sack and rested near a protruding collar bone, circling a small birthmark. Hands with long fingers gripped the thin upper arms, holding the shoulders in place against a pair of jean-clad thighs. Smallish breasts were visible on the bony chest, and the woman's back was arched as if she were attempting to twist free. Another set of hands, tanned with well-bitten nails, dug into the slender hips, pulling them toward a manly thrust.

She swallowed thickly and looked up. "Did you touch anything?"

Edith shook her head, biting her lip as the fluttering hand danced toward the phone next to the outside door. "I stopped when I realized what those were pictures *of,* and used that phone to call 911." Tears tumbled down her face. "It was an accident. She didn't do that on purpose. Not with the kids."

"Ma'am?"

"Angie." Edith raised watery eyes, and for the first time Cass realized how old the other woman was, probably in her seventies. "Lenny's stuck on the hay dolly."

———————

CASS RELISHED THE SILENCE as she circled the corral and checked the sparkling dew for signs of footsteps. The clover was darker and flattened along a narrow path that trailed from the corral to the feed troughs, presumably left by the fat cows grazing in a nearby pasture. She'd spoken to Mitch, telling him to get out to the Scarborough's place with Munk as fast as he could. The paramedics had called Grey and he was on his way, bringing Bernie with him. There was nothing to do but wait and document the scene. Cass entered the corral, passing paramedics who murmured quietly while tending to a small, dark-headed woman leaning against the rear wheel of a rusty pickup truck. The heavy dew had been knocked from the grass in a patch roughly the size of a human body, and along a wavering trail that led from the back of the truck to the driver's door. Cass stepped forward to examine Lenny Scarborough.

She guessed that he was in his late thirties or early forties and looked pretty fit. What she could see for certain was that Lenny was dead. He'd been run through with the hay dolly, one of its long spikes entering his body at mid-chest, pinning him against the loading chute's wooden slats. The force of the impact had lifted him off the ground and he hung from the metal spike, work-booted toes dangling like a ghastly ballet dancer caught mid-flight. The taste of death in the air was strong; the coppery tang of blood blending with the waste released from Lenny's bowels and bladder. A dark pool soaked the earth beneath him. Syringes and small glass vials were scattered near his feet, and a toolbox lay on its side, contents spilled and spattered. Cass shivered in the barn's shade as she bent to take pictures. Miraculously, the dolly's spikes angled up between the top two planks and several cows stood quietly in the loading chute, one placidly chewing her cud while she rested in the headlock, waiting to be released. Cass walked to the front of the barn and through the enclosure to snap a few pictures while speaking quietly to the cows. She returned to the corral to take a wider shot of the truck and hay dolly.

One of the paramedics ambled over to stand beside her. The wintergreen smell of his chewing tobacco followed, and she knew it was

Randall Mahaffey. "I didn't know people still used these things," Cass said, gesturing at the hay dolly.

"They're not easy to find any more, but farmers keep them to move a single round roll at a time. Cheap and easy."

"Has she said anything?"

Randall shook his head. "She's in shock. Found her propped up against the truck's rear wheel. Looked like she fell there, maybe trying to get to him. Truck was still running."

"Is she all right?"

"The left side of her face is pretty banged up. Nasty cut near her eye."

"Lenny took a swing at her?"

"More than one, given the state of his right hand."

Cass cocked her head to study the body as a cow lowed from the barn enclosure. Lenny wore a comic expression of surprise. "Pretty gruesome way to go."

"She had to be moving fast to catch him like that. Or maybe he was looking the other way, turned around right before she hit him. She managed to stop before she busted into the loading chute and the cows. Good shot."

"You sure it was Angie?" Cass asked, thinking of the pictures scattered on the kitchen floor.

Randall took a step backwards and spat into a Dr. Pepper can. "Don't see sign of anybody else, but I reckon that's up to you to figure out."

"That's a lot of blood," Cass commented, taking in the stain that spread across and down Lenny's faded overalls. It was darkened and looked stiff, turning a deep rust color as it dried. "It had to hurt."

"Amen." Randall turned to look toward the house. "Where did the old lady go?"

"She's in her car. Edith Lovil. Do you know her?"

"Name's familiar, but no. You know Lenny and Angie?"

"Not really. Lenny's about the same age as my oldest brother, maybe a little older. They might've known each other."

Randall cut his eyes at Cass. "That'd be Jack?"

"Yeah, it would."

"How's he doin'?"

"'Bout like you'd expect," Cass answered, trying to keep the edge out of her voice.

"When does he get out?"

"I'm not sure. It's been twenty-one years, but they gave him life. I'd imagine they meant it for what he was accused of."

"For what it's worth, I always liked Jack. He was a jock, but cool." Cass turned and looked more fully at Randall, taking in his hair, parted down the middle and slicked over his ears, and the heavy frames of his glasses. He was a few years younger than Jack, and she realized that in high school he would've been one of the nerdy kids, those with brains but few social skills. "What happened to him didn't make sense to me. I never thought he did it."

Relief brought a flush to her cheeks. Jack went to prison when Cass was four years old, and she'd never been able to reconcile the older brother that she'd adored to the crimes he was accused of. She studied Lenny's body where it hung. "Who do you think did?"

He turned to check on his fellow paramedic, monitoring Angie as she lay unmoving on the stretcher. Randall shrugged and the polyester of his uniform sighed with the motion. "There were lots of people who were more likely candidates than Jack. He just didn't seem the type. And if you look at it logically, Jack never went without."

Cass glanced at him to find color creeping up his neck. "What do you mean?"

Randall looked down at his shoes and tapped one toe against a tuft of grass. She thought it an odd reaction from a grown man. "Jack never had any trouble gettin' laid, that's all," he finally blurted.

She smiled grimly. "I've never wondered whether Jack had a sex life before all that happened."

"He had plenty of girls chasing him. There was no *reason* for him to do what they said he did. Other people had more motive, if you know what I mean."

"People who couldn't get laid?"

"Not just that. Guys who resented the fact that men like Jack had it easy with girls. And this girl, she was kind of simple. Sweet and gentle, an easy target for anybody who was nice to her. If they'd had DNA testing back then, I don't think Jack would've been arrested."

"Randall, what are you saying?"

He searched her face before continuing. "If you're into conspiracy theories, you'd say that Jack was a fall guy. I mean, I don't think your average bubba is sophisticated enough to set someone up like that, but the way it all happened, it just made me wonder."

Cass fought a surge of warmth at the thought that someone else questioned her brother's culpability for his crimes and again wished desperately that old Comfrey hadn't lost Jack's case file. An engine growled and she turned to see the medical examiner's county issue van picking its way between vehicles as it edged toward the barn. "Who's the uniform?" she asked, lifting her chin toward the figure hovering near a tree, Lenny's body safely out of his line of sight.

"Chad Garrett. He's got no stomach for the wet stuff. I'd better go check on the old lady, see if she's all right. I'll be back in a minute."

"Randall," Cass called as he trotted away, "stay out of the house."

"HE'S BEEN DEAD ABOUT an hour, maybe an hour and a half. Are you done taking pictures?" Grey asked, glancing up at Cass. She nodded. He unwound his long frame from its squat, carefully maintaining his balance as he inched toward his full six foot eight inches. "Mitch, we're going to need some help with this." Grey scratched his head with his forearm, keeping his gloved hands away from his scalp.

Mitch cocked his head to look at the corpse. "How do we get him off that thing?"

"We cut the spike off and transport him with it still in him, or we pull it out. From a forensics perspective, I don't think the spike is too important. Do you?"

"We know that's what killed him. No way to drive that thing through a man's body but by putting your foot on the gas. Truck had to be in reverse. Can't see any point in dusting the spike for fingerprints." Mitch stepped to the side to look at the loading chute where the spike had run through Lenny's body, and he stopped to rub the silky ears of the cow in the headlock. "Only Lenny's gore and cow hair on this side of the spike. And before it slid through him, it would've been covered in hay and manure. You gonna lose anything from the body if we pull it out here?"

"Just blood. Call Kado and make sure he's comfortable that we pull the spike out and he does forensics on it later." Grey glanced at Bernie, who stood beside the pickup's front fender where Munk was labeling fingerprints from the truck's interior. "What do you think?"

"Brutal."

Grey looked at him in astonishment. "You think it was intentional?"

"That's quite a mistake to make. Lining the spike up, putting the truck in reverse, accelerating aggressively and failing to stop when you realize that you're headed toward your husband with a lethal weapon? This was an angry woman."

"I agree," said Cass as Mitch closed the phone on his call to Kado and rejoined them. The ambulance had left shortly after Grey arrived, taking Angie to the hospital. Cass had sent Edith Lovil on her shaky way home, instructing her to be available for further questioning and not to repeat what she'd seen. Officer Chad Garrett had kept his distance, weaving crime scene tape through the fences around the barn. "When I got here, Edith took me to the house. There are photos, several of them, of men having sex with other men and raping a woman."

The four men stared at her.

"Photos where?" Munk asked.

"On the kitchen floor. Looks like Angie saw them and came out after Lenny. Randall said she was pretty banged up, like Lenny had hit her. Maybe she lost it and decided to kill him."

"Whoa," Mitch breathed, stepping back to look at the parallel ruts dug by the truck as it had been driven backwards. "Running somebody through with a hay dolly. And doing it in reverse, that's a special skill."

"She's a farmer's wife. Like they said about Ginger Rogers," Cass replied grimly, "she did everything Fred Astaire did, only backwards and in high heels."

Grey snorted a laugh and Bernie nodded appreciatively.

"There are some fingerprints in the car, but I imagine they're Angie and Lenny's. I'll take a look at the house and process the kitchen," Munk said. "I've known Lenny for a long time. Hard to believe he'd be involved in anything like that."

"I haven't seen sign that anybody else has been out here," Cass said. "We can check with the neighbors to see if they saw or heard anything."

"We'll put a couple of patrol officers on it, but there aren't many people out this way," Mitch said. "It won't take them long. We need to talk to Angie. If she did this, there's no point wasting too much time looking for another suspect."

"I wouldn't expect to talk to her too soon," Grey said. "I called Dr. Ramasubramanian and he's meeting her at the hospital. She'll be sedated for a while."

"How did you know Rambo was her doctor?" Mitch asked.

"Small community."

Mitch scratched his head. "But you're the dead doctor. Rambo's a live doctor."

"We transcend life and death."

"I believe it," Mitch replied, turning to Cass. "How far did you go into the house?"

"I stepped into the kitchen. Edith said she didn't go any farther, either. Just used the phone on the wall by the outside door."

"All right," Mitch said, glancing at his phone. "Kado's fine if we pull the spike out of Lenny as long as we protect the hay dolly. Only way to get it out is to drive the truck forward. Bernie and I can hold Lenny against the chute so he slides off. Grey, you maneuver the gurney to catch him. Munk, you take photos and Cass, you drive. Everybody ready?"

CHAPTER 12

DR. RAMASUBRAMANIAN STOOD BESIDE his patient's bed and listened to the steady rhythm of her heart through a stethoscope. Angie Scarborough was resting quietly, her breathing deep and slow thanks to the wonders of Valium and Demerol. The paramedics had described her as being in a state of deep shock when they arrived at the scene, finding her slouched against the tire of a pickup truck and unresponsive. Wisely, they secured her tightly to the gurney for the short ride to the county hospital. She'd woken during the trip and begun flailing and screaming, a mournful keening that could be heard before the doors to the ambulance were opened at the hospital. Dr. Ramasubramanian had joined the paramedic in the back of the heavy vehicle, speaking quietly to her while preparing the sedative.

"Dr. Rambo," she'd moaned, suddenly aware. "Don't let them take my babies. Oh my God, what has he done?"

He'd soothed her with his oddly inflected voice until the drugs had her in their grip, her swollen eyelids growing heavy, the jerking of her head stilled, her mouth sagging in a silent plea. She was in a private room now with a police officer posted outside. Dr. Ramasubramanian motioned to the nurse and she followed him from the room, pulling the door shut behind them.

"You are waiting for her to awaken?" the doctor asked as the officer strained to understand the gently percolating cadence of Ramasubramanian's speech.

He pushed his wire-rimmed glasses up on his nose. "Detective Stone said to call when she wakes up."

"What is your name?"

"Officer Greg Newton, sir."

"I am pleased to make your acquaintance, Officer Newton. I am Vijay Ramasubramanian. You can call me Dr. Rambo if you wish," he said, smiling shyly.

"Nice to meet you, sir," Newton replied, shaking the doctor's thin hand.

"It will be some time before Mrs. Scarborough is alert."

"How long?"

The doctor shrugged, his pristine lab coat rising with the motion. "I cannot be precise. Perhaps no more than three hours. I will stop to check on her periodically."

Dr. Ramasubramanian walked down the hall, his movements sleek as he selected a chart from its holder on the door, examining the contents before knocking gently and entering the hospital room.

"He's a weird one," Newton said to the nurse. "Muslim?"

"Hindu. He's from India," she replied, checking her pockets and wrapping a stethoscope around her neck. "Dr. Rambo's all right. He's a lot smarter than some of the quacks wearing doctor's badges around here. Coffee?" she asked, peering at him over her half-moon spectacles.

Newton adjusted his chair and sat, squirming until he found a comfortable spot. "I guess so. Looks like it's gonna be a long day." He watched the nurse stride down the hall and turn toward the cafeteria before digging his cell phone from a pocket and pushing a speed dial button. Voice mail answered and he left a brief update on Angie's condition, snapping the phone shut and sliding it in his pocket as the nurse rounded the corner with his coffee.

He accepted it with a smile and pulled a second phone from his pocket. "Detective Stone? This is Officer Newton. I'm at the hospital waiting for Mrs. Scarborough to wake up... Dr. Rambo said it would probably be a few hours. I'll keep you posted... Yes, sir."

He snapped his phone shut and settled back in the chair, pushing his glasses up on his nose, satisfied that his work was done for the time being.

CHAPTER 13

MUNK AND CASS SLIPPED on gloves and booties and stepped through the door. Munk scanned the kitchen and beyond before finally focusing on the photos littering the floor. "God almighty," he said, lifting the camera with a shaking hand. "I don't think that's a woman, Cass. Looks more like a girl to me."

A shift occurred in her perception, and the slender hips suddenly belonged to a child in puberty instead of a thin woman. She had viewed that photograph through the ugly filter of her own experience, and her vision hadn't been wide enough to encompass the thought that these men could be raping a child. But Munk's could. His own child had been missing for seven, or maybe it was eight, years. Her stomach twisted again; for some reason, knowing that this was a child was worse. How he managed to keep hold of his sanity in the face of such a horrible image was beyond Cass. She cleared her throat. "I told Edith Lovil to keep quiet about what she'd seen, but I don't know how long she can keep her mouth shut. This is some juicy gossip."

Munk drew a deep breath, tore his eyes from the photo of the child and studied the rest of the images. "I don't see any faces in the ones that are right side up, do you?"

"No."

"How many are there?"

"I counted seventeen."

"If this is what Angie got worked up about, how did she know Lenny was in the pictures?"

"Maybe she just uh, knows what he looks like?"

Munk smiled grimly. "Maybe so." The house was quiet. "Don't Angie and Lenny have kids?"

"No idea. There are breakfast dishes for two in the drainer."

"Where do you think the pictures came from?"

"With that kind of content, they were hidden. I wonder how Angie found them?"

Munk followed Cass as she stepped gingerly across the kitchen. She paused at the open door to a room containing a desk and what looked to be hundreds of books. "Do you smell vomit?"

"Yeah." He looked around the tidy office. "Probably in the trash can."

Cass followed his glance and waited until Munk had taken several shots before checking. "You're right. You think he kept them in here? What is this, a library?"

"Or a study. There are plenty of places to hide photos. They'd fit in any of those books." Munk scanned the floor-to-ceiling bookshelves, checking spines for titles. "There's a lot of religious stuff. I didn't realize Lenny was into all that."

"How do you know him?"

"We were in school together; he's about my age, maybe a little older."

Cass frowned. "Angie's in her late twenties, early thirties? He's what, fifteen years older than she is?"

"Something like that."

"No offence Munk, but what's a young chick like that doing with such an old guy?"

"Gotta be something about Lenny. He always had some magic pull for women. He didn't marry until he was older, and it seemed odd that he picked Angie."

"Why?" asked Cass, opening a desk drawer and scanning the labeled folders.

"She just wasn't his type. Too racy." He spotted a group of family photos on a far wall and moved to examine them more closely. "Looks like three kids, the oldest boy and girl are teenagers if this picture is recent."

"Those must be Angie's parents," Cass said, pointing to another family grouping that included an elderly couple with a strong resemblance to the young mother. "Are Lenny's parents still alive?"

"No. His mom died when we were in high school and his dad passed about five years ago." He shook his head. "Let's check through the rest of the house. You can get to the hospital, see how Angie's doing. I'll start on the hay dolly and sort out the pictures in the kitchen." He reached for his phone with a sigh. "Guess I'd better call Kado and make sure he's happy that I touch anything."

———————

CASS EASED HER TRUCK into an empty space as a plump ginger cat reluctantly abandoned his watch over the trio of chickens scratching at the courthouse lawn and moved out of her way. She knew the chickens were safe. The cat had lost an eye to an aggressive rooster when he was just a kitten, and although he loved to stalk the birds that roamed Forney County's square, he kept his distance. The day remained comfortable as the sun played hide and seek with the massive cotton ball clouds that drifted across the wide sky. Shops on the square were closed on Sundays, but the restaurants were busy. Congregants recently released from church services waited good-naturedly under wide awnings or beneath the shade trees on the lawn while those who finished church early ate lunch.

"Mornin' Cass," a familiar voice growled behind her. "Makes me want to convert to Methodism just to get fed first. They beat us Baptists to lunch every Sunday. I've heard the preachers aren't as long winded, and they don't sing all the verses." Cass turned and smiled into the broad, friendly face of David Wayne Rusted, Arcadia's mayor. Two teenage boys hustled over to where they stood.

"Hey Dad, Matt and Mark Grove are over there. We want to hear about the bones they found last night. Call us when the table's ready."

"No climbing the trees or the war memorial, all right?" They grinned in acknowledgment and trotted away. "My son and one of his friends, Jed Salter's son. Good boys, but lively at times. Those bones sure got some tongues wagging."

Cass laughed. "There's no keeping a secret in this town."

"Certainly not something that exciting. Any leads on who the bones belong to?"

"No, sir, not yet."

Mayor Rusted dabbed the sweat beading his upper lip, taking in her blue cotton blouse, khaki trousers and boots. "You working?"

"Yes, sir. Do you know Lenny Scarborough?"

"I do. What's wrong?"

"He died this morning."

Mayor Rusted's smooth, fat face contracted. "That's unexpected."

Cass paused as a watery gurgle sounded from his bowels, and wondered at his reaction. "Yes, sir. Murder usually is."

He blinked at the word. "What happened?"

"We're not sure yet, but we found him impaled on a hay dolly."

"One of those metal contraptions, with two spears on it?"

"Yes, sir."

"Good Lord," he breathed, eyes growing wide. "How did that happen?"

"Angie was in shock when the paramedics got to the Scarborough's place, and we haven't been able to speak with her."

"Was it an intruder?"

"We don't know yet, but please keep the details to yourself."

Mayor Rusted ran a dimpled hand over his sweaty face. "Those poor kids. Lenny had an investment in one of the insurance companies in town. Angie and the kids will be taken care of, but as you know too well," he said, his gaze somber as he recalled the Elliot family history, "there's no compensation for growing up without a parent."

———————

MAYOR RUSTED STRODE ACROSS the courthouse lawn, moving easily for a man of his size. The hanging tree stood near one corner of the lawn and a group of elderly men, ill at ease in their Sunday best, spat discreetly and gossiped under its ample limbs as the Mayor nodded an absent greeting while fumbling a cell phone from his pocket. Cass watched him go, wondering whether she had correctly interpreted his reaction to Lenny Scarborough's death as fear. She tried to recall the men in all the photos and compare their body compositions to the mayor's. If she had to choose one word to describe David Wayne Rusted, it would have to be "rotund". His body was a collection of various sized balls resting one atop another. His round head sat directly on a very large, round torso, by-passing any neck he might possess. The torso rested on two bulging thighs that gave way to bulging calves. His arms were oblong clumps of fat that ended in sausage-shaped fingers. But it was his gut that interested Cass the most. From what she remembered, none of the men in the photos she saw possessed the degree of girth owned by the mayor. He called to his son that it was time for lunch and disappeared into Arcadia's only Italian restaurant.

She turned at last, walking slowly up a wide sidewalk to the old building, eyes scanning its curious architecture. Constructed in the late nineteenth century from cream-colored Texas sandstone, Forney County's courthouse was a blend of plantation home and European castle, with steep gables sporting tall windows and shutters. The town's clock clanged in its tower as Cass keyed a code into a security pad and opened the front door. The building had been modified over the years and two leggy additions splayed to either side of the main entrance, housing improved court facilities on one side and the police department's offices on the other. Increasing demand for residence in the jailhouse meant that it was moved off the square many years ago and was now located a short walk away. Many counties had moved their courthouses when the big retail centers sprung up on the outskirts of town, but Forney's remained on the square and its residents seemed determined to keep the downtown area alive.

Cass crossed the dark, silent lobby and pushed through the swinging doors that led into the police station in the north wing. Once past the main hall that housed the administrative offices, she keyed in a second code to enter the secured area, designed to give the department some independence from the rest of the courthouse. She found Mitch in the squad room, pouring a cup of coffee as he finished a call.

"That was Dr. Rambo. He said to give Angie another hour or so. She'll be groggy but able to answer questions."

"Has he called her parents?"

Mitch nodded. "Her mother is down there and might have to be sedated, too. Seems she thought the world of Lenny. The kids are with Angie's father."

"That seems strange for a mother-in-law, but I guess Darla's mom would be tore up if something happened to you," Cass chuckled.

He grinned. "Don't I know it."

"Did you know Angie was so much younger than Lenny?"

Mitch glanced around the squad room before speaking. They were alone. "Angie was a prostitute when Lenny met her, working over on Whiskey Bend." Her eyes widened. "I don't remember it all, but she was going downhill fast. Arrested for drug possession. Anyway, they got married and not long after that they had a kid. Been together ever since."

"You think he's always beat her?"

"I've never heard anything about it if he has. I checked the system. Her record's still there, but there's nothing on Lenny." He glanced at the clock on the wall and rubbed his trim middle. "Can you handle some lunch? I told Grey we'd bring something to the ME's office. He should be done with Lenny pretty quick now."

Cass was surprised to hear her stomach growl. "You think they've got any chicken fried steak left out at the barn?"

Mitch smiled. "Only one way to find out."

CHAPTER 14

"WHERE ARE YOU?" DAVID Wayne Rusted demanded.

"Why Mayor," the old man answered. "How nice to hear from you on this fine Sunday. We're over in Shreveport for lunch. What can I do for you?"

"Have you heard about Lenny Scarborough?"

The old man paused, glancing at his wife as she waited for him to settle the bill. He'd brought her to a swank new Creole place and from the way her foot was tapping under the table, he knew she was fairly hopping to get home and report in to her sister. He pulled a set of keys from his pocket and held them out to her. "Go start the car, sweetheart. I'll be right there."

She flashed him a look of irritation and tapped her watch, but took the keys and swept from the restaurant. Her head swiveled from side to side as she walked and the old man wondered if those eagle eyes would spot a familiar face. He clamped his cold pipe between his teeth as he watched her go, and smiled at the attractive waitress bringing him the check.

"I have, Mayor, and it's a tragic thing," the old man said as he scanned the bill and pulled his wallet from a hip pocket. "Where did you hear about it?"

"From Cass Elliot, one of Hoffner's detectives. You know her?"

The old man grunted a positive reply around his pipe, running a finger between shirt collar and neck. His hungry gaze followed the young woman's form as she wove through the tables to pick up his payment. She smiled at him over her shoulder as she headed for the cash register.

"Did you hear how he died?" Mayor Rusted sputtered. "Do you know who killed him?"

"Yes, I heard what happened, but I understand the police are still investigating."

"This is a problem. Who's going to gather his things?"

"Don't worry, Mayor, it's been taken care of."

"What about the Circle? It has to be closed as quickly as possible."

"All in the Lord's good time, Mayor," he answered, face flushing as irritation flooded up his spine at David Wayne's panic. He reached for the credit card slip, smiled his thanks at the waitress and pushed up from the leather booth, pocketing his pipe as he surveyed the room. The food had been good; his wife had a nose for excellent restaurants. And the atmosphere was nice as well – they had a three-piece jazz band, which was pretty ritzy for Shreveport, and the waitresses looked too good to stay away for long. He'd be more generous with his tip next time. He pushed through the revolving door and raised a hand to shield his eyes from the bright sunlight.

"I'll put things in motion when I'm home, David Wayne. If you would, call the other members and let them know what's happened, but ask them to take no action until they hear from me." The old man heard a deep breath from the phone, and knew the Mayor was calming down.

"Fine. I'll keep in touch as I hear more."

"You do that Mayor," the old man replied as he opened the car door and slid into the driver's seat. "You do that."

LENNY SCARBOROUGH LOOKED PEACEFUL on the autopsy table, even with his chest and abdomen splayed open under the harsh lights. He was as fit as Cass had imagined, the long taut muscles of his legs connecting to a relatively flat stomach. His shoulders were narrow but carried a wiry strength that flowed down arms bearing a farmer's tan. Bernie worked quietly across the table from Grey, responding to requests for instruments and weighing organs.

"Cause of death was the spike. Mechanism was exsanguination. The spike missed his heart, and he was probably conscious for at least a few moments."

"What a way to go," whispered Mitch.

Grey nodded, head bent over the open chest cavity. "I won't be able to rule on manner of death until you speak with Angie, but I agree with Bernie at this point," he said, stopping to lift his head, "I'll have a hard time believing this wasn't intentional."

"Is there anything else from the autopsy that's relevant?" Cass asked.

"Other than having a spike driven through his chest, a banged-up right hand, one scar on his hip and another on his right rib cage, Lenny Scarborough was a pretty healthy man. Any questions?"

When the others remained silent, Bernie lifted his nose to the air, sniffed once, and asked, "Do I smell lunch?"

———————

THE OLD MAN TUGGED at his tie and wrenched open the shirt's top button, relishing the rush of air across his sweaty throat. He hated Sundays. All that sanctimonious 'praise the Lord' and 'what a glorious day, Brother' bullshit. They'd be right back to their snide gossip and little white lies before lunch congealed on their plates. But appearances mattered, so there he was on Sunday morning with the rest of them, shaking hands and greeting with gusto. Lunch was Sunday's only redeeming quality.

He clamped his teeth on a cold, empty pipe and sat on the bed, grunting as he leaned down to untie his dress shoes. The situation with Lenny Scarborough was disturbing – and created two problems in one: promoting someone to fill Lenny's position and selecting a new member from among The Brethren. They were always prepared to replace a member of the Circle of Illumination, but the current candidates for new membership, those belonging to The Way, were weak. It was getting harder and harder to find like-minded men who were prepared to commit themselves wholly to The Church's goals. He needed a certain breed, those lacking in self-confidence but with an undercurrent of anger or fear driving them toward success and powerful office. Someone requiring guidance and willing to do the unthinkable for approval. Through the years, the old man had come to realize that there was an important difference between men who hold power regardless of their position, and those who hold powerful office regardless of their nature. To ensure the longevity of The Church, he needed a balance of both.

Above all, the old man was a pragmatist. He recognized that his beloved Church was changing. Its origins were rooted in the social upheaval of the early twentieth century, when the voices of those who felt they were entitled to live off the sweat of another man's brow began to gather volume. Women, blacks, immigrants. They forgot their place in society and began acting on their yearning for those things, those rights, other men had earned. A select group, the old man's grandfather among them, came together and searched the Bible for instruction on dealing with those who wished to usurp their rightful place in society. They created a new text designed to enlighten and inspire. And began pushing against the usurpers using those tools with which they were best equipped: economic sabotage.

These men held sway over jobs, loans, medical histories and official police interest in a person's activities. Manipulation in any one of these areas could force a change in the direction of a person's life. Rumors of a woman diagnosed with syphilis, true or not, could upend her job and marital prospects. Denial of a loan, or the calling of an existing loan, could ruin a man's chances for advancement. But times were simpler then. Nowadays, with the changes brought about by Kennedy, Johnson and that damn Martin Luther King Jr., The Church had to move with more caution, and in some cases, exercise more extreme means of admonishing those who proved a challenge to the norm. With a slight smile, the old man once again thanked the good Lord for providing such a valuable tool as Hitch.

His mind left its reminiscing, and returned to The Church's current problem. Yes, they'd have to be careful with the selection for The Circle of Illumination and also for the new member. The old man mentally shuffled through the current candidates until his crafty mind landed on a fresh recruit to The Way. The man had been tested and performed well. Perhaps it was time to take a chance and initiate him as one of The Brethren. And having another police officer as a member of The Church was no bad thing. He gripped the tips of his socks and pulled them off, wiggling his moist toes. He'd have to make some time to think about Lenny and his replacement.

So, that redheaded Elliot woman had dealt with the Scarborough situation. He stuck a yellowed nail up one nostril and scraped, inspecting the stiff residue before flicking it from his finger, wondering why in the world Hoffner allowed women on the force. It was bad enough with all the coloreds and spics, but women? Never would have happened under the old sheriff. Women were weak, unable to meet force with force. He conceded that some women were better peacemakers than men; that old nun from India, she was a good example. But women weren't equipped to deal with the complexities of the modern world. They simply didn't have the smarts or the grit. All this equal rights nonsense had been running the country into the ground for decades, and now it was impacting his little slice of the world.

He listened to his wife prattle to her sister about lunch and watched her hang up the phone with a satisfied smirk. Tutting, she tugged the unlit pipe from his mouth and deposited it in an ashtray before swooping down to gather his socks and shoes. She placed them in the laundry basket and closet, fussing gently about the pills he'd forgotten to take with his lunch. *Now this is more like it*, he thought, admiring her still firm bottom as she bent over to stuff cedar blocks into his shoes.

He pulled his tie over his head and handed it to her, and then reached for his phone as he lowered his glasses to examine the buttons. He needed to know how things were progressing out at the Scarborough's.

CHAPTER 15

"ARE THE COWS HURT?" Angie Scarborough asked as they entered her room. She struggled to keep her eyes open as Dr. Ramasubramanian checked her pulse. The left side of her face bloomed red and raw in the fluorescent lights, the white of her eye now a slit of angry scarlet between her swollen eyelids.

A narrow hand snaked from a dim corner next to the bed, reaching to stroke her dark hair. "Now sweetheart, just calm down."

The younger woman pulled away, eyes clearing. "Are they hurt?"

"Ma'am, were you driving the truck?" Mitch asked.

"The cows," she demanded, straining to push higher on the pillows.

"They're fine," Cass answered, closing her eyes briefly against the hospital's antiseptic scent and the memories it evoked. "None were injured."

"Thank God." She found the position she'd struggled for and settled with a tired sigh. "I guess you want a statement."

Cass glanced at Dr. Ramasubramanian. The thin man nodded once, balding head gleaming in the overhead lights. "Yes, ma'am, if you're strong enough to talk."

"Now Angie, you should wait until we've got a lawyer down here." A pinched woman leaned toward the bed, her face strained in the bright lights. "Think of the children."

"For once Mother, I am," she said, softening her words by reaching for the slender hand. Angie drew a shuddering breath and focused on Cass. "I killed Lenny. You found the pictures?"

Cass nodded.

Angie's eyes filled with tears. She pointed to her face. "He did this when I confronted him. He's hit me before, but never like this. He's usually smarter, tries to hide the damage. Maybe he knew what was coming and didn't care." She fingered the smooth sheet. "He didn't deny it. Any of it.

62

Just laughed when I told him I'd found him out. He *laughed*, can you believe that?"

"What are you talking about?" her mother asked.

"Your perfect son-in-law is – was – a homosexual and abusing your granddaughter." The older woman gasped as the sound of Angie's choked laughter filled the small room.

"Lenny was no such thing," her mother said, voice sharp. "He has always been a kind and gentle husband, and has given selflessly for the children. Detective," she added, watery voice growing stronger as she pulled herself into the light, "I insist that this stop right now. She's suffered a severe shock seeing her husband killed like that. And she's confused from the sedative the doctor's given her. I may need one myself if this goes on."

"That's enough, Mother! You have no idea who Lenny was. I will not bend to him any longer." Her words were firm, eyes bright as she found Cass again. "I told him I'd take the pictures to the police. That's when he started to laugh, and he hit me. It must've knocked me silly, because next thing I knew I was flat on the ground and Lenny had gone back to working on the cows." She drew a deep breath.

Dr. Ramasubramanian shifted his slight weight and placed a hand on Angie's shoulder. "The police can wait, Mrs. Scarborough. I would like for you to rest now."

"Not yet, Dr. Rambo. I need to finish it." She focused on Cass. "I don't know if it is my daughter in those pictures. Maybe it doesn't matter. All of Lenny's preaching at me for all these years, and it was nothing but lies. I knew it wouldn't stop. So, I climbed in the cab, punched the accelerator and speared him." A ghastly slash split her face when she smiled. "He turned at the last minute and I watched his face in the rearview mirror. He didn't think I had it in me."

"Did he say where the photos came from?" Cass asked.

Angie shook her head. "He just laughed."

"What photos are you talking about?" her mother asked.

Cass had looked to Mitch when Angie spoke, her tired voice flat. "Pictures of your son-in-law screwing other men and raping at least one child. Pictures don't lie, Mother."

"Oh my goodness," the older woman whispered, skin growing sallow as she looked at Cass. "Lenny? Is this right?"

"There are photographs, but we haven't confirmed identities yet."

"Lenny's in them," Angie replied. "He has scars on one hip and on his chest. The right side. Match them to his body."

"Good heavens," her mother breathed, eyes rolling back in their sockets as she slid toward the floor. Mitch lurched for her as Angie started to giggle, developing a deep belly laugh that brought tears to her eyes.

Dr. Ramasubramanian shouted for a nurse and rushed to help Mitch move the older woman to a chair. He checked her pulse, his dark, solemn eyes watching Angie as she cackled.

"Fainting is a suitable Southern response to anything vulgar, Dr. Rambo. Wave smelling salts under her nose and give her some attention. She'll be fine," Angie assured him, blowing her nose. She sighed, cheeks glowing and good eye twinkling. "Lord, I feel better. Look, you might as well sit down. I need a Dr. Pepper and I'll be fine. Who has change for the machine?"

CHAPTER 16

OFFICER SCOTT TRUMAN SCRAPED the cow muck off his boots and joined Kado and Munk near the Scarborough's back door. Tall and slender, his fair hair and skin confirmed a Scandinavian ancestry. But instead of the traditional clear blue eyes, Truman's were hazel and fringed with gold-tipped lashes. Their color almost matched the tawny shade of a lion's eyes, and women found them irresistible. He watched Munk wipe mustard from the corner of his mouth.

"Thanks for the burgers," Munk sighed. "I was starving. I can't believe it's almost five o'clock."

"Speaking of being hungry, I put out more feed for the cows. The ones that Lenny finished with this morning ate everything and the cows stuck in the chute looked hungry. Is two bags enough for forty head?" Truman asked, leaning against a patrol car.

Kado raised his eyebrows, gray eyes thoughtful. "I've never even wondered how much a cow eats. Munk?"

"They'll make it until morning," he grunted, squinting toward the barn. "Looks like Lenny put fresh hay out. Must be why the dolly was still out there. Did you open the side gate?"

Truman grinned. "They headed straight for the pond."

Munk stretched his pudgy arms over his head, yawning as Mitch's truck turned into the drive and pulled to a stop. "How'd it go with Angie?" he called.

"Unbelievable," Mitch said. "She confessed."

"Did you arrest her?"

"Not yet."

"Why not?"

"There might be mitigating circumstances."

"What could mitigate spearing your husband? That was pre-meditated."

"According to Angie, Lenny was involved with a group of men that had some religious connection and they'd meet once a month, always at night. Lenny seemed to think he was special because there weren't many men involved. He had a briefcase that he kept stuff relating to this group in, including some sort of purple choir robe and a religious text that he read instead of his Bible."

"What's wrong with a little fellowship? Maybe the text was inspirational. Sounds normal enough," Munk said.

"Lenny wore some kind of choir robe when he was with these guys, and Angie said that sometimes it came home smelling like smoke and dirty with mud or blood."

Munk raised an eyebrow. "That's a little bizarre, but I still don't see why you didn't arrest her."

"Two reasons," Mitch answered. "First, she said that Lenny had hit her before today, so the abuse could be long term. Second, she thought that was her daughter in the photographs, and she suspects they were taken while Lenny was with this group of men. If so, there's a whole group out there abusing kids."

"But she *killed* him. She admitted it."

"Angie's not going anywhere, Munk. We need to deal with the murder, but abuse is the real issue." Mitch hesitated, eyeing Munk and wondering how his personal history would impact the investigation. "There's at least one girl being raped in those pictures."

Color flushed up Munk's cheeks and he rubbed clenched fists into his eyes. "You're right. And given what I saw in the rest of the photos, the ones that were upside down, it could be gang rape."

They were silent for several moments, the ticking of the engine and the rustling of the cows the only noise in the golden afternoon.

"How badly is Angie hurt?" Kado asked.

"She was pretty beat up," Mitch answered. "Her face is bruised and Dr. Rambo said she probably has a concussion."

"Could she be making this stuff up?"

"She was lucid, if that's what you mean."

Munk shook his head. "It just seems strange to think of Lenny Scarborough being messed up with something like the Klan and abusing kids."

"I don't think what she described is the Ku Klux Klan."

"Why not?"

"The Klan tends to stir things up, not just meet at night and prance around in robes. They also recruit actively, not limit their membership. I'm sure they're around, but things have been quiet for a while now." Mitch stood and stretched. "Have you moved anything in the house?"

"No. Just took photos and prints, and inventoried the pictures in the kitchen." Munk rolled his eyes toward Kado. "After I checked with the forensics guy."

Mitch ignored him. "Good. I wasn't sure we needed the prints, but I talked to Sheriff Hoffner, and he thought the men in the photographs might've been inside the house at some point. We may be able to ID them that way." Mitch's eyes wandered over the frame house. "Did you have any inkling that something like this might be going on around here?"

Munk shook his head and Kado just shrugged.

"Truman?"

He stared at the ground, young face pale. "I've never heard about the kind of things Angie told you."

"But?"

"But, I have been asked to join a group of men."

"And?" Mitch asked, frowning as he rested an elbow on the side of the pickup's bed.

"It's probably nothing. I haven't even gone. Just haven't had time."

"Why is it bothering you?"

Truman took a deep breath and ran a hand over his short blonde hair, trying to smooth his cowlick. "I guess it sounded weird to me. It's this elite group, membership by invitation only. They try and make a difference in the community."

"Sounds like the Lion's Club or the Masons."

"Yeah, but they meet in the woods. And," he said, "I wasn't supposed to tell anyone about it, not even my family."

"Why not?"

He shrugged. "I haven't given it much thought."

"When were you approached?"

"Six months ago. After I joined the force. That's why I haven't done anything with it, I just haven't had time."

"Who approached you?"

Truman hesitated again.

"Scott," Mitch continued, "if you think there's a link between this group and the men that Angie believes are molesting children, you're obliged to report it."

"Mitch," Munk interrupted quietly. "I think we should go in the house. Give Truman, Kado and yourself a chance to see these photos and look for more. If Truman's got any doubts, that'll clear them up."

———————

TRUMAN SAT WITH HIS head between his knees, Mitch's hand on his back. "You all right?"

"Yes, sir," he answered, voice muffled as he spoke to the floor in Lenny Scarborough's study. "I've never seen anything like this, that's all." He gulped a breath of air and slowly raised himself upright to look at the computer monitor. "I mean, pornography's one thing, but this…"

"Girly magazines are in a different league, huh?"

The young man blushed and glanced at Cass, who burst out laughing from her position next to the bookcases. The room had grown murky in the early evening gloom and she flipped on the overhead light as she regained her composure. "Truman, my six brothers must've collected a copy of every *Playboy* and *Penthouse* magazine ever printed. I've probably seen more of them than you have."

A shaky grin crossed his face.

"You all right?" Mitch asked again.

Truman nodded and pointed a trembling finger at the computer's screen. "This is definitely Lenny. The scar matches the photo Grey sent to you." He flipped the phone shut and handed it to Mitch. "There are no bookmarks or cookies linking to pornographic websites, nothing to indicate that he's used the computer for pornography other than the photos."

"You think they were all taken in the same place?"

Truman flipped between several shots. "The background never changes. There's no natural light. Looks like wooden walls, maybe paneling. I can do more with them at the station." He paused and scanned the other directories. "What do you want me to do with this? There's homework and stuff on it."

"That was risky, wasn't it? Keeping the photos on the same computer? I mean, kids are pretty smart these days. Why didn't they find the pictures?"

"The file with the photos in it is password protected. Lenny taped the password to the bottom of his desk drawer. It's a combination of Lenny's and Angie's initials and birth dates. A kid wouldn't have figured that out," Truman answered. "Kado, do you want the whole computer? There are 49 shots in this folder."

"Yes." He held up a digital camera. "There are no shots in memory but we can try and pull images from the chip."

Munk returned to the room, placing the damp wastebasket next to the desk. "Kado, I took a sample and washed the rest of the stuff out."

"Thanks, Munk. That was a nasty job."

He grunted, color returning to his pockmarked face. He turned his back to Kado and faced Cass at the bookshelves. "You want help with those books?"

"Finish checking those two bottom shelves for pictures. I'm almost done with the rest," she answered, flipping the pages of a slim volume by C.S. Lewis. "This," she hefted a heavy tome and looked at its spine, "is the book Angie found the photos in. *The Church of the True Believer.*"

"How did she know to look there?" Munk asked.

"She said she'd seen Lenny sliding it into the bookcase and thought he was hiding a birthday card in it. She found the photos when she came to look. Did you find the briefcase?"

"I checked the house after you called," Munk answered, awkwardly settling into a cross-legged sitting position on the floor, "but didn't see it. Searched through the closets looking for that robe, but there was nothing in any of them. You sure nobody's been here?"

"I don't see how," Cass replied. "We've had an officer here since Edith Lovil called it in and nobody else has been out here. Anything from the prints?"

"Angie keeps a clean house. At first glance, it looks like two or three sets of adult prints and several kids. Who's the officer on duty?"

"Chad Garrett," Mitch said. "I'll speak to him before we leave. You check the attic?"

"And the root cellar," Munk answered. "Nothing down there but cobwebs and mason jars."

Mitch knuckled his eyes, stifling a yawn. "Seems strange that we found the book but not the other stuff. Angie said she didn't know what was in the briefcase, that Lenny kept it locked. But, she knew about the purple robe because she'd washed it for him. Said she hung it in the closet but it would disappear and she figured he put it in that briefcase. Truman, are you done with the computer?"

"Yes, sir," the young officer answered, folding the last of the cables and placing them in a box for transportation to the courthouse.

"Go have a look out in the barn for this briefcase and robe. While you're at it, check the car out front. I think the keys are by the door."

"Yes, sir."

Mitch waited until he saw Truman take the keys from their hook and leave the kitchen before speaking again. "If what Angie told us links up with this group that approached Truman, I don't think he fits the profile."

Kado's head popped up from behind the desk, where he was flipping through the files in a bottom drawer. His gray eyes were clouded. "Mitch, are you thinking cult?"

Munk scowled at them from his spot on the floor. "That's ridiculous. Lenny's not the type."

"How well did you know him?"

"I haven't really spoken to him since high school," Munk said, slipping a thin volume from a shelf. "But it's stupid to think that a man from a family like the Scarborough's would be messed up in something like this."

"Based on the photos," Kado retorted, "he molested that kid and got a blow job from some guy who needed a shave. He must've changed plenty after high school."

Munk released a sigh, deflating a bit. "It just seems far-fetched, that's all."

Mitch studied the other man, whose round face was tilted down as if he were examining the floor. He needed Munk on this case. The man was good with evidence, consistently deliberate and thorough. But the emotional strain of working on an investigation involving molested children, while not knowing what had happened – or *was* happening if she was still alive – to his own daughter might be too much. Mitch cleared his throat and spoke in a low voice. "Are you going to be okay with this case?"

Munk slowly twisted his head to look up, and the pain Mitch saw in his eyes stabbed into his heart. "I have to be. They're somebody's kids," he said quietly.

Mitch nodded and exhaled slowly, and then answered Kado, picking up on the man's earlier question. "Yeah, maybe cult. Except Truman doesn't seem the kind they'd want to recruit. I mean, the point of a cult is to get someone to do something they wouldn't normally do, like donate all their money, follow blindly and steal or kill, right? Truman's too well grounded for any of that. He's a smart kid, comes from a good family, knows what he wants and seems like he's willing to work for it."

Kado frowned. "I don't know much about cults, but I keep going back to your question from earlier: Did anybody have any idea that something like this was going on? Seems that the answer is 'no'. This has to be a small group or someone *would* have heard about it."

Munk grunted from his kneeling position next to the bookcase and held out a cream colored card. "Found this in one of those books on Satan."

"What is it?" Kado asked, switching on a desk lamp against the intruding evening gloom. They leaned forward to examine the small square of paper. "That's unusual writing."

Cass pulled a loose strand of hair to the back of her neck, hooking it around her limp French twist. "It says," she squinted, "'You are cordially invited to a Celebration of Illumination on the Eighteenth of October 1988 at The Sanctuary.' No names." She raised her head. "What's a celebration of illumination?"

"No idea," answered Mitch, sitting back in the desk chair.

"Bag it," Kado instructed as Munk was slipping the card into a plastic bag. Munk glared and Kado smiled ruefully, holding his gloved hands up in apology. "Sorry."

The screen door slammed against its frame and Truman's boots thumped across the kitchen. He shook his head as he came into the study. "Nothing in the barn or the car."

"All right," Mitch said. "So far, we've got a dead man, photos showing homosexual acts and the rape of a child, a study loaded with books on Christianity and the devil, and an invitation to a celebration." He held the bagged invitation out for Truman to inspect.

"And a woman with a shady past who admits she murdered her husband," Munk added.

"That, too." Mitch sighed deeply and stood, stretching his long frame. He glanced at the fair-haired young officer standing near the door. "Truman, are you ready to tell us who invited you to join this group?"

Truman drew a deep breath and expelled it slowly. "Officer Petchard."

Munk snorted a laugh. "There's not a cult around that would have Hugo Petchard as a member."

"I didn't say he was a member of a cult. He's just the one who asked me to join." He hesitated. "What'll happen to him?"

Mitch pulled on his lower lip. "Nothing, for now. We'll do some discreet checking to see if there's anything about Officer Petchard that warrants additional attention." He studied the young man for a moment. "Officer Truman, I'll make a formal request to have you and Officer Munk moved from patrol to this investigation. Do you have any problem with that?"

Truman's smooth face broke into a wide grin. "No, sir."

"Munk?"

He flicked a glance at Kado. "If the forensic guy wants me, I'm happy to help."

Kado nodded. "Fine by me."

"All right," Mitch said. "Now, what should we do with Angie?"

Munk rose to his full height and rubbed his rounded stomach as his eyes wandered over the family photos on the walls. "Lenny Scarborough was well respected. We've got nothing to support Angie's claim that he beat her on a regular basis. She never reported it." He held up a hand to stop Cass's protests. "I know. Lots of battered women never report the abuse, and somebody *did* beat her up today, so it could be true. We've got speculation from Angie about a secret group of men who meet at night and wear choir robes." He shrugged. "There's no evidence of that, either."

"What are you saying?" Cass demanded.

"Maybe she made it all up."

"Come on, Munk."

"Cass, she was a prostitute. She had a problem with drugs. Maybe she got back into them. Maybe she was still woozy from the sedative Dr. Rambo gave her and got confused. Maybe she got pissed off because her husband was having sex with men and raping girls. All I'm saying is that we've got no evidence to support her story, other than the pictures. Maybe they could drive a woman to murder, and to lie about the reasons why."

CHAPTER 17

A CAR DOOR SLAMMED and a curtain twitched in a softly lit window. The old man opened the front door and strode across the wide porch, down the steps and across the lawn to where Officer Chad Garrett waited. Even in the wan glow of a dim moon the old man could see bits of clover and rye grass clinging to his uniform's trousers. The shine on his black shoes was clouded with muck.

"Evening, son. Good work calling this morning."

"Thank you, sir," he said, holding out a chunky legal style briefcase and thinking it odd that, in his late forties, anyone would call him 'son'. "Is this what you wanted?"

The old man scowled at the case's weight. Twisting the locks and snapping the clasps open, he glanced up at Garrett and used the hood of the patrol car to balance the briefcase while he poked through it. His eyes narrowed to slits. "You take anything out of here?"

"No, sir. What's missing?"

The old man ignored the question. "Where'd you find it?"

"In an office."

He shut the briefcase, twirling the locks before placing it carefully on the ground and leaning against the patrol car to examine the younger man through the evening's gloom. Digging a pipe from one pocket and a tobacco pouch from the other, he rubbed and fluffed the thin strands before trickling them into the bowl. With the cold pipe clamped between his teeth, he replaced the pouch and withdrew a silverish object he used to tamp the tobacco. He lifted one foot to scratch a lucifer across his shoe sole and waved the flame gently over the pipe, drawing steadily through the stem. Again he tamped and passed the match over the bowl, sucking the flame into the tobacco. His weathered face flickered as the flame rose and fell, fat puffs of smoke layering a veil around his head. Ritual complete, he speared Chad Garrett with his eyes. "Who was out there?"

"The paramedics came first. Then Detective Elliot showed up. John Grey, Officer Munk, Detective Stone and some foreign guy came out and worked on Lenny and the truck."

"Foreign?" the old man asked.

"Yes, sir. He was with Grey."

"Anyone else?"

He paused, thinking. "Scott Truman and the new forensics guy came later."

"Who went in the house?"

"All of them but Grey and his friend."

"They take anything with them?"

"Yes, sir."

"What?"

"A few boxes of stuff. I don't know what was in them."

"Then find out."

"I, uh, I'm not sure I can do that."

The aroma of cherry scented smoke filled the evening air. "Why not?"

"I don't have access to the evidence room."

"Then get it."

"It's not that simple, sir."

"Damn it son, who does have access?"

"It's mostly the receptionist and Kado who go in there."

"Get yourself assigned to this case."

"Sir?"

"You heard me."

"But I'm patrol," Garrett protested. "We don't work on investigations."

The old man waved a dismissive hand as he bent to retrieve the briefcase. "Show some initiative, boy. I don't care how you do it, but I want you to find out what they took from the house and I want it tomorrow. I'll double the payment."

The smoky veil dissolved and Garrett swallowed as he looked into the old man's eyes. Their flat surface glittered in the early starlight and gooseflesh broke out on his arms at the absence of anything human in them. He searched his mouth for moisture. "Y-yes, sir."

"Tomorrow. Or I'll let your wife in on our little secret," he grinned, baring nicotine stained teeth. "And that would be expensive, wouldn't it?"

CHAPTER 18

MITCH EASED HIS TRUCK into the carport and watched through the window as Darla puttered around the kitchen. He couldn't suppress a grin at the sight of her. Even after all these years, he was still amazed she had agreed to marry him. And equally amazed that her father hadn't simply shot him and left his body for the hogs when he had asked for Darla's hand. Their married life had been imperfect at best, thanks mostly to his insecurity and bone-headedness. But his wife had always found the courage to tolerate him, and at times forgive him, even when he was at his worst.

He had first seen her at the Dairy Queen when they were both freshmen at the local college. Mitch was still reeling from his best friend's arrest for rape and murder earlier that same year. He and Jack Elliot had been inseparable since their first day in kindergarten. They came from vastly different backgrounds, and perhaps that was what had drawn them together. Mitch's parents had died in an automobile accident when he was a toddler. And although the childless aunt and uncle who had taken responsibility for him met all his needs, he sensed that their expressions of affection came from duty, rather than from the heart.

Jack, on the other hand, was the first-born and adored by his parents and his younger siblings. In kindergarten, he had only two. In the years to come, the Elliot clan would expand to encompass six boys, each separated by two years, and one girl, born four years after the youngest boy. The Elliots were a poor family, considered white trash by some because of Abe Elliot's problem with booze. But Mitch had never felt more at home than when he was with Jack. And in spite of being surrounded by siblings, Jack's bond with Mitch had only grown through the years. Both were smart and ambitious. They had planned and schemed their way out of Forney County a million different ways. But they knew the only realistic path of escape was to leave through education. And so, as their senior year in high school had drawn to a close, the two applied to and were accepted by Forney County's college, meager scholarships in hand. But then Jack was arrested. And everything changed.

Although more than twenty years had passed, Mitch still didn't understand what had happened to Jack. His best friend had never spoken to him about that night. Wouldn't even see Mitch until after he had been in the state prison at Huntsville for two years. After Jack's arrest, Mitch was left with waves of confusion and pain crashing through his brain, threatening to derail his plans for escaping Forney County. The chaos in his head didn't quiet until he spotted Darla. She walked into the small restaurant, ordered a hot fudge sundae, smiled at him as he waited for a burger and fries, and took his breath away. From that moment, his life had purpose again. And strangely enough, with Darla by his side, he had been content to settle in Forney County.

Darla glanced out the kitchen window and smiled when she heard the pickup's door slam. That gentle curve of her lips was all it took to wash the imprint of Lenny Scarborough's impaled body to the back of Mitch's brain. She opened the kitchen door and Zeus tumbled down the steps, a slimy tennis ball in his mouth. Mitch wrestled it from the dog and tossed it out into the backyard. Zeus darted into the night and returned within moments, whining around the ball and wagging so hard his hindquarters swayed with each stroke of his tail. Mitch grabbed the ball again and strode out into the yard, throwing farther this time. They carried on until the greyhound by-passed Mitch, dropped the ball beside his water bowl and slurped loudly.

Mitch pushed open the kitchen door and breathed in the welcome aroma of meatloaf. His stomach let loose with a high-pitched growl and Darla laughed as she stepped into his embrace. "No lunch?"

"Lunch was a long time ago," he muttered, breathing in the fresh citrusy scent of her perfume. At five feet four inches tall, Darla stood a full twelve inches shorter than her husband. Her head nestled perfectly into that hollow beneath his collarbone, and he loved the feel of her soft, warm body against his. This was the time of day he lived for. Holding Darla was the one thing that could make his world right, no matter how wrong it had gone.

"Sit down," she ordered, pulling away and stepping to the stove. "The meatloaf is just coming out of the oven. Were you out at the Scarborough's?"

He settled at the kitchen table and yawned so widely he felt his jaw pop. "Yeah."

She glanced at him over her shoulder, her soft brown eyes concerned. "Gruesome?"

"You heard?"

She put food on the table and sat next to him. "Something like that? How could I not hear?"

"It was gruesome," Mitch said as he scooped generous portions of meatloaf, mashed potatoes, butter beans and carrots onto his plate.

"Was Cass there?"

"She did great. Had no problem with Lenny's corpse." He paused to scoop more carrots out of the bowl. "I still can't help but want to look after her."

Darla sighed as she took the serving spoon from him. "She's not a little girl anymore, Mitch."

"I know she's not. She's different since she finished college and came back to Arcadia. There's part of her that's changed. She's harder, in some ways, than I remember. But there's this other part of her that's so, vulnerable, I guess." He lifted a forkful of butter beans to his mouth and hesitated. "That family has had so much tragedy to deal with, I don't know what they would do if Cass got hurt."

Darla took a sip of iced tea. "She'll be fine. Cass has a level head on her shoulders, she's been through the Academy, and she's got you as her partner. What better training could she have?" She watched as Mitch took another big bite of meatloaf. "It's so unfair."

"What is?"

"That you can eat like that," she pointed with the spoon to the mountain of food on his plate, "and still stay thin."

"It's my metabolisms," he said around a mouthful of carrots.

"You don't even know what a metabolism is, do you?"

"Nope. But if it lets me eat as much of your meatloaf as I want, I'm all for it." Mitch glanced up at Darla. "You're right about Cass."

She chuckled. "Of course I am. Hey, I also heard that Angie Scarborough killed her husband."

"She did." He hesitated, and then told her everything. "There were some photographs in the house. Well, scattered on the kitchen floor. Men having sex with men and raping at least one girl. Lenny was in them."

Darla recoiled. "A girl?"

"Young teenager, from the development of her body."

"Who else besides Lenny?"

"We don't know. None of their faces, even the girl, were visible. Angie knew Lenny was in the photos because he had certain scars that she recognized."

"So you can't arrest anybody for raping that child?"

"Not until we know who they are."

Darla took a bite of meatloaf and chewed thoughtfully. "Who's working with you?"

"The new forensics guy, Tom Kado. He just turned up yesterday. Or maybe the day before. Seems to know his stuff. One of the younger officers, Scott Truman, got pulled onto the scene because he was working with Kado at the fire pit this morning where we found the foot bones last night. Kado brought him along as an extra pair of hands. Grey has a friend in town. An English guy named Bernie Winterbottom."

"Strange name. What does he do? I take it he's not a civilian if he's helping you on an investigation."

"Bernie works mostly with bones. I think Grey said he's a forensic anthropologist. He's a little strange, but seems competent." He toyed with the food on his plate. "Munk's on the investigation, too."

"Ernie? Is that wise?"

Mitch shrugged. "I asked if he was comfortable working on a case where we're looking for child rapists, and he said he was."

"Wow," she breathed. "I'm not sure I could do that."

"Me either. But I'm not sure I could've survived everything Munk and Gabrielle have survived, either."

"Good point." She watched as Mitch pushed back from the table and started clearing their dishes. A frown drew lines across her brow. "What's gotten into you?"

"Things are going to be busy over the next few days." He waggled his eyebrows at her, blue eyes mischievous. "I thought we could spend a little quality time together tonight."

Darla laughed and rose to help him. "You devil."

"Every chance I get," he confirmed.

CHAPTER 19

"THAT IT?"

"YEAH, THAT'S everything. I'll leave the inventory for the receptionist…," Kado stared off into space.

"Elaine," Cass prompted.

"For Elaine to process tomorrow." Kado drew a deep breath and glanced at his watch. "Thanks for staying, Cass. It's almost eight o'clock. I hope I didn't keep you from anything."

"It's fine. I didn't have plans tonight," she answered, pulling her latex gloves off, unclipping her French twist and quickly re-knotting it. She caught Kado watching as she moved. Cass would have sworn that his tanned skin darkened before he turned abruptly to his paperwork. Again she was unsettled at the response his glance raised in her. Since the rape, Cass had studiously avoided feeling attraction for any man, and she'd only dated so she wouldn't be the target of petty gossip. Her body's response to Kado – the warm tingle deep in her gut, the catch of breath – was unwelcome, and since she wasn't able to control or kill it, downright irritating. She cleared her throat. "What do you think about what Truman told us?"

He leaned against a clean counter, crossing one leg over of the other and examining the tip of a worn boot. "Could be nothing."

"He was nervous."

Kado looked up at her. "Have you seen him like that before?"

"No. Seemed like he was ratting out his best friend. I didn't know Truman and Petchard were that close."

"I haven't met Hugo Petchard. Can you see him as part of a cult?"

"You bet."

"Really? Why?"

Cass flipped open the latches on her crime scene kit and began replenishing the contents from the evidence room's cabinets. "He's an arrogant little man, always trying to take credit for things somebody else did, wanting attention. But he just uses all that bluster to hide his insecurity. He would fall for someone telling him how smart and important he is. Flattery would buy his loyalty."

"Interesting. I think Mitch's idea about holding off before talking to him is sound."

Cass shuffled through boxes. "You don't believe Angie's story either, do you? Where are the gloves?"

"Next drawer down," he answered absently, gray eyes clouded. "It's not that I don't believe her. It wouldn't be the first time a cult set up shop in a rural area. It's just that the pieces don't fit and there's no point stirring up trouble with Petchard without a good reason. The things Angie described, other than that book," he said, glancing at *The Church of the True Believer* where it sat on the evidence table, "weren't in the house. Officer Garrett said nobody had been inside but us." He shrugged. "Talking to Angie tomorrow, after the sedatives have worn off and she's had a night to rest, is a good idea."

Cass flipped her crime scene kit closed and helped Kado load evidence bags into a milk crate. She looked around the room and found the order that Kado was imposing helpful. The place had been comfortable chaos when Comfrey was in charge, but it took forever to find what you needed. "Are you still working on the fire pit?"

"Truman got through it this morning. There's nothing out there. It's down to Grey and Bernie to deal with the bones. I'll run some tests to see what accelerant was used, but I'm guessing gas or kerosene." He gathered their scattered paperwork and sealed it in an envelope, jotting Elaine's name and a note on the front. "You want to start on the book in the morning?"

"Yeah, I'll be in early. I'm curious to know what *The Church of the True Believer* is about."

He lifted the milk crate and placed it in the evidence cage, locking the gate and pocketing the keys. Cass wiped the table while Kado grabbed the envelope for Elaine and turned off lights. She followed him from the room, waiting as he locked the door and sneaking a peek at the way his jeans molded to his hips, then shaking her head in irritation at herself. The station was quiet this time of the evening, any prisoners bedded down for the night and the second shift still out. Sundays were one of the more tame nights of the week, outside of football season. If the Dallas Cowboys were playing, all bets on civilized behavior were off.

"I meant to tell you earlier," he said, pushing through the swinging doors into the lobby, "thanks for being open to hear what I'm saying. I don't think Officer Munk is too interested in my input."

Cass shrugged. "Ernie Munk is all right. Old Comfrey treated him like a right hand, trained him on forensic procedures. If you're running down Comfrey and changing everything, Munk is probably wondering what you think of him."

"I think he's got a good eye for detail and if he's interested in forensics, I'm glad he's working on this case. He just seems pissed off with me, regardless of the situation. I guess I don't know how to reach the guys around here," Kado said, and slipped the envelope in one of Elaine's desk drawers.

She grinned. "Can I give you some advice about donuts?"

———

HE WAITED ON ONE of the side streets off the square, watching until the last of them left the courthouse. He'd been so proud of himself today. The call to the old man was perfect this morning, made when the ambulance had gone and everyone else was at the barn with the body. He'd crept into the house and was out within minutes, stowing the briefcase in the patrol car's trunk before returning to string yellow tape through the fence. Stealing from a crime scene was beyond the normal task he was asked to perform, but he'd been promised a payment that would make a serious dent in the credit card debt his wife continued to build. And the old man had assured him that the briefcase contained nothing related to Lenny Scarborough's death, just papers for the insurance business. It seemed like a no-brainer.

But this. This was more than a no-brainer. Chad Garrett had to assume that anything Kado took from the Scarborough's place was relevant to the investigation, and here he was, thinking about passing that information to an outsider. He considered the consequences of what he was about to do, tapping his fingers on the steering wheel while Lynyrd Skynyrd's "Gimme Three Steps" rolled from the patrol car's radio. Could the old man be involved in Lenny's death? Garrett didn't think so. It was pretty clear that Angie Scarborough had snapped, and since he'd seen the pictures on the kitchen floor of men screwing each other and that chick, he figured she had a pretty good motive for murder. Garrett ran both hands over his buzz cut. Maybe the old man had the pictures planted for Angie to find. Something like that wasn't beyond him.

Granted, he had no option but to find a way into the evidence room. Consequences. If his wife found out he'd been balling her stepsister, she'd make sure he knew all about consequences. How the old man found out about it was beyond Garrett. They'd always been discreet. But the old man *did* find out, and so here he was, planning to break into the police station's evidence room to find out what Kado had taken from Lenny Scarborough's house. All because he liked big tits.

He tensed at movement through a window and watched Kado and Detective Elliot stop near the receptionist's desk in the lobby. Kado disappeared from view, as if he had bent over, leaving Garrett with an unfettered view of Cass Elliot's curves. Now *that* was worth the wait. Kado reappeared and they left the courthouse, climbed into their trucks, and drove away. Garrett watched the clock for another five minutes to make sure neither returned before he drove to the back of the courthouse. He climbed out of the patrol car while tugging a ball cap over his forehead, and then punched a code into the keypad to enter through the police station's door.

He passed quickly through the deserted halls, grateful for the darkness and the quiet. Garrett stopped at the door to the evidence room, pulled his shirttail out and tried the doorknob. Locked. He stood silently, thinking through procedure. Kado would have inventoried the evidence this evening with Detective Elliot as a witness. But it was Elaine who normally took care of any paperwork. Maybe...

Garrett squatted as he reached the swinging doors leading from the police department's offices into the lobby and duck-walked to the receptionist's alcove. Bent over, he couldn't use his shirttail to avoid leaving fingerprints, so he reached up and tugged a tissue from a box on the counter. He searched quickly through the desk drawers and found the envelope Kado had left, and then exhaled in frustration. It was sealed. There was nothing to do but open it, copy the papers and slide them into a fresh envelope. Kado's note to Elaine would be lost, but who was to know? Guilt tweaked his intestines. *It wasn't like he was breaking into the evidence room,* he silently chided. *This was just some paper. A list. No harm in it at all.*

He drew a deep breath and slid a pocketknife from his trousers, slicing open the envelope before he could change his mind.

CHAPTER 20

BRUCE ELLIOT SAT AT the kitchen table amid a sea of papers, red marking pen dangling from his lips. He scratched at the day's growth of dark beard covering his square jaw and glanced up as Cass opened the door. "Herman the German out on patrol?"

"Goose-stepping away. What's his deal?"

"He was in the war, but I thought he fought for our side." He shrugged. "Had any supper?"

"Anything left?"

"Harry went and got the girls and they had macaroni and cheese — there's some in the pot. The grownups had Mexican chef salad. Meat and beans are on the stove, salad stuff's in the fridge."

"How are the girls?"

"Seemed fine to me. A little quiet maybe. But it is Sunday night and they go back to school tomorrow." Bruce shrugged his solid shoulders. "Who knows with kids? Anyway, where've you been?"

She sighed. "Lenny Scarborough is dead. Did you know him?"

"No. Who was he?"

"Farmer outside of town, had an interest in one of the insurance businesses."

"What happened?"

Cass turned the burner on under the mixture of beef and kidney beans used to top a salad of greens, tomatoes and avocados. She gently pulled the duct taped handle on the fridge and found the container of salad, answering over her shoulder. "Looks like his wife killed him."

"Whoa. Gun?"

"Hay dolly."

Bruce lifted an eyebrow. "Creative. Is she in jail?"

"Not yet. He beat her up. She's still in the hospital."

"Stupid man. Women may be smaller, but they're meaner," Bruce replied, pen hovering over a handwritten diagram.

Cass rolled her eyes. "Where's Harry?"

"Gone to take the girls home. He should be back any time now."

"Are you grading papers?"

"Yup, they've just finished half term." Bruce taught woodworking at the local college, and despite the hands-on nature of the course, seemed always to have mounds of paperwork to plow through.

"What are they working on?"

Bruce flashed a wicked grin and in that moment Cass saw beyond her older brother to the handsome man most of the eligible, and some of the not so eligible, women in Forney County drooled over. "Rocking chairs."

"You are cruel."

He chuckled, clearing an open space on the table. "The Dean of the Business School is in my class this term. I must admit, it's satisfying to watch him scratch his head on occasion. I don't want them to fail or anything, but it is funny to see what they come up with." He swiveled a large piece of paper toward her chair. "Look at this."

"What is it?" Cass asked, settling down with her salad and examining a complicated floor plan.

"New kitchen."

"Whose?"

"Ours."

"What?" she exclaimed, fork clattering against her plate.

"The front porch is about to fall off. The kitchen is barely functional. The whole house needs remodeling. It's about time, don't you think?"

"No, I don't. What's wrong with the kitchen the way it is?"

Bruce sat back in his chair and glanced around the small room, cracked and worn beneath its clean surfaces. "It's never been updated. Every time something goes wrong with an appliance or one of the cabinets, we stick a little duct tape and spit on it to hold things together for a while longer."

Her violet eyes clouded as Cass fiddled with her napkin. "This is Momma's kitchen, Bruce. Her cabinets, her pots and pans, her stove."

"But it's been over twenty years, Cass. And it looks like it'll be more than just Daddy living out here, for a while anyway. Even if it was just him, he needs a fridge with a handle that isn't attached with duct tape, and we could do with a new oven and stove."

"Have you talked to him about it?"

Bruce ran a hand over his dark hair. "No. Thought I'd talk to you first and see how you reacted." He reached for the plans and carefully folded them. "Just think about it, all right?"

She nodded slowly and picked up her fork, eating and watching Bruce grade papers. He frowned as he studied the homework in front of him, heavy brow drawn in concentration. After he'd written a final score and short note at the top of the paper, she spoke.

"I've got some questions for you, but they're kind of peculiar."

"Shoot."

"How many homosexuals are there around here?"

Bruce choked a laugh. "Why are you asking me?"

"I'm not questioning your orientation, if that's what you mean. I just figured you'd have some idea about this stuff given that you're out at the college."

The screen door opened and Harry smiled. "Hey."

"Thank goodness you're back. Cass wants to talk about homosexuality."

"What?"

"Come on, Bruce," Cass chuckled, using her foot to scoot a chair out for Harry. "How are the girls?"

"They're fine," he answered, swiping a tomato from her plate. "Said to give you a hug. What are you talking about?"

"All I wanted to know was how many homosexuals we've got around here."

Bruce grinned. "Harry should know, he's in design. Bound to be a fag or two in that line of work."

"Hey!" Harry protested. "I do the architecture. Carly deals with the interior decorators."

"No bashing." Cass carried her dishes to the sink. "Seriously, what do you think?"

Harry pursed his lips, hands linked over his cottony hair. "I reckon there are a fair few. Certainly more in the closet than out. Bruce?"

"I agree. And there must be some married gays, trying to pass for straight."

"What's for dessert?" Cass asked.

"Ice cream. Homemade. Grab an extra bowl," Bruce answered.

"One for me, too."

"And me," said Abe as he swung through the kitchen door. "You get the girls home okay, Harry?"

"Yeah. They weren't too happy to be back."

"Carly's the bad guy right now, making 'em get up and go to school, take their vitamins, all that stuff," Abe chuckled.

"Not according to Chloe," Harry replied. "She's still plenty mad at me."

"She's just trying to protect her momma. She'll come around."

Cass finished scooping and passed bowls around the table. "Chocolate syrup?"

"Hand me that pot of macaroni and cheese," said Harry.

Motion in the room ceased.

"You're kidding, right?" asked Bruce.

"You should try it. The sweet and the salty are pretty good. The girls taught me," he said, scooping clumps of unnaturally orange pasta into his bowl and stirring the gooey mixture.

"If that's what having kids does to you, count me out."

Harry shoveled a creamy spoonful into his mouth. "Mmmm."

"You're as bad as Cass," Bruce grumbled, raking a stream of syrup over his ice cream. "She wants to know about butt bandits."

Their father raised a hoary eyebrow. "Why?"

"Just something I'm working on," she answered. "I wanted to know how prevalent homosexuality is in this area."

"I've got no idea. Boys?"

Harry swallowed. "I figure we're not that much different than the rest of the country, maybe a little more conservative. So whatever the average is, drop it by five percent or so. That's probably a good estimate."

Cass licked syrupy ice cream from her spoon. "You don't know anybody who's out of the closet?"

Both Bruce and Harry shook their heads.

"Next question. How many child molesters are there?"

Harry choked on an elbow of macaroni. "Come on, Cass."

Abe rattled his spoon in his empty bowl. "You're separating abuse from sexual activities?"

She nodded.

"I'd imagine there are a few people who still hit their kids harder than they need to. A spanking is one thing, but leaving bruises," Abe shook his head, "that's something else. As for molestation, I'm sure it goes on but I've never heard anything."

Harry sniggered. "I'd think bestiality would be a bigger problem in this neck of the woods."

Bruce's eyes narrowed. "Who got arrested a couple of years ago for abusing their kid?"

"John Lee Grifford," Harry answered.

"Yeah," Bruce agreed, waving his spoon at Cass. "Talk to him."

"Can't. He's in the loony bin."

"But that's what you need, a real live molester."

"Not a bad idea. One more question. Cults. Know of any?"

"Jeez, Cass. Like in Forney County?"

"Yup."

"Other than the Klan?" Abe asked.

"Any type of cult."

Their father shook his head. "Klan's the only cult I can think of, and I haven't heard anything about them in a long time."

"You looking for religious nuts, like the Koreshian thing?" Harry asked.

"Maybe."

"Never heard of anything. Bruce?"

"Not unless you count the Goths out at the college, but they're harmless." He gathered their bowls and stacked them in the dishwasher before collecting his paperwork. "I'm going to bed. See you in the morning?"

"Thanks Bruce," Cass answered. "I'll be up and out early."

"Me too," said Harry, pushing back from the table. "'Night."

Cass began preparing the percolator for the morning as the kitchen door swung closed. Abe cleared his throat. "Those were some strange questions you asked."

She glanced over her shoulder at her father. "It's a strange case we're working on."

"If there's a cult around here, Cass, and you rile them up, things could get dangerous."

"Things could always get dangerous," she answered, settling across the table from him.

Abe sighed. "I've never treated you any different than the boys, Cass, and your momma wouldn't have tolerated it if I'd tried." His eyes, the color of honeyed oak, lit up briefly at the thought of Nell. "But you've always been special, and not just because you're my only girl. I was so proud when you got your accounting degree. You had the whole world in front of you. I still don't understand why you decided to join the force." She shifted and he slid a hand across the table, reaching for hers. "We never talked much about it, but I suspect that it has something to do with Jack."

Cass blinked. She'd never told anyone what had happened in her junior year at university. That night, and the days that followed, had changed her. She'd been extraordinarily self-possessed when she had woken the next morning, bloodied, nauseated and aching. As she had bandaged the cut along her breast, swabbed semen from her thighs, combed her pubic hair for traces of his and used clear tape to lift his fingerprints from any possible surface in that dingy hotel room, her mind had latched onto a tiny, burning seed of fury that eventually found purchase in her soul. In the years since that night, she'd drawn the hazy memories into a tight ball of pain and nursed it, experimenting with the emotions fighting to wrap around it. Fear was first, but it only hollowed out her core. She tried cloaking the pain with forgiveness and forgetfulness, but the infusion of emotions left a bitter taste in her mouth. At last she settled on an unblemished rage with a chemical taint to it, and a cold wrath blossomed, which had been the only real option all along. Her life changed course that night, shedding the search for a respectability her white trash family had never known, and becoming a calculated hunt for the man who had hurt her.

She drew a breath and glanced at the dark kitchen window, unable to look her father in the eye while she lied. "Maybe I was just too young when it all happened, but I've never believed that Jack was guilty." She let him take her hand in his. "What are you trying to say?"

Abe pursed his lips. "I couldn't pick a better partner for you than Mitch. He kind of took Jack's place as your oldest brother when Jack went to prison, and I trust him not to let anything happen to you. But it worries me to think you could be in harm's way. And Jack," he continued as she began to speak, "would be devastated if anything happened to you, especially if he thought that it was because of him that you were on the force."

Anger sparked in the violet depths of her eyes. "That's playing dirty. I am capable of doing my job and staying safe at the same time, Mitch or no Mitch. And I love what I do. I'm good at it. I want your support, Daddy, but I will stay on the force, even without it."

His eyes were clouded as he squeezed her hand. "You are more like your momma every day, Cass. And I guess I should be grateful for that. I'll try not to mention it again. But please," he said, "stay safe. After losing your mom and Jack, none of us could stand to see you hurt."

CHAPTER 21

Monday

CASS YAWNED WIDELY AS she pushed opened the door to The Golden Gate, waving the folded newspaper she carried at the lawyers and farmers who were getting a jump start on the day, and letting the warm smells of coffee and maple syrup wrap around her. She stretched and grinned at skinny Stan Overheart as he crossed the café with a mug in his hand.

"Hey Cass, you're early."

"Hey Stan." She frowned, tipping her head toward the jukebox as she slid into a booth covered in burgundy vinyl. "What *is* that racket?"

He slid into the seat across from her, throwing his gray ponytail over his shoulder and pushing the full mug toward her. A tattooed tiger rippled across one hairy forearm as he leaned forward. "I've got a deal with Wallace and Wilbur Pettigrew. They get one country song first thing in the morning, then we listen to my stuff. But they had a spat today about who they'd listen to. Wallace wanted Hank Williams and Wilbur wanted Tanya Tucker. It got pretty heated." Cass cast a disbelieving glance at the sturdy Pettigrew brothers in their customary booth, silently hunched over steaming coffee mugs. She'd never seen either of them do anything more aggressive than lift a chin in greeting. Stan nodded in confirmation. "Seriously. Looked like they were gonna come to blows over it. So, I took matters into my own hands and picked the Farmer Boys, "You're a Humdinger"."

Cass listened to the lyrics. "What exactly is yeller puddin'?"

"I'm not sure, but I needed something drastic." He cut his eyes at the men. "They've calmed down now. This track has about a minute left. Listen

91

for some Creedence followed by "The Man Who Sold the World" by David Bowie. You watch," he said confidently. "Wilbur won't move until he's heard something by Bowie. He'd never admit it, but I think "Life on Mars" is his favorite."

"You have some funky stuff in that jukebox," Cass said, grinning.

"All the greats," he agreed, pulling an order pad from his apron. "What can I get for you?"

"I need some breakfast burritos to go, enough for me and Mitch. And two," she yawned again, "make that three, large coffees."

"No problem."

Cass added cream to her mug and sipped gratefully, opening the paper and scanning the headlines. This was a ritual she had enacted every morning since leaving the Dallas Police Department and forsaking access to the swirl of fact and rumor that kept her informed about rapes in the metropolitan area. She spoke occasionally with her former colleagues, but there were only so many times she could ask whether a rape victim described her attacker as a former president before they began to wonder why she was interested. As happened almost every morning, Cass found nothing of note in the newspaper. It reported only the most serious assaults, and she was beginning to wonder if she should again try to expand her monitoring to the Internet. Her previous attempts to identify similar crimes using Google had resulted in masses of useless information about Nixon and the Vietnam War. She would have to rethink her search strategies before using the Internet again. Refolding the paper, she glanced across the café to see the Pettigrew brothers engaged in a silent battle of wills, and watched with interest as one of them slid from the booth and shuffled in her direction. She smiled as he approached, his head bobbing in greeting.

"Morning, Cass," he said, blushing.

"Morning, Mr. Pettigrew. How are you?" she asked, unable to determine whether this was Wilbur or Wallace.

"Just fine. Would you mind if I sit for a minute?" he asked, shifting from one foot to the other while fiddling with the shoulder strap on his overalls.

"Not at all," she replied, folding the paper. "What's up?"

He cut his eyes at his brother and took a deep breath before sitting opposite her. The fat licks of "Bad Moon Rising" bounced from the jukebox. "We, uh, heard there was some trouble out at the Scarborough place."

Cass nodded.

"Is Lenny dead?"

"I'm afraid so."

"I heard he was speared on a hay dolly."

Cass nodded again, unsurprised that he knew. It was impossible to keep a secret in a town this size. "Yes, sir, he was."

"What happened?"

"We're investigating, Mr. Pettigrew, but at this point, we're considering it an accident."

"It was Angie, wasn't it?"

"We're still investigating," she answered patiently.

"If she did it, and we reckon that she did, he only got what was coming to him."

"Sir?"

"Wilbur and me," he jutted his chin toward his brother, "thought about calling the police, but didn't figure it was any of our business if she was happy to tolerate it."

"I'm sorry Mr. Pettigrew, but you've lost me. What was Angie tolerating?"

"Lenny hit her," Wallace answered simply.

"How do you know that?"

"We seen it. We did some work for Lenny now and again, and she'd try to hide it, but sometimes she'd be limping. And her t-shirt sleeve would ride up. There were bruises on her arms." He shook his head. "She never said nothing. Not a word. But we knew what was going on."

"When was this?"

Wallace sat back in the booth and poked his bottom lip out. "Must've been eight or nine months ago."

"Is that the only time you saw bruises on her?"

"Naw, that's just when we quit going out there."

Cass cocked her head to one side. "Why did you stop going to the Scarborough's place?"

"Lenny started getting all religious on us. It kinda spooked Wilbur, and I didn't much take to it either."

"Religious how?"

He shifted in the booth and hitched one shoulder. "Just quoting the Bible at us, only it didn't feel like real stuff from the Bible. Sounded like it was kinda made up."

She tapped a finger against the side of her mug as John Fogerty faded and David Bowie picked up his slack. She glanced across the café. Stan was right. Wilbur's work boot was tapping rhythmically beneath the table. She wouldn't have believed it if she hadn't seen it for herself. "Mr. Pettigrew, we may need for you and uh, Mr. Pettigrew to give us a statement about what you've just told me. Would you be willing to do that?"

He frowned. "Ain't that what I just done?"

"You need to come to the station and make a formal statement. We'll type it up and you can sign it."

Wallace sighed deeply and glanced at his brother. They had been hewn from the same gnarly old oak tree, shoulders broad, faces weathered and stoic. He leaned toward Cass and lowered his voice. "Can't you bring it tomorrow? We'll sign it here."

"You don't want to come to the station?"

"It's not me, it's Wilbur." Wallace stretched his face closer and Cass leaned to meet him. "He spent a night in jail when he was in high school. Bought some of your daddy's moonshine and ended up exposing himself on the courthouse lawn." Cass bit her lip to suppress a smile. Wallace nodded sagely. "He had to take a leak and just lost all sense of where he was. They kept him overnight and said there'd be no record, but it's been over twenty years now and he still won't go in the courthouse. Too embarrassed. Hasn't touched a drop o' drink since, so I reckon there's some good come of it."

"I see the problem. I'll type up what you told me and bring it tomorrow morning. The two of you can read it and make changes. I'll fix it and bring it for you to sign on Wednesday. Would that be okay?"

"It sure would," Wallace said as he slid from the booth and bumped into Stan. Muttering an apology, he shuffled back across the café as Stan placed two paper sacks on the table. "What was that about?"

Cass shook her head. "Motive or defense. I'm not sure which."

94

CHAPTER 22

THE OLD MAN ROLLED up the window to keep the dust out of the cab. He lifted a Styrofoam cup from its holder and sipped his coffee while he fingered the envelope that Officer Garrett had left in his mailbox last night, eyes focused through the windshield. A wetback construction crew was working on the new automobile dealership near downtown Arcadia. The slab was in and the crew had started framing the building. The old man was one of several investors in the establishment, and even though he had hand-picked the construction boss, he planned to ensure his funds were well spent.

Given its location and the fact that only a residence had previously existed on the site, this was a prime piece of real estate. Obtaining the land for this project had proved especially difficult as Toby Waller, the young man who had inherited the property, was disinclined to sell. At any price. But Toby's reticence hadn't been enough to stop the project. The old man had never been one to take no for an answer, and his special means of persuasion had resulted in a lower price for the property. Significantly lower. He watched the men scrambling over the studwork for a moment longer, and then satisfied that this crew knew what they were doing, he replaced the cup in its holder and peeled open the envelope's lip.

Three pieces of paper slid into his lap. He scanned them quickly, grimacing when he saw the titles of the books taken from Lenny Scarborough's study. The man had grown sloppy. He should have kept his copy of their sacred text in the briefcase, along with the rest of his material. His eyes moved rapidly down the first page, and he turned to the second. *Photographs – explicit content*, he read. Quite a few of them. He scanned the next page, and then rested the papers in his lap while he thought.

The inventory said the photos were found in the kitchen, on the floor. They weren't described in detail, yet an itch of anxiety clawed at his bowels. Lenny had embraced The Church's philosophy wholeheartedly, perhaps too intensely for the old man's comfort. And lately he had become somewhat fanatical. The Church had rituals, of course. They were necessary to build commitment and solidarity. But they could be... misconstrued. He rubbed a gnarled hand over his lean belly, feeling the gurgle of nerves. The old man had no fear for himself. He was past the point where he could have a direct involvement in sexual activities of any sort and rarely stayed down at the cabin past the closing of their ceremonies. The men were always careful to keep their hoods on when a stranger was at The Sanctuary, but in the heat of passion caution was known to slip. And someone with a camera. Photographs could do irreparable damage.

The grumble of a compressor brought him back to the present, and he raised his hand at the construction boss in farewell. He needed to know what was in those photographs. He cranked the engine and dialed Officer Chad Garrett's number as the cab cooled.

CHAPTER 23

"YOU'RE EARLY."

"I HAD the most fascinating conversation at The Golden Gate," Cass answered as Mitch unwrapped a burrito.

"With who?"

"One of the Pettigrew brothers."

He stopped mid-bite. "They have vocal chords?"

"Indeed they do, and Wallace knows how to use his. Did you know Wilbur was locked up for peeing on the courthouse lawn?"

"Come on Cass, I'm trying to eat," Mitch whimpered before stuffing the burrito in his mouth.

"Wallace told me that both he and Wilbur have seen bruises on Angie, on more than one occasion. And they'll put it in writing."

"When was this?"

"Nine months ago, when they stopped helping out at the Scarborough place because, get this, Lenny started quoting religion at them."

"Anything in particular?"

"Wallace didn't think it was direct quotes from the Bible. He thought Lenny was making the stuff up."

"I guess that fits with the idea of Lenny belonging to a cult."

"And it supports what Angie told us about Lenny hitting her." She stirred cream into her coffee and opened the newspaper again as the squad room filled with the noise of shift change. "Munk didn't seem willing to believe Angie's story, did he?"

"No. But now we've got witnesses to Angie's bruises and Lenny's preaching to the Pettigrew brothers." Mitch stifled a belch with a fist over his mouth and waved across the room. "Hey Carlos."

Detective Martinez left his duffel bag at his desk and came to shake Mitch's hand. "Thanks for that tip on John Doe's real name. I went around to the churches yesterday and found a few people who remember the name

Humberto Gonzalez. But they connect it with a young man who was trying to find his father not too long ago."

"That must be his son. I reckon that explains why he disappeared from Arkansas. Where is he now?"

"Gone. They figured he'd moved on to keep looking for his father."

"Did they have a description of the son? His car, anything?"

"He was bumming rides. They thought he was staying down in the river bottoms near that old camp I searched last week. You want me to keep asking about him?"

"He illegal?"

Martinez nodded, crossing his arms over his broad chest and leaning a hip against a nearby desk. "The community knows about the skeleton. They're more willing to talk given that the old man was murdered. But they won't say anything on record."

"His son is the only link we've got to Humberto Gonzalez. See if you can find somebody who gave him a ride, maybe got him to talk."

A disturbance rippled through the squad room as a scrawny man was greeted by a smattering of applause, puffing his concave chest in reply. He moved with a limp, stopping to take a shallow bow, basking in the attention. Spotting the trio talking by Cass's desk, he sauntered over, holding his loose cotton trousers away from his legs.

"Hey Cass," he called. "I hear you're stealing all my glory about that wetback skeleton. Just so we're clear, I get credit for finding him, yeah?"

"We keepin' score Petchard?"

"Just want to make sure Sheriff Hoffner knows it was me that found him. Hate for him to think a *girl* was taking credit for my finding a murder victim." He hitched up his trousers and grimaced. The sound of cloth scraping over gauze escaped from beneath his clothes.

"Yup Petchard, you've been instrumental in helping us identify Humberto Gonzalez, laid up at the hospital with burns like you were." She smothered a grin. "Have you got a new pair of pants for your uniform yet?"

"That fire was blazing, babe. Somebody had to do something. Hey Mitch, hey Beaner," he sneered.

Martinez threw his head back and laughed at the insult. "Yeah, you're a real fireman, *Hugo*. That name doesn't quite suit you, does it?" Petchard blushed and Martinez glanced at his legs. "It's a shame you passed out like you did, and Cass had to pull your clothes off to keep you from burning up. I hear they're doing great things with dick implants these days."

Petchard huffed and muttered under his breath.

"Come on now boy, if you're going to throw insults, you need to do it out loud. Let's hear you," Martinez said, cocking his steely head in Petchard's direction. "Nothing? That's what I thought, *cabrón*," he grinned, standing to wrap a strong arm around Petchard's narrow shoulders. "Yeah, you're a *Hugo* all right."

Petchard's blush rose to the roots of his thinning blonde hair and he squirmed out of Martinez's grip, reaching down to touch his shin. "I deserve a medal," he whined. "That whole forest would've gone up if I hadn't done something."

"Nobody's interested," Martinez said, flicking his fingers at the small man.

"Time for roll call anyway," Petchard muttered, limping around the desks.

"Why do you put up with him, Carlos?" Cass asked, watching the slight man leave. "Why not report him?"

"What, for the 'beaner' comments? He's harmless. And it's more fun to torture him – he'll toddle home and grab his English – Spanish dictionary to look up *cabrón*, and that makes it worthwhile." Martinez cocked his head at Cass. "Why don't you report him for the sexist stuff?"

She shifted in her chair. "It'd cause *me* more trouble than him."

"Sheriff Hoffner wouldn't take you seriously?"

Cass rolled her eyes. Martinez grinned and turned to Mitch, who was watching Petchard with a scowl as he left the squad room. "What's up?"

Mitch continued to watch until the door swung shut behind him. "How much do you know about him, Carlos?"

"Petchard? Not much. From up north somewhere."

"He hasn't been in Arcadia that long, has he?"

"Year or two, maybe. He moved down to join his parents. They've been here a while."

Mitch shot a glance at Cass and pursed his lips. "Has he always been like this?"

"What, an idiot?" Martinez scratched his chin and leaned into the edge of Mitch's desk. "Now that you mention it, no, he hasn't. He started off pretty normal, but lately he keeps ragging on the racial stuff. Cass, have you had much problem with him?"

She shook her head. "We haven't had much contact." She hesitated. "He does that eye thing whenever I see him."

"What eye thing?"

"Like guys do, when they're checking you out. You know," she demonstrated, using Martinez as a point of reference, "up and down the body, with strategic lingering. It's like lifting a leg to mark territory."

"Women notice that kind of thing?" Martinez blushed as Cass laughed. "Guess we're not as smart as we think. Why are you asking about Petchard, Mitch?"

"He's full of himself, and he's got no reason to be. It's almost like he's got a chip on his shoulder."

"I figure the food chain will take care of him," Martinez said, stretching his arms over his head. "Something that weak can't survive for long by itself." He grinned and headed to his desk.

"Any word on the old lady?" Cass called.

"Iris Glenthorne? Nothing yet," Carlos answered. "We found her car back in some trees. The keys were still in the ignition and her purse was on the seat."

"You think she just wandered off?"

Carlos shrugged. "Maybe. Her friends say she was losing her memory. I've asked for tracking dogs from Watuga County, but they're working on a missing teenage girl. In the meantime, I'm headed out to see what else I can learn about Miss Glenthorne." He locked his desk and waved over his shoulder as he headed for the door.

"What's up this morning?" Mitch asked as Cass started putting files in her desk.

"I'd like to go see Angie Scarborough again, tell her we didn't find everything she told us about."

"Think they'll let us in this early? It's barely seven."

"Good point. Is Kado here? I want to take a look at that book from Lenny's study."

"Y'all finished the inventory last night?"

"We did. I'll check with Elaine. If she's got everything logged in, she can grab it from the cage for me."

———————

CASS SLIPPED INTO THE receptionist's alcove and watched as a small woman recorded a message before pulling the headset off and fluffing her wild curls. She started as she turned and found Cass behind her, her heart-shaped face warming into a smile. "Hey honey, what do you need?"

"Hey Elaine. Have you found Kado's inventory yet?"

She frowned and shuffled a stack of papers on her desk. "Where'd he leave it?"

"Second drawer."

She pulled it open and took out an envelope, peeling it open and sliding out the paperwork. "It'll just take –"

"Turn that over," Cass interrupted, watching as Elaine flipped the blank envelope in her hands. She plucked tissues from the box on the counter and took it from Elaine. "Kado left a note on the envelope, saying that we went through everything from the Scarborough's place last night. All you need to do is load the inventory database."

"What happened at the Scarborough's?" Elaine asked as she switched on her computer.

"Lenny was killed."

"Oh no," Elaine said, hand flying to her mouth. "What happened?"

"He was impaled on a hay dolly," Cass answered. "What's wrong?"

"Lenny was my brother-in-law, Brian's half-brother."

"Oh Elaine, I'm sorry you found out this way. I didn't realize you were related."

She waved a hand, the color returning to her cheeks. "I haven't had much to do with them since Brian died. I was thinking about Angie and those kids. She must be so relieved. Lenny was an intolerable jerk." Cass arched an eyebrow and Elaine blushed. "I couldn't stand him and Brian didn't think much of him either."

"Why not?"

The small woman leaned back in her chair and reached for her coffee cup, warming her hands around it. "Lenny tried to recruit him into some religious group. He told Brian there was a need for strong men to stand up in the community and keep things on an even keel. To keep the minorities and what he called "freeloaders" in their place. That to be a real man Brian

101

had to take charge of his family, get me under control." She rolled her eyes. "What a load of crap. He didn't tell me all of it, but whatever Lenny said really made Brian mad. He wouldn't speak to Lenny after that."

"Did he tell you anything specific about this religious group? Did it have a name?"

Elaine shrugged. "If it did, Brian didn't tell me. Just said he wouldn't be caught dead out in the woods with that bunch."

"Any names?"

"Of members? Other than Lenny, no. Why does it matter? This was years ago."

Cass shook her head. "I don't know yet. Angie's in the hospital. We'll be going over to see her later."

"What happened?" Elaine asked, concern cleaving a line between her eyes.

"Lenny hit her."

"Oh my God, and she ran him through with the hay dolly?"

Cass nodded.

Elaine's lips narrowed to a tight line. "Tell her I'll see her tonight. That bastard."

"Whoa," Mitch said, swinging around the corner and into Elaine's alcove. "Who's a bastard?"

"Lenny Scarborough, that's who."

He frowned and Cass shook her head at him. "I'll fill you in later." She waved the envelope at him. "I need to see Kado."

"I came out here to find you. He just got in."

CHAPTER 24

KADO GLOVED UP AND turned the envelope over in his hands. "Where was it?"

"Right where you left it."

"Come with me," he said, grabbing a forensics kit and striding down the hall. He stepped into Elaine's alcove and she turned with a smile on her lips. "I need to process your desk," he said, face drawn. The smile vanished and she slipped the headset off, pushed a button on the phone and hurried to stand with Cass and Mitch.

"What have you touched?"

She looked around the alcove. "Everything, just about. I haven't used the fax machine or the copier yet."

"Cass, go check the trash cans in the foyer." He worked rapidly, muttering to himself as he dusted, lifting several fingerprints from Elaine's desk. The laser printer spat pages of court transcription, whirring rhythmically. Kado sighed in frustration when he dusted the copier. "It's clean."

Cass returned. "They're empty."

"Kado, what is it?" Elaine asked.

"The envelope I put the paperwork in is gone. Someone opened my envelope but left the inventory from the Scarborough's place in a clean envelope."

"What was in your note?" Mitch asked.

Kado stripped off his gloves. "Nothing. I just asked Elaine to update the database first thing so we can start checking the evidence in and out."

"So that wasn't what they wanted."

"Nope, it was the inventory. The copier has been wiped down, so they must've used it and slipped the papers into a clean envelope thinking that you wouldn't miss something that wasn't there."

"Why would somebody want the inventory?" Elaine asked.

"To find out what we took from the house, I guess." Kado pinched the bridge of his nose. "Who has access to the courthouse after hours?"

"Everybody with the code," Elaine snorted. He stood behind her as she called up the courthouse security system and scrolled through the entries from Sunday night. "I can't tell you who came in, only what time someone punched in a code."

"What time did we leave, Cass?"

"Eight-ish? A little after?"

"Did anybody come in about that time?"

Elaine pointed at the screen. "Eight twenty-two. The next entry's not until nine seventeen."

Kado ran a hand over his dark hair. "Cass, did you see anybody else here?"

"No. And I don't remember any other vehicles in the parking lot."

Mitch snapped his fingers. "Cameras. Show me the back entrance."

Elaine swiftly maneuvered to a new software package and found the time they wanted.

"Roll it," Kado commanded.

Elaine released the mouse and they watched as a patrol car pulled into a parking space and the headlights were cut. The driver's side door opened, interior light flaring to reveal a muscular figure wearing a baseball cap. Stepping from the car, he rubbed a hand across his lip as he looked around the parking lot. He strode quickly to the station's back door, keyed in the code and slipped inside where he was lost from the camera.

"Unbelievable," said Mitch.

"Run it forward," Kado said, watching until the door opened and the figure hurried back to the car, clutching a large envelope to his chest with one hand. "That's our boy. Back it up to where he parks."

Elaine rolled the image back and released the mouse.

"Again."

Elaine obliged.

"Good. Freeze it there. Send that shot to me on email." He spun on his heel and trotted through the swinging doors to the police station.

"Thanks Elaine," Cass called as they hurried after Kado.

They found him hunched over his computer in the evidence room, tapping at the keyboard.

"Have you had any coffee?" Mitch asked.

"No. You offering?"

"Sure, black?"

"Uh huh," Kado answered absently, and began maneuvering the mouse. Mitch raised an eyebrow at Cass, she nodded, and he left the room. She stood behind Kado and focused over his shoulder at the screen as he enlarged the digital image and tried to sharpen it. He stretched forward and she leaned with him, catching the gentle scent of his cologne. Her body flooded with warmth. Irritated, her jaw tightened and she dropped her eyes from the screen, noticing that Kado's wavy hair was so dark it carried a blue hue. She fought the urge to touch a curl and stifled a burble of hysteria at her reaction to this man.

"Cass, could you just…," he said, waving a hand.

She cleared her throat and moved away, taking in the room where Kado spent so much of his time. Glass fronted cupboards housed jars and cans of forensic chemicals and potions. The wide evidence table was switched on, illuminating a set of paperwork from underneath. She peered between the bars of the gate into the evidence cage. Metal shelves were stacked with brown boxes, those near the front neatly labeled and stuck with a barcode tag, others toward the back of the cage shoved haphazardly on the shelves, apparently waiting for Kado's organizing touch. They stretched from floor to ceiling and across the wide room.

"Got it," Kado called.

She hurried to stand behind him as he sharpened the image one more time.

"Whose plate is that?" he asked himself as he opened a database and scrolled through the list of department issued vehicles.

"Gotcha," he whispered as the evidence room door swung open. They turned at the sound. Mitch filled the opening behind the newcomer, mugs of coffee resting uneasily in his grip. "Officer Chad Garrett," Kado said, gesturing them into the room. "Just the man."

CHAPTER 25

"WHY'D YOU LET HIM go?" Cass asked. "He's the one."

They had questioned Garrett in the conference room and then moved down the hall to the evidence room, stopping on the way for fresh coffee. Kado leaned over the backlit table, copies of the inventory sheets spread in front of him. "It's circumstantial. He came into the courthouse at the right time and took paperwork with him when he left. We've got that on film. He used a brown envelope. Most likely, he took that from Elaine's desk — brown's only for forensic stuff. We use white for all the patrol information."

"He said he was here to look for his softball glove. At eight thirty at night, four hours after his shift ended, and he's got no practice or games for a week. It's lame."

Kado lifted his arms over his head in a stretch that grew into a yawn. "I've got no fingerprints and I can't prove that someone didn't leave a forensics envelope in the squad room."

"Why would Chad Garrett care what we took from Lenny Scarborough's house?"

Mitch shook his head slowly, eyes unfocused. "I don't know. But Garrett was on duty out at the Scarborough's yesterday until four."

"He arrived after the ambulance," Cass said. "He was never out there on his own."

"He could've gotten in the house."

"When?"

"He had a couple of opportunities. One was when we were out at the barn with Lenny, getting him off that spike. The second was when just Garrett and Munk were at the house. Munk went out to the barn to work on the hay dolly. There was nobody in the house and Garrett could've slipped in then."

"Let's talk this through," said Kado, sitting down and turning off the table's light. "Garrett slips into the house while everybody else is occupied. What does he see?"

"We didn't process the photographs for evidence until late afternoon," Cass answered. "If he came in through the kitchen, he would've seen them."

"What else?"

Cass squinted into the distance, thinking. "From what we saw, there was nothing disturbed. Angie's vomit would have still been in the wastebasket. Other than that…"

Mitch straightened. "Maybe he took the briefcase."

"You're talking about tampering with a crime scene, removing evidence. He could be prosecuted for that. You saw him just now. He was adamant that he hadn't done anything. And Garrett's too close to retirement to screw up. He has too much to lose."

"Kado, do you have the photographs Munk took before lunch?"

He turned to the computer. They scrolled through the shots of the kitchen and study, stopping to count the photographs on the floor. "Seventeen. Same number Cass counted, so he didn't take any of those. But there's no briefcase in the study," Kado said, turning to Cass. "When did Munk take the photos?"

"Right after we pulled Lenny off the hay dolly."

"If Garrett slipped inside the house, he did it early," Mitch said. "Print those shots of the study, Kado. It's almost eight. Cass, let's go to the hospital and show them to Angie, see what else she can tell us."

CHAPTER 26

CHAD GARRETT PULLED TO the side of the road, hands trembling as he dug the phone from his trouser pocket. He rested his head briefly on the steering wheel, letting the air conditioner cool his sweaty face. Cars flew past, brake lights flashing as drivers realized they were speeding past a patrol car.

There was only one way out of this. Things had gone too far. Reporting on somebody's movements, passing along gossip, even planting gossip, that was one thing. He'd tossed a handgun into the Sabine River last autumn when the old man had squeezed him, and *that* had been questionable. But tampering with an investigation? This was something else entirely. He couldn't do it. He *wouldn't* do it. It was like he told the detectives, he wasn't unethical. What he did last night was slipping a toe across the line, but he wouldn't go any farther. He'd just have to live with the consequences. The police radio burbled and he reached to turn the volume down, pushing the speed dial button before his composure broke completely.

The voice that answered was sharp. "Bring them to the house."

"I uh, I didn't get them," Garrett answered.

"*Goddamn* boy, what did I tell you?"

"I know, sir. I tried, but they know I was in the courthouse last night, and think I took the inventory."

"So what?"

"I can't jeopardize my pension. You're asking me to interfere with an investigation," he answered, voice rising. "I could go to jail for that."

"You'd rather she cut your balls off?" came the grim reply. "Be a hell of a way to spend those golden years, wouldn't it? No balls. No wife." He chuckled. "No pension."

"What do you mean?" Garrett asked in a small voice.

"Son, if I don't find out what's in those photographs, I reckon this here inventory will find its way to Sheriff Hoffner. Maybe with a confession from your good self. And if that happens, retirement will be the least of your worries."

Garrett shivered. "I know what's in them; I saw them out at the house."

The noise of a pipe clacking against teeth came through the phone. Garrett had grown to hate that sound. The old man spoke. "Tell me."

He swallowed thickly. "They were pictures of men having sex with other men. One showed a guy with his dick in another guy's mouth, one being jacked-off by somebody else."

"You're sure it was men and men, not women?"

"Not unless the women had hairy knuckles and a five o'clock shadow. But yeah, there was a chick, as well."

"Faces?"

"No."

"You sure?"

"*Yes*," he answered emphatically. "I can't do this anymore. I don't mind what you've asked for before; there wasn't any harm in it. But this is illegal. I want out. And," he added, "I don't want your money. Keep it."

The phone exploded with laughter. The old man coughed and sputtered before speaking again. "As you wish. I'll let you know where to drop your phone."

CHAPTER 27

ANGIE SCARBOROUGH WAS FINISHING a bowl of oatmeal when Officer Greg Newton tapped on her door. He pushed it open a crack and she waved him in. He opened the door wider and Cass and Mitch stepped through. A small girl darted between them, snatching a pink backpack from the corner and giggling a good-bye to her mother.

"You be good at school, you hear?" Angie called after the tiny figure. The bruises on her cheek were darkening to purple, and Cass saw a flash of pain cross the woman's face. "I haven't told them that their father is dead. I just couldn't do it," she said. "I hope they don't find out at school today."

"I'm sure they'll be fine today," Mitch said. "But tell them this evening."

"Dr. Rambo said I could go home if I ate all my breakfast." Angie looked at the tray on her lap with a grimace. "Disgusting, but it's gone."

"Are you up to answering a few questions?" Cass asked.

"What do you need?"

"A few things. I want to go over your statement to make sure we got it right. And I want to show you some photographs."

Angie's eyes flew wide and she shook her head, pushing a hand out in front of her. "I - I don't want to see them again."

"Not those," Cass said. "These are shots that we took of your house. I just want to know if anything is missing, okay?"

She nodded, face relaxing.

"Before we start, did you have help at the farm?"

"No, it was just Lenny and me."

"You never had anybody out to help around the place?"

"The Pettigrew brothers used to come help Lenny now and again with the heavy work. But," she pulled a face, "all of a sudden they got right smart and wouldn't come back. It made no sense to me. We paid them well, fed them lunch. They always did good work for us."

Cass glanced at Mitch, who nodded. "I talked to Wallace today. He told me he'd seen bruises on your arms on occasion." Angie closed her eyes. "He also said Lenny started talking about religion, and it made them uncomfortable. That's why they quit."

"That man," she breathed. "And all this time I thought they just got uppity. I'll have to call and apologize for Lenny. He did that sometimes, started preaching to people. Usually after those meetings of his."

"We need to know more about this group that Lenny belonged to."

"I don't know what else I can tell you."

"I'll ask a few questions. We can try it that way."

She adjusted herself against the headboard. Mitch drifted into a corner and listened silently. "What do you want to know?"

"Who was in this group with Lenny?"

"I have no idea. I wanted to ask him, but I didn't think he'd be too happy about it."

"He was never with anyone you were surprised to see?"

"He never spent time with anybody other than me and the kids. There was church on Sundays and Wednesdays, and sometimes he'd go into town about the insurance business, but that was it."

"Did anybody ever come to your house and spend time with Lenny?"

"No. The only visitors we got were from my side of the family, and sometimes the kids would have friends over. Very few adults."

"What made you suspicious of this group?"

"You live with a man long enough," she shrugged, "you know things about him. He was involved for a long time, before we were married. He would go out once a month or so, always called it business. Said he had to meet some of the men from the community. The meetings were at night and he never told me where he was going." She reached for a cup on the table and sipped through the straw. "Normally, he'd have a phone with him, even if he was just out with the cows, and tell me to call if we needed anything. But on those nights, I was forbidden to contact him."

"Even if something happened to one of the kids?" Cass asked.

"Yes. And that was unusual for Lenny. He was a good father, in spite of everything else." Her eyes drifted across the room before coming to rest on her hands where they lay in her lap. "He'd come home from these meetings all glowing. Sometimes he'd be like a rooster, strutting around and almost crowing. It made me think he'd got a promotion or a prize. He'd be happy for a few days after, but more demanding."

"Demanding how?"

"Quoting more scripture at me. More likely to put me in my place. 'Correction', he called it. That's when he'd hit me."

"You had no idea where he was going?"

"No. But he almost always had mud on his boots when he came home. Not heavy like clay, more sandy. And there was that purple robe. Sometimes it was dirty, too. A couple of times it was sopping wet and he smelled like he'd been in the river. But after every trip out, he'd have me wash it. I'd hang it in the closet and it would disappear."

"Where to?"

"Probably his study, in that briefcase. I wasn't allowed in there." Angie paused. "And then sometime last year it got worse. He was cross a lot, even after these meetings, and he spent more time on the other cell phone."

"What phone?"

"He had one that wasn't from our plan. I think he kept it locked up, but sometimes I'd peek through the door into his study and see him talking on it, real quiet and in a strange voice."

"What kind of voice?"

"It was...," Angie thought for a moment, and then nodded in recognition. "Subservient. Almost like he was kissin' ass." She squinted. "No, it was more respectful than that, but for the life of me, I can't imagine who Lenny would talk to in that tone of voice."

"You don't know where he kept the phone?"

"The only place I can figure is in that briefcase of his. Did you look in there?"

"We found the book you told us about, *The Church of the True Believer*, but we didn't find a briefcase, Angie."

She blinked slowly. "It was right next to his desk. I kicked it on my way out of the study."

"It wasn't there when we went through the house."

"You sure?"

Cass pulled out the digital photos and handed them to Angie. "These are the shots from the study."

Angie examined each photo, frowning in concentration. She plucked one from her lap. "It was here. I threw up in that wastepaper basket," she pointed, "and on my way out of the room I slammed my foot into his briefcase."

"What did it look like?"

"Dark brown, old. It was a big rectangle with flaps on the top that laid over each other and locked." She demonstrated with her hands. "Did you find the robe or the phone?"

Cass shook her head.

"Where did they go?" she demanded. "That briefcase was there when I left the house and ki –," she caught her breath, "killed Lenny. Did you search the barn and the cellar?"

"Yes."

"The attic?"

"Yes."

"And the robe wasn't there, or the phone?"

"No, neither."

"Well then, someone took it all," she announced, crossing her arms. "I don't want to be prosecuted for killing Lenny, and I wouldn't make up a story like this. He did belong to some group and he wore a purple robe and there was a briefcase in that study yesterday morning." Her brows drew together. "The man was a rapist. Him and his friends. You've got pictures of him raping that girl. Isn't that enough?"

"I don't know," said Mitch, stepping from the corner. Angie started as if she'd forgotten that he was in the room with them. "We need to talk to the district attorney. If Dr. Rambo lets you go home today, go. Just don't leave the county. The study's been sealed. Don't go in there. The hay dolly is still evidence, so you can't use it yet. All right?"

Angie buried her hands in her dark hair. "Good Lord. What a mess. And tell me Mitch Stone," she challenged, lowering her hands, "if I can't use that hay dolly, how are my cows gonna get fed?"

He grinned. "Call the Pettigrew brothers."

———

CASS PULLED THE DOOR shut and cranked the engine. "Well?"

Beside her, Mitch sighed. "I think she's telling the truth. But, we need to talk to Sheriff Hoffner and the DA, to see what they want to do with her."

She crossed her arms over the steering wheel, staring sightlessly through the windshield. "Whatever happened to Lorena Bobbitt?"

Mitch shivered. "The woman who sliced her husband's hoo-hoo off?"

"Hoo-hoo? *Hoo-hoo?*" she said, chortling.

He shifted. "There are some things a man can't discuss comfortably. Bobbittizing is one of them."

"Whatever," she said, smile dying as she glanced across the cab. "Didn't she get off with battered wife syndrome, or something like that?"

"You think that might be a defense for Angie?"

Cass shrugged and slipped the truck into reverse, looking over her shoulder. "You think we should charge her?"

He hesitated. "In terms of pure justice, no."

"But in terms of the law?"

"Maybe."

CHAPTER 28

MUNK AND TRUMAN SAT, heads together, hunched over the Scarborough's computer. They'd dragged a desk into a corner of the dingy conference room for privacy, scanned the photos from the kitchen floor, and were scrolling through those images and the shots that had been stored on Lenny's computer. The blinds were drawn and a murky light filled the room. Munk shook his head and pulled away from the screen.

"I just can't see Lenny involved in any of this."

Truman pointed at an image. "That's his hip." He clicked to another. "And this one."

Munk ran a hand over his pocked face and smoothed his thinning hair into place. Reaching for their empty cups, he stood. "Coffee?"

Truman nodded as Munk ambled across the room to the stout old coffee machine. He swung open the refrigerator door. "Cream?"

"Please." Truman reached for the fresh coffee when Munk settled next to him again. "Thanks. I needed it."

"I've been thinking," Munk began.

"Yeah?"

"I don't know much about computers, but I know you can manipulate images with them. Could those pictures have been changed?"

Truman scrolled back and forth between the photographs. "They look genuine to me, but I imagine that's the idea." He shrugged. "Maybe. You'd have to have the original pictures to start with, wouldn't you? Shots of two different men?" He flipped to an image and double clicked. It filled the screen and they looked over their shoulders to check that the room was still empty. "You could use that one, I think. His…" He pointed to the screen, blushing. "His, the uh… it isn't touching the other guy's mouth. So that should be simple. But this one." He reduced the image and found another, again filling the screen with it. "I don't know how you make an arm curve around somebody's body like that, or wrap their fingers around… you

115

know."

"Who would know about something like that?"

"Somebody out at the college might."

"Is there a computer class out there?"

Truman shrugged. "I went to college in Chambers." He jumped as the conference room door swung open and quickly minimized the image.

"Hey Truman. You working on Lenny's computer?" Mitch asked as he strolled across the room. Cass stopped at the coffee machine, filling two mugs before joining them in the corner.

"Yes, sir. Munk wondered whether the images could've been altered. Maybe taking two photographs and putting them together. Anybody around here know about that stuff?"

"There's software that'll let you do that," said Cass, handing a mug to Mitch. "Bruce should know somebody out at the college. You want me to call him?"

Munk sighed. "We'd better check with Sheriff Hoffner first. Whoever knows about this stuff will need to see the image to figure out if it's been manipulated." He lifted his chin toward the computer. "How do you explain that stuff?"

"And what if they recognize themselves in one of those shots?" Cass asked quietly.

"Whew," Mitch answered, blowing out a long breath. "I don't suppose," he started, looking at both Munk and Truman, "that you recognized anybody in those pictures?"

Munk choked a laugh while Truman blushed. "No, sir. You want to have a look?"

"No thanks," he grinned, holding up a hand. "Maybe I should've asked if you noticed any unique characteristics that could help us figure out who these people are, or where they are, particularly in relationship to that girl. Somebody missing a finger, or like Lenny, with a scar in a certain place? I mean, it's not like we can ask all the guys around here to drop their trousers and let us have a look, but if there's something obvious, we should use it."

Truman cleared his throat. "One guy has red hair. That's got to be unique."

"Show me," Mitch said. They watched as Truman scrolled through several images showing a fair-skinned, freckled hand or a splash of orange pubic hair. "This is worse than a John Doe. How do we figure out who these men are? They may not even be from around here."

"I've got an idea," Truman said, leaning back in his chair. "What if we tried to figure out how many men are in these pictures? It'll take some work, and a strong stomach, but if we can figure out how many there are, and what characteristics each has, that might help us narrow it down."

"And see if you can pull anything out of the background in these shots. Knowing where they were taken would help." He eyed Truman closely. "I'd prefer it if we keep distribution of these pictures limited. You up to this?"

"Yes, sir. I'll be fine."

"Munk, what are you working on?"

"I'll do the comparison on the prints from the house. Did you bring back Lenny's prints from the autopsy?"

"They should be in the evidence room. Cass?"

"I want to take a look at *The Church of the True Believer*, see what it's about. If Lenny kept the photos in it, it must've meant something to him. Maybe it'll give us a clue."

"All right. I'll talk to Sheriff Hoffner and the DA. See you around lunch time?"

CHAPTER 29

THE OLD MAN'S TRUCK bumped across the rutted pasture and stopped under the protective shade of an ancient pecan tree. He had the phone snugged between his ear and bony shoulder. The air was blowing on high, and he turned the knob to slow the blast so he could hear.

"You get any details?"

"Not really," Officer Greg Newton confessed. "She was talking about a group Lenny belonged to, same as yesterday. She was worried that his briefcase has gone missing from the study. Said it was there yesterday morning when she went to kill Lenny."

"She said that?"

"Yes, sir. That's at least twice she's confessed."

"Why haven't they arrested her?"

"I don't know, sir."

The line was silent for a moment. "When are they releasing her?"

"Today."

"You going home with her?"

"My orders were to stay with her at the hospital. I'll find out."

"Good," the old man grunted.

"Is there anything else? I need to get back to her room."

"That's fine, Newton. The Celebration of Illumination will be soon, on short notice. Make sure you're ready." He snapped the phone shut and stared into the distance for some time, searching the quilted patterns of the past and wondering if it was possible for one damaged thread to unravel all the others. Movement in the pasture broke his concentration. A tall, slim man broke away from the crew and trotted to the truck. He pushed the cowboy hat back on his head, exposing a strong face with narrow features and golden eyes, and placed a strong arm on the doorframe as the window rolled down.

"Morning, sir."

118

"How's it going?"

"Just fine. Another couple of days and you can get your herd back out here." Hitch turned to look at the sleek shine of the five-strand barbed wire fence. A shirtless youth glistened in the early sun as he lifted and dropped the heavy driver over a gleaming silver and green fence post.

"Men any good?"

"Yes, sir. Picked them up this morning." Hitch nodded toward a burly man with a bristly moustache. "Victor's the boss. How is your construction project going?"

"No problems. Seemed to be a good crew over there." He dug in his trouser pocket and clamped the cold, empty pipe between his teeth. "Got a job for you."

"Sir?"

The old man jerked his head at the passenger side of the truck.

The heavy pickup barely rocked when the door opened and Hitch sat down. The interior smelled of cherry tobacco and was cool in tree's shade.

"What do you need?"

The old man sucked at his empty pipe, studying the man opposite. His accent gave nothing away, but the old man suspected he'd spent time inside. Even after all these months, Hitch refused to discuss his past and the old man thought that best. Sometimes, the less known the better.

"I got a situation."

"A problem?"

"Of sorts," the old man allowed. "But it's delicate."

"How so?"

"I need to send a message to the po-lice. One of the officers is stirring things up."

"How strong a message?"

"Permanent." The old man shifted and looked in the amber eyes opposite. "And public."

"Pain?"

"Up to you."

"Souvenirs?"

"Just the usual."

Hitch took in the name and details of his prey. "How soon?"

"Tonight."

He arched an eyebrow.

"I know it, son. But I've got faith in you. You'll find payment plus a bonus in the customary place in the morning."

CHAPTER 30

CASS JUMPED WHEN MITCH tapped her shoulder. She leaned back in her chair and rubbed her eyes, then smiled crookedly up at him and patted the open book on her desk. "This is some funky stuff."

"Funky how?" he asked, pulling a chair up to her desk and flipping through the creamy pages covered with elaborate script and colorful scenes.

"It's all sorts of religious stuff. I don't think it's the Bible, even though it sounds like it. Listen to this. It's supposed to come from First Thessalonians: 'For we believe that Jesus has died and risen again, and that through Jesus, God will bring with Him the True Believer and their beloved who have passed away. For this we declare to you on the Lord's own authority—that the True Believers who are alive and continue on earth until the Coming of the Lord, shall certainly forestall those who in darkness would extinguish The Light. For the Lord Himself will come down from Heaven with a loud word of command, and with an archangel's voice and the trumpet of God, and the dead in The Church will rise first and through Christ smite the darkness. Afterwards the True Believers who are alive and are still on earth will be caught up amid the clouds to meet the Lord in the air. And so The Church shall be with the Lord forever. Therefore encourage one another with these words.'"

"Sounds like the Bible to me."

She grimaced. "I need to talk to Deacon Cronus this morning. Maybe I can borrow a Bible from the church to compare it to."

"You'd better get going, it's nearly lunch time. I'll go pick something up. Chubby's all right?"

"Fine with me. See if Grey and Bernie can free up from whatever they're into. I'd like to know what's going on with those bones from the fire pit." She closed the heavy volume on her desk. "Would it be all right if I showed this to Deacon Cronus? Ask him what he thinks?"

"Sure. I wouldn't expect a preacher to be involved, would you?"

DEACON CRONUS WAS SLOUCHED forward as far as his bulk would allow. A beefy hand supported his bearded face as he read the document on his desk. Framed photographs of his family dotted the credenza behind him, showing the Deacon as a proud husband and father of three boys and two girls. The photos showed the family's progression from infant and toddler stages, with the Deacon's wife looking particularly exhausted, through to the most current, which showed the oldest two boys as teenagers, the youngest girl as around seven years old. Other photographs dotted the walls, commemorating the various mission activities Deacon Cronus had organized. Cass spoke softly from the door.

"Good morning, Deacon. I hope I'm not disturbing you."

His head jerked upright and he forced a smile. "Hello Cass. What a beautiful morning God has made for us. It's good to see you," he answered in a voice crafted to hold a congregation's attention, waving her toward a chair. His eyes snagged on the book folded in her arms. She sat and balanced it on her lap, out of his line of sight. "Is there something I can help you with?"

"Yes, sir. Two things actually. I'd imagine that you've heard we found a skeleton last week."

"God rest his soul."

"He was an older man from Arkansas, named Humberto Gonzalez."

"Humberto Gonzalez," he repeated. "It's familiar, but I can't place him."

"He was in the country illegally. Could he have attended one of your outreach services?"

"Perhaps," Deacon Cronus shrugged and then his eyes, dark raisins in the doughy softness of his face, narrowed in thought. "There was one elderly man late last year. He came to several of the services but wouldn't tell me his name."

"Why not?"

"He was afraid."

"Of what?"

"Something he called *diablo de luz*."

"A devil of light?"

Deacon Cronus nodded.

Her mind flew to Goober's "anonymous" phone call Saturday night, reporting that a devil made of light had started a fire in the forest. Could it be coincidence that someone else had been afraid of a devil of light? "What do you think that meant?"

"I have no idea, but the man was terrified. He asked that I sprinkle him with holy water, and while that's something more in line with what a Catholic priest would do, I collected some water from the infant baptismal and," his hands fluttered, "sprinkled it over him while I prayed for his protection."

"From a devil," Cass stated.

"Yes."

"Okay. Well, we'd appreciate if you'd ask your Mexican congregation about Humberto Gonzalez." She snapped her fingers. "Although a missing person's report hasn't been filed, the sheriff up where Mr. Gonzalez lived believes that his son has gone missing as well."

"How bizarre. I suppose it's good that we have a name for the elderly man now, and know something about him. Do you have any suspects with regards to his death?"

"We don't, which is why your help is so critical."

Deacon Cronus nodded solemnly, chins multiplying with each downward movement. "I'll mention both Humberto Gonzalez and his son and be in touch if I hear anything. There was a second matter you wanted to discuss?"

Cass lifted the heavy volume from her lap and balanced it on his desk, preparing to speak. Deacon Cronus shoved back from his desk and his mouth formed a comical 'o'. Her gut contracted. Instinct told her to move slowly.

"I wanted to ask your opinion about this book," she said, placing one hand on its cover.

"Wh –," he cleared his throat, "where did you come across it?"

"It's part of an ongoing investigation. Do you know it?"

"I, uh," he said, dabbing at his damp forehead with a snowy handkerchief and squinting at the book's title. "*The Church of the True Believer?* No, no I don't think I've seen it before."

The knot in her stomach twisted. "Deacon? Are you all right?"

He smiled weakly. "I had a tummy virus this weekend. Must not be over it."

"Then I won't keep you," she replied, standing and balancing the heavy tome on one hip. His eyes stayed locked on her face. "No offense, Deacon, but you're looking a bit peaked. You might want to see a doctor."

With effort, he shook his head. "No, I'm fine. Really," he answered. "I'm glad you stopped by. I'll be in touch about Humberto Gonzalez."

"Thank you. I'll let myself out."

She pulled his office door closed and waved good-bye through the window before walking slowly down the hall. Her boots clunked on the bright linoleum as she passed offices humming with life, and her mind gnawed over the Deacon's reaction to the book she carried. He'd seen it before; she was sure of it. But why would he lie? Only if, she reasoned, he was involved in this group of men and their sexual activities. The thought of Deacon Cronus as a sexual being brought a hushed gasp of laughter to her lips. Cass tried to remember the various shapes of the men in the photographs from Lenny Scarborough's house. One in particular had a sagging gut. But as she had with Mayor Rusted, Cass discounted Deacon Cronus as a candidate for that man, simply because his girth was too great. She shook the image from her mind. Short of asking him to expose himself, she had no way of knowing whether he was in any of the photos. Glancing at the book she carried, she remembered that she'd wanted a Bible for comparison. She'd stopped at a door labeled 'Pastor's Office', and on impulse tapped lightly. After a moment, it opened and a fair-haired man smiled at her. "Good morning."

"Uh, hello," she said, startled at his youthful appearance. "I'm Detective Cass Elliot, with the sheriff's office. Are you the pastor?"

"I am," he smiled, pulling the door open. She shifted the book in her arms and shook his hand. "Luke Knightman. Is there something I can help you with?"

"I just wondered if I could borrow a Bible."

"Of course, Detective Elliot," he answered, gesturing to the low bookshelves lining one wall of his office. "What version do you want?"

"Call me Cass," she answered. "Um, something modern? Without the thee's and thou's?"

He motioned her toward a chair and squatted next to the bookshelves.

Vertical blinds moved gently with the breeze from a ceiling fan and late morning sunlight rippled across the blood red carpet. He reached for a fat volume and placed it on his desk. "Is there something specific you wanted?"

She hesitated, examining him across the desk. He wasn't as young as she'd initially thought. His hair was thinning and laugh lines had started to carve themselves near his eyes and alongside his mouth. He exuded an air of ease with himself and his world. Of comfort and dependability. But if it was possible that Deacon Cronus was one of this secret group, then wasn't it also possible that Pastor Luke Knightman could be, as well? He was trim and his hair fair. She thought that most of the men in the Scarborough photos would be a bit heavier than this man, and perhaps a little hairier in the abdomen and groin area than she judged Pastor Knightman would be. Suddenly, she found herself blinking hard against the laughter caught in her throat. There was absolutely no point in trying to guess whether any man was part of this group. He looked at her expectantly. *What the heck*, she told herself. *In for a dime, in for a dollar.* The knot in her stomach untangled itself. "Pastor Knightman, can I ask you to look at something? Confidentially?"

"Of course. But please call me Pastor Luke. Pastor Knightman is my father."

She smiled and lifted the heavy book to his desk. "This is part of a murder investigation."

"Oh," he said. "How can I help?"

"It's called *The Church of the True Believer.* Have you heard of it?"

Pastor Luke pursed his lips and shook his head. "Should I have?"

"I don't know. It's not part of the materials you'd normally use?"

"No. I don't think I've come across it, even as a reference in a footnote." He turned to his computer and typed. "I don't see any references to it on the internet, either."

She hesitated. "Is it something Deacon Cronus might have seen before?"

"I doubt it. Why?"

"I stopped to see him on my way in, and he reacted strangely to it."

"Well, he had a stomach bug over the weekend, so maybe he still isn't feeling well. I don't know where he would've come across it."

Cass nodded, still uncertain at the explanation. "I started to read it this morning and got confused. It reads like it's a religious text, or maybe a set of instructions, but," she blushed, "I don't know the Bible very well, and I wanted to compare some passages."

He chuckled and reached across the desk. "May I?"

Pastor Luke flipped through the pages, taking his time and stopping frequently to read. "I see why you're confused." He checked the publication date and quickly scanned the book's opening paragraphs. Drawing a deep breath, he glanced again at the bookshelves, seeming to consider his words. "It's very well done. Bottom line though, this book is the basis for a cult."

"Cult?" She moved forward in her chair. "I tend to think of Waco or the Kool-Aid guy. Is that what you mean?"

"Cults are about control, simple as that. David Koresh isolated his followers from their families and other support networks, forcing them to rely on him alone and increasing their vulnerability. Jim Jones took his control to an extreme and demanded that his followers sacrifice themselves as a demonstration of their commitment. I'd need to study this more closely to understand what this group is trying to achieve. But from scanning it," he fanned the pages, "it's twisting the Bible for some purpose."

"Have you heard of any cult activity around here?"

"No." He flipped again to the publication page. "And given the length of time that has passed since this book was published in the 'twenties, you'd think word would've gotten out."

"That's one of the reasons this is so confusing. Can I show you one of the passages, and get your reaction to it?"

"Of course." She found the page for him. He read through the paragraph and frowned. "It's close to First Thessalonians Chapter 4, but it's been doctored," he said, reaching for the Bible. He turned translucent pages and read, eyes distant as he finished his comparison, then tapped *The Church of the True Believer*. "This passage is based on verses thirteen to eighteen. More restrictive as to those who will share in the rapture..."

She closed her eyes as she listened, opening them when he stopped mid-sentence. He was smiling shyly. "Members of the congregation do fall asleep during a sermon, but they're usually much older than you."

Cass grinned. "I'm sorry. Closing my eyes helps me concentrate," she said, checking her watch. "This will sound a little forward, but do you have lunch plans?"

Pastor Luke's smile widened and he scratched the back of his neck. "No, I don't."

"I should tell you that I have an ulterior motive. We're a pretty ignorant bunch. I'd like to buy you lunch from Chubby's if you'll join me at the courthouse, and give my partners a lesson in cults. Does that sound like a fair trade?"

"Throw in a chocolate shake and you've got a deal."

Cass reached for her phone. "Onion rings, fries, or both?"

CHAPTER 31

DEACON CRONUS SAT IN silence after Cass left his office, eyes closed as he hunched over the papers on his desk. This was dangerous. For those who don't possess the wisdom to understand the message of *The Church of the True Believer*, misinterpretation is a possibility. He wondered if the book would have to be burned since a woman had soiled it. And now that it was in the possession of the police, how would they ever get it back?

He drew a long, shaky breath. Lenny Scarborough's death, he fervently believed, was Satan clawing at The Church, trying to unravel the tightly knit group. If that happened... he shuddered at the thought of what would be lost. Deacon Cronus jerked upright when the phone vibrated against his hip. He snatched it from its holster and snapped it open.

"Did you know the Elliot woman has the book?" he demanded.

The old man was silent for a beat. "Not her, specifically, but yes, I knew the police had it."

"What do we do now? A woman has... has *handled* it. The book is lost to us. It will have to be destroyed."

"Slow down, Deacon. You sound upset."

"I am. Lenny has jeopardized us all. And his book," Deacon Cronus breathed heavily into the phone, "has to be retrieved and destroyed. How will we replace it?"

"Calm down, Deacon. Be mindful of your heart."

Cronus grimaced. The old man was an expert at manipulation. "It's too much, that's all. Lenny's death. His *murder*." He ran a hand across his damp forehead. "Good Lord. We have his briefcase, but lost the book. The *names* in the book. This is a nightmare. Have you warned them?"

"Those who need to know, yes."

"Are we safe? Shouldn't we do something?"

Again the old man was silent. When he spoke, his voice was thoughtful. "You were chosen for a reason, you know that, don't you Deacon? You have a powerful gift from the Lord, the ability to understand and translate His Word for those who have ears to hear, the True Believers. You alone are The Light of this generation." He paused as the other man's breathing slowed. "Your distress over these issues is why I've taken The Church's operational burden on myself. To spare you the frustration of running The Church and its day-to-day activities. We need you focused on the Lord, not on these matters. And we need you now, more than ever before."

Cronus held his breath and let the warmth of the old man's praise seep into his bones. He bowed his head and spoke softly. "I understand. And I... I recognize and appreciate the weight that you carry on behalf of us all. Your strength continues to amaze me. You are a blessing."

"I am only pleased to do the truth that I may come into The Light." The old man drew a quick breath. "We need to move ahead quickly. With Lenny's death, the Circle of Illumination cannot be closed. Have you given thought to the selection?"

"I um, well," the Deacon blustered, "I have read through Acts Chapter 1 and reviewed the footnotes in the text. What are your thoughts?"

On the other end of the call, the old man smiled. "I'll ask the others to come to the house tonight. You'll need to spend some time considering an opening prayer and an invitation to The Brethren."

"Your house? Is that wise?"

"The missus has no idea what we're about, Deacon. She'll be only too pleased to make cookies and brew coffee."

"If you're sure that there's no risk now that the police have the text..."

"I'll tell her that we're gathering to mourn a respected man, and that'll be the story that hits the grapevine."

Deacon Cronus nodded into the phone, respectful of the man's deviousness. "Fine."

"As you open the invitation for tonight, make sure you give The Brethren the option to remove themselves from the selection process."

"Of course. I uh, wonder if there are any members that should be encouraged not to participate."

"Someone in particular?"

"Jed Salter is still distressed over his oldest son's death," the Deacon said cautiously.

"It's unfortunate that his grief is so deep, but God works in mysterious ways. Like you, I don't think he's ready for the Circle of Illumination. I'll encourage him to take additional time for reflection before he chooses to participate in the selection."

"Good. We'll need to choose a new member of The Brethren tonight, as well."

"Yes, we will."

"This will be an open debate, but I suspect you have someone in mind."

Through the phone, Deacon Cronus heard the clacking of teeth against pipe and knew that the old man was content. "I'm thinking about Hugo Petchard."

"The police officer?"

"He's done a good job for us as one of The Way, and he can be... molded."

Anxious thoughts scurried through the Deacon's mind. It was always a risky business, indoctrinating someone into The Church. The bond between members was sealed through what some might consider harrowing rituals, and complete obedience and loyalty were demanded. As far as the Deacon knew, only one man had left The Church while alive, and he must've made a powerful argument to be allowed to leave and live. Members were selected carefully and over time, were subtly formed to fit The Church's mold. Petchard certainly had a need to belong, to be recognized. The old man could ensure that Sheriff Hoffner promoted him to detective before too long. And having a detective as a member of The Church would be beneficial. But still, he was one of the more unpredictable members of the police force.

"He may be too volatile to function effectively inside The Church. Perhaps he's better suited to remain a member of The Way," the Deacon proposed, scratching his beard.

"He is passionate," the old man agreed. "We could use an infusion of emotion right about now. Someone to work from the bottom of The Church, to complement your work from the top. To generate enthusiasm."

"I see what you mean," Deacon Cronus said, picturing Petchard as an assistant of sorts. "How will he react to the rituals?"

The old man sighed. "That's always an unknown, isn't it? We've been blessed with men who are completely committed to The Church's work. Petchard is an astute enough young man to realize the benefits he'll gain,

THE DEVIL OF LIGHT

and will understand the rituals for what they are – an outward and visible sign of our bonding in the name of the Lord."

Deacon Cronus grunted into the phone, satisfied. "I'm not sure who the others will recommend, are you?"

"No, but I'll do some campaigning. We won't have a problem getting Petchard approved. We need to move quickly. Wednesday night?"

"Do we have the elements?"

"Yes. We'll use The Sanctuary."

"Do you think Jed Salter's younger son is ready to serve?"

"I'll speak to him about it. The child's involvement might be just what Jed needs. Getting back on the horse that threw you, so to speak," the old man said. "Are your two girls available?"

"I'm sure they will be. I'll have invitations printed and delivered." Frown lines creased folds in his fat forehead. "What will we do without Lenny's book?"

The sizzle of a match hissed down the phone line, followed by gentle puffing as the old man lit his pipe. "More operational stuff, Deacon. Let me worry about that."

CHAPTER 32

OSCAR MUCKLEROY STOPPED TO rub his left leg. He'd spent the better part of Sunday and all of Monday morning trudging along disused trails in East Texas' piney forest, checking for unusual activity, and his leg made sure he knew it was working overtime. But after seeing the fire pit Matt and Mark Grove had found, and realizing that it contained human bones, Oscar was worried about what was going on in *his* woods. He'd spent the better part of his fifty-some-odd years as a forestry man and felt justified in claiming the land as his own. A fire would be devastating, environmentally and economically. But what mattered to Oscar was the beauty of the place, the peace he felt as he watched the forest ebb and grow over time. In today's disposable world, he wanted something of substance left for future generations. If that meant his leg and back suffered, so be it.

He wiped the sweat from his forehead with a brightly colored kerchief. It was threadbare, but he couldn't stand to part with it. His wife had always purchased loud kerchiefs for him, believing that if a hungry animal spotted her husband in his mundane forestry uniform, a colorful piece of cloth might save him from becoming lunch. Madge had died a couple of years ago, but Oscar wasn't ready to let go. He carefully folded the kerchief and tucked it in his back pocket. Stopping to rest had eased the aching in his leg and he surveyed the surrounding area before deciding which way to go. He was on an old fire trail and believed it led to a natural clearing just ahead. If someone was horsing around with campfires out here like they did in that clearing the Grove boys discovered, the one with those foot bones in it, a clearing in this remote area of the forest might prove just as attractive.

Taking a swig of water from a canteen he carried on his belt, Oscar swung his heavy leg forward to get his momentum going and headed for a cluster of azalea bushes covered in papery purple blooms. Fifteen clumping strides forward and he shouldered through the heavy foliage, jerking to a stop and straightening as far as his hunch would allow.

"Oh boy," he whispered as his eyes darted into the shadowy underbrush. "Grey's going to love this one."

CHAPTER 33

"STOP HOGGING ALL THE food, Mitch," Cass moaned. "Pass that bag around, we've got company."

Mitch snagged a handful of onion rings before scooting the bag toward Scott Truman, who pushed it to the center of the table. "You know Pastor Luke, given what you've described, I'm not sure this is a cult."

"Why?"

Mitch studied the preacher before glancing at Kado and Munk, who read the question in his eyes and nodded. "What I'm about to tell you relates to Lenny Scarborough's death and is extremely confidential. It cannot be discussed outside of this room."

"I understand."

Mitch drew a deep breath. "You described leaders who are interested in power, in increasing the number of people who follow them. They want attention, glory, and eventually, they end up attracting negative scrutiny from the local community and perhaps the authorities. Angie Scarborough described a group of men that Lenny has belonged to since before they were married. She said they met at night and Lenny wore a purple robe to those meetings."

"That could be something like the Lion's Club or the Masons. They have their own rituals, their own garb. But you seem to think there's something sinister about this group."

"There is. We have evidence that several men are involved in the gang rape of a child and homosexual activities."

Pastor Luke blinked and carefully placed his cup on the table. "What kind of evidence?"

"Photographs."

"Good Lord," he breathed.

"There can't be many men involved, since they've operated without detection for so long in such a small community. Does this sound like a cult?"

Pastor Luke reached for *The Church of the True Believer*, flipped to the opening pages and read aloud. "'For we are locked in a battle of proportions to rival the end of times. Satan grows and groans, shaking the foundations of the earth and threatening the blessings so graciously poured upon us. We labor to fight the good fight, seeking the few True Believers for our sacred charge from the many who worship in hypocrisy. The Brethren cling one to another, drawing strength from strength, protecting our mission from the clutches of evil. The innocence of the lamb feeds our virtue, expands our knowledge and fuels our lust for the fight.'" He exhaled slowly, eyes distant as he considered his next comment. "Depending on the reader, the words are simply an encouragement to the True Believers to seek out and draw strength from one another, to continue the fight against Satan. Similar to Paul's letters in some respects." He scanned the text. "But, given what Angie told you and knowing about the photos, the tone changes. It becomes exclusive – the 'few True Believers' versus those who 'worship in hypocrisy'. 'Clinging to one another' could imply a physical relationship between members and again, exclusivity. 'The innocence of the lamb' could refer to children."

The room was silent for a beat.

"What are you saying?" Munk asked.

"To me, it sounds like a cult. Still focused on control and the acquisition of power, the power of exclusivity rather than numbers. But the definition of this group as a cult isn't important."

"Why not?"

"From the perspective of wanting to find child molesters and rapists, the *question*," Pastor Luke said, "is who in this community has the power to convince men like Lenny Scarborough that homosexuality, rape and child molestation will give them strength and knowledge?"

THEY CALLED THEIR GOOD-BYES as the door swung shut behind Pastor Luke Knightman, and then collapsed into chairs around the table. Kado broke the silence. "Fascinating."

"How do you mean?" Mitch asked, digging a ringing phone from his pocket.

"We haven't focused on who Lenny was in the community. He was a pretty powerful man, right? He owned some real estate and a piece of some insurance company. Not too shabby in terms of financial wealth. Maybe it is about power, money."

"Pastor Luke wanted to know who has the power to recruit men like Lenny Scarborough," Cass said. "If power equals money, there aren't that many around here that fit the bill."

"You'd be amazed," Munk injected. "There's a lot of money in this area. Old money from agriculture, but also from oil and gas. People just don't flash it around."

"Maybe we should start with the folks Lenny knew. Angie told us that they didn't have many visitors. Let's find out how active he was in the insurance business."

"Was he," Cass began, wondering how to phrase this question. "Did he know Deacon Cronus, over at the First Baptist Church?"

Kado shrugged and looked to Officer Truman, who shook his head and spoke. "I don't know. Why?"

"I stopped to see him when I went to the church to look for a Bible. When I showed him *The Church of the True Believer*, he kind of freaked out."

"Freaked out how?" Munk asked.

"He just looked spooked, like he was shocked to see me with that book."

"So now you think David Cronus is involved in this thing?"

"I don't know. I guess I've been trying to size up the guys I've come into contact with."

Munk's look was blank. Kado and Truman exchanged glances and snickered.

Cass blushed. "All we've got to go on are those photos from Lenny Scarborough's kitchen floor. Some of the men were big, and I wondered about Deacon Cronus, and even the Mayor."

Munk let fly with a disgusted laugh. "That's probably not good for your mental health, Cass."

"I know." Her grimace morphed into a grin. "You're right, it's stupid. The Deacon said he'd had a stomach bug over the weekend. He's probably not over it."

Mitch had spoken quietly on the phone while the others talked. He snapped the phone shut and reached for the coffee pot and cups. "Grey and Bernie are on their way over. They've got some news on the bones from the fire pit and Lenny's autopsy. Kado, are you done with the fingerprints from the Scarborough's house?"

"There's nothing unexpected. I've got Lenny's, Angie's and four sets of child-sized prints. There are two adults that came back with no hits. Maybe relatives."

"All right. Truman, tell me how you figured out how many men are involved."

The young officer shifted in his chair, heat climbing his cheeks. "I just compared one photo to another. Some guys were easy to identify because of the color of their, um, pu-pubic hair," he stuttered as the blush deepened, "or because of the shape of their hands. One guy bites his nails. A couple have moles in certain places. One consistency is that where I could see it, they each have a scar on their sides," he pointed to his right rib cage. "I marked the photos to show the similarities and gave each man a letter to keep track of them. But there are some shots that I'm not sure about. It could be one of the same men, or a different one."

Mitch smiled grimly. "Good work. That can't have been easy."

Truman drew a shaky breath. "No, sir, but there's more. I was able to work with the photos using a commercial software package. We might be able to do something more with a professional package, but I think all the photos were taken at the same place. Let me show you." He reached for a thick envelope on the counter behind him as the conference room door swung open.

Sheriff Bill Hoffner sauntered into the room and checked the coffee counter for spills before leaning into it. He was a vulture of a man, eyes set close to a long, hooked nose, snowy hair cropped short, Adam's apple riding high in a long neck. His eyes swept the room, skipping over Cass. He crossed his arms over his chest and grunted a greeting. "You working on Lenny Scarborough?"

"Yes, sir," Mitch replied. "Truman's done some work on the photographs this morning and was about to show us some similarities in location. You have time for a look?"

"I do," he said, carefully pouring from the coffee pot. He snapped a paper towel from its holder and wiped the cup's rim, the chair seat and the edge of the table before sitting down. "Let's see what you've got."

"Yes, sir," Truman answered, pouring the photos on the table. They were printed on standard letter-sized paper and each bore notes in Truman's neat handwriting. "They're pretty graphic, sir. I've been able to find at least seven different men who appear in these photos. There are several more that I have questions about. I'll keep working on that. But I noticed that the background never changes." He shuffled through the stack and pulled several pages out, turning them to face the group. "It's most clear in these. They've done a good job of picking a dark place – the paneling on the walls doesn't give off a reflection, the windows are covered and I haven't come across a mirror. But I see the same furniture in each shot. There's a bed." He pointed to a snip of white in one photo and a narrow expanse of rumpled sheets in another. "But it doesn't have a headboard or footboard. In some shots you can see the curve of a rocking chair runner. The floors are unfinished wood but they're old and look pretty smooth. The windows are covered with what looks like dark blankets. The light in the room never varies, but I haven't seen the source. From the shadows, I think it's an overhead fitting."

Sheriff Hoffner used the tip of one finger to pull a page toward him and leaned over it. "Looks rustic."

Kado leaned over another page. "Can you bring this up on the computer?"

Truman moved to the computer and unlocked the screen, scrolling to the right shot. Kado pointed to a corner of the photo. "See if you can enlarge that."

Truman selected the area and clicked to magnify and sharpen the image. "That's about as good as it'll get. What do you see?"

Kado squinted at the screen as the others gathered behind Truman. "Those points. Is that a rack?"

Collectively, they leaned forward. Sheriff Hoffner grunted. "Buck?"

"Hunting cabin? Deer camp?"

Truman nodded. "That would explain the rough floors and walls, and the blankets over the windows."

"And why they'd have enough privacy to do all this," Cass added, noting the stiffening of Sheriff Hoffner's face at the sound of her voice. "If it's a cabin down in the river bottom, Lenny could've picked up the sandy mud Angie said was on his boots."

Mitch heaved a sigh and sat at the conference room table. "How do we narrow it down? I mean, how many deer camps do we have around here?"

Sheriff Hoffner straightened a staff notice on the wall as he returned to his chair. "Officer Truman, can you identify anyone from the characteristics you spotted?"

"No, sir. Most were close up shots of the uh, acts, and showed only the chest, hips and thighs."

"How about the woman?"

"There are at least two included in the photos, sir. Their faces are always covered, but I think they're teenage girls, like Munk suggested."

Hoffner paled. "What makes you think they're girls?"

"Just comparing their size to that of the men. They could be very slender women. But even compared to the smallest man, the girls have small bone structures." He blushed. "Their uh, breasts are small and their hips are very narrow. They also don't have much pubic hair."

"Any moles, tattoos?"

"Moles or birthmarks, yes."

Hoffner rubbed his face with both hands. "Compare their descriptions with any missing teenagers here and in the surrounding counties. Maybe we can identify them that way."

The conference room door swung open and Elaine stepped through, curls bouncing. "Sheriff, Grey is on the phone for you," she said, color in her cheeks from her dash through the station. "Oscar Muckleroy just called. He's found a body down near Logan's Quarters. Grey and his friend Bernie are on their way. He said to bring shovels."

CHAPTER 34

CASS WAS SURPRISED THAT the clean scent of pine and cedar were all that met her nose when she and Mitch stepped from the truck. Grey's van, a patrol car, and a battered pickup were pulled to the side of the road. Kado rolled to a stop and they gathered forensic equipment and shovels from the pickup's bed.

Mitch breathed deeply through his nose. "I don't smell anything."

"Me either," answered Munk. "Grey said Oscar found the body down a fire trail," he pointed to a narrow path that disappeared into the forest. "Ready?"

Their eyes swept the ground, checking for evidence without knowing exactly what they were looking for. The dense canopy of pine branches provided relief from the sun's heat, but gnats and mosquitoes hummed in the air, sticking to the layer of sweat that coated their faces.

"It sure got hot in a hurry after last week's storm," Mitch groused, pulling a handkerchief from his pocket to mop his brow.

"It's supposed to rain again," said Munk. "Big storm coming, apparently. And we haven't hit Easter yet. We'll have a cold snap around then."

"I hope the storm will wash some of this humidity out of the air. Can't hardly breathe." He stopped and peered farther along the path as he pulled his phone from its holster. "Where are they?"

He dialed Grey and continued deeper into the forest until they saw a latex glove hanging from a tree branch. They pushed through the undergrowth, following the trail beaten by Grey and Bernie, emerging into a clearing isolated from the surrounding forest by huge azalea bushes heavy with blooms. The scent of decay was raw in the air. Oscar Muckleroy leaned against a tree talking to Bernie, breathing through the kerchief clutched over his mouth. Grey squatted on his haunches at the edge of the clearing and directed their gaze to its center with a lift of his chin. The tattered remnants of a decaying forearm protruded from the sandy ground, its bony middle finger fully extended in a defiant gesture.

Cass chuckled. "Not very dignified, is it?"

Bernie smiled. "No, but expressive. The killer secured the arm, hand, and finger to a length of metal, ensuring his greeting would remain intact for some time."

"Metal?"

"Re-bar," clarified Oscar.

"Well," said Mitch, "I guess we have to dig him up."

"And sift for trace at the same time," sighed Kado. Munk grunted in disbelief. "Grey, is he on his back?"

Grey uncurled his long frame and raked a hand through his dark, bushy hair. "If it's a full body, that's my guess. I can't see somebody digging a man-sized hole straight down, even if he's folded into it. It's easier to dig shallow but long."

"How long has he been out here?"

"Given the arm's decomp, a few weeks, but we'll need to see the full body before we can tell for sure."

Mitch eased around the edge of the clearing and stood next to Oscar Muckleroy. "How did you find him?"

Oscar pointed a gnarled finger to a narrow path cutting into the clearing. "That's an old branch off the fire trail. After I saw the Grove boy's fire pit, I figured I better check some of the older sites and see if they're being used. Kids like to come out here and horse around. I pushed into this clearing and, well, there it is."

"Who's in the patrol car?" Cass asked.

Grey grimaced. "Hugo Petchard. He was closest when dispatch asked for assistance."

"Where'd he go?"

"Took a smoke break before coming out here, of all things," Oscar grunted, lowering his kerchief to sniff for smoke. "The fool. Here he comes."

Petchard pushed through the azalea bushes, stopping short when he saw the rotting forearm thrusting toward the sky. "Whoa."

"Come on, Petchard," Cass said as a sly grin crept across her face. "After finding that skeleton last week, surely seeing a little old rotting arm is no big deal for a tough guy like you."

He coughed a reply and about-faced toward the patrol car.

"Where you goin'?" Mitch drawled.

"I, uh, I'd better go secure the scene for y'all."

"Mighty considerate, but you'll be more valuable with a shovel in your hand." Mitch grinned. "Grey, where do you want him to start?"

"Digging up bodies from unmarked graves is right up Bernie's alley," Grey said as the Englishman bent to scrounge in a case and stood with a delicate paintbrush in one hand and a small pick in the other. "I'm sure Officer Petchard will learn a lot."

BERNIE AND GREY HOVERED over the fully exposed corpse while Kado and Cass sealed containers of soil samples. The afternoon had worn away as they dug, the sun falling behind nearby pine trees, leaving a soft blue sky above and cooling the clearing. Oscar left shortly after the digging began, realizing that he wasn't suited to the task and pleased to be out of the way. Mitch and Munk finished taking photos while Cass watched Petchard disappear into the woods and listened for his dry heaves. She smiled sweetly when he trudged into the clearing, face devoid of color, wiping his mouth with the back of one hand. He scowled in reply, checking the ground carefully before sitting down and leaning against a pine tree. Sandy soil streaked his uniform, arms and face. In spite of the warm temperature, Petchard had dug delicately where directed by Bernie, and without complaint in spite of the discomfort his burns must've caused. But in fairness, so had the others. Petchard had controlled his revulsion until the digging was done, even though the sickly sweet smell had grown more intense with every shovel of dirt, until the clearing was so thick with the stench of death that everyone but Bernie had given in and smeared Vicks under their nose. He insisted that his unfettered sense of smell was just as important as his eyesight. Cass debated silently before taking pity and tossing Petchard a bottle of cold water.

"Thanks," he muttered, turning to watch the scene in the middle of the clearing.

Bernie and Grey had murmured between themselves as the corpse was exposed bit by bit, and were engaged in a debate about how to process the decomposing body. They seemed confused by the state of the naked corpse, which had a desiccated, leathery appearance. As the others watched, both nodded, satisfied with whatever decision had been reached. Bernie dug a fresh pair of gloves from one of the pockets on his safari vest, then crouched and crept around the body, gently brushing away debris. He stopped suddenly. "This is most unusual," he said, poking a gloved finger into matted tufts of dark hair on the corpse's head. He turned to Grey. "I've rarely seen a gunshot wound to the top of a skull, have you?"

Grey squatted next to Bernie, examined the skull, and then looked up and down the body. "This isn't a short man. He must be close to six foot." Grey squinted into the distance. "How do you shoot someone in the top of the head?"

"Maybe he was bending over," said Kado.

"Or kneeling," Munk offered.

"I saw a show once," Petchard volunteered. "Some dude fired a shot up in the air and the bullet came down in a driveway, a few blocks away. Drilled this chick in the head. An accident." He pointed at the open grave. "Coulda happened to this guy."

Mitch cocked an eyebrow. "And this dude who fired the gun, did he know he'd hit this woman a couple of blocks away?"

Petchard scratched his head. "Don't think so. The TV show was a re-creation thing. They figured out where she was standing and that the bullet had to have come from the sky and started asking people in the area about firing guns on the day she died. Pretty smart, huh?"

Mitch raised the other eyebrow. "So, you're thinking maybe there's somebody out here in the middle of the woods, right? And they point a gun up in the air and pull the trigger. And this guy," Mitch points to the corpse, "is standing in the clearing, naked as a jaybird, right next to an open pit. And he gets that bullet in the head, and somehow survives long enough to tie a metal pole to his arm, hop in the grave and pull some dirt over his body."

Petchard listened with an open mouth, and then blushed. "It was just an idea."

Mitch winked quickly at Cass and turned to the others. "Bernie, what do you think?"

Bernie leaned closer to the wound. "I need to look at this more closely. I'm not sure it's a bullet hole."

Grey frowned. "What else could it be?"

"I don't know." He shook his head and repeated his earlier statement as he continued to creep around the body. "Most unusual."

The group watched as Bernie muttered to himself, gently prodding the corpse and occasionally speaking to Grey, exchanging cryptic comments in a language only the two of them understood. Bernie finally stood and stripped the gloves from his hands. "I can be more precise when I've examined him at the ME's office, but this is the body of a middle aged male."

"Time since death?" Mitch asked.

"I'm getting different information from the portion of the body that was above ground, the arm, and the rest of the body. We'll need more analysis, but at this point, I would hazard a guess that he's been out here for several weeks, perhaps longer."

"Was he killed here?"

"From examination of the grave, I cannot say. Kado?"

"We found a Dubble Bubble wrapper and a very old condom, but I doubt they're relevant. I didn't find any evidence that he was killed here. Once we have his identity and cause of death, we can work backwards on location."

"Any idea on cause of death?" Mitch asked.

Bernie shrugged. "Grey will need to perform an autopsy to be sure."

"But your initial thoughts?"

"With limited analysis, all I can say with certainty is that the presence of a hole in the skull is suspicious, as is the state of the body. Grey?"

"We'll work on the autopsy this evening." Grey twisted to stretch his spine. "Kado, are you happy that we leave his arm attached to that bar until we get to the ME's office? You can have it after we finish with him."

"No problem," Kado answered, packing samples into his forensic kit.

"Mitch, would you pass me that body bag? We're ready to move him."

Mitch carried the bag to shallow grave. "He kinda looks like a mummy. Think he'll hold together while we lift him?"

Bernie squatted again, eyes alight as he examined the corpse. "Ah yes, good observation Mitchell. This dried appearance is confusing. He looks as if decay has stopped." He snapped on a fresh pair of gloves and looked to Grey. "I have some theories, but we need your examination equipment. Lift on three?"

––––––––––––

MITCH FOLLOWED KADO AND Grey out of Logan's Quarters and back toward town. The sun had dropped lower, drawing a veil of tangerine across the clear evening sky. A lone hawk circled high above on a thermal and looped out over the forest.

"You want to grab something to eat?" Mitch asked.

"Just drop me at the courthouse. I need to finish the Pettigrew brother's statement. I promised I'd bring it to The Gate tomorrow morning and let them proofread it." Cass yawned, shaking her head. "Might even wake up early and run."

"When was the last time you ran?"

Cass wrinkled her brow. "Six weeks ago."

"Ouch."

"Yeah, I figure it'll burn for the first few days. But I have to start some time." She turned in her seat to look at Mitch. "You remember Randall Mahaffey?"

"The paramedic? Sure. Why?"

"We ended up talking about Jack at the Scarborough's place yesterday, while we were waiting for Grey to arrive."

"What did he say?"

"He didn't think it made sense that Jack went to jail for what happened."

"Why?"

"He said Jack never had any trouble getting laid," she answered, watching as a smile teased at the corner of Mitch's mouth.

"You could say that about Jack. He sure was a ladies' man," he cut his eyes at Cass. "Didn't hurt that he was an athlete, but the boy had looks and brains to go with it all. Randall was younger than we were. I don't remember him having much to do with us."

"He said y'all were older, but he knew who you were. Anyway, he thought Jack might have been set up."

Mitch drew wind through his teeth in a low whistle. "I wonder how many other people think that, and how many were just happy to see Jack out of the way?"

"Why would anybody want him out of the way?"

"Petty jealousy, maybe. What better way to get rid of the competition?"

"It seems extreme to try and put somebody you don't like in jail." She drew a deep breath, feeling the familiar ache of frustration about her oldest brother settle into her chest. "Maybe Randall was just trying to be polite."

Mitch flipped on the blinker, eyes focused into the past. "Maybe. But it sure is interesting that he brought it up. It didn't make sense to me then, Cass. And Jack's never talked about it to me. He refuses to discuss it. Has he told you what happened?"

At her silence, he glanced across the cab to see her staring out the side window, her red hair shot through with gold in the late sun. Her face was smudged with dirt, her clothes brushed off but still dusty. She sighed as Mitch turned into the courthouse parking lot. "I was only four at the time, and it's been totally off limits between us. We don't even talk about it at home. Not about Jack or Momma." Cass shrugged. "His file is gone, anyway. Comfrey lost it."

"I know," Mitch answered softly. "So until Jack tells us something new, or evidence falls from the heavens, there's nothing we can do for him."

CHAPTER 35

CASS SETTLED BEHIND HER desk and listened to the ancient computer whir through its start-up routine. Sheriff Hoffner had convinced the good people of Forney County to cough up sufficient taxes to update the department's primary communication and research channels and set aside enough money to keep critical functions approaching the leading edge of technology. Unfortunately, the computers used by the department staff in their day-to-day office activities were teetering on the lagging edge. They had an internal network that allowed for email and file sharing, but the sophisticated upgrades were reserved for forensics, links with other investigative bodies and communications between officers and dispatch.

The station was quiet again this evening, supper served to those in the holding cells and cleared away. The sound of canned laughter drifted through the halls and Cass wondered if the prison at Huntsville sounded the same. If Jack had finished dinner and was watching comedies or was in his cell, reading. Glancing once more at the still chugging computer, she wandered across the empty squad room to pour a decaf coffee and returned to her desk as the login screen finally appeared. She reached for a small radio she kept in her desk and flipped it on. KOIL stuttered to life. The tiny station was fairly rigid in dispensing a diet of solid country music and football scores, but recently they'd relented to community pressure and offered a few hours of rockin' greats during the week. Monday night was music from the sixties and seventies. Cass logged onto the department's system and started typing a statement for the Pettigrew brothers. Jim Croce thumped into "You Don't Mess Around with Jim" and she sang along while she tapped at the keyboard.

"Don't give up your day job, babe," sneered a voice from across the room. Cass jerked her eyes from the screen to see scrawny Officer Petchard leaning against the coffee counter, legs slightly apart to avoid bumping his burned calves. He'd changed into street clothes and his hair was still wet from the shower. His eyes darted into the corners, checking for eavesdroppers. "Great bags, bad pipes," he sneered, cupping his hands at his chest.

"What do you want, Petchard?"

"Good to see you doing *proper* work for a woman. Typing's about as far as the allegedly fairer sex should go when it comes to work outside the home. Better off on your hands and knees, scrubbing the floor and taking care of business," he thrust his hips toward her, "while you're down there."

She arched a brow. "I've seen all you have to offer, remember? Gotta give a woman something to work with. That scrawny little worm you call a dick wouldn't pass for bait."

He crossed arms over his chest and pushed his bottom lip out as his face bloomed crimson. "That was uncalled for," he pouted.

Cass threw her head back and laughed until her sides ached. "Jeez Hugo, I had no idea you were so *sensitive* about that tiny dick." Her voice hardened. "You come in here dishing out sexual harassment and racial abuse, you little prick, you better expect some of it back. And be man enough to take it."

"Growing up with all them brothers of yours and no momma didn't do your manners any good. Guess your daddy was too busy drinking to know what a little bitch he'd raised."

A flash of rage, white hot and liquid, seared her spine as it raced toward her brain. Cass snapped from her chair, fists balled. "What did you say?" she growled, taking a step forward.

Petchard lurched upright and rubbed a hand across his mouth as Cass stalked toward him. "N-Nothin'. I didn't say anything," he sputtered, sliding along the counter.

Cass caught him before he could reach the door, grabbing his slender wrist and spinning him around to face her. She stabbed a finger into his chest. "You want to screw with me, that's fine Petchard, I'll take you on." She jabbed him again. "But you talk about my family and I will rip off those marble size balls of yours, batter them, fry them and shove them down your little chicken neck." She leaned forward until her nose was millimeters from his. Fury sharpened her vision and she saw every blocked pore on his nose and the black dots that patterned his murky green irises. "Are we clear?"

Petchard swallowed, a dry clicking sound in the quiet room. "Whatever," he muttered, breath sour with fear, then slunk from under her finger and out the squad room door.

She watched him leave and took a deep breath, exhaling as she crossed the room to her desk. Her hand shook as she reached for her coffee and she sat back, burning with anger, brain spinning. *Who did that little freak think he was? How did he know anything about her?* Cass lowered her head into her hands and took several deep breaths. *Would she ever outlive the shadow of her family's mistakes?* Her mind was alive with memories of her brothers and the bonds they shared. Her father's alcoholism had threatened their security, and if it weren't for her mother's sheer willpower, Cass was sure the family would've crumbled long before her birth. Jack's imprisonment twenty-one years ago for rape and murder had destroyed her mother, and Nell had died a young but broken woman only a year later. Those tragedies had bound the Elliot children closer together, and any threat to one was a threat to them all. Cass was the youngest of the seven and the only girl. To a man, each of her brothers had protected her in their own way, whether by using their fists or their sharp wit. Her reaction to Petchard's taunt about her family had been pure animal instinct to protect them in return.

She drew another deep breath and knew she was out of line in her response to Petchard's goading, but he'd pushed too far. Absurdly, she chuckled at the thought of his face. Sheer terror. Maybe he'd gotten the message that it wasn't safe to mess with her, which was a much better result than filing a complaint would have drawn.

Laughter cleared her brain and she focused again on the Pettigrew brothers' statement, working for another twenty minutes before she was satisfied she'd captured the details Wallace had given her that morning. She clicked a button and listened to the printer hum. Snagging the single sheet of paper as it slid into the tray, she scanned it quickly before reaching for an envelope. Her fingers brushed an unfamiliar surface and she looked down to see *The Church of the True Believer* nestled in her drawer.

The book was heavy, and she needed both hands to lift it. She'd meant to spend more time with it today, but that was before Oscar Muckleroy had found the corpse in the woods. Resting her weary head on one hand, she flipped through the thick, creamy pages, stopping to look at the colorful illustrations of Biblical characters and the events impacting their lives. A vivid scene showed Abraham with a sharp dagger raised over his son Isaac's breast, a ram struggling in nearby bushes. Another depicted a wise Solomon dangling a sword above the naked body of an infant stretched between two women, one whose face was twisted in anger, the other's in anguish.

Deeper in the book a disturbing image portrayed Christ on the cross after his side had been pierced by a centurion's spear. Blood spurted from the wound, drenching the disciples kneeling at the foot of the cross. The caption read *Washed in the Blood of the Lamb*. Cass frowned, unable to recall the crucifixion story clearly. As she remembered it, few of the disciples were present at Jesus' crucifixion. But women. Several women had been present, including Jesus' mother and Mary Magdalene. Why weren't they in this picture?

A pattern emerged as Cass again worked through the images. If a woman was depicted, she was in a subservient position, on her knees at the foot of one prophet or another with her face averted or eyes downcast. Cass turned through the book to a story she knew well, or thought she knew well – that of the birth of Christ. In most of the paintings she'd seen, Jesus was in Mary's lap or cradled in her arms, Joseph and the wise men standing to one side, worshipful of the baby. In this illustration, Joseph held the chubby infant Jesus on his lap and the wise men knelt in front of them. Perhaps not so strange, until she noticed what had drawn her attention back to the image in the first place. Mary was visible, but standing to one side, head lowered in an attitude of sorrow. And most curious was that while one of Joseph's hands cradled the Christ child, the other was held palm out toward Mary, as though pushing her away.

Cass sat back in her chair, a frown on her face. The quality of the illustrations was good and to her untrained eye they appeared professionally drawn. This caption read, "Adoration of the Magi," a title she thought belonged to another painting, but that also suited this one. A footnote near the bottom of the page offered an interpretation of the image: "The Christ child's power and fate are recognized by the wise men, who foretold of His coming and traveled from afar to worship Him and God who sent Him. For it is through Him alone that we are saved, His immaculate conception in the filthy vessel of woman serving to remind man of the weakness she has wrought in us. Joseph's authority as head of his wife is manifested, and his obligation to ensure her subjection to him is complete."

"Oh boy," Cass breathed. That wasn't how she had understood Mary's role in Jesus' birth, life and death. Nor was it the interpretation of millions of Catholics, who ranked Mary pretty high in the holy hierarchy. She thought back to Pastor Luke's tutorial on cults. He'd said that cults were about power, and if that were the case, the illustrations in *The Church of the True Believer* were designed to ensure that men held power over women. And not in a good way. Cass reached for her cold coffee and grimaced at a sip as she flipped through to the end of the book. The last few pages stood upright and she noticed writing on the page before the cover. Four lines were included, each written by a different hand but with bold, proud strokes, ink more faded on the first entry than the last. She squinted to read the words and numbers. The most recent name was Lenny Scarborough's, dated 1988. The other entries were each dated years or decades earlier.

Cass closed her eyes as the full meaning of the handwritten words hit her. The short list was a genealogy of the book's ownership, extending back to the nineteen-twenties. If this group was involved in the same activities back then, some of the most powerful men in the community had been molesting children for decades.

CHAPTER 36

THE OLD MAN'S WIFE pulled the study door closed and bustled to the kitchen, turning on the coffee pot before peeking into the oven. Her cookies were just beginning to brown and she checked the timer on the stove. She could bake off another three or four batches before the men were ready for a break.

Inside the shadowy study, the group shuffled between furniture to greet one another and the heady smell of excitement and uncertainty quickly filled the small space. The old man took a step to the center of the room and held his hands out to each side. The men formed a circle, grasping one another's hands and bowing their heads. Deacon Cronus began, his voice barely a whisper.

"Father, we thank you for taking our brother Lenny Scarborough into the beautiful light of your presence. We are grateful for the work Lenny completed in your name, in the fight against the evil one. We pray for his family in this, their time of need, and ask that you would comfort and provide for them. Give us wisdom as we follow your command and prayerfully adjust the membership of your sacred Church. As you guided the disciples in the upper room, show of these our Brethren the one whom you have chosen to complete the Circle of Illumination. Bless our charge, Father, and give us your protection as we prepare for the battles to come. Amen and amen."

"Amen," the men murmured, releasing hands. They took up positions on the couch, unfolded metal card chairs and rested hips against the desk. Windows in the room were closed and the curtains drawn, and the small space grew warm as the men moved about. The old man flipped a switch to turn on the ceiling fan. Deacon Cronus huffed his bulk into a wide chair set before the cold fireplace and took in the men before him. Each represented a successful business or an influential position within the community. Chosen not only for his personal qualities, but for the authority and connections he brought with him. Judges, doctors, lawyers and bankers. Each had a role to play in ensuring that Forney County remained on an even keel, safe from the ravages of those who would challenge the balance of power: minorities, feminists, non-believers. Even newcomers were suspect until they proved their willingness to live within the bounds of established society. Cronus was still amazed at times that these powerful men deferred to him, but he was growing accustomed to the authority of his office. He cleared his throat and the men settled into an expectant quiet.

"We are here tonight to follow in the sacred footsteps of the original disciples, when they gathered in the upper room to elect a new disciple to replace Judas Iscariot, betrayer of our Lord. Lenny Scarborough was no traitor; he was an obedient follower of Jesus Christ and a powerful contributor to the works of The Church of the True Believer. To continue our hallowed mission on earth, our number must be restored to thirteen, representing the holy alliance of Jesus and his twelve disciples."

He paused, searching the faces watching him. Each was rapt, serious. The fullness of their attention was not lost on him, and Deacon Cronus hefted himself straighter.

"There are two matters before us tonight. The first is ascension. Lenny was one point on our compass, the Circle of Illumination, and must be replaced by a member who can steadfastly travel the long road before us, guiding, interpreting, and protecting The Light." His fat face contracted momentarily in pride and he hurried to hide the emotion from his audience. "Of our eight Brethren, one will join the Circle of Illumination. He must possess strengths suitable for the battles to come, and characteristics complementary to the Circle's three existing members. We will replicate the actions of the disciples described in Acts Chapter 1, and our selection will be by lot." Deacon Cronus examined the men. "You have been instructed to prayerfully consider your suitability for ascension. Joining the Circle is an honor that carries with it sacred duties and at times, requires that heavy burdens be shouldered. There is no shame in choosing not to be considered for ascension, only respect for your obedience to the will of our Father. Does anyone wish to withhold their name?"

The group of men were subdued this evening, each mindful of Lenny Scarborough's gruesome end. Jed Salter slowly raised his hand, and two others joined his. Deacon Cronus closed his eyes briefly. "Do any of you care to speak before lots are drawn?"

One hand remained in the air and Deacon Cronus nodded, jowls wobbling with the movement. "Since Lenny's death, I have spent considerable time in meditation and prayer," Officer Greg Newton said, pushing his wire-rimmed glasses up on his nose. "I am still young in my understanding of The Church and its ways. For that reason, I believe another member will be better suited to support The Light and provide direction."

Several men bowed their heads at his words and one reached out to clasp his shoulder. Deacon Cronus counted out five matchsticks from the pocket on his shirt. He broke the match head from one, and aligned the clean ends so that all five protruded from his pudgy fist, level with one another. Stretching his arm toward the middle of the room, he watched as the five Brethren stepped forward to select a matchstick, hiding it until all had drawn. The old man watched from the chair at his desk, cold pipe clasped between his teeth. On instruction from Deacon Cronus, the five simultaneously opened their hands. A smile creased Dr. Tom Warner's face and the group of men surged around him, reaching to shake his hand and offer words of congratulation.

As the men settled into their places, relaxed now that this important task was complete, Deacon Cronus stood and motioned for Warner to kneel. He placed one dimpled hand on the man's bowed head and raised the other toward heaven. The others lowered their heads, hands clasped before them.

"Gracious Father, we give thanks that You have chosen Tom Warner to serve in Your Circle of Illumination. We ask that Your strength and wisdom flow through him, directing him and his skills as a businessman and surgeon in Your holy service. Amen and amen."

Deacon Cronus removed his hand and held it out to help Warner to his feet. They embraced and Warner, face flushed, stepped back to join the others. The Deacon settled again in his chair and glanced at the old man, who nodded once for him to continue. He drew a deep breath and began to speak, his voice gaining strength and conviction with each sentence.

"The second matter before us is the restoration of The Church to its full membership of thirteen. Selection of a new member carries great responsibility, both for the member and the existing Church. We require men with strength of character and conviction, who will stand beside us as we fight the good fight, protecting the community and truly, the world, from the threat of Satan. We need a man who will commit his life to our Lord and His cause. A True Believer." Beady eyes alive, Deacon Cronus examined each man in the room. "The topic is open to a fifteen-minute debate. At its close, we will vote anonymously on our new member. Who among us will begin?"

A middle-aged man raised a freckled hand, and at a motion from the Deacon, he blushed to the roots of his red hair and cleared his throat. "Before we start, I've heard that the police have Lenny's book. How do we provide instruction to the new member without it?"

The old man shifted in his chair. "If the Deacon doesn't mind, I'll address this question," he said, waiting for agreement from Deacon Cronus. "The police do have Lenny's book and it's been handled by a woman."

A collective gasp rose as anger and fear flooded the men's faces. The old man raised a hand and the crowd grew silent.

"To our knowledge, this has never happened before. The purity of Lenny's volume has been sullied, and it must be destroyed." Several men protested, but the old man nodded sadly. "It must be done. To satisfy the need for instruction, I've contacted a trusted friend and commissioned a replacement copy. The new book will be an exact replica of the twelve that remain, in both materials and presentation."

"How long will this take?" the redheaded man asked.

The old man grimaced. "About three months, I'm afraid." He shrugged at their dismay. "There is no alternative. The book must be reproduced exactly, and since the original plates were destroyed, much of the work will be done by hand." The group murmured in reluctant agreement. "As we've seen with Lenny's death, Satan acts swiftly and with determination. Let this be a reminder to us all to remain diligent in protecting the sacred tools of our faith."

Deacon Cronus glanced around the room. "Shall we continue?"

Voices rose and fell over the next half hour, as names were suggested and rejected. At the end of the debate, three names remained and after an anonymous vote, Officer Hugo Petchard had been selected as the newest member of The Church of the True Believer.

The old man looked at Greg Newton. "You'll instruct him in what to expect?"

"Yes, sir. He'll be thrilled."

"Your invitations to our most sacred ceremony, the Celebration of Illumination, will be delivered tomorrow evening at the latest. Keep Wednesday night open. We'll meet at The Sanctuary." The old man pushed up from his chair and sniffed the air. "And if you've got time, I believe the wife has some fresh cookies coming out of the oven."

CHAPTER 37

Tuesday

HITCH CHUCKLED AS FLAMES licked the base of his cooking pot. A shimmer skated across the oil's surface, and he knew it wouldn't be long now. He was back in his clearing, at home in its isolation and suitability. Over the bright crackling of the wood, the Sabine River gurgled as it sucked at the riverbank, its surface black in the moonlight. The old man had called Monday evening with an interesting modification to the evening's plans. Hitch shook his head in admiration. He had thought himself creative; but the old man, he was in a different league altogether.

Checking his watch, he dug in his pocket for a cigarette. It was well past midnight but the hardest part of the night was behind him. Sucking the smoke deep into his lungs, the nicotine hit his system, his body relaxed and he let his gaze wander. As Hitch glanced around the clearing, a spark of awareness shot through the lizard part of his brain that housed survival instincts, and a prickle of discomfort skittered across his neck hairs. He grew still, watchful, muscles bunched and senses preternaturally alert, his nose lifted to the air. The evening's tranquility was broken by the fire's sizzle and the creak of rope. With a whisper of ruffling feathers, a night bird swooped through the treetops and Hitch felt a flush of adrenaline as he instinctively ducked before sensing the creature's passing. He shivered, and then chuckled at the absurdity of his reaction. Grinding his cigarette against his boot and shoving the butt in his pocket, he took a few steps into the heavy foliage for a piss. Zipping his fly, he coughed up a wad of phlegm and spat into the underbrush.

Turning to the fire's serene glow, Hitch shook off the lingering sense of unease and considered his next steps. He lifted the top of the toolbox in the pickup's bed and examined the drill bits inside. The half-inch hadn't worked fast enough last time, so he planned to up the ante. He selected a one-inch hole saw and tightened the chuck, squeezing the drill's trigger to hear it whine.

A groan sounded. Hitch turned to see a pair of dazed eyes darting around the small area, body jerking as awareness seeped past the pain. Hitch tugged his heavy leather gloves more securely over his fingers and watched to see what would happen when his prey came into himself enough to understand what was happening.

The man's face and torso were glossy with sweat. Thin streams of blood ran across the flat plane of his stomach, caught in the dark hair that covered his chest and formed a pool in the soft flesh beneath his chin. Three wide-mouthed buckets rested on the ground to one side. His damp body shone in the moonlight as he twisted, a macabre ornament hanging from a tree accustomed to slaughter. A longer moan emerged from his lips, followed by a contracting of stomach muscles as he struggled to pull himself upright. He collapsed with a gasp of pain, grew still for a moment and exploded into frustrated motion. His violent thrashing started the overhead limb swinging and drops of blood and sweat sprayed from his body.

Hitch climbed a stepladder and peered at the rope running through the block and tackle on a sturdy branch about ten feet above the ground. Everything was holding nicely. He grinned as he climbed back down and squatted, examining the spikes, careful to stay away from the swinging crossbeam. "How you doing there, Officer Garrett?"

"Help me, man, let me down!" He panted, struggling against his bindings, groaning with the effort, eyes searching the long, thin face before him. "Oh God, what happened? I can't move!"

"You're right where you're supposed to be this evening. Lovely night, ain't it?"

"Fuck you!" Garrett howled, his face contorted with pain and rage.

"Temper, temper," Hitch chided. "Guess I'll just suppose it's the pain talking." He stood and stepped away from the tree, smiling at his handiwork. He'd chosen crucifixion because he knew the old man practiced one flavor of Christianity or another. Garrett was secured to a cross of four-by-four Southern Pine, arms splayed wide and secured to the timber through the palms with six-inch cut clasp nails. His feet were crossed one over the other and nailed through their thinnest point, just behind the toes. Since he'd needed to hang the cross upside down, Hitch hadn't been comfortable that a single nail would support the man's weight, so he'd taken the precaution of wrapping baling twine around Garrett's ankles and the cross. All in all, a job well done.

"What do you want, man?" Garrett pleaded, his agonized face clouded with confusion. "Who are you?"

Hitch squatted. "Just so we're clear, there's nothing personal about this. Between you and me, I mean. I've got a job to do, just like you did." He paused. "Did you really think you could just walk away?"

Garrett's eyes cleared. "Oh my God."

"'Fraid God won't be any help now. The old man's the one you should be praying to."

"Oh Jesus," Garrett whispered, again attempting to contract his stomach muscles to pull himself upright, grunting in pain. "He can't be serious. I'd never say a word. He's got too much on me. Come on, man," he groaned. "Cut me down. I won't tell. Nobody has to know."

"I've got my orders," Hitch replied with a small smile, golden eyes flat. "We have work to do, you and me. See that pot?" He pointed to the brightly burning fire.

Garrett focused across the clearing.

"That's where your supper's coming from. A last meal, you might call it," he said, ambling over to peer into the kettle. The oil had reached an agitated boil. Garrett moaned as Hitch brought a metal bowl to him. "I picked peanut oil, concerned for your cholesterol and everything. I thought about using corn meal for the batter, but figured flour would be easier to swallow. Corn meal's more of a catfish thing, know what I mean?" he asked, tilting the bowl so Garrett could see its contents. Blood seeped through the outer dusting of flour, pink spots marring the small, irregular bundles.

Garrett strained to find Hitch's face, searching those unusual amber eyes, firelight sparking red in their depths. The confusion clouding his brain suddenly cleared and he howled, body jerking with rage as the stench of fear stained the night. Clear lengths of snot flew from Garrett's nose as he swung, tears tipping over his eyelids to flow into his crew cut and spatter the ground. "You're fucking nuts! Get away from me. Oh dear God, SOMEBODY HELP ME!"

IN THE DANK, DENSE undergrowth near the river's edge, where the foamy eddies swirl and the fetid mud and mosquitoes suck, a pair of dark eyes blinked at the scene unfolding by firelight. Their bluish whites and the reflection from their liquid surface were the only indication that human life was present. She was clad in black, and with the inky darkness of her skin had only to close her eyes to disappear. The acrid stench of urine was strong where the ghost had sprayed out into the woods, a glistering stream arcing golden into the velvety night. Heart fluttering at her breast and eyes unfocused, she found the form in the clearing, an indistinct sliver woven into the kaleidoscopic glow of the fire; a devil made of light. The scene swam, the grisly spectacle of Christ on His cross wavering in her fuzzy vision. A whining scream rose and her bleary eyes experienced a moment of unnatural clarity at the sound. He was familiar to her clouded brain, this upside down Jesus. The mournful call of a whippoorwill sliced through the horrible calm as the whine faded. Her thoughts and vision blurred and she uttered a silent, jumbled prayer begging mercy for the Christ-man suffering in her forest. Hiding beneath the next shrill shriek, she inched her stealthy retreat.

CHAPTER 38

CASS SAT BOLT UPRIGHT, heart pounding, scream struggling toward her throat, stomach muscles clenched. Instinctively, she grabbed for the gun on her bedside table, flicked the safety off and racked a round into the chamber. Her eyes darted into the shadows and she drew a quick breath, swinging her torso over the bed's edge, arm extended and ready to fire as she cleared the area beneath. She jerked herself upright and slowly took in the rest of the room, smiling grimly as she remembered the nightmare. A grotesque caricature of Richard Nixon wasn't lurking under the bed or in the closet.

She sank back onto her pillows, damp with sweat, and carefully traced the scar circling her breast. It was on fire again, as it always was when she had the dream. Glancing at the clock, she groaned. Four thirty. After discovering the names in *The Church of the True Believer* last night, she'd stumbled home, eaten leftovers, mumbled goodnight to her brothers and father and fallen into bed. She'd slipped easily into the old nightmare and now fought the temptation to ponder what had brought it on. No matter. Nixon didn't frighten her when she was awake. He just pissed her off.

Cass rubbed her fists into her eyes and swung her legs off the bed. Quickly pulling on her running gear and securing her hair in a ponytail, she crept from the house. A security lamp snapped on as she opened the door and the soft yellow light stretched shadows across the garden toward the trees bordering the backyard.

She stretched and then started off at a slow pace, her body creaking until it settled into a familiar rhythm. Moving past the garden, she entered the woods on a dirt path, the beat of her footfalls quiet on the soft soil. The land beyond the backyard was owned by the Craven family who, out of pity, had rented the two room shack on the northern edge of their vast property to a very young, very pregnant, and very poor couple – Abe and Nell Elliot. Over time, Abe had added rooms to the house to hold his expanding family, the severity of tilt of a new room against the old in direct proportion to his degree of inebriation at the time of construction. The woods were an extension of home to the seven Elliot children, and as they grew, they had ventured deeper, learning its twists and turns, the flow of the streams trickling through the dense underbrush, building rickety forts and fighting mighty imaginary battles against Indians in its quiet shade.

Cass lengthened her stride, unafraid of the heavy blackness wrought by the thick branches overhead. This was the place she felt safest in the world. Her body knew the trail she ran; the sudden dip where erosion had eaten a small crevasse around tree roots. The bough that hung too low to either duck under or leap over, demanding that a runner break her stride to hoist herself onto its girth and swing her legs over before continuing. Her brother Lloyd was the second oldest child, and at one time, held the distinction of being the fastest white boy in Forney County. Cass had spent her childhood chasing him through these woods, and the reflexive memory of her muscles bore testament to Lloyd's patience and her persistence.

She reached a smooth length of trail that followed the edge of the Craven's pasture and felt her thighs start to burn. The spring growth on bushes and trees reached for her hair, and she shifted her route slightly to move out of their grip. Cass had no idea how many acres the Craven clan owned, but she knew they were one of the wealthiest families around. This stretch of land ran unbroken for several hundred acres and was bordered on its east side by a large house still occupied by the eldest Craven, old Mr. Lucius. Easily in his seventies, he still ruled his family's vast land and cattle holdings with an iron fist. His daughters were long since married off, both of them grandparents in their own right. Several of his sons and grandsons worked the family business with him, but one or two had left Forney County to seek their fortunes elsewhere.

From her childhood, she remembered Mr. Lucius as a kindly old man, larger than life and smelling of sweet tobacco, always ready with a ruffle of the hair and the occasional stick of chewing gum secreted for the children. The family was generous in the community, hosting Halloween hayrides and Easter egg hunts. For some reason, the Cravens had taken special care with the Elliot family, eventually allowing Abe to buy the house and five acres surrounding it, with generous repayment terms.

A stitch seared her side as she left the pasture and turned into the woods to follow the trail winding behind the massive Craven home. A match flared near the backyard fence, and Cass stopped in her tracks, breath heavy and sweat dripping from the loose tendrils of hair curling around her face. It was too early for anyone to be out, and she automatically reached for her gun, which was still on her nightstand. She narrowed her eyes at a rustle from the yard, and realized that someone was lighting a pipe.

"Who's there?" a gruff voice barked.

"Detective Cass Elliot," she answered, injecting authority into her voice as she took a quiet step behind a tree. "Who are you?"

"Cass? I don't believe I've seen you since you finished university."

"Mr. Lucius?"

"Of course. Who else would be out in my backyard this time of night? Come on over here, let me look at you. I had no idea you still used these old trails. Thought they would've grown over by now," he said, leaning on the top fence rail as Cass stepped forward, wiping sweat from her face with her arm. He wore the clothes she remembered from her youth – khaki cotton trousers and matching work shirt. "My goodness. You sure have grown up. Where did you go to school again?"

"Texas A&M, sir," Cass smiled, feeling the gentle security of being a child again in his presence.

"Fine school. What did you study?"

"Accounting."

Mr. Lucius grunted. "Good choice, accounting. There's money in it. How'd you end up a po-lice officer? I remember hearing about it when Hoffner hired you onto the force, and again when you were promoted to detective. I figured you had some sort of criminal justice degree."

"No, sir," Cass sighed. "Education was important to my daddy, so I went to A&M and got my accounting degree. Even interviewed with some of the big firms, got offers and everything. But it just didn't feel right." She shrugged. "Those people are boring."

Mr. Lucius threw his head back and laughed, long teeth gleaming in the dim moonlight. "That's one of the things I enjoyed about you, Cass. You always did speak your mind. I know what you mean. Accountants are all kind of gray."

She smiled with him. "That's it. Anyway, I just couldn't get excited about working in accounting." *Well*, she thought, *that was one version of the truth.* "I decided to join the force in Dallas. When I told Daddy what I was doing, we had an awful fight."

"I'd imagine he wanted you to be safe, Cass. And po-licing can be a dangerous job."

"He wanted me to come home right away, but I wanted to work in a big city, first. I guess I was lucky that Sheriff Hoffner had a vacancy when I did move home."

"And you made detective quickly. First woman and the youngest detective we've had."

A rueful smile touched her lips. She still wondered what had motivated Hoffner to promote her. "Yes, sir."

"Abe should be proud of what you've accomplished." He scrutinized her through a thin veil of smoke. "And so should you."

"Thank you. How are you? How's your family?"

He sucked reflectively at his pipe, tobacco glowing orange in the bowl, the soft scent of cherry floating on the night air. "Doing just fine. Got several grandchildren now, mostly girls. They're sweet little things." He paused as he smoked. "Reckon you heard about our Timmy. Lost him in a car accident a few years back, probably while you were away at A&M."

"Yes, sir, I do remember hearing about his death. I sure am sorry for your loss."

"The good Lord gave him to us for thirty-two years. That's more time than some fathers have." He shifted and Cass caught a full view of his face in the moonlight, glasses pushed high on his forehead. He hadn't changed much over the years. The wrinkles were etched deeper and his hair was thinner, but he was still dignified and full of authority. Mr. Lucius eyed her before speaking again. "I suppose your father knows about losing a son."

"I imagine you're right," Cass answered, heart growing heavy.

"How long has he been in prison now?"

"Twenty-one years."

Mr. Lucius scratched a thick ear. "I sure hated what happened to Jack. That's his name, isn't it?"

"Yes, sir, it is."

Cass paused, and he cocked his head toward her. "What is it?"

She debated whether to pursue the topic of Jack's innocence with him. But Mr. Lucius was a powerful man and he certainly would've known the circumstances of Jack's arrest. Given the confusion Cass was feeling about her brother's situation, it couldn't hurt to ask. "It was a long time ago, but do you remember his arrest?"

Mr. Lucius tapped his pipe against his work boot and began the ritual of refilling it, eyes averted from her face. He pulled the flame from a lucifer into the bowl with a deep draw on the stem, and raised his gaze as he tamped the tobacco down with a silverish object. He spoke in a quiet voice. "Yes, I do. I've never seen people so devastated as your family after he was arrested, and certainly after your momma's death. That's a lot of tragedy for one family to bear."

"I've heard talk recently that maybe," she hesitated again, "he was framed."

He was silent, pipe clamped between his teeth, absently running a thick nailed thumb over the object in his hand. "It's been a long time ago, and you were small when it all happened. With crimes like Jack's and how it all went down, people can think up all sorts of theories to explain something they can't understand. And I'd expect you to believe your brother to be innocent, regardless of the evidence. I'd do the same if it was one of my children."

Cass sighed silently to herself, reaching down to massage a tight calf muscle. Perhaps he was right, and the Elliot's were like every other family who wanted to believe their kinfolk innocent of such terrible crimes. She glanced up at him. "Yes, sir, I imagine you're right." She smiled weakly. "It's early, what are you doing up?"

Mr. Lucius belched quietly. "Had some Rocky Mountain Oysters last night. Didn't sit well with me. Ever tried 'em?"

"No, sir, can't say that I have."

"I don't recommend that you do," he said, glancing at his watch. "I'd better start the coffee before Mary wakes up. Keep praying for rain, Cass. We need it."

"There's supposed to be storms before the week is out."

"Let's hope so," he answered, glancing up at the lush sky dotted with stars. "Maybe I'll see you out here again before too long."

"If I keep my motivation up," Cass grinned, "and if you keep eating those oysters, I imagine you will."

CHAPTER 39

MITCH STROLLED INTO THE Golden Gate to the sound of the Beatles asking to hold her hand, and stopped short. Two steaming cups of coffee and an unopened newspaper sat at his and Cass's customary table, but she wasn't in the booth. He lifted a chin in greeting to two bankers arguing quietly at a corner table and an unfamiliar figure seated near the kitchen before glancing across the café and grunting in amazement. He stopped to grab his coffee and walked quietly across the room to join Cass and the Pettigrew brothers at their booth. She sat with one of the brothers, bent forward over a piece of paper, the other brother leaning in from the opposite side of the table. Each was clutching his coffee mug for dear life.

"Morning," he called, grinning as all three jumped upright from their hunched positions.

"Hey Mitch," Cass replied, smiling her relief.

He swung a chair from a nearby table, straddling it and balancing his mug on its back. "How are y'all this morning?"

The Pettigrew brothers glared at each other across the table before one of them reluctantly spoke. "Fine. You?"

"I'm good, thanks. What's up?"

"We're just going over the statement I typed up last night about Angie Scarborough's bruises. Mr. Pettigrew," Cass looked across the table, "had a few changes, and once I've made those, we'll be fine. Right?"

She glanced between the two brothers until each of them agreed. "Good. I'll bring the new version tomorrow morning." She slid from the booth, taking the single sheet with her. "Thanks very much for doing this. You're helping Angie."

One of the brothers blushed while the other simply nodded. Cass wove through the tables as skinny Stan Overheart appeared with plates of eggs and bacon. Mitch returned his chair to the table it came from and slid into the booth across from her. "Morning Stan. Man this looks good," he grinned, rubbing his hands together.

Stan leaned a bony hip into a nearby table and crossed his hairy arms over his chest. "How you doing Mitch? Cass ordered for both of you. Everything all right?"

"This is perfect. Thanks." He motioned for Stan to lean closer, flicking his eyes toward the unfamiliar figure near the kitchen. "Who's that?"

"Wally Pugh. Works for the radio station."

"He must be new."

Stan glanced at the young man whose face was drawn in concentration as he scribbled in a notebook. "Gave me his life story this morning. He was raised over in Stanton and studied down at UT Austin. Went to Chicago for a while and then came home to look after his folks. Found a reporting job with KOIL and thinks he'll make his name there."

"Why in the world would you give up Chicago for Arcadia?" Mitch mused, taking in the small tape recorder Wally was shoving into a backpack. He looked up suddenly, catching Mitch watching him. His pointed features were reminiscent of a weasel. They moved in a caricature of a smile as he left a wad of crumpled bills on the table and quickly made his way to leave. Mitch watched him go, murmuring, "Thanks, Stan."

"No problem. Holler when you need a refill," he said, swinging toward the warming counter where the Pettigrew brother's breakfasts waited.

Mitch glanced at Cass as she rubbed her eyes. "How are you this morning?"

"All right," she chuckled, passing the bottle of Tabasco sauce. "The changes were minor, but it's so hard to get them to talk, you'd think the Pettigrew brothers had taken a vow of silence. Anyway, we have a statement they're both happy with."

Mitch swallowed a bite of egg. "What are you doing up so early?"

"I ran."

"Really?"

Cass speared a piece of bacon. "Yup. Ran into Lucius Craven, no pun intended. You know him?"

"Sure. One of his boys was in mine and Jack's class in high school. They've got a big spread over there next to y'all, right?"

"Yeah, his family's always been good to us." Cass stopped suddenly, brain singing with the memory of the names written in the heavy book.

"Listen, I need to tell you what I found last night –"

Her voice caught as The Golden Gate's door thumped open and Goober staggered in. His mouth was slack, one strap of his overalls had fallen from a shoulder and his wild eyes jumped around the small café until they found Cass. He stumbled to the booth, its vinyl shrieking in protest as he collapsed on the bench seat beside her.

"Goober? What's wrong?" Cass asked as Mitch watched, forkful of eggs and bacon suspended between the plate and his open mouth. Goober stared at her, glassy eyes trancelike, mouth moving but no sound escaping. Mitch called to Stan for another cup of coffee.

Stan appeared with a steaming mug and placed it in front of Goober, who shifted his gaze from Cass to the coffee. Gently, she lifted his hands from his lap and wrapped them around the hot mug, speaking softly. "What happened, Goob? You look like you've seen a ghost."

Goober shuddered, a deep spasm that shook his body from head to toe and sloshed coffee from the mug. The searing liquid seemed to penetrate his stupor and he grabbed the table's edge, pulling himself from the booth, color flooding his face. "C-Come on," he pleaded. "You have to help him."

"Help who, Goober?" Cass asked.

"I c-c-couldn't. I'm sorry Cass. I tried," he whispered, voice breaking as he took her hand and tugged her from the booth.

"Sorry for what, Goober? What's wrong?"

"It was the vampires," he answered. "They got him."

GOOBER BOLTED FROM THE Golden Gate with a worried Cass and Mitch scrambling after him. He hurried across the street that wrapped around the courthouse without bothering to check for traffic, pulling a red kerchief from a back pocket to blow his nose. A rose-streaked sky was building in the east, but traffic was still quiet as Cass and Mitch trotted along behind him. A lone engine coughed to life nearby, screeching as its owner changed gears.

"He's over here," Goober called, stumbling as his feet hit the lawn. He rounded the tall war memorial and stopped suddenly, bending to place his hands on his thighs as he heaved great breaths. Cass bumped into him as she lifted her eyes to follow the direction of Goober's outstretched arm and gasped as Mitch thumped into her.

Parallel trenches slashed across the courthouse lawn, grass and mud churned up and spat out across the grisly scene. A long wooden cross bearing a human body rested against the war memorial's cool stone, half hidden in its tall shadow. The cross leaned at an angle, the body's head directed toward the ground, arms tilted so that one pointed at the sky while the other dug into the soft earth and provided stability. The man's flesh looked as pale and cold as marble in the early light. A cloth was draped over his hips and narrow gashes marred his forearms. His face was turned away from them but a feeling of familiarity tugged at Cass's memory. She took a step forward.

"No," Mitch commanded. "You can't help him now. Goober, go sit on the courthouse steps. Don't move until someone comes for you. Don't talk to anyone except a police officer, understand?"

Goober nodded, dragging his eyes from the grisly corpse and staggering toward the front of the courthouse.

"Cass, call Kado and find out where he keeps those tent things. I'll call Grey and Sheriff Hoffner. We don't have long before this place will be swarming with people. We've got to protect any evidence and," his voice trembled, "we need to cover Officer Garrett up."

CHAPTER 40

JOHN GREY STEPPED BACK from the cross, checking the thermometer. "He's been dead four to five hours," he sighed, snapping his gloves off in an angry gesture. Mitch's call had pulled him from the shower and his normally bushy dark hair was flattened against his head, emphasizing the sharp angles of his face. He stood slightly hunched to avoid brushing the top of the forensic tent as his eyes ran the length of Garrett's body. "Who could do something like that to another human being?"

The forensic examiner fidgeted beside him, snapping and unsnapping the front of his white coveralls. Kado had done a cursory examination of the tire tracks and was irritated at their apparent uselessness. "You done?"

"Yeah. How long until I can move him?"

"I don't know. Jesus, what a mess." He pulled the hood over his head and nodded at Cass, who was dressed in a similar protective suit. "Snap up. We're gonna go slow."

CASS STOOD UNDER THE pounding shower, enduring its scalding power as she tried to scrub away the images of Chad Garrett's tortured body. She'd helped Kado process the scene, painstaking work at first, covering the area around the corpse on their hands and knees, turning up nothing. He'd meticulously examined the cloth covering Garrett's groin, which turned out to be a large swatch of gauze taped over the area. Moving to the cross, Kado had run a magnifying mirror on a pole underneath the timbers and along Garrett's body, looking for additional wounds and obvious evidence before moving him to the ME's office. A lone fly buzzed in the tent as they worked, dive bombing the dark, sticky smears on Garrett's head, forearms and abdomen.

By the time they finished with the ground, cross and body, the sun was well up and the tent had grown stifling, thick with the heady scent of death. Watchers had gathered on the courthouse lawn and Wally Pugh's excited murmuring into a tape recorder was the only sound audible. Word was out that an officer was dead – sadistically mutilated in what looked like a ritualistic killing. A stunned hush hung over the square until Garrett's wailing widow arrived, leaving her still moving car in the street as she darted across the lawn. She howled, a primal cry of disbelief, clawing and scratching at the strong arms that wrapped around her waist until Grey sedated her, calling an ambulance and Dr. Ramasubramanian to let him know the circumstances around her arrival at the hospital.

The old coots normally resident on the courthouse portico had moved their vigil to the hanging tree. A pearly haze of pipe smoke snaked through its branches as their gnarled, wrinkled forms leaned into its trunk for support. Wise eyes gazed from beneath papery eyelids, wandering the crowd and searching memories from long ago, seeing other tragedies that threatened the tranquility of their little town.

Tempers grew as the sun climbed the gloriously clear blue sky and the temperature and humidity rose. The smell of fear filled the air as officers, reporters and ordinary citizens jostled for position near the hastily strung crime scene tape. On Mitch's instruction, Elaine collected Goober from the courthouse steps where he'd waited, mute and lifeless. The receptionist coaxed him into the lobby, wrapping him in a rough blanket from the supply kept for inmates. Tears streaked her face as she held Goober to warm him up, shed for the loss of an officer's life, but also for the confused, trembling man-child who had found the body.

Grey decided to remove Garrett from the cross before taking him to the ME's office. To protect the tire tracks and the scene, Kado erected a second tent next to the war memorial, linking it to the first to keep the morbidly curious from seeing the body. They used pliers to pull the heavy nails from his hands and feet, cringing at the sucking sounds the metal made as it was pulled from his still moist flesh. Grey backed the ME's van to the flap of the second tent and Garrett's bagged body was slipped quickly inside, the doors slammed shut in the respectful silence that lingered as he was driven away. Kado and Cass had done as much work as they could in the tent, but in the end, Kado decided to leave the bulky cross intact for the move into the forensic room. They tried to disguise it, but a gasp escaped from the crowd as they realized how Garrett had died.

Once the body was gone, a ripple of anger surged through the crowd. The watchers, police officers included, began grumbling for information. Munk left his job pouring casting mix into the tire tracks to prowl the police tape and demand order, the wet bag swinging from his tense fingers as he moved, spattering those immediately behind the tape. The quiet murmur grew insistent when Officer Hugo Petchard arrived and strutted through the crowd, demanding action from the 'elite' team of Forney County detectives. Sheriff Hoffner physically hauled him into the courthouse, bellowing at the crowd to disperse and let the police department do its job. As punishment, Petchard was sent to help with crossing duty at the elementary school, spittle from Hoffner's tirade still wet on his cheeks.

Wally Pugh had cursed himself when news of violent happenings on the courthouse lawn finally reached his ears. He'd left The Golden Gate to get to the radio station early. If only he'd waited a few minutes, had an extra cup of coffee, he would've seen the body before it was covered up. As tension and the temperature around the war memorial grew, Wally had given up his 'live' commentary and, taking his cue from the newspaper reporters covering the scene, stowed the tape recorder in his backpack and used his trusty digital camera to catch the action. He was glad he'd taken the time to charge the batteries last night, and visions of a Pulitzer danced in his beady black eyes. He had several good shots – one of Hoffner pulling a flailing uniformed officer up the courthouse steps; another of the one-eyed ginger cat perched on a branch above the tall war memorial, gazing down on the traumatized widow with disinterest; and one of the cloth-draped cross.

Cass turned off the shower's powerful stream and rested her forehead against the cool tiles, letting the water drip from her body. Her mind had been able to compartmentalize what she'd seen while she worked on Garrett with Kado. His skin's alabaster hue let her pretend she was examining a figure carved from marble rather than a man who had drawn his last tortured breath only a few hours previously. The wounds in his hands and feet had torn, suggesting that Garrett struggled while he was nailed down. And the damage to his skull. Her imagination fluttered, picturing the agonized man straining to pull himself free – while what? While someone drove another spike into his head? Her mind jumped to the image of the mummified corpse from Monday. Did the hole in his head somehow link him to Garrett?

Drawing a deep breath, she roughly dried herself before reaching into her locker for a sports bra. Her fingers brushed the lace of a regular bra and she hesitated. She'd brought it to work just in case she got up the nerve to risk someone seeing the scar unfurling beneath her blouse. But now wasn't the time to exorcise old demons. She stretched the sports bra over her head and gently shook her breasts into it before pulling on panties, a fresh pair of Dockers and a pale blue button-front shirt. She combed her wet hair and pulled its heavy weight into a ponytail. A pale, drawn face stared back at her from the mirror and she closed her mind to the horrible image of Garrett's punctured hands and feet before striding out of the locker room and into the evidence room.

Kado stood from his hunched position over the cross as she entered, lifting the magnifying glass hooked around his head. Drawing a deep breath, he dug his fingers into the back of his neck before checking the clock on the wall, his bleary eyes taking a moment to focus. Three hours had passed since Goober had found Garrett's body. "I need food," he said. "Let's go to the morgue."

CHAPTER 41

THE OLD MAN FOLDED his phone closed and watched the bulldozer grumble forward, heavy blade lowered to the ground, scraping away a layer of soil for a new pond. Officer Greg Newton had called to let him know that Chad Garrett had been found on the courthouse lawn, nailed to a cross. The old man smiled. He'd asked for something dramatic and Hitch had delivered. As promised, he'd left payment and a generous bonus for last night's services, and given this morning's news, the old man considered every penny well spent.

His phone rang again and he lowered his glasses to check the screen before answering. "Good morning, Deacon," he said in greeting. "How are you?"

"Have you heard?" Deacon Cronus whispered into the phone. "About Officer Garrett?"

"I've just received a call."

"Good heavens, it's horrible. I've been across the street to the courthouse – you couldn't help but go," he babbled. "What a commotion. I've never seen anything like it. Reporters kept coming. I don't know how they hear about these things. And everyone who works on the square was out on the lawn. I think they were all shocked. Goodness me, I'm shocked."

"What did you see?"

"I suppose not much, really," he hedged. "They had two of those tents up, the kind you see on the news when there's an accident. I didn't see the body, but they took the –," Deacon Cronus gulped into the phone, "– the cross away while I was there."

"They took it out in the open?"

"No, no. They had it under a plastic cloth, but you could see what it was. What a horrible way to die."

"I agree," the old man answered slowly, further pleased with Hitch's efforts. "I suppose we'll need to start looking for another new recruit for The Way."

Deacon Cronus was silent for a beat. "Of course. I hadn't thought of that. You don't think someone found out he was involved with us, do you? And killed him as a warning?"

"No, I don't," the old man reassured him. "Sounds like some nut who has a problem with religion."

"It seems a risky thing to do then, to pick Officer Garrett. I mean, the whole police force will be focused on this investigation. Whoever did this will have a hard time escaping."

"Possibly, Deacon," the old man agreed, reaching for his pipe. "But I'd imagine that somebody sophisticated enough to kill a policeman in this manner will cover his tracks."

"Yes, I suspect you're right," Deacon Cronus agreed. "I don't see any reason to postpone tomorrow night's ceremony, do you?"

"I certainly regret Officer Garrett's death, but we shouldn't let anything interfere with closing the Circle."

CHAPTER 42

MINNIE PECK STOOD BEHIND the glass door to the ME's office, thin arms crossed over her bony chest, chin jutting at a ferocious angle toward the crowd gathered outside. A photographer had already captured Minnie in all her blue-rinsed beehived glory and now waited for a more interesting shot. Stan Overheart muscled his way through the few dozen people straining for a glimpse of Garrett's body, even though it was sheltered in an autopsy room far removed from their prying eyes.

"Excuse me," he muttered, shouldering past a bear of a man with a TV camera on his shoulder. Stan hefted the bulging paper sacks bearing the Golden Gate Café's logo to catch Minnie's eye. She frowned as she unlocked the door, slipping an unlit cigarette between her heavily glossed lips as she bolted it again behind him.

"Buzzards," she barked with a husky voice scraped raw from years of smoke.

"Who are they?"

"A few gawkers. Some reporters. Stanton and Shreveport have turned up."

Stan lifted bags and asked a question with his eyes. Minnie glanced out the front door before pointing to Grey's cluttered desk. "Let me move that crap for you. Better to be over there. They can't see past my desk."

"Cass and Mitch here?"

Minnie nodded, beehive tilting dangerously with the movement. "That new forensics man, they call him Kado, is here, too. They're in the back with Grey and Bernie."

"How long you been with the ME's office?" Stan asked as he unloaded jugs of coffee and stacked breakfast burritos in a pyramid on the desk.

"Too long," she replied, dropping her birdlike frame into Grey's chair. She gestured at the front door. "I've never seen anything like this. Even when that school bus caught on fire back in the 'seventies," she shuddered.

"That was truly awful, all those children. But even that didn't attract the likes of this crowd. Arcadia rarely makes the television news."

Stan had followed quickly behind Cass and Mitch as they ran from The Golden Gate. Not from curiosity, but in reaction to a deep dread that built in his chest as Goober spoke through his tears. Stan Overheart and his wife Sally had spent most of their lives running a music shop in the Haight-Ashbury section of San Francisco and were accustomed to graphic drug overdoses and the results of occasional street violence. But the sight that greeted Stan as he rounded the tall war memorial had taken his breath away. He'd covered his eyes and breathed a silent prayer for the man's soul before quietly pivoting and trotting back to The Gate to refill the Pettigrew brothers' coffee with a trembling hand.

"I guess this one's pretty spectacular. It's not every day that a police officer dies, and well..."

"And well is right. Even Grey was shook up by Garrett's wounds." She held up a hand tipped with nicotine stained fingers and arched a penciled eyebrow. "I don't know what they all are, but he came out of the autopsy room for a breath of air. I've got a feeling about this one, Stan. A bad feeling."

He folded the paper bags into a neat pile on the corner of the desk. "You hang in there, Minnie. Give me a shout if there's anything else you need, okay?"

She smiled, baring yellowed teeth. "You can get rid of those reporters for me. I can't have a smoke until they're gone."

CHAPTER 43

SHE SWAM TOWARD A consciousness punctuated by harsh clanging and lifted a hand to cover one ear. Her stinking body was doused in sweat, mouth cottony dry. One eye opened, a bleary slit, and she sighed with relief. She was at Nana's. On the tatty old couch that smelled of Icy Hot and the soft peppermint candies the old woman loved. The ringing jangled again and her head throbbed with a pulsing stab as she swung an arm toward the rickety table at the end of the couch, snagging the phone's heavy handset.

"'Lo?" she breathed, throat aching with the effort.

"Blackie?"

"Uhn umm."

"Where were you last night?" a voice hissed; urgent, frightened, relieved. "Nana was out of her mind with worry, girl. You're too old to be doing this kinda thing."

"Jerome?"

"Where were you?"

A memory flashed in her mind – black night, dancing fire, a vision of the devil woven from light. She inhaled the fetid depths of the river bottom on her skin and in her hair, and fear clawed at her stomach. Blackie sucked in a deep gulp of Icy Hot and peppermint before pushing herself upright. "I'm gonna be sick, Jerome. I'll call you back."

CHAPTER 44

THEY ATE IN SILENCE, each acutely aware of the small crowd milling outside the ME's office. Minnie had snuck out back for a quick smoke as Stan launched a marketing campaign with the reporters out front, taking orders for coffee and food before heading across the square to the Golden Gate Café. Munk had finished with the casts of the tire tracks and set out with young Officer Truman to try and locate Garrett's vehicle. A quick drive past his house in Mole Hill community found his patrol car out front. His wife's two-seater sports car was parked on the square after she'd driven it into town. But Garrett's truck, a new fire-engine red Chevy, wasn't at his house or the courthouse. And no one occupying a branch on his considerable family tree had seen it since Monday afternoon.

Bernie patted a splatter of picante sauce from his safari vest while Cass emptied another small carton of cream into her cup. Grey drained his coffee and wiped his mouth with a napkin before snagging his left earlobe between his thumb and forefinger and beginning to rub. His assistant, Porky Rivers, recognized the signs that his boss was thinking and pushed his chair back from the desk.

"Stay with us," Grey ordered as the painfully thin black man stood. "I want you to hear all this." Porky silently sat down, the wealth of small studs and barbells lining his ears and eyebrows, providing the source for his nickname of Porcupine, glittering in the overhead light.

Mitch spoke first. "Kado, was there anything of forensics value on the cross?"

"Cow manure and Garrett's blood. The manure makes it pointless to try for epithelials. There were bits of flesh in the holes where his hands and feet were secured – most likely Garrett's. The wood has no markings and the end cuts are clean, probably made at a lumber store. I did find tiny scraps of leather snagged in a couple of splinters. Maybe from a work glove." Kado ran a hand over his weary face. "He used standard six-inch cut clasp nails, available in any hardware store. These are rusty, so they've probably been in somebody's barn for years. They're covered in Garrett's blood and have no fingerprints on them. We found nothing on the courthouse lawn."

"Anything on the tire tracks?" Mitch asked.

"Maybe. The sprinklers come on early. The ground was soft and damp but the tracks were a mess where he spun out. Munk got a few good casts – tires look big enough to come from a pickup. I'll run them through the database."

Mitch took a deep breath and turned to Grey. "What have you got from the body?"

"A lot. There's some sticky residue over the lower part of his face. His mouth was taped shut at some point. Neither Bernie nor I saw anything other than dirt stuck in the residue, but Kado, you can check it for trace." He rubbed his earlobe. "Mechanism of death was exsanguination, excessive blood loss. And given the way the wounds on his hands and feet are torn, it looks as if he was," Grey cleared his throat, "crucified upside down."

Cass frowned. "What do you mean?"

Grey released his earlobe and massaged his forehead, stopping to pinch the bridge of his long nose. "It's easier if we show you. Think you can keep your breakfast down?"

––––––––––

THE BRIGHT OVERHEAD LIGHTS sputtered to life as Grey wrapped a fresh gown over his scrubs. Garrett's body lay on a stainless steel table in the middle of the room, a clean sheet across his waist. The Y-incision had been folded closed but not stitched, and the edges of the skin were puckered and had a leathery look to them. Grey tugged on a clean pair of gloves.

"He was secured to the cross through the palms, with the palm itself facing away from the wood." He beckoned them forward, picking up one of the pale hands to show them the angry wound. "If the cross was upright, the hands would've borne most of Garrett's weight. The flesh would've pulled or torn up and away from the palm toward the index fingers and thumbs as his weight pulled him down, and bones would be broken in that direction. Instead, the flesh is torn, but only slightly, as if his full weight wasn't dragging on the palms. Also, the flesh is torn from the palm toward the little finger." Grey replaced Garrett's hand and moved down the table. "His feet were placed one on top of the other and secured with one nail. If the cross had been upright, we'd expect to see the flesh torn toward his ankles as his weight bore down. Instead, it's ripped toward the toes, as if he was suspended by his feet."

"If he did hang upside down," Mitch asked, "wouldn't the weight of his legs and upper body be enough to pull his feet right off the nail?"

"Good question," Grey answered as he lifted Garrett's lower leg. "We think he was bound to the cross around the ankles and calves to stop what you described from happening."

"What kind of binding was used?" Kado asked, leaning forward to examine the marks cutting into the bloodless tissue.

"The individual marks are narrow. Some sort of fine, tight rope."

"Did you swab for trace?"

"Yes, and we picked up some fibers. Swabs are on the counter behind you." Grey lowered the leg to the table, choosing his words carefully. "As to cause of death, we think the cuts to his forearms and the hole in his head were placed there to drain the blood from his body."

"Drain his blood?" Mitch asked, frowning. "What made the hole in his head?"

Bernie cleared his throat. "I believe it was a drill bit of some sort."

Mitch paled, making his blue eyes even brighter. "Somebody drilled a hole in his head?"

"That's what markings on the skull indicate."

"Was he alive?"

Grey moved to the top of Garrett's body. "Initially. As the bit ate through the skull, it sank into the brain. Trauma to the tissue indicates that Garrett wouldn't have died from the injury, but if he were conscious, the pain from the drilling would've caused him to pass out. Regardless, given the size of the opening," he lifted Garrett's head, "blood would have drained quickly and he wouldn't have lived long."

"Good Lord," breathed Cass. "Goober wasn't far off with his vampire theory. Why would somebody do that?"

"To collect the blood," Bernie volunteered.

Kado's eyes narrowed. "Why?"

"Perhaps a ritual of some sort."

"It's some voodoo thing," Mitch announced. "Like Humberto Gonzalez and his foot. That's downright creepy."

"Yes, it is," Bernie replied. "And combined with the upside down crucifixion, it also appears torturous."

"What do you mean?"

"Crucifixion is a particularly horrendous way to die. The mechanism of death is usually asphyxiation over a long period of time – how long a period determined by the victim's general health and upper body strength. Upside down crucifixion is not as well understood, but asphyxiation seems a reasonable cause of death given that the diaphragm will become exhausted from keeping the contents of the abdomen lifted from the lungs. However, if the person is in good physical condition, they could die due to exposure, shock or starvation, which could take much longer than death by traditional crucifixion." He searched the faces in the room. "It has been suggested that death in this manner may be linked to the occult, or that it is something of an insult, indicating a lack of worth. Although unconfirmed, there are suggestions that Christ's disciple Peter was crucified upside down at his request, stating that he was not worthy to die in the same manner as his Lord."

"Great. A ritualistic murderer." Mitch pressed the heels of his hands into his eyes. "What about the cuts on the forearms? Were they made with a knife?"

"Yes," answered Grey. "Smooth edge, very sharp. Possibly a hunting knife. And, there's something else." His quiet tone drew complete silence in the room. "We left the bandage on Garrett's groin in place when we moved the body," he began, reaching for his earlobe. "Once we looked underneath it, we realized that Garrett's testicles had been removed. I think the same sharp knife was used, but the cuts hesitate. Either because the cutter had difficulty with the mechanics of the action, or due to the psychological difficulty of what he did." Mitch and Kado covered their crotches in a defensive gesture. Grey smiled grimly as he nodded at Porky, who took a steel bowl from the counter and silently handed it to Grey. "These were lodged in his esophagus. He probably hadn't eaten since lunch. His stomach contents were mostly bile." He angled the container over Garrett's body so the others could peer inside, swirling the dark, cloudy liquid to reveal two small, rounded mounds resting on the bottom of the bowl.

Three pairs of eyes found the pasty lumps at the same moment. Mitch tightened the grip on his jeans and the color drained from Kado's face as his jaw dropped. Cass sensed rather than saw both movements and her mind understood the horror that both men had instinctively known: Garrett's testicles had ended up in his throat.

"Did he –," Kado cleared his throat and glanced at Mitch, "did he swallow them?"

"There's no trauma to his throat and the testicles appear to be intact, so yes." The medical examiner gulped convulsively, Adam's apple bobbing in his long neck. "He swallowed them. Given that they were lodged in his esophagus and he wasn't able to cough them up, I suspect that they were fed to him shortly before he died."

"Tell them about the coating," Porky prodded, thin frame shifting in his purple scrubs.

Mitch slowly released the front of his jeans. "Coating on what?"

Grey motioned for Porky to continue. "When we extracted them, the testicles looked like they had something on them. A golden color, maybe brown."

"Like they were cooked?" Mitch blurted.

"Battered and fried."

"Oh my God," Cass moaned, her legs buckling. She leaned against the counter and locked her knees. "I can't believe this."

"What is it?" Mitch demanded.

She closed her eyes. "I had words with Petchard last night. He got nasty about my family, and I snapped."

"Snapped how?"

"Just got in his face," Cass said, clenching the countertop for support. "I told him if he talked about my family again I'd rip off his balls, batter them, fry them, and...," her voice caught, "shove them down his throat."

CHAPTER 45

THE ROOM WAS SILENT for several beats, the silvery sluicing of water through a drain the only sound. Mitch folded his arms across his chest. "You can't think Petchard had anything to do with this," he stated.

Cass shook her head. "No, but how likely is it that the exact thing I threaten him with comes true for Garrett?"

"Not very," answered Kado. "What time did you talk to Petchard?"

"Must've been eight thirty, maybe nine o'clock."

"What did he do after your...," a smile touched his lips, "encounter?"

"We were in the squad room, and he just slunk out the door. I don't know where he went."

"What did you do?"

"I worked for another half an hour maybe –," she stopped, eyes jumping to Mitch. "I need to tell you something about Lenny Scarborough's case."

"Later," Mitch said. "What happened when you were done at the courthouse?"

"I went home. Had supper and went to bed."

"No sign of Petchard as you left the courthouse?"

"None."

"Did he have any problems with Garrett?"

"Not that I've heard of."

Mitch studied the floor for several moments. "I can't see Petchard doing something like this, at least not by himself. For starters, he's not strong enough to overpower Garrett or do the kind of heavy lifting it would take to move that cross with a body on it. Beyond that, the man is a wimp. He couldn't have handled cutting off Garrett's balls. If we rule out Petchard, there are two possibilities. One is that Garrett's murder is completely random. I think that's unlikely, given that this," he gestured toward the cold body, "took some planning. Second, someone who knew Garrett decided to crucify him and cut him up, for some reason. If you forget that he's a cop and think of him as a man, then having his balls sliced off could mean that he was involved in something of a sexual nature."

"Like molesting girls, raping them?" Cass asked.

Mitch's exhaled. "I hadn't thought of that. I was thinking that maybe he had an affair, or was still having one, and got caught."

"Perhaps as with Abelard and Heloise, someone acted to extract vengeance for a perceived wrong to the lady?" questioned Bernie.

Mitch blinked. "Who?"

"They were lovers in the twelfth century. Abelard was a theologian and philosopher, much older than Heloise, entrusted with her education. She became pregnant, and after delivering their son Astrolabe –"

"That's straight from Frank Zappa," Porky murmured.

"– they married in secret. Heloise's Uncle Fulbert was furious. She withdrew to a convent to escape his wrath, but Fulbert believed that Abelard was simply trying to rid himself of the girl, and ordered his servants to castrate Abelard in retribution."

Porky shivered. "He survived?"

"Oh yes," Bernie said. "He and Heloise continued their passionate relationship through correspondence. Quite tragic."

Mitch squinted across the autopsy room, gaze unfocused. "Garrett's always been one of the boys, but I haven't heard any rumors about him. We'll talk to his wife and friends, find out if he had anything on the side." He moved to the table containing Garrett's body. "Truman said that all the men in those photos had scars on their right sides. Garrett doesn't."

Grey moved alongside him. "What does that prove?"

"Nothing yet. But, it's less likely that Garrett was involved in molesting those girls. Which means that if there was something sexual going on, it probably involved another adult." Mitch fingered a button on his shirt. "Grey? Was he, you know, abused?"

Grey frowned. "Sexually?"

Mitch nodded, holding his breath.

"No, his body showed no sign of penetration."

Mitch released the breath. "Good."

Bernie cleared his throat and smoothed a hand over his unruly hair, flaxen in the overhead light. "There is a third possibility," he began, looking to Mitch, who motioned for him to continue. "The crime may be primarily ritual in nature, with its focus on the collection of blood." Bernie moved to the second metal table in the room, which held the remains of the man they'd dug up Monday afternoon. "Until I'd seen Officer Garrett's body today, I was confused about what had happened to our friend here. But now, well, let me tell you my hypothesis. Porky, would you put x-rays of both craniums on the light box please? Include the one of this man's neck, as well."

As Porky snapped the films in place, Bernie donned a fresh pair of gloves and moved to the head of Monday's corpse. "There is a slight subdural hematoma near the base of the skull, suggesting that he was struck on the head before death. I was confused by the hole in the top of the head, and we speculated that it could have been the result of a gunshot." He peeled scalp away to expose the skull and leaned closer. "But we found no exit wound, nor did we find a slug in the brain or neck and none appear on the x-rays. I am now sure that this hole was not caused by a bullet, but by a drill bit, as was Garrett's. A smaller one, perhaps a twelve millimeter bit."

Mitch frowned at Grey. "Translate?"

Grey lifted his eyes toward the ceiling, mouth moving silently. "Half inch," he announced.

The others drew near to the corpse and in turn, took the magnifying glass to examine the hole. "Unbelievable," Kado exclaimed. "You can see the spiral where the bit ate through the bone." He shivered as he stood to let Cass examine the wound. "Brutal."

"Indeed," answered Bernie. "I was also confused by the mummified appearance of the body. The arm that protruded above the soil was decaying as expected, but we saw little evidence of decomposition on the rest of the body. Burial slows the process, but our corpse should have been well into the state of decay known as putrefaction, where gas builds in the body, forcing fluids out and into the surrounding soil. We should have seen insect activity, or at least evidence of such."

"But there weren't any insects, right?" asked Mitch, straightening from his examination of the skull.

Bernie moved to the light box. "Very few. I believe this man's blood was drained from his body, in the same fashion as was Officer Garrett's. Look closely," he said, pointing to a spot on the neck x-ray near the collarbone. "The horseshoe shaped bone is the hyoid, which can be damaged when someone is strangled or hung. In this case, the absence of ligature marks around the neck indicates strangulation."

Mitch frowned and started to speak, but remained silent when Bernie lifted a finger and moved to the corpse, pausing near the foot of the table. "There *are*, however, ligature marks on the legs. They wind along the calves," he pointed to a long section of discoloration on the legs. "The color of the marks suggests that he was alive when his legs were tied, and that they were secured very tightly." He moved to the torso and lifted an arm, drawing their attention to the different areas. "The arms and wrists are clear of marks suggesting binding. However, long slits have been cut in the forearms, along the radial arteries." Bernie paused expectantly.

"And that means…," Mitch prompted him.

"I believe that this man was stunned by a blow to the back of the head, then had his legs bound before being strangled to death. At that point, we believe he was suspended by his legs, his wrists were slit and the top of his head drilled to drain the blood from his corpse." The room was silent as they took in Bernie's description. "The absence of blood would explain why decomposition has not progressed as expected, and why the corpse has taken on a mummy-like appearance."

Mitch closed his eyes, as if to erase the gruesome image painted by his brain. "If you're right Bernie, and blood was collected from Garrett and this guy, the same person or people killed both men. What kind of creepy ritual is this? Who would want somebody's blood? And what would they do with it?"

Cass started, lips rounded in surprise. She held a finger up in the air and darted from the examination room.

"What is it?" Mitch called after her.

"Don't move," she answered, voice fading as she dashed toward the front door. "I'll be right back."

CHAPTER 46

SHE RETURNED WITHIN TEN minutes, tendrils of dark red hair clinging to her forehead and sweat beading her upper lip. She carried a large-ish object wrapped in a white towel. Breathing heavily, she asked Porky to pull out a third examination table and carefully placed the bundle on its surface. "I ran into Sheriff Hoffner, Grey. He wants to know when he can talk to the press. They're milling around outside your office and on the courthouse lawn. I had to barrel my way in and out."

"Not yet," Grey answered distractedly. "What's that?"

Cass unwrapped the towel to display *The Church of the True Believer*. The others surrounded the table, faces drawn in curiosity. "I didn't put it together until just now," she said. "I was flipping through this book last night, and there are several strange things in it. Look." She flipped to the colorful crucifixion scene portraying blood pouring onto the disciples from Jesus' wounded side. "Maybe they're using the blood in some sort of ritual. Washed in the blood of the lamb, see? And those scars Truman saw on their sides? Maybe that's supposed to be some symbol of Jesus' sacrifice. Replicating the mark the spear left when it pierced his chest."

Grey's dark eyebrows jumped high on his forehead as he considered what Cass had said. "Interesting."

Mitch leaned into a counter, crossing one long leg over the other. "What in the world makes you think Chad Garrett's death is linked to that book from Lenny Scarborough's house? That's a mighty big leap."

"I know." Cass paused, gathering her thoughts. "Lenny's briefcase was missing from his study, and Garrett had the opportunity to take it. We're also pretty sure he took that inventory from Elaine's desk Sunday night. The only people who would be interested in Lenny's death are the men in those photographs, right? And those pictures were in this book, which means that the members of The Church probably had something to do with raping those girls." She shrugged. "Even if Garrett wasn't a card carrying member, maybe he was involved in some other way."

"But why would they crucify him? This took some planning, and a pretty devious mind."

"Maybe Garrett did something wrong and this is punishment. Or a warning to someone else. The way he was killed has a dark feel to it, like Bernie said. The whole thing does."

"Bernie," Kado interrupted. "Does the mummy have any scars on his chest?"

"No, he does not."

"So he wasn't part of this group, either. You think he might've been involved on the outskirts, Cass?"

"Maybe. Or maybe they needed the blood and he was in the wrong place at the wrong time."

"What are they," Mitch snorted, "devil worshippers?"

"Cass may be right," Bernie said thoughtfully, examining the picture of the crucifixion. "This could be a bonding of some kind. Think of the blood brother ritual. Individuals were brought into a family of sorts by the mingling of blood and on occasion, the drinking of blood. Perhaps they use it in a rite of passage. Blood is also symbolic of birth, death and even re-birth. Maybe...," he paused, one finger pressed to his lips. "Cass, is there a description of The Church? Its membership?"

"I think so." She flipped through the pages and read. "Given what Pastor Luke told us about cults yesterday, I'm assuming that everything in this book is based on the Bible, but it's been a little distorted. This is an extract from First Corinthians. It talks about how the members of The Church are of one body, but each has a unique role to play and shouldn't be jealous of the others. Here's the structure part: 'Now ye are the body of Christ, and severally members thereof. And God hath set the design for His perfect Church: the first is The Light, God's holy vessel; secondly, The Circle of Illumination, who protect The Light and travel the road as steadily as the points on a compass; thirdly, The Brethren, who keep themselves alert and are ever vigilant against the acts of Satan. At no time shall The Church extend beyond the holy number established by Christ Jesus and his disciples, sacred for the taking of the blood and the body. Therefore, outside and with equal honor but anonymous glory are The Way, the blessed eyes, ears, feet and hands of The Church.'" She looked up at Bernie.

"Is that what you meant?"

"Let me think for a minute." Reaching for a note pad, he began drawing, scribbling out sections and re-writing them. Stopping to chew on the cap of his pen, he tore off a clean page and, checking his original diagram and the text, he drew a three level pyramid of several blocks. Finally, he turned the pages around so the others could see, and smiled.

"What is it?" Kado asked.

"A graphic representation of what Cass described. There were thirteen 'official' members of Jesus' group – himself, plus the twelve disciples. They were the only ones at the last supper, where Jesus gave his symbolic body and blood." Bernie tapped the page as he tucked his pen into a pocket. "Consider this in organizational terms. The top box, or the head of the organization is The Light, accountable to God. Four people report to The Light, this Circle of Illumination. I believe there are only four due to the reference to the points on a compass, and because there were four canonical gospels: Matthew, Mark, Luke and John." Mitch chewed his lip, but remained quiet. "These people called The Way should be excluded from the formal chart, because they are discussed after the number of members is defined and they are referenced as outside and anonymous. That leaves eight available spots from our total of thirteen, which gives us the number of The Brethren."

The others nodded slowly as they studied the page. "I guess it makes sense," said Mitch, stepping away from the table to lean against a counter. "But what about the blood?"

"We know that Lenny Scarborough was a member of this group due to his possession of the book and the scar on his chest, yes?"

"Yes," Cass answered.

"Then they'll need to replace him. Perhaps they gather the blood as some sort of initiation, welcoming new members or moving the members from one level to another."

"Like a promotion?" she asked.

Bernie paused. "Possibly, yes."

Her eyes widened as she looked to Mitch and Kado. "Do you remember that invitation Munk found out at Lenny's? Something about being invited to a celebration?"

Kado answered her with a question. "You think that's a promotion?"

"Why not?"

"Man, this is bizarre," Kado said, running both hands through his dark hair.

"And it doesn't get us any closer to figuring out who these guys are, does it?" Mitch asked in frustration.

"There's something else I wanted to show you. I was trying to tell you this morning when Goober came into The Golden Gate," Cass said, turning the large volume around and flipping to the last page. "Take a look at this."

Mitch and Kado bumped heads as they leaned in to read the handwritten words. Kado stood first, gray eyes confused. Mitch followed, mouth open in disbelief. "What is that?"

"I think it's a list of the people who have owned this book."

Mitch blinked. "These are… I mean… These were some of the most influential families in Forney County in the last hundred years," he replied, sighing heavily. "Good Lord. You know what this means?"

Cass nodded. "We've got a lead."

———————

THEY LEFT THE ME'S office through the back door while Minnie slipped out the front to share a cigarette with the reporters. Circling the short block, they trotted quickly through the police department's parking lot and entered the courthouse through a rear door, avoiding the crush on the front lawn. Glancing in the Sherriff's office, they found him pacing the room, phone mashed to one ear, the knuckles of one hand white from gripping the handset, the fingers of the other combing through his short, snowy hair. They covered the distance to Elaine's alcove in the lobby and stood watching as a news van bearing the logo of a station in Dallas pulled to a stop across several parking spaces. A fresh-faced woman jumped from the passenger seat and hurried the burly cameraman and a weedy sound guy climbing through the van's side door. The trio began pushing toward the courthouse steps. Elaine checked the doors again to ensure they were locked and trudged back to her alcove.

"I've never seen anything like this… this pandemonium," she said, brushing a curl from her forehead as colored sparks of light twinkled wildly on her telephone. "We've shut down all business in the courthouse today, except the critical stuff. I can't imagine…," she said in a low voice. "How could this have happened to someone like Chad Garrett?"

Cass leaned against Elaine's desk while Mitch stood motionless next to the busy fax machine, watching sheet after sheet of requests for interviews from news agencies spool out and puddle in the receiving tray. Kado scratched his head and leaned into the copier. "How does somebody overpower a trained officer like Garrett? Is that what you mean?" he asked.

"I guess so," she answered slowly, dropping her gaze to her lap. "But I've heard awful things. That he was crucified, tortured. That he was beaten and even sod –," she took a breath before whispering, "sodomized."

Mitch turned to face the receptionist. "Elaine, I know you'd never do it, but you can't speak a word about what you hear concerning Garrett's case. Every scrap of information has to be kept confidential to give us a better chance of finding his killer. If there's incorrect information out there, that's fine. It'll keep this guy guessing about what we really know and what we just suspect. Understand?"

"Yes," she answered with a hitch in her voice.

"Garrett was crucified. He wasn't beaten, but I'd imagine he was in some pain. He wasn't sodomized, okay?"

Elaine caught her breath. "Thank you. I didn't really know him, but he just seemed like a normal guy, know what I mean?"

"Yeah, I do," answered Mitch, lips twitching. "I wouldn't wish this on an abnormal guy."

A reluctant smile tugged at Elaine's mouth. "I stopped by to see Angie Scarborough last night."

"How is she?" Cass asked.

"About like you'd expect. Angry. Sad. Still in shock." Elaine spun back and forth slowly in her chair. "She's a tough cookie. Said Mitch told her to call the Pettigrew brothers to come help on the farm, and that's what she was planning to do this morning."

"Life goes on," Kado said.

"Hungry cows have to be fed," Elaine answered as an angry burp erupted from her phone. She lifted her headset and spoke quietly. Disconnecting, she gestured toward the police station. "Sheriff Hoffner's off the phone. He said to hurry before he gets another call."

Cass frowned. "How are people getting around you to call him, Elaine?"

The other woman smiled wickedly. "Silly man. He's given out his direct number all over the county. All those election contributions and favors people gave him over the years? Looks like they're calling them in for information."

CHAPTER 47

THEY STOOD IN SHERIFF Hoffner's office, waiting. He was pacing again, phone pressed to his ear with one hand while he straightened pictures on the wall with the other. His brow was drawn into an impressive frown, pulling his bushy eyebrows together over his close-set eyes and long, hooked nose. A younger Hoffner stared from a framed photo, auburn hair still vibrant and blue eyes piercing.

"I understand Ob, but there's nothing I can tell you until Grey finishes the autopsy." He held the phone away from his ear as a voice screeched over the line. Hoffner's scowl deepened and he growled a reply. "Obadiah, I intend for you to have the first interview as soon as I have the information. But if you keep up this attitude, I'll go with Stanton. Understood?"

Nodding sharply at the reply, he withdrew a snowy handkerchief from his pocket and wiped the ear and mouthpieces before replacing the headset in its cradle. "Obadiah Graham over at the Forney Cater. Been hounding me for a story all morning. Not like he's going to print until tonight," he grumbled, re-folding the handkerchief into a precise square and replacing it in his pocket. Hoffner ran a hand over his weary face and drew a deep breath. "What a mess. Garrett's wife is still knocked out at the hospital. Grey must've given her enough sedative to keep a horse down. What have you got?" he asked, plunking into the chair behind his desk and motioning them to sit.

Mitch leaned forward, placing his elbows on his knees. "What we think happened is pretty screwed up. Hear me out, then poke holes in our theory."

Sheriff Hoffner was silent for the twenty minutes it took Mitch to walk through the forensic and autopsy findings; their theories on what the absence of blood in Garrett's body and that of the corpse found on Monday meant; and lastly, Bernie's structure chart for The Church of the

True Believer and Cass's interpretation of the crucifixion image. The expression on Hoffner's face alternated between fascination and horror. Mitch ended his monologue by opening the heavy volume to its last page and turning it to face the sheriff.

Sheriff Hoffner leaned forward to examine the handwritten names, adjusting the book to align with the edge of his desk. Color flooded his cheeks. "Salter, Peavey, Shepherd? You think these men were fags?"

Mitch grimaced. "I don't care about their sexual preferences, sir. I care about whether they raped girls or women."

Hoffner grunted. "They're all dead. What do you propose? Harassing their kinfolk?"

Mitch ran a hand over his blonde hair as he leaned back in his chair. "Yes, sir, that's exactly what we propose. These are the kind of men who could convince Lenny Scarborough that homosexuality and child molestation could give him power."

"Are you out of your mind? Jed Salter's a bank president and Peavey, well, how much land and oil does that man own around here? These are powerful men, Mitch, they control money and votes. And John Earl Shepherd? His daddy's name is in this book, but that boy's a complete waste of time. He can't help with any of this."

"Respectfully sir, we've got a dead officer to think about."

"I am well aware of that *fact*," he growled, icy eyes narrowed. "This is all *speculation*. You think this is some sort of generational thing? Passed down from grandfather to father to son?"

Mitch shrugged, keeping his voice even. "Maybe, although if it were, it seems that the father would pass his book on to the son, rather than to someone else. Maybe there's no connection between father and son regarding membership in this group."

"If not, is there any reason to go upsetting Salter and Peavey?"

"If there isn't a connection, it shouldn't upset them if we ask questions. And they might remember something about their father's or grandfather's involvement." Mitch stopped to eye Hoffner across the desk. He leaned forward again, clasping his hands loosely between his knees. "It's worth a shot."

Hoffner was silent for several moments. Finally, he shook his head. "I can't leave this building right now; reporters are still on the lawn. Call

Sammy and tell him to get over here. Let's hear what he has to say about this."

"Sheriff," Mitch said, a flush spreading across his cheeks, "I can't believe I'm gonna say this, but can we trust him?"

"You think the District Attorney's involved?" Hoffner barked.

Mitch held up his hands as if to ward off a blow. "The Peavey, Salter, Shepherd and Scarborough families' names are in that book. These men are, or were, pillars in this community. Upstanding, God-fearing, *righteous* men. Without those names, we never would have considered that men like that could've been involved in something like this... this cult, or whatever it is. But with the names," he said, disgust heavy in his voice, "in what must be their own handwriting, there's little doubt that they were involved."

"What is your point, Mitch?" Hoffner enunciated with care.

"If men like that could be involved, how the hell do we know who we can trust?"

CHAPTER 48

BLACKIE COCHRAN TURNED OFF the rusty, tepid water and stepped gingerly from the shower, trying to keep her head steady. Nana's plumbing needed serious work, but the woman refused to consider moving to city water. Too expensive, she claimed. And Blackie's skin was a beautiful nutty brown, just like Nana's, so a little rust wouldn't hurt, would it?

She lifted a wrist to her nose and sniffed, tentatively at first, and then more thoroughly. Satisfied that the mucky smell of the river was gone, Blackie slathered on Nana's rose-scented lotion and examined herself in the full-length mirror behind the bathroom door. In spite of her pounding head, she looked pretty good for thirty-something. Gently, she probed her face, satisfied that the worst of the damage was gone. Her skin was again luminous and – she leaned into the mirror – still wrinkle free. She sighed as she pulled on clean clothes from a stash she kept at Nana's. Life as a prostitute was profitable but unpredictable, a state the beating from her pimp had reinforced. She'd been out of work for several weeks now, but had gotten a call from the DA's office only yesterday to let her know that they had enough evidence to prosecute. Sammy Mathison believed Brent Small would be a multi-year guest of the state prison system for rape and assault. While frightened of testifying when the time came, Blackie was content.

She slipped into a pair of Nana's old slippers and padded to the kitchen. Sitting at the chipped Formica table while coffee perked, she swallowed four aspirin with a glass of water and cradled her head, willing the thrumming to stop. Last night was a terrifying blur. She'd been so tickled about Small's prosecution that she'd driven to Booger's rotting bait shack near the county line. His hooch was nasty stuff, its quality variable at best, but Booger was the cheapest moonshiner around and her funds were low from being away from work for so long.

The percolator's wet sputter snagged her attention. She poured the dark liquid into a heavy old mug, adding a healthy dose of real cream and sugar. Blackie tried to rationalize what she'd seen last night to her degree of inebriation. She'd been smashed, no doubt about it. Frowning, she wondered if Booger hadn't slipped something extra into her bottle. Maybe thinking he could barter his 'shine for some time between her legs. But she'd left Booger before she opened the bottle *or* her legs, and drove to a secluded grove down near the river. It was peaceful there, and at this time of year, isolated. Toasting herself and Small's upcoming trial, Blackie sat on the hood of her tiny car, intending only to have a few sips before heading home and changing to meet Nana at the church. Monday was Bible study night, and Nana was sure it was only a matter of time before exposure to the Good Book would straighten her granddaughter right out. *Jesus loved the Magdalene*, Nana often reminded her, *even though we think she was a harlot. He showed Himself to her first after His resurrection, so* she *was His favorite, no matter what that self-righteous John thought.*

But Blackie hadn't made it to church. Instead, she'd woken in a stupor to find herself resting in slimy, sticky mud reeking of dead fish. A sixth sense had kept her still, letting the night's sounds seep into her addled brain before she began, ever so slowly, to raise her head. The sight in the clearing still burned in her memory, and she fought with herself over whether it was real or imagined. A familiar Jesus on a cross, head toward the ground. A devil with burning eyes, slim form iridescent in the firelight. The stench of urine and fear, the slick feel of muck against her cheek.

Thanks to the aspirin and the caffeine, the throbbing in her head had slowed to a tolerable level and Blackie checked her watch. She reached for Nana's phone on the kitchen wall and traced the cracks in the linoleum tabletop as she listened to Jerome's cell phone ring.

"What took you so long?"

"I'm fine Jerome, thanks for asking."

"Girl, I oughta turn you over my knee. You scared Nana to death last night. Why didn't you make it to Bible study? She found you passed out on the sofa this morning, stinkin' to high heaven."

Blackie sighed into the phone. She and Jerome were cousins, as close as brother and sister while they were growing up. And although he'd spent time in prison for auto theft and armed robbery, Jerome came out convinced of the error of his ways. He lost everything while he was inside –

wife, children, job – but started again without complaint. He lived with Nana and worked at a retirement home, taking care of a rich old widow whom he adored, and who adored him in return. Jerome knew about Blackie's professional life and she knew he worried about her. Especially after her pimp's beating. And although she fiercely protected her independence, she warmed to Jerome's devotion.

"Where were you last night?" she asked, hoping to change the subject.

"Out here at Pecan Grove, with Mrs. Forrester."

"She not doing well?"

Jerome sighed. "Havin' bad nightmares for some reason. I'll be out here tonight, too." Blackie heard him yawn near the phone. "But we were talking about you."

"I think I got some bad booze out at Booger's."

Jerome chuckled. "You should know better. He brews that hooch with alligator pee. What happened?"

"Something kinda weird," she answered, slowly telling him what she'd seen. Jerome was silent when she finished speaking. "Well?" she prodded, pouring and doctoring a second mug of coffee.

"How'd you get to Nana's?"

"I have no idea." She stood and lifted a curtain patterned with roses to check the drive. "My car's here. Booger must've slipped something in the bottle, right?"

"You need to talk to the po-lice, Blackie."

"What?" she exclaimed, half laughing. "Why the po-lice need to know some two-bit whore been seein' devils dancing in firelight 'round the river bottom?"

He sighed. "They found a body this morning. On the courthouse lawn. A man on a cross."

"That ain't funny, Jerome," she whispered, wrapping her hands around the hot mug.

"I mean it Blackie. You best go tell them what you saw." She heard scratching and a murmured conversation as the phone disappeared into Jerome's large hand. The crackling cleared and he spoke again. "Mrs. Forrester said it's all right if I leave now. I'll meet you at the courthouse. Park out back."

CHAPTER 49

IT TOOK SAMMY MATHISON a solid half hour to make the short walk from the District Attorney's office off the square to the courthouse. A few members of the press waited in front of his small office and their numbers grew as he stepped outside and word spread that an official was available for comment. He pushed gently against the expanding crowd, quietly refusing to answer the questions that swelled from a peppering to a bombardment as he struggled against the tight crush of sweaty bodies. Sammy's image appeared on several news programs that night and on the front page of a few newspapers the next morning, his cowboy boots, pearl-button snap front shirt, giant belt buckle and broad brimmed hat considered too emblematic of quirky East Texas to pass up.

Elaine hopped up to open the courthouse doors and quickly re-locked them behind him. "Is that crowd getting worse?"

Sammy gave her a slow smile as he lifted the cowboy hat from his head, running a hand over his hair before reaching behind him to check that his can of Skoal was still in his back pocket. "It ain't too bad. Hoffner will talk to them, give them something to chew on and they'll quiet down," he drawled. "Is he in his office?"

"Sure is. I'll bring some coffee."

"Thanks, hon," he replied, turning toward the swinging doors leading to the police station. He stopped outside Hoffner's office and took a deep breath. "How y'all this morning?" he asked as he pushed the door open and found Kado, Mitch and Cass inside.

"How was it, Sammy?" asked Mitch, standing to shake the DA's hand.

He shook Kado's hand and smiled at Cass, touching her shoulder as he moved to lean against one of Hoffner's credenzas. "Pretty bad. You need to make a statement, Bill. Just to keep them quiet."

Sheriff Hoffner nodded. "I need your advice before I go out there. Listen to what Mitch and Kado have to say."

Cass resisted the urge to roll her eyes as Hoffner excluded her from the group of people permitted to speak, and settled in her chair instead, listening once again to the facts and conjecture they'd woven together this morning. Sammy crossed one long leg over the other, fingering a lamb chop sideburn where it ended near his jaw. He grunted once or twice as Mitch spoke, but asked no questions.

As Mitch finished, Elaine knocked on the door, carrying several cups of Golden Gate Café coffee. "Stan's set some food up in the conference room for whoever wants it."

Cass looked at her watch, astonished to find it was after noon. Sheriff Hoffner shooed Elaine from his office and watched as Sammy emptied cream and sugar into his take-out cup, stirring slowly with a wooden stick. He stared blankly at the smudge of condensation left in a precise circle on his desk when the DA lifted his cup, watching until it evaporated.

Sammy drew a noisy slurp before speaking, face contracting as the scalding liquid hit his lips and tongue. "Let me get this straight. You want to go dig around in Chad Garrett's house, see if you can find some link to this cult."

"Yes," Mitch said.

"That part sounds all right. And then you want to go talk to John Earl Shepherd, Mr. Peavey's son, and Mr. Salter's grandson, find out what they remember and whether their... ancestors, were involved in this cult?"

"Yup."

"That part sounds all right, too. But then you want to ask the doctors in town if they've got any male patients with scars on their right sides, somewhere on the rib cage or under the arm."

Mitch nodded.

"That part's not all right," Sammy said, taking another slurp of coffee as he stood to walk the small room, head cocked to the side in thought. "Well, maybe it is all right. You've got men out in the woods sodomizing one another, but that's among consenting adults. And you've got photographic evidence of at least one female being raped. That's a crime. You have photographs of these scars?" he asked, stopping to glance at Mitch and Kado.

"Where the right rib cage is visible," Mitch answered.

He started to pace again. "We've got perpetrators we need to identify, and a pretty unique characteristic. Technically, we could request a subpoena for medical records in a search for men with that particular scar. Judge Shackleford might even sign it, given the photos. And the doctors will follow through and give us what we want – they have an obligation to protect those children in the photographs. But we've got how many doctors in town? Twenty-five, thirty? Maybe more," he answered himself. "How long is it gonna take to go through all those records, and how much gossip is gonna be out there about what we're doing? How many men are we gonna find that have a scar on their sides for some perfectly logical reason?" He stopped, thinking. "Maybe not that many, but still, that's like sifting for a grain of sugar in a pile of ashes."

An indistinct memory slammed into Cass's brain and she mentally tugged at it until it crystallized. She was kneeling beside Officer Hugo Petchard's prone form, pulling his uniform and white undershirt up so she could slice his smoldering trousers from his body while flames skittered through dry underbrush. She bit her lip.

"Got a better idea?" Sheriff Hoffner asked.

"Nope," answered Sammy, coming to rest again against the credenza. "But I'd go through Garrett's house and talk to Shepherd, Peavey and Salter before I tried stirring all those ants up."

Cass took a quiet breath and steeled herself for the outrage she suspected would follow her statement. "Sir?"

Hoffner grunted, eyes swiveling to take her in. "What, Elliot?"

"I have an idea."

He sighed and leaned back in his chair. "Go on."

"Last week, when Officer Petchard tried to stomp out that trash fire and caught his uniform on fire, I cut his trousers and undershorts off to keep them from burning him. In the process, I hiked up his t-shirt and," she paused, "he has a scar on his chest."

Sheriff Hoffner thumped forward in his chair, eyes glacial. "What are you suggesting, Detective?"

Cass glanced at Mitch, who nodded silently. "Sir, I've noticed that Officer Petchard's behavior has become – uhm – aggressive over the past few months. And the men named in the back of that book," she gestured toward *The Church of the True Believer* where it lay open on his desk, "were powerful and, I guess, wealthy. Petchard's father is pretty well off, and maybe –"

Her voice was lost in Sheriff Hoffner's honk of incredulity. "You must be joking. You think Sam Petchard is involved in this? That man's a doctor. You've come up with some stupid ideas before Elliot, but this one –"

"– maybe he and Petchard are both involved," she finished, raising her voice over Hoffner's to do so. The room went silent, the staccato tap of feet hurrying past in the hall penetrating the closed door. "If Petchard is part of this group, he's been indoctrinated into a world where women and minorities are 'less than', and would explain why he's been such a –," *an asshole*, the voice inside her head pronounced, "– a loud mouth."

Sheriff Hoffner snorted and opened his mouth to speak. Mitch cut him off. "I know it sounds unbelievable sir, but Cass may have something with this. Petchard has been a real jerk lately, not just to Cass but also to Martinez, using racist language. Technically, what's he's done to Cass is sexual harassment."

The sheriff's face blossomed with red blotches as he snapped his jaw shut and placed both hands on the desk, leaning forward, blue eyes blazing. "Then why haven't you reported it?" he thundered.

Cool anger coursed through Cass's body, driving her forward to face Sheriff Hoffner across the desk. Her eyes flashed as they meet his, her voice low in contrast to his bellow. "I didn't think it would do my career any good to complain. Sir."

Hoffner paled and his glance darted among the men in the room. His voice was slow and considered. "You think I wouldn't believe you, Elliot, because you are a woman?"

Inadvertently, she had scored a point, but the man was her boss. Her heart rate slowed as the flare of anger died and Cass considered her answer carefully. "I was worried about how the other officers would perceive me if I reported Officer Petchard."

Mitch shifted, his plastic chair creaking with the motion. "Martinez has said the same thing, sir. Both he and Cass just tolerate it and push back where they can."

Hoffner sighed, glancing at the lean DA, hip again braced against a credenza. "I'm sorry you're hearing all this, Sammy. Petchard's performance out on the courthouse lawn this morning is the first I've seen of it."

The DA lifted a shoulder in a casual shrug. "It's the same everywhere, just to different degrees."

Cass cleared her throat. "Sir? There's more."

Hoffner glared. "Go on."

"Petchard and I had words in the squad room last night. He ended up insulting my family and I threatened him."

"With what?"

"I told him that if he talked bad about my family again, I'd rip his balls off, batter them, fry them and shove them down his throat," she answered, voice fading.

Sammy smirked in appreciation, seeming to consider that if Cass Elliot intended to emasculate Hugo Petchard, she was fully capable of doing so. "Sounds reasonable punishment to me," he drawled. "Why is that relevant now?"

Mitch glanced at Sheriff Hoffner, who dropped his chin in a curt nod. "What Cass threatened actually happened, but to Garrett instead of to Petchard."

The DA froze; his voice was brittle when he spoke. "Garrett's *testicles* were removed?"

"With a sharp knife, according to Grey. They were probably battered and fried, and he," Mitch coughed into his fist, "swallowed them shortly before he died."

The color drained from the DA's face and he slouched against the credenza as the full impact of the words hit him. "Good God, he was alive?"

Mitch and Kado nodded.

Sammy picked up his coffee and started pacing again, eyes blind to the room and its inhabitants. Hoffner watched him, waiting for the DA's brain to finish its considerations. Sammy drained the last of his coffee, carefully placed the empty cup in a wastepaper basket, and then faced Mitch. When he spoke his words were clipped, direct, as if he were examining a witness. The drawl was almost mitigated. "You've ruled Officer Petchard out of this?"

"Not explicitly, but logically, yes. We'll go through the motions once we've got the okay from the sheriff."

"Cass, you think he told someone about your threat?"

"Yes," she answered, pushing a loose strand of red hair from her forehead.

"And that someone acted on it, but using Chad Garrett instead?"

"Yes."

"Why Officer Garrett?"

"Tell him everything," Hoffner ordered. Kado explained the circumstances surrounding the envelope missing from Elaine's desk and their confrontation with Garrett on Monday morning. Mitch took over and told the DA about the briefcase that Angie had reported missing from the Scarborough's study.

"If Chad Garrett sneaked into Lenny Scarborough's house while y'all were out at the barn, and stole this briefcase with a robe and maybe a phone in it, what did he do with it?"

Mitch and Cass exchanged glances. "We don't know."

"And then he came into the courthouse and made a copy of the evidence inventory from the Scarborough's place?"

"Yes," Kado answered.

"Why would he do that?"

Mitch exhaled in frustration, burying his hands in his hair. "We don't know."

"So you're speculating that Officer Garrett is involved in this cult." He stopped and leaned over Hoffner's desk to look at the notes on The Church's structure earlier. "In what part?"

Cass leaned forward to look at the notes with Sammy. "He doesn't have a scar on his rib cage, but we need to search Garrett's house for a briefcase or one of these books," she said, tapping *The Church of the True Believer.* "If he's one of the thirteen members, he'll have a copy with his name in it. If he doesn't have one, maybe he's a member of The Way."

"And everything he's done has been for someone in this group? Man, this just sounds too weird to be true. But, you have the pictures," he said, coming back to the only piece of solid evidence they'd found. "All right, check out Garrett's place. Get authorization from his wife if possible, but if she's still sedated, you can go in as part of your investigation into his death."

Hoffner frowned. "You sure about that?"

"A crime was committed, but we don't know where. It's reasonable that you'd search his house to try and determine his last movements. Then talk to Peavey, Shepherd and Salter. And while you're doing that, check up on Petchard and that scar."

"How do we do that without asking him to lift his shirt?"

Sammy smiled. "Got his personnel file? He should've had a medical before he joined the force."

THE DOOR CLICKED SHUT and Hoffner released a heavy sigh. He knew he needed to call Obadiah Graham over at the Forney Cater and give the man his exclusive. And then he had to talk to those reporters on his lawn. Vultures, every last one of them. He caught a faint scent and recognized it as the light perfume Cass wore. It was similar to the scent her mother had worn and the smell of it swept him into the past.

Lord, but she was like her mother. He could hardly stand to be in the same room with her, much less listen to her voice or watch the animation in her face. She was as sharp as Nell, as fierce, as tenacious. And with the same body. He'd accepted her application to the force with reluctance, not because Cass wasn't qualified, but because he didn't know how he'd handle being reminded of the past every day. *Not very well, it seems*, he thought, rubbing his face with open palms and breathing deeply, pushing her scent from his nose.

In control again, he stood and unlocked a cabinet, reaching for Officer Hugo Petchard's personnel file. A sharp knock sounded. "Come in," he called.

Elaine's curly head poked through the narrow opening. "Sorry, Sheriff. The mayor's on the phone."

"What does David Wayne want?"

"To know when you're going to talk to those reporters."

"Might as well get it over with," he murmured, suppressing a shudder. "Ask him to come to my office."

CHAPTER 50

MITCH, CASS AND KADO reconvened in the conference room, drawing Truman and Munk into a corner to strategize the afternoon. Bolting sandwiches stuffed with Stan's mix of whole food ingredients, they brought the two men up to date on Garrett's autopsy and their suppositions about The Church. The mood in the room was subdued, disbelieving. Their senses were numb from their encounter with a scene from a horror flick featuring one of their own. A scene played out in full-blown Technicolor, with an unmistakable reality driven home by the smells of death and the faint, metallic taste of blood in the air.

Munk and Truman had spent the morning cruising the northern part of the county for Chad Garrett's truck, with no luck. They volunteered to cover the south and western areas, stopping to search Garrett's house on the way. Kado wanted to work on the gauze and tape taken from Garrett's body, to see if he could lift any trace or find fingerprints. Mitch and Cass decided to talk with Salter and Peavey. Energized by the thought of action, the group stood to leave the room as Mitch's phone rang. He frowned at the unfamiliar number on the screen.

"Mitch Stone."

"Good mornin' sir. It's Jerome, Blackie Cochran's cousin? We met when Blackie had her trouble with Mr. Smalls."

"Of course," Mitch answered, wondering at the road noise in the background. "What can I do for you?"

"I need to talk to you for a few minutes, down there at the courthouse."

"This is a bad time. Would tomorrow work for you?"

"No, sir. You need to hear what my cousin has to say."

"About what?"

"That man y'all found this morning."

Mitch lowered his long frame into a chair. "What about him?"

"I'm almost at the courthouse, and Blackie should be gettin' near there, too. I heard there's a crowd out front, so we'll park in the back. Can you meet us?"

"How far away are you?"

"'Bout five minutes."

"I'll wait by the rear doors," Mitch said, snapping the phone shut and meeting Cass's curious stare. "Remember Jerome? Blackie Cochran's cousin?"

"Big guy, tattoos. Not long out of Huntsville for armed robbery. Seemed genuine when he took care of Blackie after her rape," she answered, shrugging. "What did he want?"

He stared, mouth open. "How do you remember that much detail?"

"I've got more brain cells than you."

"No doubt. Seems she might know something about what happened to Garrett."

"You don't think he was —"

"Screwing Blackie?" he finished for her, shaking his head. "It wouldn't surprise me. If that's the case, we might just solve his murder this afternoon. If she found out, I reckon his wife would've been pissed enough to take his balls right off."

———————

BLACKIE COCHRAN SHIFTED IN the plastic chair, unable to find a comfortable position. She'd dealt with both detectives when she'd reported her pimp's rape and beating and had been inadvertently impressed with Cass's ruthless attention to detail and Mitch's compassion. Regardless, she didn't like being in a police station, even if she was in a nice meeting room with a cup of decent coffee, talking like normal people. She cut her eyes at her cousin as he sat beside her. In spite of his status as an ex-con, Jerome looked perfectly calm, and she tried to imitate his demeanor. Cass took copious notes as Blackie spoke, and she was encouraged that they were taking her so seriously.

"Tell me where you were again?" Mitch was asking.

"Down near Deuce's Flat, where the Sabine River cuts underneath 323?"

"I know that bridge."

"Before that, there's an old trail leads down by the river bottom. Just wide enough for my car. There's this little glade, looks out over the river. It's real peaceful and I go there sometimes, to be alone."

"And where did you end up?"

"I'm not sure," Blackie shrugged. "It must've been right in that area, and near the river, 'cause I was filthy with muck."

"Can you find it again?"

She nodded hesitantly. "Maybe."

"You're sure you didn't recognize this man, this," he looked at Cass's notes, "devil made of light?"

Blackie grimaced. "It sounds silly, but that's what ran through my mind when I saw him. His eyes burned, and the fire kinda cut through him."

"I'm not saying it's silly at all. That's what your brain told you, under pretty stressful circumstances. But you didn't know who he was?"

She shook her head.

Mitch sucked his teeth. "How do you know Officer Garrett?"

Her eyes flew wide. "The dead man's a po-lice officer?"

"You didn't recognize him?"

"I – no. I didn't. I mean, there was something familiar about him, but I don't know any Officer Garrett."

Cass turned to the computer behind her, tapping a few commands on the keyboard. She swiveled the screen to face the table. "Have you seen him before?"

Blackie clapped one hand over her mouth and reached for Jerome with the other. "Sweet Jesus," she breathed through her fingers. "I – I think that's the man on that cross. And…" She hesitated and Jerome squeezed her hand. "He's been with one of the girls over at The Donkey."

The Ronkey Donkey was one of the strip bars that dotted the highway just over the county line. One notch above the other joints on Whiskey Bend, The Ronkey Donkey was air-conditioned and its tobacco-spattered floor was swept nightly, clean sawdust spread the following morning. The girls who worked The Donkey were usually younger and viewed the work as a way to make a quick buck. A few had even worked their way through college, stripping on weekends. Some turned tricks, as did Blackie, but always away from The Donkey's premises.

"What do you mean by 'been with'?" Cass asked.

"I'm not sure," Blackie began. "But I've seen him in The Donkey with Mo."

"Doing what?"

She smirked. "Them things that go on before a man and woman get together."

"Blackie," Cass said, turning the computer screen away. "Did Officer Garrett and Mo have sex?"

"I don't think he paid her, if that's what you mean," Blackie hedged.

"I'm not interested in whether some of the dancers pick up extra cash, but Chad Garrett is married."

Blackie harrumphed. "Girl, you oughta see the married men come piling in The Donkey. You'd think that sticky ol' sawdust covered floor was some kinda magnet for a wedding band. They can't keep away."

"Why?"

"'Cause the girls are discreet out there. Don't want no problem with the law *or* the wives."

Mitch followed the exchange, frowning. "This Mo, is that Maureen Davidson?"

Blackie nodded, hand still resting in Jerome's.

"That's interesting." Mitch scratched his chin. "Garrett's wife Charlene and Maureen Davidson are stepsisters."

"He was messing with his wife's sister?" asked Blackie.

"Her stepsister, yes. When was the last time you saw Mo and Garrett together?"

Blackie tilted her head. "Maybe early this year. A couple months ago."

"Could someone have seen them?"

"At The Ronkey Donkey?"

"Yes."

"Of course," she snorted. "The lights may be low, but we don't turn them off. And it don't matter whether you rich or poor, fat or thin. *All* men are equal at The Donkey, long as you got folding money."

Cass frowned at Mitch. "What are you thinking?"

"Don't know yet." He stood and stretched. "Blackie, we need to take a ride out to Deuce's Flat with you. Jerome, you're welcome to come if you'd like."

She tightened her grip on Jerome's hand. "Y'all can follow us," he said.

CHAPTER 51

ELAINE UNLOCKED THE COURTHOUSE doors and Hoffner stepped through, followed by the larger than life figure of Arcadia's mayor, David Wayne Rusted. The noise level rose as reporters and their cameramen scrambled for a position at the base of the courthouse steps. Hoffner spotted a young reporter from The Forney Cater, and smiled to himself. He had honored his word and called Obadiah Graham moments earlier, giving the man a few more details than he would share with this group, ensuring Ob got his exclusive for tomorrow morning's paper. Forney County's only newspaper had been steadfast in its support of Hoffner's election campaigns over the years, and opportunities to repay the favor with an exclusive on such a spectacular case were few and far between.

Tom Kado had left his forensic tents in place, ringed with yellow crime scene tape and guarded by sullen officers, threatened to within an inch of their pensions if they so much as breathed too loudly in the vicinity of a sharp-eared reporter. A breeze gusted the tent's fabric, gently snapping the soft sides. The early afternoon sun seemed unnaturally bright, and with the exception of one carefully coiffed woman, the cluster of reporters sported a slick sheen of sweat. The crowd was larger than Hoffner had expected, and he adjusted the angle of his cowboy hat, tilting it to expose more of his strong jaw but leaving his exhausted eyes in shadow. Framed by the elegant old courthouse, he felt more at ease with his position, better able to cope with speaking to the hungry crowd before him. Mayor Rusted shifted at his shoulder, restless for the press conference to begin. Digging his fingers into his trouser pockets to still their trembling, Hoffner waited until the noise and jostling on the lawn abated, and then spoke into the cluster of microphones.

"I'm Bill Hoffner, Forney County's Sheriff and this," he moved his head to the side, "is David Wayne Rusted, Arcadia's mayor. Given the circumstances, this'll be a short one. This morning, at approximately six fourteen, the body of Officer Chad Garrett was discovered on the courthouse lawn. Officer Garrett's death has been ruled a murder by Forney County's Medical Examiner and we are appealing for any witnesses to Chad's last movements to come forward. We believe he died in the early morning hours, sometime after midnight. Officer Garrett was a twenty-two year veteran of the police force and is survived by his wife and parents. His death has shocked the community and the force, and we extend our heartfelt condolences to his family."

The crowd of reporters came to life when he paused, waving notebooks and hands in the air, seeking his attention. He pointed to the coiffed woman, figuring she was from one of the larger stations.

"MaryAnn Jefferson, Channel Seven News, Dallas. Sheriff Hoffner, how was Officer Garrett killed?"

"I can't release that information at this time."

"Is it true he was tortured?"

"Again, I can't release that information."

"Was he killed here, in front of the courthouse?" she asked, gesturing toward the forensic tents.

"No, ma'am, we don't believe he was." He pointed to a narrow man wearing a shirt with an Alma newspaper logo on the breast.

"Jim Long, Sheriff. Was Officer Garrett murdered because he is a police officer? Could someone be targeting your department?"

"None of the evidence points to someone who's targeting police officers, and we have no indication that Officer Garrett's death is related to his job."

"Any leads?"

"We're pursuing several lines of inquiry, but I can't be more specific than that. We are retracing Officer Garrett's steps from about mid-day yesterday. I'd ask anyone who saw him or had contact with him to call my office as soon as possible."

"Who found him?"

"A local citizen."

"Who's that?"

"I'm sure you'll understand, but this person was upset by Officer Garrett's death and has asked to remain anonymous."

The questions continued for several minutes, with reporters requesting details about manner of death and specific evidence, which Sheriff Hoffner refused to discuss. He turned to Mayor Rusted, asking quietly if there was anything he wanted to add. Planning to draw the conference to a close, he turned to the microphones to see the well-groomed reporter from Dallas raising her notebook into the air. He nodded at her.

"One more question. How much confidence should the citizens of Forney County have in your ability to find this man, given the current unsolved murders in the county?"

Hoffner's fingers tightened into fists inside his pockets and he fought to still the surge of irritation that flashed hot across his face. "Ongoing murder investigations are a normal part of police work, Miss Jefferson, as I'm sure you're aware."

"Yes, but the murders of Humberto Gonzalez and another Hispanic man are particularly grisly, are they not?"

"Murders are grisly by nature, Miss Jefferson." Mayor Rusted shifted in his position behind Hoffner's shoulder, but remained silent. "I've lost an officer today, in terrible circumstances. I'm sure you'll appreciate that my energy, and that of every one of my officers, is focused on finding his killer. I do not wish to dilute our efforts by discussing another case at this time."

"I understand," she replied, brushing fair hair back from her forehead with a manicured hand. "But you didn't answer my question. Should your residents feel safe given that two murders are unsolved, a woman who killed her husband this weekend – a Mrs. Scarborough – is still free, that one of your own officers has been brutally murdered in what you called terrible circumstances, and that a…," she checked her notebook, "Mrs. Iris Glenthorne, an elderly woman, has disappeared without a trace?"

Who the hell has been talking to this glitzy bimbo? Hoffner thought, nostrils flaring. "Yes, ma'am, they should. Officer Garrett will be greatly mourned and missed by his family, his colleagues and the residents he served. But the people of Forney County are resilient. And despite today's tragic events and other open investigations, I think you'll find that Forney County is a safe community." He scanned the now quiet crowd, predators evaluating the strength of the prey they stalk. "That's all for now. I'll provide an update this evening."

Hoffner spun on his heel and marched up the courthouse steps, David

Wayne Rusted following in his wake. A collective rustling rose as the reporters reached for cell phones or rushed for vans to file their stories. Elaine was waiting behind the locked doors and quickly opened them, stepping out of his way. Hoffner barreled through. "Any comment?"

"No, sir," she answered, meeting his angry eyes. Elaine had worked as receptionist in the courthouse for years, and Hoffner held no threat for her. She knew his greatest weakness was fear of looking foolish and she'd watched as that fear had just materialized, and on film, no less. He was smarting and looking for someone to take his frustration out on, but it wouldn't be her. "I'll just lock these doors again. Can I get you anything?"

He paused, flustered by Elaine's cool response to his belligerence. "No," he replied gruffly. "I'll be in my office."

Elaine and Mayor Rusted watched him stride through the swinging doors to the police department. "They caught him off guard, didn't they?" she asked.

"'Fraid so," Mayor Rusted answered. He patted Elaine on the shoulder as he headed across the foyer to the opposite corridor leading to his office. He stopped at the matching set of swinging doors, and turned to look at her. "Keep an eye on him and call me, all right?"

Elaine nodded, curls bouncing with the motion.

CHAPTER 52

THE SMALL GROUP WALKED along a path barely wide enough for a compact car and after a short distance came upon the glade Blackie had described. Near the Sabine River the air smelled fresh and was filled with the sounds of rushing water and the screech of squirrels. Narrow tire tracks clearly showed where she had driven into the clearing and parked. Matching tracks ran in the opposite direction.

"How long were you here?" Mitch asked.

"I don't know," Blackie answered, walking close to the river, shivering in spite of the warm afternoon. "I came out about six o'clock. Sat on the hood, took a few sips and," she shrugged, "that was it until I woke up in the mud."

Cass snapped a few photos of the tire tracks and circled the clearing, finding brushy undergrowth damaged in one small area. "You went this way?"

Blackie nodded hesitantly. "I expect so," she answered. "Should I go in?"

"I'll go first. You follow and make sure I'm going the right way." Blackie's eyes bounced to Jerome. "He'll be behind you and Mitch behind him. Ready?"

"Do you think he's still here? The killer?"

"No, but it doesn't hurt to be cautious."

Cass moved into the gap between two trees, pushing brush from her path. Three startled deer lunged from the dense tangle where they were bedded down for the day, leaping gracefully away from the intruders. The small quartet jumped with fright, laughing nervously at their reaction. Cass stopped several times to look ahead for damage to the undergrowth before moving on. The path Blackie had forged last night followed a shallow angle toward the river's bank. In spite of their attempts to move quietly, Cass imagined that they sounded like a herd of buffalo. If anyone was nearby, no doubt they thought an army was approaching.

After no more than fifty yards, her skin prickled and she glimpsed another clearing through the trees. She continued to follow Blackie's path toward the muddy bank near the river, a dank, loamy smell growing with each step. Cass stopped near an area of recently churned muck. Snaking knee and handprints were visible for some distance along the water's edge. She turned to the other woman. "Familiar?"

Blackie's eyes were wide as she pointed toward the clearing. "That's where he was."

"Show me."

Trembling, Blackie followed her to the edge of the clearing, where Cass took several photographs. Barring a fire pit at its center, the entire area had been brushed smooth. Cass supposed pine branches had been used to weave the feathery marks sweeping across the soil. The sharp scent of a campfire hung in the air, providing confirmation that someone had used the clearing recently. Branches from several large trees swung heavy over the area and as Cass's eyes roamed along their length, she swallowed a gasp. Each bore evidence that it had been used to hold heavy burdens in the past, bark rubbed away from the surfaces and weathered gray over time, scraps of rotting rope dangling from their smooth scars. One thick limb, however, showed fresh marks, pale wood shining through an older wound. Her gaze dropped to the ground, finding a darkened patch of soil directly beneath the freshly damaged branch and her stomach contracted at the thought of Garrett's blood soaking that small patch of earth.

"No footprints or tire tracks," she said to Mitch as he joined them. She led his gaze to the damaged limb with her eyes. He blinked once before quickly looking away. Jerome stood behind Blackie; a tall, silent sentinel from which she seemed to draw strength.

Mitch turned to Blackie. "Tell us again what you remember, no matter how strange it seems."

She cleared her throat. "There was a fire," she said, gesturing with her chin. Her eyes jumped to the edge of the clearing. "I think there was a truck parked over there, but I'm not sure. A man was moving between me and the fire, a white man, but he looked skinnier than a man ought to be. He knelt and there was a loud sound, a cry, or a whine." She frowned. "And there was the man on the cross."

"Do you remember where he was?"

"He was –," she began, mind straining to fit her hazy vision into the reality of the clearing. "He was upside down. On a cross, head pointing toward the ground. I think –," she stopped briefly. "He might've been hanging." Her eyes raced along the branches spreading above the open area and flew wide as she found the fresh marks. "Oh my God," she whispered, swaying into Jerome's strong embrace. "It was real."

Mitch flipped open his phone and dialed Kado. He described the scene, asked for instructions from the forensics examiner before they disturbed anything, then snapped the phone shut and looked to Cass. "Kado said to keep out of the clearing. He'll see if he can find Bernie and they'll be here as quick as they can."

"Is this where he was killed? That Officer Garrett?" Blackie asked.

"We need to do some tests, but yes, it might be." Cass watched as the other woman closed her eyes. "Are you all right?"

Blackie straightened from Jerome's arms. "I thought it was just some bad booze. Who would do such a thing?"

"That's what we'll try to find out," Mitch answered. "I know it wasn't easy for you to come to the station Blackie, but I sure am glad that you did."

She looked up at Jerome with a sniff and poked him with her elbow. "When Jerome decides what's gonna be, that's what's gonna be. Some police officers're just not good to my type. But y'all ain't so bad."

Mitch stifled a proud grin. "We'll take you back to your car now, but is there anything else you remember?"

Blackie glanced toward the river and then smiled shyly. "He went to the bathroom out in the woods."

Cass started. "Where?"

"Over there, where I was. I thought he was gonna pee on me."

CHAPTER 53

SHERIFF HOFFNER SLAMMED OPEN his office door, fury coursing through his body. That arrogant reporter. She had no idea what was involved in keeping a community safe. That woman sat on the sidelines, an armchair quarterback. Safe from danger, taking no chances. Happy to sit back and criticize. And how did she find out about Humberto Gonzalez and that mummy from Monday? And old Iris Glenthorne? Good Lord, in all the ruckus about Lenny Scarborough and now Chad Garrett, he'd completely forgotten about her. He ran a hand over his close-cropped white hair, exhaling a slow stream of air. Gossip was their business, those reporters. She must've heard something from one of his officers while she waited for the press conference. He'd rip new assholes across the squad room, just to make sure they knew to keep their mouths shut.

With a glum sigh, Sheriff Hoffner opened his eyes to see a manila folder centered on his desk. He chuckled grimly as he crossed the office and plopped down in his chair. He'd been avoiding this moment, not wanting to know the answer to this particular question. He fidgeted, adjusting the phone to align with the desk, straightening a pencil, opening drawers to look for a fresh pen. Unable to find further reasons for evasion, he jerked the folder open and with a trembling hand, turned the pages toward Officer Hugo Petchard's medical exam.

CHAPTER 54

CASS AND MITCH ITCHED to process the site where a fellow officer had been tortured and murdered. Instead, they obeyed Kado's instructions and contented themselves to circling the clearing's perimeter. They found an overgrown camp trail leading deeper into the forest, away from the river. Slender trees to either side of the narrow path had been crushed beneath a heavy vehicle, very recently, confirming Blackie's belief that she'd seen a pickup the night before. The same feathery pattern in the clearing's dirt was whisked in the sandy path, eradicating tire tracks. They walked on either side of the trail, shoving spiky honey locust branches and willowy limbs from their faces, relishing the cool space beneath the soaring pine trees.

"Mitch?"

"What?"

"What do you think of Tom Kado?"

He shrugged. "Seems on the ball. Knows his stuff. In spite of all the grief he's getting, he'll be good for the department. Why?"

"It's just that," she began, eyes following the trail that wound away from them, "you'd think that Munk would be glad for someone competent to be here."

"Maybe what happened to old Comfrey hit too close to home." The previous forensic examiner was well known for his love of burgers, booze and cigarettes and it was a shock to no one when he dropped dead of a heart attack while processing a crime scene. "Munk could afford to go on a diet."

"He could," she agreed. "What do you think it'll take for him to ease up on Kado?"

"Munk is a smart guy and he loves forensics. I figure he'll warm up to Kado when he sees what kind of work the guy can do. He's just sore right now because he lost a good friend in Comfrey."

They fell into a comfortable silence, following the path for a quarter of a mile until it dumped into a slightly larger trail leading to an isolated fire tower. Disused, its graceful angles were marked with graffiti, the most colorful and poetic blazing from the rust-streaked cab that sat at its top, peeking above the trees. Its external ladder crossed back and forth over the structure's steel frame and at its base rested a blazing red Chevy, driver's door hanging open.

Cautiously, they circled the truck. A key ring was visible on the driver's seat and a Styrofoam cup bearing Chubby's logo sat in a console near the dash. The feathery pattern in the dirt continued beyond the fire tower and disappeared as a cracked blacktop road emerged from the soil. Cass sighed in frustration. The small road would become more civilized and better maintained, eventually joining a county highway. Chances were slim that they would find any evidence along that route.

Mitch flipped open his phone and although the signal was faint, was able to reach Munk. He and Truman were at Chad Garrett's house searching for evidence linking the officer to The Church. Mitch let them know about the truck, instructed them to finish their search and join them down near Deuce's Flat.

"We're close on this one," he told Cass.

"Really?"

"Yeah. We know where Garrett was killed, we've got his truck. Munk and Truman are going through the house. We're bound to turn something up."

"I don't know, Mitch." Her shoulders sagged. "There are no clear tire tracks to work with, here or at the courthouse. The cross and Garrett were both clean." She leaned into the truck's cab for a quick look, careful not to touch anything. "I doubt there's anything useful in here. Unless we learn something when we talk to Mr. Peavey and Mr. Salter, I don't know where we go after that."

Mitch smiled bleakly. "Keep the faith, girl. You never know where help'll come from. Who would've thought an ex-con and a hooker would've gotten us to the spot where Garrett was murdered?"

CHAPTER 55

KADO AND BERNIE STOOD with Cass and Mitch on the edge of the clearing. Bernie's nose was in the air, and he sniffed gently. "Wood smoke, no accelerant, fresh blood. Something heavier. A cooking smell?"

"That nose is a gift, Bernie," Mitch teased.

"And a curse at times Mitchell, believe me," the Englishman answered, digging in a pocket on his vest for a pair of gloves. "Given the fresh marks on that branch, we should focus our attention on the darkened area directly beneath it, and on the fire pit."

"And the urine," Kado added.

Mitch glanced toward the disturbed area of mud where Blackie had hidden. "How are you gonna find it?" he asked as Kado circled the clearing, staying near the edges.

He grimaced. "If he's like most guys, he'll have aimed at something."

"A tree," Mitch chuckled. "Of course."

Kado moved into a squat and shuffled slowly from tree to tree, examining the bark and surrounding area of each, sniffing reluctantly. "I think this is it." He swabbed the bark and carefully lifted several trowels of dirt from around the tree's roots, bagging and tagging each. Pausing, he stooped to examine a leafy fern and hissed with delight.

"What is it?" asked Mitch

"Phlegm," he answered, scraping the sticky substance from the plant into a plastic jar. Holding the evidence out to his side, he made his way back to the others. "For some reason, that's more disgusting than the stuff I usually do."

"What will you do with it?"

"DNA."

"From pee?"

"And snot."

"Jeez, that's scary."

"Kado," interrupted Bernie. "How do you want us to proceed? There are no footprints or tire tracks, but presumably you wish the scene to remain as undisturbed as possible?"

"We'll handle it like we would any other site. Minimum disturbance to process the pit and the area under that branch. Then we'll decide where to go next. Bernie, you and Cass take the fire pit. Mitch and I will work on the soil."

Cass pulled on latex gloves and followed in Bernie's footsteps across the clearing. The ground was a mixture of silt and heavier compost and it readily formed impressions around their soles. "The perpetrator of this crime was quite cautious," stated Bernie.

"How so?"

"It seems he took the trouble to loosen the soil before he swept it, perhaps with a rake, to ensure that pressure from any objects that might dig into the ground would be eradicated. Clever fellow."

Cass knelt beside Bernie. "Looks like he dumped dirt on the fire to put it out."

Bernie grunted in acknowledgement, holding a gloved hand near the rocks circling the pit. "A bit of warmth remains in these stones." Lowering his face over the ashes, he sniffed again. "Definitely no accelerant," he said, bending further to examine the rocks. Pulling a swab from its protective case, he swiped at a stone and held the tip close to smell it. "Some spatter, possibly cooking oil."

Cass popped the top from an evidence bucket and placed a sieve over the opening. "Should I start digging?"

"Small amounts at a time."

"Bernie," Cass asked. "Did you finish with those bones from the other fire pit?"

"Ahh yes," he answered, watching as she scooped ash and spread it over the sieve. He stopped to pluck a hardened glob from the pit with his tweezers, shaking his head as he dropped it into an evidence bag. "I've no idea what that was, but it's silverish and has melted. Yes, I finished with the bones last night. Complete skeletons for two birds, chickens most likely, were in that pit, along with the shattered remains of one human foot."

"Is it from our skeleton?"

"I am reasonably confident, eighty-six percent so if pushed, that the foot came from our elderly gentleman from Arkansas, Mr. Humberto Gonzalez."

Cass chuckled. "Why just eighty-six percent?"

"To allow for error. The bones are from the left foot of an adult, which matches our skeleton. But they were banged up, as if someone had smashed them. Also, I was unable to locate the bones of the small toe, which would either mean that someone snapped the toe off and it wasn't placed into the fire pit, or again, it could provide further confirmation that this foot belonged to our victim."

"Eighty-six percent sounds pretty good to me. Mitch, what do you think?"

"I'll take it. Guess we need to figure out why somebody bothered to saw Humberto Gonzalez's foot off last autumn, keep it all this time, then toss it in a fire along with two whole chickens. Gotta be voodoo."

"You should also be aware that the foot bones had charred flesh on them," Bernie added as he sealed a bucket of ash.

"That means it hadn't decomposed?" Cass asked.

"Correct. The foot has been stored somewhere cool to retard the decomposition process."

"How cool?"

Bernie considered her question. "Fairly cool. A cellar might suffice, but if I were to save a foot for future disposal, I would choose to freeze it."

Mitch and Kado straightened from their kneeling position under the damaged oak branch, brushing dirt from their knees and snapping lids on the buckets of soil. "Most of this is old," Kado said, eyes wandering around the clearing and over the trees. "Hunters probably used this place. They might still."

"Any human blood?"

Kado examined the ground. "If we assume that Garrett hung upside down from this branch, blood from the hole in his head would've drained directly underneath, but there's nothing fresh here." His eyes moved along the circumference of an imaginary circle. "And since his wrists were sliced while he was nailed to that cross, blood from those cuts should've dripped a couple of feet out from where his head hung. But again, there's no sign of blood." Kado knelt near the closest tree, examining its bark and running a swab over its craggy surface. "There's no spray from the wounds, confirming that he was dead when his wrists were cut." His face grew somber as he realized the implications of what he had observed. "Guess you were right, Bernie."

"Yes? About what?"

"That Garrett's blood was collected. There's no spatter here, no –," he shrugged, "– waste."

Bernie nodded, tightening the lid on the last container of ash. "If that's the case, then the buried gentleman found on Monday also had his blood collected. Now that we are reasonably certain that we know how and where Garrett died, we can suppose similar circumstances of death for our buried man. But that raises another question – where was the buried man killed?"

"We don't even know who the guy *is* to begin tracing his movements before death. I don't know how we'd figure out where he died," Mitch said, pulling his gloves off and rubbing his sweaty hands on his jeans.

"Then let's begin at the beginning. How sure can we be that Officer Garrett was killed here?"

"What do you mean?"

"There is no physical evidence that he was actually in this clearing, is there?"

Cass heaved a tired sigh as the weight of Bernie's comment settled in. "We've got loads of circumstantial evidence – his truck is nearby, the fresh marks on the branch, what Blackie saw, someone's urine and phlegm, the swept ground. But you're right, we have nothing of Garrett's that places him here."

"Given the head wounds and cut wrists, chances are that the same person killed both men. If we believe that Garrett was here, it could also be possible that our buried man was killed, or at least his blood was collected, here."

Kado cocked an eyebrow at Bernie. "The only consistent points of contact are the fire, which will have destroyed most evidence; the bloodied soil, which will contain little evidence if the blood was collected; and," he said, looking up the thick trunk, "the branch, where Garrett and the other man could've hung."

"Indeed."

Kado circled the tree and pointed to fresh rub marks around the back of its thick trunk. "Block and tackle?" he asked as Mitch leaned in for a look.

"Maybe," Mitch agreed. "With a pulley system, one person could've got Garrett and that cross up on the tree by themselves."

"Give me a leg up to that first branch," Kado said, tucking a digital camera in his shirt pocket. He scrambled up the gnarled trunk, stretching to reach the lowest limb, and stepped easily from one branch to the next. Reaching the limb that spread over the clearing, he flattened himself along its length, examining the marks across its surface. He pulled the camera from his pocket and snapped several photographs before inching his way farther out.

"What is it?" Mitch called.

"I'm not sure yet," Kado replied, twisting slowly to pull a pair of tweezers and a paper bag from his back pocket. "There are two sets of marks up here. One is raw. The other is fresh, but starting to heal over. And there's," he added, tongue poking from his lips as he extended his arm out with tweezers at the ready, "something stuck on a nail."

He squirmed back along the branch and worked down the tree, landing with a soft thud at its base. Mitch took the bag and tipped the contents into a freshly gloved hand. It was nothing more than a scrap of leather, stained golden from use. "Any good?"

A smile lifted the corners of Kado's mouth as he plucked the fragment from Mitch's palm. "Those are sweat stains. More DNA."

CHAPTER 56

MITCH AND CASS WAITED on the bridge's guardrail, feet dangling over the murky Sabine River. Kado and Bernie had returned to the courthouse to process the meager evidence they'd collected from the killing site. Truman rolled to a stop behind Cass's truck before he and Munk climbed from the cruiser.

"Find anything?" Mitch called.

"Only Garrett's prints in the truck," Munk answered. "Whoever got him lured him away from it first."

Truman climbed over the guardrail and sat next to Cass. "Nothing from Garrett's house, either," he said. "But boy, you should see it. He has some serious entertainment equipment."

Munk nodded. "Something was going on with him. We flipped through his bank statements. He was making cash deposits now and again. Was he moonlighting?"

"Not that I know of." Mitch answered. "Was Charlene working?"

"The only regular deposit was Garrett's paycheck."

"How much cash?"

"A few hundred here, couple thousand there. Seemed to start last year. And," Munk added, "they have some hellacious credit card bills. That woman can spend money."

"Where was it coming from?" Mitch asked.

"We need to ask Charlene. You found the spot where Garrett was killed?"

"We've got a scrap of leather, some ash and a few solids from the fire, lots of dirt soaked with what's probably old blood, and a swab of urine and some snot."

"Kado found pee and boogers?" Munk asked.

"He's pretty thorough." Munk grunted in reply as Mitch continued. "Best chance we've got is if Kado can pull some DNA out of that leather or from the urine. Might get a match through a database. In the meantime, we start on interviews. Can the two of you come with us this afternoon?"

"Sure," Munk said.

"We need to talk to Garrett's wife Charlene, and to Maureen Davidson."

"Why Mo?" Munk asked. Mitch told them what Blackie had said about Garrett spending time at The Ronkey Donkey. Munk chuckled grimly. "You ever met either woman?"

"I know them by sight," Mitch answered.

"Wildcats, both of them. This should be fun. All right, who else?"

"Mr. Peavey and Mr. Salter. Maybe John Earl Shepherd, but I don't know if we'll get anything out of him. I thought Cass and Truman could take the men; you and I can take the women. Sound good?"

"You current on your rabies shots?"

Mitch barked a startled laugh. "Why?"

"With those two girls and what we're gonna ask about, you'll need 'em."

MO DAVIDSON WAS HUDDLED on a tall stool, slouched over the gleaming bar, one arm stretched along its length, the other clutching a tumbler of amber liquid. Tendrils of smoke curled from a cigarette resting in an ashtray near her blonde head. Munk glanced in her direction as he spoke to the bartender, a beefy man, the sleeves of his crisp shirt rolled back to reveal thick patches of hair matting his arms. A long runway dotted with gleaming brass poles sliced through groupings of small tables. Paint blackened windows gaped open to allow fresh air to circulate, and the sawdust scattered over the floor was clean. Fading afternoon sunlight spilled through the still air. The scent of mown grass mingled with the bite of Brasso and a lemony furniture polish.

Munk nodded his thanks as the bartender poured another drink for Mo. He motioned for Mitch to follow and ambled along the bar, one hand gliding over its polished surface. He paused next to the woman and cleared his throat quietly.

"Not today," she mumbled from beneath a heavy hank of hair.

"I'm not here to buy, Mo," Munk replied.

She drew her arm along the bar, skin stuttering against the surface, and scraped the platinum strands back to swivel a bloodshot eye toward them. "Great," she said in greeting. "Pigs."

Munk took the full tumbler from the bartender, lifting it into her line of sight. "We need to talk about Chad Garrett."

She pushed herself abruptly upright, hair swinging over her face with the effort. Snagging the cigarette, she plunged the filter between matted strands toward her lips, and slowly lifted the hair from her face, pushing the heavy weight over her head. The white-blonde wig slithered to the floor, revealing wispy brown curls flattened against her skull. A startlingly attractive woman was revealed, her face a mottled red, angry eyes swollen with tears threatening to tumble down her cheeks.

"What, you think I did it?"

"No. The bartender confirmed that you worked until five this morning. We just need to talk about Chad."

"There's nothing to say, is there? Not anymore."

Munk slid onto the barstool next to her. Mitch sat quietly at a nearby table. "I think there's a lot to say. How long were you involved with him?"

Mo drew an angry drag, chin quivering as she held the smoke deep in her lungs. A blue-white stream flew from her lips as she challenged him. "Who says we were involved?"

"Lots of folks. Bartender for one," Munk said. "The Donkey's not the most discreet place to carry on, and you wouldn't be crying your eyes out over a nobody, would you?"

With a savage thrust, she smashed the remainder of her cigarette into the ashtray. "What happened to him?"

"He was murdered, Mo," Munk said gently.

"I know that. *How* was he murdered?"

"Brutally." Her eyes snapped shut at the word. "We need your help to figure out who. And why."

Mo drained her tumbler in several trembling gulps, replacing it carefully on the bar. She fingered the rim. "I don't know who would do that. Or why."

"Tell us about your relationship."

"I don't want any trouble," she said, wrapping a thin arm around her waist in a defensive gesture.

"We'll keep you out of it as much as we can," Munk replied. "It's obvious that Garrett was important to you. The more you tell us now, the less likely it is that we'll need to involve you any further. Okay?"

"Fat chance," she snorted. "You'll have me on prostitution charges. Got to make your arrest goals, right?" Munk sat impassively, waiting. Finally she nodded once, trancelike. "I don't suppose it matters now. Neither of us meant for it to happen. We've known each other forever, me and Chad. There's always been something between us. I knew, just in the way he looked at me. But he married Charlene. And that was that."

"When did it start?"

"Last spring," she answered slowly. "The attraction never went away, even though he was married. I guess it just got the better of Chad. He showed up out here and we sat in that booth," she lifted her eyes toward one corner of the room, a single tear sliding down her cheek, "and just talked between my sets."

"And then?" Munk prompted.

"And then one day he was waiting outside after my shift ended, and we went back to my apartment." She stood suddenly, bare feet balanced on the brass boot rail, and leaned over the bar's gleaming surface to pluck a handful of paper napkins from a stack. Tight jeans pulled down from her waist, revealing a tempting fraction of red lace. Mitch's eyes widened as he took in her curves – full hips and breasts, trim waist – and he understood Garrett's attraction. She lowered herself back onto the barstool and patted her eyes.

"Were you still seeing each other?"

Mo shook her head, reaching a shaking hand for the new tumbler. "He stopped coming by early this year, all of a sudden."

"Why?"

She lifted a slight shoulder, irritation on her face, voice sharp. "He didn't call to tell me why he was dumping me. I didn't see him again until a few weeks ago, when the family got together. He didn't want to talk to me, but I made him. All he said was that it was better this way, for everybody."

"How did he seem to you?"

They watched as she struggled with a new cigarette, lighter quivering in her hand. Munk took it from her and held it steady. She took a quick drag and released the smoke through her nose. "Nervous."

"How?"

"Always watching, eyes darting all over the place."

"You know who or what he was watching for?"

"No, but he'd never been like that before."

"Did Garrett ever mention anything he was worried about? Any *one* he was worried about?"

She shook her head, eyes filling again. "No, never. We talked a lot about me, what I was doing here, what I'd do when I got older. Chad was sweet. Brought me flowers, talked about the future. For a while I even thought he meant it."

"What about Charlene?"

Mo snorted. "Charlene never knew nothin' about it."

"You sure about that?"

"Chad was scared to death she'd find out. He only came out when he was on night shift, so she wouldn't wonder where he was." She took another drag, chased by a healthy belt from the tumbler. "No," she continued. "Charlene didn't have a clue."

CHAPTER 57

CASS AND TRUMAN PULLED to a stop in front of the Peavey's rambling farmhouse. He and his wife were childless, and old man Peavey was the last of his line. Their wealth was invested in land, oil and cattle, and Cass idly wondered what would happen to it all when they died. She cut the engine and a trio of hounds roused sleepily from their position under the wide arms of a shady elm, baying in greeting as they loped out to the truck.

Truman trotted up the porch steps and rapped on the front door. When he got no answer, they walked around the side of the house and were met by the bleating of a nanny goat straddling a row of early tomato plants. Her twins cavorted among the pansies growing near the house. Old man Peavey emerged from the barn's gloom, pulled a pipe from his mouth and waved. "Grab that goat for me Cass, bring her out here."

"Yes, sir," she hollered. She took hold of a small, curved horn and gently led the goat through the gate to re-join the rest of the herd, Truman following. The kids bounced happily behind their mother to the nearest feeding trough where she butted through the throng to dinner. Cass picked her way around the cow patties and goat droppings, dodging a busy chicken as she and Truman came near the barn.

"That goat'll be the end of me. I don't know how she gets out of the pen, crafty little devil. Eating Mrs. Peavey's garden before it even gets up. Won't have a moment's peace until I sell her," he said, wiping an arm across his wrinkled brow. He was looking older now, back showing a slight hunch, but he still radiated strength and assurance. "Hate to, though. She drops twins every time."

"Is Mrs. Peavey out?" Cass asked, suppressing a smile.

He pulled a cell phone from his grease-smeared overalls and lowered his glasses from his forehead to check the screen. "She's at the church cooking and getting ready for a revival meeting tomorrow evening. Don't know why they try to do a full revival in one night. The opening prayer starts at six o'clock and we usually don't finish until gone midnight. It's hard on the families with young children." He tucked the phone into a pocket and turned toward the barn. "Come inside, it's cooler. I'm working on the tractor. Don't build anything to last nowadays."

Cass looked past him into the dusky barn and caught sight of his ancient John Deere as she followed him into the weathered structure. "This is Officer Scott Truman, Mr. Peavey. We need to ask you a few questions, if we may."

"Hello, son," old man Peavey greeted him, pushing his glasses back up to their perch on his forehead. "What do you need?"

"We're looking into a group called The Church of the True Believer. Have you heard of it?"

"No, can't say as I have," he answered, bending to examine the tractor. Truman stepped to his side and squinted into the engine before pointing into its grease-blackened depths. Old man Peavey nodded and pulled a wrench from a pocket, putting it to use where Truman had pointed. "Why?"

"You've heard about Lenny Scarborough's death?"

"That something to do with this church?"

"We're not sure. But we found some information at his house that links your father to it."

"Daddy?" he asked, standing from the tractor's engine, wrench gripped in one hand. "What are you talking about?"

"We found a book, kind of like a Bible. It had Lenny Scarborough's signature in it, and your father's. Did he belong to a group of men with some sort of religious affiliation?"

Old man Peavey frowned, eyes piercing from beneath hoary eyebrows. "My daddy was messed up in the Klan, that's no secret. But all that ended a long time ago. And in spite of that, he was a good man. He did a lot for the community, Cass. Especially the children. He donated the money for Arcadia's playground."

"Yes, sir," she replied, wondering just how much old man Peavey's father had loved children. She held her ground in spite of an urge to step back. "Your father was very respected. People still talk about the Peaveys and what your family has given Arcadia."

He sniffed, mollified. Truman reached for the wrench and squatted down to work, sneezing at the dust the movement stirred.

Cass continued. "This is a different group. We're not sure what their purpose is, but we believe that they meet in the evenings, about once a month. Your father would have had possession of this book, it's a great big thing, and he might've had a lawyer type briefcase that he kept it in. One of those big rectangles with flaps on the top. Does that sound familiar?"

Peavey grew still, seemingly captivated by the motes dancing in the shaft of sunlight spilling through the open barn door. When he spoke, it was as if from a trance. "Haven't thought about that briefcase in years. Got myself in a world of trouble when I tried to open it once. Daddy tore me up, told me to mind my business, not go digging into other folks'." His eyes narrowed. "And he did go out at night, had a robe he wore. Always thought that was unusual, but what do you say to your daddy about something like that?"

"Does the year 1947 mean anything to you, or would it have been important to your father?"

"Daddy would've been thirty-two that year. I was six. Can't think of anything important about it. Why?"

"That was the date written next to your father's name. We believe that's when he took possession of the book from its previous owner."

"Who else is involved?"

Cass shifted uncomfortably. "I'm not at liberty to say. For the same reason that you might prefer your name, or your father's, not be mentioned to anyone else."

He grunted in acknowledgement and considered his next words before speaking. "Has someone in this group done something wrong?"

"Possibly."

Old man Peavey's mouth dropped open, revealing long teeth. "Not that po-lice officer?"

"Again sir, I can't talk about details."

He shook his head as he bent to watch Truman work, lowering his glasses for a better look. "That's a terrible thing. You two should be careful." He motioned Truman out of the way, grabbed a ball peen hammer from a workbench and whacked the engine, a solid gong vibrating through the old barn. They leaned in again and, satisfied, Truman went back to work. "Don't know what else I can tell you, Cass."

She hesitated. "Did your father have a scar on his rib cage?"

Peavey shrugged. "Never saw him without his clothes on. And I don't remember Mother ever talking about him being hurt."

"When did your father pass, Mr. Peavey?"

"Nineteen hundred and eighty-five. He was seventy years old."

The date clicked in Cass's mind as the year Mr. Shepherd took possession of the book. "What happened to the briefcase after he died?"

"I don't know, to tell the truth." He squinted in thought. "I don't remember seeing it after the funeral. Everything was such a jumble." He paused. "Lots of people were in and out of the house for the wake and again after the burial. I suppose one of them could've taken it."

"Mr. Peavey, we have some indication that membership in this group might be passed from father to son."

His eyebrows shot high on his forehead. "And you think I might be involved?"

Cass shifted. "Well sir, it's a possibility we have to consider."

Old man Peavey wiped his forehead with his arm, smudging it with grease. He turned to the tractor's engine, pointing. "Tighten that for me, son." He watched Truman work for a moment. "Sounds like you're asking me to prove a negative, Cass. I'm not sure how to do that."

"I – uh, would you mind if we took a look at your house, sir?"

He sighed heavily, wiping his hands on red work rag. "For that book and the briefcase?"

She nodded and watched as he pushed his glasses back up on his forehead, pulled a pipe and tobacco pouch from his hip pocket and went through the ritual of lighting it. He puffed quietly, tamping the cooled tobacco with a silverish object, and then topping the pipe up, tamping gently and lighting it again. Truman reached for a different wrench and went to work on the oil filter as the scent of cherry flavored smoke filled the barn. Peavey sighed with satisfaction, yellowed teeth gleaming as he spoke around the pipe's stem.

"You ever change your mind about po-licing, son, you give me a call. You've got a future as a tractor mechanic." He replaced the tobacco pouch and glanced at Cass. "I don't reckon it'll hurt. Ain't nothing in that house to worry about, certainly no briefcase or robe. And Mrs. Peavey just polished the furniture, so she won't mind company. Come on," he said, marching toward the barn door, heavy boots thumping on the tired plank floor. He stopped suddenly, swearing under his breath. "Son, put that wrench down and go get that goat for me. She's in Mrs. Peavey's garden again."

CHAPTER 58

"OF *COURSE* I KNEW he was screwing her. What do I look like, an idiot?" Charlene Garrett stood outside the hospital's service entrance, cigarette dangling from one hand, the other wrapped tightly around her waist. Her designer handbag sat on the ground at her feet, gaping. The scent of rotting food wafted from a nearby dumpster. A clutch of reporters had formed near the hospital's main entrance and the emergency room doors, alert for her first appearance. After clawing her way up from the sedative Grey had given her, she'd demanded to be released. Dr. Ramasubramanian refused, insisting that she stay through the afternoon for observation. But he had relented on her demands for a smoke, perhaps hoping that once the nicotine hit her system she would calm down. Charlene had grabbed her short leather skirt and white t-shirt, yanking them on before stomping angrily through the hospital. "*Everybody* knew he was sleeping with her," she continued, cutting a chilling glance at Mitch. "Almost everybody."

"Did you confront him with it?" he asked.

"Are you asking if I killed my own husband?"

"Did you?"

"I dreamed it a thousand times, but last night I was over in Stanton in the hospital with my sister. She's pregnant. Is that good enough for you?"

"Did you ever confront Chad with what you knew about him and Mo?"

"Didn't have to," she grunted.

"I don't understand."

She flipped her cigarette to the ground, grinding it impatiently with the delicate tip of a sandal. "Here's some free advice. You ever cheat on your wife, wash your dick afterwards. He *stunk* of her. And watch your checkbook. If she's smart, she'll make you pay. Literally."

"I'll keep that in mind," Mitch replied, glancing at Munk as Charlene squatted to dig in her handbag, tapping another cigarette from the pack and flicking open a fancy silver lighter. She was a pretty woman, not voluptuous like her stepsister Mo, but trim and athletic. Muscles rippled in her thighs and calves as she pushed herself into a standing position. "We've been out to the house, Charlene. Where'd you get all that new entertainment equipment?"

She stopped mid-drag, a fog of smoke circling in her open mouth. "Who said you could go in there?"

"We needed to figure out Chad's last movements," Mitch explained. "You were sedated, couldn't give us permission, but we went in as part of the investigation into his death."

"Amazing," she breathed. "Can't believe people are spying on me even after he's dead."

Munk spoke as he and Mitch exchanged a glance. "What do you mean, spying on you?"

"Chad was flipping out the last few months," she answered, tugging her skirt down with one hand. "Kept looking over his shoulder all the time, like somebody was watching him. Even made me nervous, but he wouldn't talk about it. Sometimes I felt like somebody was watching me, but I never saw anybody."

"When did his behavior change?"

"Around Thanksgiving, maybe before. At first, I thought it was because I was spending so much money," she said grimly. "But he didn't even notice. He was too busy with that slut."

"You had extra money going into your bank account Charlene, cash payments. Where'd they come from?"

"How do I know?" she shrugged. "Chad got the money, I just spent it."

"Was he working a second job?" Mitch asked.

"He was too busy trying to slip it into Mo to have time for a second job." She plucked a piece of tobacco from her tongue and inspected it before flicking it away. "I wondered if he was dealing drugs."

"Why?"

"The money. And because he was acting so paranoid. But Chad didn't have the balls for something like that," she answered casually, and Mitch flinched mentally at her words.

"He ever say anything to you about the money?"

She paused, cigarette poised to slip between her lips. "He joked once, about blackmail."

"What about it?"

She sucked in a lungful of smoke and released it in a slow stream. "Just that he had no idea blackmail could be so profitable."

Mitch paused, stunned. "Garrett was blackmailing somebody?"

Charlene shrugged. "The money came from somewhere, didn't it?" Her face brightened. "Hey, when will his life insurance pay out?"

CHAPTER 59

TRUMAN CRANKED THE TRUCK as Cass waved through the windshield to Mr. Peavey. "Nice old man," he commented, sliding the gear into reverse and backing the truck around.

"Mr. Peavey's all right. I can't imagine that he's involved in any of this, but I guess you never know."

"You happy with the search?" Truman asked as he pulled out onto the black top road leading to the highway. They'd examined the house quickly but thoroughly, checking in drawers and the tops of closets, surreptitiously looking for loose floorboards or joins in the walls. Nothing was out of place.

"We did what we could do," she answered, checking the clock on the dash. "It's already six thirty. Man, it's been a long day. It still doesn't seem real."

"Garrett?"

"Yeah."

"I know what you mean. He wasn't that old, and what happened to him sounds bad."

"It was," Cass said, pushing the images of Chad Garrett's body from her mind. "Swing by the bank, Truman, and let's see if Jed Salter is there. I can't imagine that he will be, but it's worth a try."

"If he's not, you want to go by his house?"

Cass sighed. Sheriff Hoffner was reluctant to upset these powerful men, and she didn't want to provoke his ire any further than she already had. "Let me check with Mitch, see what he wants us to do. We could go find John Earl Shepherd and ask about his daddy."

"What about his momma?"

"Whose momma?"

"John Earl's. Isn't she still alive?"

Her face brightened. "Of course, Truman. She's in the same nursing home as Big Momma. Forget the bank," she ordered, flipping her phone open and pushing Mitch's speed dial button. "Hit the Loop and let's go to Heavenly Hills. If we time it right, Marguerite'll feed us leftovers."

———————

MARGUERITE CLUCKED WITH SATISFACTION as Truman held his plate out for another helping of roast beef and mashed potatoes. As Cass had predicted, the chubby chef was more than pleased to have another two mouths to feed. The woman who owned Heavenly Hills Assisted Living Center, Karen Adamson, sat with them, her hands wrapped around a cup of coffee. Marguerite served Truman and turned back to her preparations for the next day's breakfast.

Karen shook her head at Truman's appetite, and smiled at Cass. "You said you wanted to talk to Mrs. Shepherd?"

"About Mr. Shepherd. Is she up to it?"

"I think so. She's still depressed about his death, but it'll do her good to know that people remember him. And it's taking her a while to settle in. She still believes her son will take her back home."

Cass snorted. "John Earl? Not likely."

Karen traced a heavy scar in the table's surface. "Deep down, she knows that. But she's still got hope. Is there anything I can help with?"

"No, but thanks. Should we talk in her room, or maybe out on the porch?"

"Probably her room. Mosquitoes are getting bad outside. I'll go check on her while you finish supper. Does Big Momma know you're here?"

Cass shook her head. "She was getting her bath when we came in. I'll stop and see her when we're done talking to Mrs. Shepherd."

Karen left them as Truman sopped up the remainder of his gravy with a thick chunk of bread. Cass eyed him while he ate. "You could put Mitch to shame," she said. "You'll have to join us one morning, see if you can't out eat him."

"I don't know if I could take on Mitch." Truman burped quietly, patting his trim waist. "Besides, I have to think of my figure. Ready for Mrs. Shepherd?"

———————

CURTAINS WERE DRAWN OVER the large windows in the great room, creating the intimate feel of a family living room. Most of the residents were in their nightclothes, settled in comfortable chairs in front of the wide screen television, canned laughter spilling through the room. In one corner, a stern woman in scrubs spooned pureed food into the toothless mouth of a wrinkled old man.

Mrs. Shepherd was resting in a large recliner when they came to find her. "Hello, Cass dear." She smiled and lifted her cheek for a kiss. "And who is your handsome young friend?"

Cass bent to hug the older woman. "This is Officer Scott Truman. He's helping me with an investigation."

She held a liver spotted hand out to Truman. "Nice to meet you, Officer Truman. Help me up from this chair, won't you? Karen said you'd like to talk about Mr. Shepherd."

"Yes, ma'am," he answered, placing a hand under her elbow to help her to a standing position. She held his arm as she shuffled toward her bedroom. Drawing the curtains and switching on a desk lamp, she settled into a rocking chair, motioning Cass into a worn recliner opposite. The soft smell of her room was a comforting combination of violets and face powder. Truman pulled a straight-backed chair in from the hall and placed it to one side of the room.

"Now," Mrs. Shepherd began, "does this have anything to do with that terrible business today?"

Cass drew a quick breath. "About Officer Garrett?"

"Yes," answered Mrs. Shepherd, shaking her head slowly. "I know Mrs. Garrett. She'll be devastated."

"Yes, ma'am, I imagine she will." She hesitated. "I don't know whether this has anything to do with his death. We've found Mr. Shepherd's signature in a book called *The Church of the True Believer*. Is that familiar to you?"

"Oh yes," she answered dismissively. "Mr. Shepherd belonged to that silly group for a few years."

Cass was stunned into momentary silence. "Could you tell us about it?"

"I don't know that it'll help much, but I'll tell you what little I know." She pushed off with her slippered toes, setting the rocker gently in motion. "Mr. Shepherd was invited to join this 'elite' group sometime in 1985. It sounded perfectly legitimate to me, Christian men with responsible jobs who wanted to do well in the community. I expected it was similar to the Lion's Club. But," she said, rocking slowing, "things changed, rather suddenly. Mr. Shepherd and I had always had an open relationship and suddenly, he became very secretive and a little more... I suppose authoritarian is the right word." Her face colored and she drew her sweater more tightly around her. "I have a university degree and worked in the bank for many years. Mr. Shepherd had always shown me the greatest respect, and viewed our marriage as a partnership, which was rather uncommon in those days."

Cass nodded slowly. "I think I understand. Men tended to go to work, women to stay at home and tend to the house and kids."

"Exactly. Things have come such a long way, my dear, and you are a perfect example of how times have changed." She glanced at Truman. "Not that there's anything wrong with a man wanting to take care of his wife and family, you understand, just that women are capable of more than giving birth and scrubbing toilets."

"Yes, ma'am." Truman shifted in his chair. "I have sisters. I know all about equality."

"It will serve you well one day."

"You said things changed, Mrs. Shepherd," Cass said.

"It happened quickly, his invitation to join and the changes in him. There was some sort of ceremony, and he came home with this new attitude, a locked case, and a row of stitches in his side." Cass's eyes flew briefly to meet Truman's and she saw the shock registered in his face. "I couldn't believe it. Mr. Shepherd had never had a sick day in his life. He was the most fastidious of men, had never been hurt in any way. And here he shows up with this long cut on his body," she pointed to her right side, beneath her arm, "holding out a dirty choir robe and telling me to wash and iron it, and won't discuss what's happened or who did this to him."

"He didn't tell you how he got cut, or who stitched him up?"

She shook her head, voice brittle. "No. And over time, he started preaching to me, quoting Ephesians five, in particular, only it wasn't the Ephesians five that I know. He left words out, and perhaps added words. I'd never heard such nonsense in my life. It was worse after those meetings. And when I challenged him – granted, this was some time later – he lifted his hand to me." Tears filled her eyes with this revelation, and she plucked a tissue from a box on her nightstand. Her voice quavered. "Mr. Shepherd had *never*, in all the years we'd been married, even hinted at violence toward me." She fluttered her tissue at Cass. "Of course, he spanked John Earl. Goodness knows that boy needed it, and probably more. But never had he threatened me."

Cass waited, allowing the older woman to collect herself. "I'm sorry this is so painful, Mrs. Shepherd."

"I tend to cry easier as I get older," she said through a watery smile. "You might find the same. I think I would like a cup of tea. Should we go to the kitchen to finish this sad tale?"

Truman again helped Mrs. Shepherd from her chair and down the hall. Following behind them, Cass stifled a smile. Mrs. Shepherd needed no help to walk and she suspected that the older woman simply enjoyed the attention of a twenty-something year old man. Given Truman's fresh, innocent appearance, Cass supposed she couldn't blame her.

They settled around Marguerite's worktable, mugs of herbal tea steaming in front of them. "Did Mr. Shepherd ever hit you, ma'am?" Truman asked tentatively.

She shook her head, silvery strands gleaming in the overhead light. "I was so appalled when he raised his hand to me the first time; I think he was ashamed of himself. It happened once or twice more, but he never followed through. 'Correction', he called it," she sniffed. "I'm not sure what I would've done if he had hit me."

"How often did Mr. Shepherd meet with them?" Cass asked.

"He would leave the house late in the evenings at least once a month, telling me that he was going to meet some of the boys. Always explaining that it was business-related and taking that old briefcase with him."

"Did you see what he kept inside it?"

She flashed a mischievous smile across the table. "All those years working in the bank taught me how to jimmy open a teller's till, if nothing else. Silly girls were always leaving their keys at home." She took a delicate sip of tea. "I picked the lock once, when Mr. Shepherd was out. There wasn't much inside. Just that choir robe and a heavy book."

"What color was the robe?"

"Plum."

"Mrs. Shepherd, you said that Mr. Shepherd belonged to this group for a few years. He passed not long ago, didn't he?"

"Yes," she answered. "Three years ago this autumn."

"He lived almost twenty years after first joining. Did he quit?"

Mrs. Shepherd nodded. "We had the most terrible fight one night when he was on his way to one of those meetings. I couldn't take it anymore." She lifted her chin in a defiant gesture. "No, I *wouldn't* take it anymore. All the secrecy. Never outright lies, but half-truths about where he'd been and what he'd been doing. The condescension, the subtle threat of violence. I told Mr. Shepherd that he could have his silly group, or he could have me. And that was that."

Cass blinked. "What happened?"

"He quit that night. Took that briefcase with him like he always did, but he didn't bring it back. And when he got home, it was almost like a burden had been lifted from his shoulders." She looked into the gloomy evening settling outside the kitchen's bay window. "I waited up for him, and he didn't come home until almost daybreak. He'd never been away that long before. He sat with me on the sofa and cried."

"Did he tell you why?"

"He only said he was sorry for everything that had happened over the past few years. He promised never to treat me like that again, and asked my forgiveness. I gave it to him, of course. And tried to ask what had happened when he quit. He wouldn't say, other than that he was glad he had quit when he had."

"Do you remember when that was?"

"It was in 1988."

Mentally, Cass linked the date to the year that Lenny Scarborough took possession of the book. "Did you ever learn who else was involved?"

"No. From the little he told me, I understood that it was a small group. *Influential*, he called it," she said, snorting in derision. "I could never be sure, but I believe that the robe came home soiled not only with mud, but with blood on occasion."

"And you never knew why?"

"I asked him about it, telling him I needed to use the right cleanser so the stains wouldn't become permanent," she smiled slyly, "but he didn't believe that for a minute."

"Ma'am, was John Earl ever involved?"

Mrs. Shepherd shook her head abruptly. "Mr. Shepherd valued his reputation too much to involve John Earl in anything that could damage it. He loved his son, but he also knew his weaknesses. And John Earl has many of those," she added, sighing into her mug of tea. She lifted her eyes to Cass and Truman. "I'm afraid this hasn't been much help."

Cass stretched her arm across the table and grasped the older woman's hand. "It's been incredibly helpful, ma'am."

"Could you, I hate to ask, but can you keep Mr. Shepherd's name out of this investigation, whatever it is?"

"We'll do our best," Cass assured her, and then smiled at a rustling in the hall.

Big Momma bustled into the kitchen, cinching a robe around her tiny waist, the soft smell of baby powder trailing her. "I thought I saw that red hair reflected in the window. Come here." The tiny woman wrapped her birdlike arms around Cass, gripping her granddaughter's shoulders tighter than she could've imagined. "I heard about that business down at the courthouse today. Lord have mercy, what's happening around here?"

Cass hugged the fragile woman gently. "This is Officer Scott Truman. He's working the case with Mitch and me. Truman, this is my maternal grandmother. We call her Big Momma."

Big Momma reached to squeeze Mrs. Shepherd's hand then sat down next to the young man, peering intently into his face. "Scott Truman. You're Bernard's boy?"

"Yes, ma'am."

"Good man, Bernard. He'll be right proud of you deciding to become a police officer." She squinted at him. "I see your grandmother in that fair hair and those hazel eyes."

"You know my family?"

Big Momma waved a hand. "Of course. Your grandmother made the best peach cobbler in these parts. She passed on a few years ago, didn't she?"

Truman smiled. "Yes, ma'am. And she did make a good cobbler."

"I never did get her recipe. Shame that. Well," she said, standing abruptly. "I imagine you have business to tend to." She patted Truman on the shoulder and pecked Cass on the cheek. "Come for a visit when you've got time, sugar."

Cass chuckled as her grandmother hurried from the kitchen. "We'd better be going. Mrs. Shepherd, thank you for being so candid. We will do our best to keep Mr. Shepherd's involvement quiet."

"Thank you, dear. That was a very difficult time in our lives. I'm just grateful that they let Mr. Shepherd go the way they did."

"What do you mean?"

"When Mr. Shepherd got home that last time, he was so relieved. I think that's why he cried like he did. He told me that members were required to join for life. And that life meant…" She paused. "Well, life. I had the impression that he was lucky to walk away with his."

CHAPTER 60

CASS GLANCED UP AT a movement reflected in the squad room's windows. Night had fully fallen, only the occasional headlight sweeping around the square or the glare of a reporter's light easing the gloom. She was sprawled at her desk, long legs kicked out to the side, one hand tangled in her mass of fiery hair. *The Church of the True Believer* lay open next to her, and she glanced at it occasionally as she read through the file open on her lap.

"Hey," she called, stretching and enjoying the popping of her spine as Kado and Mitch crossed the room, cups from The Golden Gate Café in their hands. She swept some papers into a pile, clearing a space for the extra coffee Mitch carried. "Heaven," she muttered as she lifted the lid and dumped in cartons of cream, mesmerized as the thick liquid swirled and lost its form to the rich roast. "Did you go out?"

Mitch shook his head. "Elaine called over for some coffee and Sally brought it in. Sounds like The Golden Gate's hopping with reporters tonight."

"She have any gossip?"

"All sorts of stupid theories going around. Satanic rituals, ultra conservative Christian sacrifices and," he snorted, "some reporter from Shreveport suggested a terrorist got hold of Garrett and crucified him."

A laugh tumbled from Cass's lips. "Why on earth would a terrorist target Arcadia for that kind of thing?"

"We *are* in the buckle of the Bible Belt. Maybe he thought some nut was trying to scare all the good Christians around here."

"No alien abduction theories?"

"Not yet," Mitch grinned.

"How's it going?" Cass asked, flashing a glance at Kado over her coffee, disturbed to again feel her stomach flutter when his gray-green eyes touched hers. His lips curved into a brief smile that disappeared into a wide yawn.

"Just sent those samples off for DNA analysis," he answered, handing another cup to Truman and leaning against a nearby desk.

"How long will it take?"

"They've got a rush on it. Should be tomorrow afternoon."

"Anything from the bandage?"

"A few more bits of leather."

"Can you do anything with them?"

"If the DNA matches between the leather from the tree and the spit or urine, I might be able to link that leather to the tiny pieces we found on the cross and in the bandage." Kado yawned again. "If this guy is in the system, and we get a hit, you should be able to tie him to killing Garrett."

Mitch struggled, gave in and yawned as well. "What're you two working on?"

"Truman's typing up our notes from Mr. Peavey and Mrs. Shepherd."

"Anything useful?"

"Truman?" Cass asked.

He finished tapping at the keyboard and saved the document, and then stood to stretch and join them. "Nothing much from Mr. Peavey. He did remember that his daddy had a briefcase like Lenny Scarborough's, but didn't know what happened to it after his father died. He let us search the house but we didn't find anything."

"You don't think he's involved?" Kado asked.

Truman glanced at Cass and shrugged. "He seemed genuinely surprised by the whole thing and only remembered that his father might've been involved when Cass mentioned the briefcase."

"What about Mrs. Shepherd?"

"She gave us the same story that Angie did," Cass answered, pausing to sip her coffee as she told them about the conversation with Mrs. Shepherd. "He had the cut on his chest, got it when he joined that group and wouldn't tell her what happened. Only difference between Lenny and Mr. Shepherd is that Mr. Shepherd quit while he was still alive. From what we can tell by the dates in the book, the others remained members until they died."

"Why did he quit?"

"She put her foot down. Said it was that group or her. Check your notes, Truman," Cass said. "What did she say about the night Mr. Shepherd quit?"

"Mr. Shepherd told her that members were required to join for life, and that life meant life. She thought he was lucky to walk away with his."

"A lifetime commitment," Mitch said, considering. "Do you think John Earl's involved?"

Cass shook her head. "No, and neither did Mrs. Shepherd. Apparently Mr. Shepherd valued his reputation too much to involve John Earl in something so elite. I tend to agree with her, but we can check it out if you want."

Mitch finished his coffee and leaned into the desk opposite, pulling gently on his lower lip. "Let's see what you get from Jed Salter. Are you planning to see him tomorrow?"

"As soon as the bank opens." She yawned and stretched. "Did anybody see how Garrett ended up leaning against the war memorial this morning?"

"No. We have officers lined up to interview the breakfast crowd tomorrow morning."

"Is Sheriff Hoffner still here?"

"He's gone out to see Garrett's wife and his folks."

"Anything happen this afternoon?"

"He held another press conference."

Cass struggled to contain a smile. "How did it go?"

"Not great," Mitch admitted. "There's nothing new to give them, at this point. And there's a woman reporter from Dallas that's giving him a hard time over the two unsolved Hispanic murders, Angie killing Lenny without being arrested, and that missing old woman."

"How did she get hold of all that?"

He shrugged. "Must've heard something out on the lawn. They've been there all day."

"Did you learn anything from Charlene or Mo?"

"Garrett was sleeping with Mo. She said it started sometime last spring but he ended it earlier this year."

"Why?"

"He just told her that it was best for everybody."

"Had Charlene found out?"

"Mo didn't think Charlene knew, even said Garrett was afraid that she'd find out. But Charlene says she knew all along." Cass raised her eyebrows and Mitch shrugged. "Something to do with how he smelled when he came home. I didn't ask too much more. Both of them said Garrett started acting funny around Christmas time. Charlene said he thought somebody was watching him."

"Who?"

"She didn't know, but she felt that way on occasion, as well."

"What about the money?" Truman asked.

"Charlene claims she didn't know where it was coming from, just that she was happy to spend it. Considered it punishment for Garrett's affair with Mo. She did say that Garrett mentioned blackmail to her once, that he had no idea how profitable it could be."

Kado frowned. "Garrett was blackmailing someone?"

"It kinda adds up," Mitch said, "given the unexplained cash hitting his bank account. What else could it be?"

"If he wasn't working on the side," Kado said slowly, "maybe that does make sense." He ran his fingers through his curly black hair. "What if somebody knew about him and Mo? Maybe *he* was being blackmailed."

Cass gasped. "The briefcase."

Kado nodded. "That would explain why Garrett took it. And why he took the inventory of Lenny's house from Elaine's desk Sunday night."

"Maybe he was being blackmailed by someone from The Church?"

Mitch frowned and pulled the diagram Bernie had drawn earlier from beneath the heavy book. "He wasn't part of The Way? The ones who help, but aren't part of The Church?"

Kado shrugged. "I guess he could've been, and might have taken the briefcase and inventory voluntarily. But it's possible that this was simple blackmail. If somebody found out that Garrett was cheating on his wife, they could've used that as leverage. And if one of the goals is to limit the number of people who know about The Church, then blackmail over infidelity is pretty powerful."

Cass yawned again, scraping the papers on her desk into folders and slotting them into her desk. "I can't think straight. Y'all staying?"

Mitch shook his head. "We should all get some rest." He turned toward the window as a camera's flash pulsed blue-white. "I don't think tomorrow's gonna be any better."

CHAPTER 61

THE FRONT DOOR OPENED at the sound of her wheels on the drive, and Abe's lean form was framed against the hall light. He ambled down the porch steps and across the lawn to meet her, wrapping her in a long hug. Cass relaxed into his strong embrace, breathing deeply against his chest, grateful that she smelled no booze on him, letting weariness settle in. Abe pulled back to look at his daughter in the faint glow of the porch light. Her face was drawn and her eyes bright with fatigue.

"You all right?"

"I'm fine. You heard about Chad Garrett?"

He pulled her against his chest, cradling her head with one hand. "It's been on the news all day." Drawing a deep breath, he led her across the damp grass toward the house. "I guess it was pretty bad."

"About as bad as I've seen," she answered as Abe pulled the front door shut behind them.

Bruce came to meet them in the hall, heavy brow drawn in concern. He hugged her briefly. "Had any supper?" he asked.

Cass sniffed the air. "Leftovers out at Heavenly Hills. What's that smell?"

"Made another one of Big Momma's chocolate cakes," he grinned. "This one didn't fall. Come on."

SETTLED AROUND THE KITCHEN table, Cass felt the comfort of home wrap around her, easing the stress from her shoulders. The microwave dinged and Bruce served giant pieces of warm cake while Abe poured milk. At last she allowed images of Garrett's body staked to the cross and later laid out on a cold metal table to flash through her mind, and she trembled before steadying herself. They were incongruous with the

251

familiar room where she now sat, surrounded by people who loved her. *This is what Garrett should be doing*, she thought, *instead of growing colder on that slab in the morgue.* She shook herself mentally and watched her father and brother work.

"Where's Harry?" she asked.

"One of the girls is sick," Abe answered, a gentle chuckle escaping his lips.

"What's wrong?"

"Phoebe had an upset stomach," Bruce answered. "Sounds like Carly don't do vomit, so Harry went over to clean up and put the girls to bed."

"You're joking," Cass said. "She can't clean up after her own kids?"

"Or won't," Bruce agreed, forking a mountain of cake into his mouth. He glanced at their father as he swallowed. "Saw both of Sheriff Hoffner's press conferences today. He didn't come across very well."

"I didn't see either one. What was wrong?"

"He looked nervous, and some reporter caught him off guard about your Arkansas skeleton, another unsolved murder, the Scarborough killing and some missing woman. Dug into him pretty good about whether people should feel safe here."

"Ouch. That points at everybody on the force."

"Yeah, but he's the only one in front of the cameras, isn't he?" Bruce smirked.

Cass grinned involuntarily. "He always wanted the limelight."

"Any reporters talked to you?"

"Nope, and that's just fine with me."

Abe cleared his throat. "Cass, are you in any danger from whoever killed that officer?"

"What do you mean?"

"Is somebody targeting the police?"

Cass sat back in her chair, fingers dancing in the condensation on her milk glass. "I don't think so. We know what happened to Garrett, just not who did it. There's nothing to indicate that this is the start of something bigger."

He nodded at her reply. "You still sleep with your gun by the bed?"

"Of course. I've always got it with me."

"Did you run with it this morning?"

"No," she answered slowly, reading the concern on her father's face. "But I will tomorrow."

———————

HIS HEADLIGHTS PIERCED THE curtain of night in the backyard and Mitch started as they swept across a pale form. He pulled into the carport and cut the engine. Breathing deeply to try and force the smells of death from his lungs, he opened the pickup's door, closed it quietly behind him, and walked across the grass to where Darla sat. She was in an Adirondack recliner, wrapped in a throw from the couch, head tilted back to drink in the night, lanky greyhound sprawled on the ground beside her.

Without looking up, she patted the empty recliner next to her. Mitch squatted and stroked the dog's silky ears, then sat next to his wife. Her dark hair held a faint gleam and her skin was washed with alabaster moonlight. He was struck again by her beauty, by how fortunate he was to have her in his life. Taking her hand in his, he tilted his head back and gazed up at the sky.

"I hate days like today." Darla's voice was soft, almost a whisper. "I heard it on KOIL, around seven o'clock this morning. They didn't say who had been hurt, or how. Just that an officer was down on the courthouse lawn."

Mitch dug his fingers into his eye sockets, realizing that he hadn't spoken to her at all today. "I should've called."

"I got through to Elaine at about eight o'clock and she told me it was Chad Garrett." He turned to look at her as her voice caught in her throat. "I feel so terrible."

"I know."

"No, you don't. My God, I'm so awful," she said, swiping at her cheeks. He looked closer and realized that her face was puffy and the tip of her nose reddened. "I was so relieved to hear somebody else's name come out of her mouth. Anybody else's name. I was desperate to know it wasn't you."

Mitch sat up and pulled his wife out of her chair and onto his lap. Her normally soft form was stiff against his chest. "I'm sorry, Darla. I can't believe I was so stupid. It didn't even cross my mind to call. Things were so…" He drew in a deep breath of her citrusy scent and dug his fingers into her silky hair. "It was bad. And things just moved so fast after that, I didn't think to call."

She pulled back to look at him, running a wrist under her nose and snuffling loudly. Her eyes blazed. "Don't you ever do that to me again. It's bad enough imagining what could happen every time you leave the house. But when a cop is injured, Mitch Stone, you call. You call and tell me you're safe."

He met her gaze with steady eyes. "I will. I promise."

She sank against him. "How is Charlene holding up? I heard she collapsed on the courthouse lawn and they took her to the hospital."

"I think maybe their relationship was on the rocks. Munk and I talked to her this afternoon, and she seemed to be doing okay." Mitch thought about the hardness in Charlene Garrett's eyes, compared it to the grief he had seen in Mo Davidson's face, and felt a stab of pity for Chad. "It might not hit her until later, you know?"

Darla shivered. Her throw had fallen to the ground when Mitch pulled her onto his lap and he picked it up and clumsily spread it over her. "Better?"

She nodded against his chest. "I heard it was brutal, the way Chad was killed. What happened?

Mitch closed his eyes, wishing he could banish from his mind the image of Chad Garrett's pale body nailed to that cross. "Are you sure you want to know?"

"It was that bad?"

"Yeah, it was."

She hesitated only a moment. "Tell me. I'd rather hear it from you."

And so he did. Describing how Goober had found Garrett's body on the courthouse lawn early this morning; the presence of a hole in Garrett's head, similar to that in the skull of the buried man discovered Tuesday morning; and Grey and Bernie's assumptions about the purpose of those holes.

Darla pushed up and placed her hand on Mitch's chest for support. Her face was twisted in disgust. "To *drain* his blood? What for?"

Mitch explained the paintings in *The Church of the True Believer* and the conclusions they had drawn about the use of blood as part of an initiation.

He also described the organization chart Bernie drew from the description Cass had found in the book.

"Dear Lord. Who did it? Who killed Chad?"

"We don't know. Tom Kado, the new forensics guy, thinks he got some DNA from the site where Chad was killed." He told her how Blackie Cochran had led them to the isolated clearing. "He said the lab will put a rush on it because a cop was killed."

"But Mitch, why Chad?"

"We don't know yet."

She shivered again, in spite of the blanket and the warmth of his body against hers. "Whatever the reason, a murder that violent can only mean more bad things to come, can't it?"

CHAPTER 62

Wednesday

DEACON CRONUS OPENED HIS eyes as the sun's first rays touched the window shade, fat face cherubic in the pale glow. His wife's breathing remained deep and even, and he enjoyed the ripple of delight that tickled his body at the thought of tonight's ceremony. He knew he should try to get back to sleep. Today would be long as he finished his preparations and made his way out to The Sanctuary, but his mind nibbled insistently at the items on his list and at last he surrendered. He rolled his bulk gently out of bed and groped with his toes for his slippers before trundling quietly to the kitchen, flipping the pot's switch and anticipating the aroma of brewing coffee.

Everything he needed was in the shed. His briefcase with robe and book, of course; the ladle, cup and platter carved years ago from the same giant oak tree that contributed The Sanctuary's roof beams; the heavy rope, grown stiff from sweat and blood; and the knife. He planned to call Pastor Luke today and let him know that he would work from home, and then spend the rest of the day in the shed. The knife had to be sharpened, the rope checked to ensure it hadn't begun to fray, and the wooden implements cleaned. He also needed to study the ceremony itself, the Celebration of Illumination, remembering its order, its cadence, as it had been many years since the Celebration had been held.

And perhaps he should think through how best to handle the new initiate, Officer Hugo Petchard. Although Greg Newton had been instructed to give Petchard a sense of this evening's events, no doubt he would be unsettled and perhaps a bit panicked when he understood the initiation rites. It had been a few years since a newcomer had joined The Church. Cronus clearly remembered the circumstances surrounding that event, and his mind contracted briefly at the horror of what had happened. Greg Newton's initiation had been a subdued affair, sorrow over the death of Jed Salter's oldest son Nathanial the week before casting dark shadows over the event. No one could have anticipated Nathanial's reaction to the ritual. Although he had participated and completed the sacred acts as was expected of him, Jed Salter had been among the living dead during Newton's ceremony. Deacon Cronus nodded to himself, staring blankly through the kitchen window into the quiet backyard. Petchard and his reaction were worth some consideration.

Cronus had already purchased the wine and wondered again at the possibility of mixing blood with it to move one step closer to purifying the communion ritual. But he was unsure about the health risks associated with drinking human blood, and decided to wait until the next meeting to allow time for research. Washing the initiate and The Brethren in the blood would have to do. He blinked, snapping his fingers. And then there was the loaf. He mustn't forget the loaf.

The coffee pot burped and sputtered and he reached for a heavy mug, filling it and adding a heavy dollop of fresh cream and two sugars, praising the Lord for His generosity and blessings. He couldn't think of a better start to the day.

CHAPTER 63

CASS ROLLED HER SHOULDERS and rubbed a palm across her left rib cage as Wilbur Pettigrew read through the statement once again before signing it. He pushed the paper silently to his brother, who scrawled his signature and scooted the statement toward Cass.

"Is that it?" Wallace asked.

"Yes, sir. Thanks very much for helping Angie like this."

"Seems like we're helping her more by going out to the place again, working with the cows," he replied, glancing at his brother. Wilbur blushed scarlet and focused on the table as he fingered the hook on his overalls.

"I'm sure she appreciates everything," she said, sliding from the booth and waggling her empty mug at Stan as the Rolling Stones swore never to be beasts of burden. Wilbur's hand trembled as he lifted his mug. Cass smiled. "I'll let you know if there's anything else. Have a good morning."

Stan sauntered over to her booth with the coffee pot, glancing up as a knot of people pushed through the café's door. "And comedy hour begins," he muttered under his breath.

"Who are they?" asked Cass.

"Damn reporters. Picking over every negative event in Arcadia's history, trying to make us out to be devil worshipping freaks."

"Oh come on," she scoffed, spreading the Dallas newspaper across the table and scanning the headlines. "It can't be that bad."

"Hmph," he snorted as the door opened again and Goober stepped inside, quickly sidling away from the reporters. "Wait until they find out you're a detective. They won't stop hounding you until they've got photos, family history and a stool sample. I'll get your breakfast to go. Pancakes all right?"

Cass nodded, shifting herself and the newspaper so Goober could slip into the booth beside her. "For Mitch, too. And a few coffees to go."

Stan grabbed a clean mug and filled it with steaming coffee, leaning into the booth and lowering his voice as he placed it in front of Goober. "You all right?"

"Yeah," he answered, his muddy brown eyes bleary. "Can I have scrambled eggs?"

"With pancakes?"

"And double bacon."

"Done," Stan replied, motioning Sally from the kitchen to come help with the reporters.

Cass warmed her fingers around the hot mug and turned sideways. Goober was a gentle soul, sweet natured and eager to help. But he looked weary today, the part in his thinning brown hair a little crooked, a patch of shadow on his jaw where his razor had skipped, and his shirt buttons misaligned. *No wonder*, she thought. *He really had seen a ghost when he found Chad Garrett on the courthouse lawn.*

"Why are you in town so early?" she asked.

He picked at the sleep in the corner of one eye. "Bad dreams."

"About yesterday?"

"That was awful, Cass."

"It was," she agreed, pouring cream and spooning sugar into his coffee. "But it was a good thing you found him that early. If it hadn't been for you, more people would've seen Officer Garrett like that, and think how upsetting that would've been for his family."

"It's just scary." He glanced at her. "With the vampires and all."

"Tell you what. If you're scared like that again, call me. You can spend the night at our house."

"Really?"

"Yeah," she grinned. "But be careful what you wish for. If my dad finds out how good your garden looks, he's likely to put you to work in ours."

He frowned. "You haven't planted any vegetables, have you?"

Not since my mom died twenty-one years ago, she thought. "Nope, not yet."

"Well, that's good, 'cause it's too early to plant. The Easter snap is still coming and it'll bring a frost."

"See what I mean? You know all the gardening stuff," she said. "Hey, I meant to ask, why were you out at Possum Creek on Saturday night?"

"Huh?"

"You called in to report the fire out there, right?"

"But I was anonymous. They ain't supposed to tell nobody," he replied seriously.

"When you call in anonymously you're not supposed to give your name. That's what anonymous means, that *nobody* knows who's calling."

"Oh," he said, watching his coffee swirl in the mug. "I ran out of potato chips and was coming back to town for some."

"I thought you were eating more salad, trying to be healthy."

"I am, but I've had the munchies lately."

Cass smiled in acknowledgement of the universal complaint about diets and then hesitated, watching the play of emotions across his face. "Goober, they said you saw a devil Saturday night. Is that right?"

A shiver ran through his body. "Yeah."

"Did you get a good look at him?"

Goober shook his head.

"Then how did you know it was a devil?"

"There was all this fire and it looked like," he leaned close and whispered, "hell."

"So you couldn't identify him?"

"Nope. I don't know any devils."

Sally huffed past, rolling her eyes at Cass and flipping through her order book. The reporters and their entourage had picked a table near the door and were busy arranging equipment in a pile against one wall. Mitch strode in and headed straight across the café to Cass, turning to look at the sullen group.

"Who're they?" he asked, hooking a thumb over his shoulder as he slid into the booth. "Hey Goob."

"Hey Mitch."

"Stan says they're reporters," Cass answered, peeking inside the newspaper again. "Gonna get us breakfast to go."

"Why?"

She shrugged and reached to massage her ribs. "Something about stool samples. Thought it'd be best if we weren't around too long."

"What's wrong with your side?" Mitch asked, pulling back from the table as Sally plopped a steaming mug in front of him.

"Wore my shoulder holster when I ran this morning. I figured it wouldn't bang around as much as if I had it on my hip."

"You ran with your gun?" Goober asked, eyes wide.

"Daddy wanted me to. He's worried about what happened to Chad Garrett."

"I think that's smart," Goober replied, slurping coffee.

"Me, too," Mitch said, eyeing the newspaper. "You done with that?"

Cass scooted it across the table to him.

"Dallas? Why don't you read the local paper?"

Because I'd know if anybody wearing a Richard Nixon mask attacked a woman in Forney County, she thought, *but chances are that he'll strike again in Dallas.* "I just like to keep up with what's going on in the big city."

Goober jumped as the café door thumped open and Officer Hugo Petchard sauntered inside. He stood, hands on his hips, eyes wandering the room, smile playing at the corner of his mouth. The group of reporters stopped talking, taking in his uniform, sniffing for a story. Spotting Cass and Mitch, he swaggered to their booth.

"Didn't expect to find Arcadia's dynamic detective duo here in The Golden Gate," he sneered, cutting his eyes at Goober. "Or our intellectual elite."

"What're you doing up so early, Petchard?" asked Cass.

"Sheriff Hoffner needed officers to pull an early shift and interview the folks who come in for breakfast. I volunteered," he preened.

"Anything to brown that nose, huh?" Mitch said as Goober giggled into his mug.

"I ain't sucking up," Petchard said, crossing his arms across his skinny chest. "Sheriff said he needed all able-bodied men helping to chase down Garrett's killer."

"And you're the ablest body we got?" Cass chuckled. "Lord help us all. How'd it go out at the elementary school yesterday? Them kindergarteners give you any trouble?"

He flushed and swiveled to survey the room. "Crossing guard's an important job. Kids get hurt if folks aren't careful."

"Course they do," Cass cooed. "Happens all the time in big towns like Arcadia."

Petchard's flush deepened. "I'll start with them," he said, thrusting his chin toward the Pettigrew brothers. "Know 'em?"

"Wilbur and Wallace Pettigrew," Cass answered, nudging Goober from the booth and reaching for the paper bags Stan brought. "Real chatty. Knock yourself out."

―――――――――

MITCH OPENED HIS TAKEOUT container and grimaced. "Sally put oats in these pancakes. She knows I hate that." He poked at his breakfast with a finger. "Darla must've called her. She was pretty mad at me last night."

"Why?" Cass asked.

"I didn't call."

Her expression was blank for a moment, then comprehension dawned in her eyes. "After we found Chad Garrett?"

He nodded, face rueful.

"She was scared it was you?"

"Apparently so. She gave me an earful and new marching orders."

Cass chuckled. "And they include?"

"Calling her any time a cop gets a hangnail. Especially if it's bad enough that she'll hear about it on the news."

"Sounds reasonable. Lord only knows why, but that wife of yours does love you," Cass said. "The oats in your pancakes are just her way of trying to keep your cholesterol low."

"Nothing wrong with my cholesterol," he groused. "And these aren't as good as the ones made with plain flour."

"They taste just like the others, and they're better for you. Look," Cass said, tilting a paper bag toward him, "Sally gave you extra syrup to make up for the oats."

"Well," he sniffed, peeling the foil top from the container, "I guess anything tastes good with maple syrup. But doesn't extra syrup defeat the purpose of the oats?"

"Quit whining and eat," Cass grinned, glancing at the squad room clock and reaching for her notebook. "I'll try to catch Mr. Salter before the bank gets too busy."

"You want some company?" Mitch asked as he forked a dripping bite of pancake into his mouth.

She shook her head. "I talked to Rose last night and she wasn't sure he'd be in this morning. I'll give you a call if anything comes up."

"All right. I'll see you back over here. I want to talk to the sheriff about whether Petchard has a scar."

CHAPTER 64

CASS STEPPED INTO THE bank's cool, dark interior, smiling her thanks at the security guard. The regular humming and gentle thunking of the escalator accompanied her to the main floor, where the soft purring of cash machines and teller gossip completed the bank's early morning symphony. She crossed the lobby's polished floor and smiled as she approached the President's office.

"Good morning, Rose."

"Hi Cass," replied the young secretary with a wave of her letter opener. She poked its point into her blonde bob and scratched delicately. A large pile of unopened mail was scattered across her desk. "What awful business with Chad Garrett, God rest his soul. I saw Sheriff Hoffner on television last night. Poor man looks absolutely strung out. Those reporters are nasty people. How's the investigation?"

"It's coming along," Cass replied.

"I guess it's best to keep things hush-hush right now, huh?" Rose said knowingly. "Are you trying to catch Mr. Salter this morning?"

"Will he be in?"

Rose glanced over her shoulder at the dark corner office before turning back to Cass. She selected a letter from the pile and sliced through its flap. "Nope," she answered, pulling a conference flyer from the envelope, placing it in a tray marked 'Non-Urgent', and reaching for a second envelope. "Sometimes after a trip he'll work from home." She sliced through the flap, extracted and examined the contents, and then tossed the single sheet into a pile marked 'Customer Service'. She reached for the next letter and Cass frowned as she saw the cream colored envelope that lay beneath.

"I can ask him to call you," Rose said, slicing and opening.

"I do need to speak to him," Cass answered as Rose tossed the bill into a pile and grabbed the cream envelope. "But in person."

Rose examined the engraved lettering, confusion drawing her sharply penciled brows together. "No return address," she murmured. "And no stamp. How odd." She shrugged and flipped it over, tugging the letter opener through the heavy flap. Her eyebrows jumped as she read the small card before sliding it partly into the envelope and onto a tray marked 'Personal'. Cass glanced at the lettering. From this angle, she could see 'The Sanctuary' engraved at the bottom of the card and her heart leapt as her mind struggled with the itch of familiarity the words brought. Rose reached out to finger the envelope before plucking it from the tray and dropping it in an oversized handbag at her feet.

"Better take that to him with the rest of his stuff. I'm sorry honey, what did you say?" Rose asked as she continued opening the mail.

"Just that I need to see Mr. Salter in person," Cass replied, glancing around the secretary's alcove to find a way to distract her. "Does he have any appointments this afternoon?"

"No, his calendar is clear –." She stopped abruptly, shaking her head and rolling back from her desk. "Let me go check his office. He's terrible about writing appointments down in there. I keep telling him that I have to know what he's got scheduled so I don't double book him. Hang on, Cass," she sighed, digging in a desk drawer and extracting a set of keys, "I'll be right back."

Rose stood and tugged at her short skirt before teetering to the dark office on four-inch high wedges. Cass's booted feet twinged in protest. As the door swung open and the fluorescent light stuttered to life, Cass stepped to the side of the desk and peered over its edge. Rose's purse gaped near a chair leg and the envelope lay slotted between a bulging wallet and a partially open compact. She plucked two tissues from the box on Rose's desk and swooped down to reach for the heavy envelope, jerking upright and in front of the desk as the other woman called out from the President's office. Cass balled up the tissues and jammed them into her pockets to hide her trembling fingers.

"Nothing on his blotter. I'm not even sure he'll be in today," she said, tottering to her desk. She settled into her chair and picked up the letter opener, cocking her head at Cass. "You okay?"

A cold sweat beaded Cass's forehead as an image of Ernie Munk holding a similar card flashed across her brain. He had been crouched in

Lenny Scarborough's study, beside the tall, orderly row of books. She was desperate to see the letter in Rose's handbag – and equally desperate to get back to the evidence room and check out the card Munk had found. Rose's expression changed from curiosity to worry.

"Cass, honey?"

"I'm fine," she said, running a hand over her hair. "It's just been a long few days."

"Can I get you anything? Some water?"

"No, that's all right. I'm keeping you from Mr. Salter's mail. Did you say you take stuff to his house?"

"If he's working from home. That man," she shook her head, glancing at a stack of neatly labeled folders balanced precariously on a nearby chair, "he's always busy. I take files and reports, correspondence. Why, can I tell him something for you?"

Glancing into the corner office, she spotted a photograph of a silver-haired man dressed in running clothes. He had the slender, lightly muscled body of a runner and his arms were raised in victory as he broke the tape to win a marathon. A family portrait was nailed to the wall above – a tight-lipped wife, adolescent son and a slender teenage girl. Cass cleared her throat. "Is that Mr. Salter's family?"

Rose swiveled to follow her glance. "His wife and kids. He had an older son," she added, lowering her voice as she spun back around. "Died a few years ago. He was only nineteen, but such a mature boy."

"What happened?"

"Dropped dead while he was out camping. They said it was a weak heart." She opened another envelope and glanced up at Cass. "The death of a child could destroy a man. And his family. Mr. Salter though, he said his faith gave him strength. Even drew his family closer together. You see them now and they can hardly take their eyes off of Mr. Salter." Rose checked her nail polish before opening another envelope. "He's even closer to his second son. That boy worships the ground his father walks on. A real charmer, that kid. His daughter's quiet, very shy. They turn that way when they're teenagers, don't they?"

"I suppose so," answered Cass, thinking that they become shy when they've been abused. "I'll just check in with you later, to see if Mr. Salter has come in, if that would be all right."

"That'd be fine. You have a good day now. I know you're busy, but try to get some rest. You look washed out, honey."

CHAPTER 65

OFFICER HUGO PETCHARD PEEKED into the squad room to see who was around. He resisted scratching the last bandage on his thigh, grateful that the slight burns had healed so quickly. Officer Truman was typing at a computer and Mitch Stone sat sprawled behind his desk, phone cradled between shoulder and ear. That smart-ass Detective Martinez stood at the coffee machine, filling his mug while he chatted with the new forensics guy, Tom Kado. Squinting through the small window in the door, he couldn't see the whole room, but this wasn't a bad audience.

He started as Cass pushed past him into the squad room, trailing a plastic evidence bag. She frowned at him before swiveling to smile at Kado. "Elaine let me into the cage for this. It's from Lenny Scarborough's."

Petchard sauntered in behind her, making a point of checking her curves as she wove between desks. She wore snug fitting trousers and a wine colored button down blouse that should have hidden her figure but instead emphasized her femininity. "I'll take this view any day," he leered, snapping to a halt when he spotted Sheriff Hoffner leaning against the coffee counter with Kado and Martinez. Color drained from Hoffner's face and Petchard flushed under his piercing stare.

"What was that?" Hoffner growled.

"Uh, nothing sir," Petchard squeaked, holding up his notebook. "I've got some info –"

"I asked you a question, Officer. What view will you take any day? You weren't commenting on Detective Elliot's figure, were you?" Hoffner asked, advancing toward Petchard with a measured stride.

Petchard took an involuntary step backward, sweat prickling his underarms. "I uh," he began, looking around the room for help. Mitch was still on the phone but had glanced up at the commotion, while Truman, Kado and Martinez were trying to suppress their pleasure at his discomfort. Cass put her notebook down and faced him, bracing a hip against her desk.

His audience had turned against him, and Petchard decided that honesty might be the best policy. "Yes, sir, I was. But she was taunting me, the way she was walking, she wanted me to notice."

Hoffner's eyes narrowed as he drew nose to nose with Petchard. "Looked like she was just walking across the room to me. You unable to control yourself when a woman is around?"

"No, sir," Petchard answered, sucking in a waft of the sheriff's coffee stained breath and wondering why the man was so worked up. "I apologize sir, what I said was inappropriate."

"What you said was sexual harassment, Officer Petchard," Hoffner replied, leaning into a nearby desk and crossing his hairy arms over his chest.

"No – no it wasn't, sir," Petchard stammered, unsure of the consequences for sexual harassment. "I was just teasing Cass. We've got that kind of relationship. It was just banter."

Hoffner glanced across the room at Cass. "I didn't realize you had a relationship with Detective Elliot at all."

Petchard blushed again. "Not that kind of relationship, sir. Just, you know, jokey."

"I don't find what you said *jokey* at all, Officer Petchard," Hoffner retorted, drawing himself up to his full height. "It's insulting. Now, since this is the first I've seen of this behavior, we'll consider it a first offence, and this is a verbal warning. I don't expect to hear a peep out of you with regards to sexual or racial abuse. And just to make sure the point finds its way home, you can pick up an extra shift tonight."

Petchard paled. "I can't, sir."

"You *can't*, Officer Petchard?" Hoffner bellowed. "You *can't* follow an order?"

"I – I've got plans tonight, sir. Plans that I can't change."

"What plans?"

"Just personal plans, sir," Petchard replied, sweat beading his upper lip. He fought the urge to wipe it away. "I'll take the extra shift tomorrow night. I'll do two nights of extra shifts, but I can't work tonight."

Hoffner let him squirm before reaching down to align a telephone sitting on an empty desk. "Two nights. Get it on the duty log. And adjust your behavior. Understood?"

"Yes, sir," he said, fighting the urge to salute as the sheriff nodded at Kado and Martinez before striding from the room. Truman locked the screen on his computer and hoisted a stack of files. He smiled as he passed Petchard and shouldered his way through the squad room door. Petchard relaxed into the nearest chair, dragging his arm over his upper lip. Kado and Martinez resumed their discussion, but not before Petchard noticed Martinez smirk in his direction.

Mitch straightened his head from its cocked position and cleared his throat. "You say you have some information?"

Petchard glanced down at his hands, amazed to see his notebook still clutched in one of them. "Yeah. I need some coffee first," he said, pushing up from the chair and moving quietly to the coffee pot.

Kado opened the cupboard door and Martinez smiled as Petchard reached for a mug. "What?" he demanded.

"I'm just pleased to see you this morning, that's all," Martinez replied.

"Whatever," Petchard mumbled, suppressing the urge to comment on the likelihood that Martinez had unnatural relations with goats. *Cabrón* indeed. He added a healthy dose of sugar to his coffee and wove back through the desks. Mitch nudged a chair out and he sat, grimacing gratefully. He reached to open his notebook and Mitch stopped him.

"You got something to say to Cass?"

He jerked his head up. "Huh?"

"You gonna apologize?"

"What for?"

"What you said earlier, you idiot."

"Jeez," he breathed, huffing back in his chair. "Fine. If that's what it takes for somebody to listen to what I've got about Garrett, then yes. Cass, I apologize for what I said."

"Thanks, that's real nice of you," she replied. "What'd you find out?"

He flipped his notebook open and scanned one page. "One of the farmers at The Coffee Shop said he saw Garrett parked on the highway Monday morning. He was sitting in his patrol car talking on a cell phone, and the farmer said he looked pretty shook up."

"How did he come to see Garrett out there?" Mitch asked.

"He was taking a cow to the vet. He's not comfortable with his trailer hitch, so he was in the slow lane, driving below the speed limit. He checked to see who was in the patrol car as he drove past, and watched in his rearview mirror. Said he was just curious."

"Did he know Garrett?"

"Nope," Petchard replied, gently touching his thigh. "Saw his picture on the news last night. Didn't think anything about seeing him parked on the side of the road until I started asking questions this morning."

Mitch studied Petchard. "It's no big deal for an officer out on patrol to use his cell. Why does this matter?"

"I've ridden with Garrett a few times, and I've never known him to make personal calls while he was on duty. And I figured that if he was talking to somebody and was upset, it would probably be his wife. I called Charlene to find out if she talked to Garrett on Monday and to see if we could have his phone."

"What did she say?" Mitch asked, frowning.

"That's the funny part," Petchard said, proud of his initiative. "She said Garrett didn't have a cell phone."

"What do you mean?" Cass asked, pushing a loose strand of hair behind her ear and leaning forward in her chair. Petchard fought not to look down the front of her blouse, gaping gently at her neck.

"Charlene said he wouldn't have one, claimed he was worried about cancer. So maybe he borrowed it."

"From who?" Mitch asked.

"Dunno." Petchard slapped his notebook closed and stood, hitching up his trousers. "That's what you get paid the big bucks for, ain't it?"

———————

CASS WATCHED PETCHARD STROLL from the room. "Why wouldn't Garrett want his wife to know he had a cell phone?"

"If I was cheating on Darla, I'd have a phone she didn't know about so I could talk to my women without getting busted."

"More than one woman?"

"Might as well dream big."

"What if Garrett took copies of the Lenny Scarborough inventory from Elaine's desk on Sunday night?" She stretched her booted feet under the desk. "Maybe he wasn't using the phone to talk to a girlfriend. Maybe he was using it to talk to whoever wanted the Scarborough inventory."

He frowned. "Somebody from The Church?"

"Who else would care what we found at Lenny's house?"

"I guess we need that phone."

"We can search for phones in his name. Want me to start an affidavit?"

"Truman can do it and take it to Sammy and then to Judge Shackleford."

Cass snapped her fingers. "Hey, Petchard's scar. Does he have one?"

"A very old one. Some childhood injury. What did you find out from Salter?" Mitch asked, reaching for his desk phone.

Cass drew a deep breath and released a long sigh as Mitch called Elaine, asking for Truman. He turned back to her, sipping as she looked over her notes. "He wasn't there," she began. "But Rose was opening his mail. There was a letter addressed to Mr. Salter, with no stamp or return address."

"What was it?"

"Remember that card Munk found out at the Scarborough's house?" Cass lifted a plastic evidence bag from her desk and handed it to Mitch. "Lenny's invitation. The paper and the engraving are the same on Salter's card."

"Are you sure it's the same thing? It could be an invitation to a charity ball or something."

"All I saw on Salter's card was 'The Sanctuary'."

"Lenny's has a specific date on it. Did Salter's?"

"I tried to distract Rose, but she didn't give me enough time." Her face flushed with excitement. "Rose is taking a load of files out to his house today. She slipped the letter into her handbag for him."

"What are you thinking?"

"That we need that card, today."

Mitch's lips puckered. "Why today?"

"I think it's too convenient that Lenny Scarborough dies on Sunday and on Wednesday morning an invitation – if that's what it is – turns up for someone whose grandfather was a member of The Church."

"We don't have enough for a warrant."

"We don't need one. Not yet," she answered, leaning forward and lowering her voice. "I think we can catch all of them, Mitch. They need to replace Lenny, and this ritual, this Celebration of Illumination, is how they do it."

"What are you suggesting?"

"That I go see Jed Salter and get a look at that card, without tipping him off that we know he's part of The Church."

"How are you gonna do that? Walk in and ask him for it?"

"I have no idea. We might have to get a warrant. But this is the best lead, the only lead, into Lenny Scarborough's child abuse and Chad Garrett's death that we've got right now."

CHAPTER 66

"I CANNOT BELIEVE JED Salter would abuse a child," stated Sheriff Hoffner, rubbing his fists into his eyes. He was pale and drawn this morning, his starched shirt creased as if he'd slept in it. Kado and Munk were slouched against the coffee counter in the conference room, and Truman straddled a chair in the corner. "We've got nothing but a card that looks like the one from Lenny Scarborough's," he arched a bushy brow at Cass and she fought the surge of anger at his mocking tone, "and the words 'The Sanctuary'. We don't even know what this sanctuary is. It could be a church."

"Truman looked through the phone book," Mitch answered wearily, sitting in a chair at the conference room table, "just in case there's a ranch or a business called The Sanctuary, but nothing has that name around here."

"Can't we follow him?" Cass asked, cheeks coloring as all heads swiveled toward her.

"You want to set a tail on the president of Arcadia's biggest bank?" Hoffner barked.

"If he's part of this group, I do. There's a chance that someone from The Church was involved in Garrett's death, to collect his blood for this Celebration of Illumination." She glanced at Mitch before continuing to speak in a low voice. "It seems silly to me that they put the invitation in writing. Why not just call each other? It's a game to them. They think nobody knows about The Church, nobody's smart enough to figure it out, and they're comfortable taking the risk that somebody will see one of those invitations and make the connection."

Sheriff Hoffner shook his head, blue eyes flat. "Do you realize what a nightmare this will be if you're wrong about Jed Salter's involvement? Rather than sneaking around trying to find this invitation in his house, I think we should go speak to the man like the upstanding member of this community he is. That was good enough for Peavey, why isn't it good enough for Salter?"

"Peavey didn't have an invitation sitting on his desk. The card was addressed to Jed Salter. There's no reason he would've received it, unless he's a member of The Church. We have to try and get a look at that card at his house." She shrugged. "If there's nothing to it, we walk away and Salter's none the wiser. If we can't find it, we have to decide whether to ask for a warrant. But if this Celebration of Illumination really is a blood ritual, and there's a date on the invitation, we could catch all the men involved."

"And do what with them?" Hoffner demanded, frustration blooming in blotches on his cheeks. "Let's say there is a group of men out there tromping around the woods, wearing robes and chanting at one another. And let's say people as important as Jed Salter are involved. So we catch them at it, dancing around a fire, what do we charge them with? Acting funny?"

"Maybe murder," Munk answered quietly, sliding into a chair. "Maybe child abuse or rape."

Hoffner scowled and shifted his glance to Kado. "You got enough evidence to pin either crime on anybody?"

Kado sighed and sat next to Munk. "Not yet, no. But DNA is coming back today from the site where Officer Garrett was killed. There are the photographs of men gang raping those girls. When we have somebody in custody, we can compare characteristics. We've also got pictures of what we believe is a deer camp. If we can figure out who is involved, we can check their properties and try to match the interiors to those photos."

"And maybe, sir," young Truman piped up, "the girls will be out there with them."

Hoffner stared at him, bug-eyed. "You think this Celebration of Illumination, or whatever, involves child abuse?"

"I don't know, sir. But from what I understand about pedophiles, once they get a taste for abusing a child, that desire becomes unquenchable." He continued once the room remained silent, digesting what he'd said. "If they meet every month, like Angie, Mr. Peavey and Mrs. Shepherd told us, it makes sense that they'd want the girls with them as often as possible."

"Good Lord," Sheriff Hoffner mumbled.

"Sir, I know you're worried about how this could be perceived if –,"

Munk began.

"Of *course* I'm worried about how this will be perceived!" he shouted, leaning into the table. Crimson blotches blossomed on his cheeks. "I've got an officer as good as ritually murdered on the courthouse lawn and we have no idea who killed him, but our suspect list includes the president of our biggest bank; reporters are camped out front, sticking a microphone in front of anybody who happens to be breathing; *and* they're digging into every move we make on this case, those two open murders, Lenny Scarborough's death and poor old Iris Glenthorne, God help us all," he roared, spit flying across the table. A bulging purple vein throbbed at his temple, and his breathing grew labored. "We need something *solid*, people. Something unquestionable. Or every one of us is out of a job."

The room was stunned into silence, people thrown back in their chairs by the force of Hoffner's furious outburst. Mitch cleared his throat. "We have something semi-solid, sir."

Hoffner frowned.

"The card Cass saw with Salter's name on it. That's it. That's our lead."

CHAPTER 67

MITCH REACHED FOR A paper towel and patted his face dry as he stood. "Sorry for barging in on you, but Sheriff Hoffner's a little emotional at the moment."

"The election?" Grey asked, pulling off a pair of latex gloves.

Kado leaned into the counter, smoothing both hands over his dark, curly hair. "And how Chad Garrett's murder will impact the outcome."

In the corner, Porky Rivers looked up from the batch of instruments he was sorting, diamond studs dotting the edge of one ear glittering in the overhead light. "Ain't no savin' the sheriff now," he volunteered. "Not according to my granny and aunties."

"He doesn't have the support of the black community?" Cass asked, watching Bernie pull a magnifying lens over his face and lean close to examine a length of bone.

"He *did*," Porky corrected, "but all this violence got everybody shook up. They're worried that if the sheriff can't protect his own officers and that old lady, not to mention those two other dudes, how safe are they?"

"The election is over a year away, and people have short memories. Even so, I'm afraid a lot of folks around here will think the same thing," Grey commented. "And while Hoffner's not perfect, who else would even want the job?"

"Not me," Mitch said. "What's up with the bones?"

The medical examiner folded his lanky frame and leaned down next to Bernie. "What do you see?"

"Nothing, which makes my suppositions slightly more fantastic."

"What are you thinking?"

"I've little fact to work with, but I'll share my hypothesis, if that would be of use," Bernie answered, pulling the magnifying glass from his head and straightening from the table. Grey nodded for him to continue. "These are Humberto Gonzalez's bones, the man whose skeleton was found last week, whose son reported him missing in Arkansas and who has now gone missing himself. I think the murders are linked, and Mr. Gonzalez's blood was drained from his body, as was that of Officer Garrett and the buried body we discovered on Monday."

"Why?" asked Kado.

"I see a progression among the three cases," Bernie answered, lifting a skull from the table. "Mr. Gonzalez died first – he was placed outside last autumn and his body wasted away to skeleton by the time it was discovered last week. He was shot in the head. Although useful for killing, a bullet wound to the back of the head would not be efficient for draining and collecting blood. However," he continued, replacing the skull and lifting a long bone, "Mr. Gonzalez's foot was cut from his leg, and I believe this was done to drain the blood from his body."

"Why do you think that, Bernie?"

He shrugged, replacing the bone on the table. "All of this is just speculation. But, I can find no other logical explanation as to why the foot would have been removed. If someone wanted to conceal the identity of a victim, he would remove the hands, head and any other unique physical characteristics from the body. But if we think of the three killings as a progression, our murderer's approach to draining the blood from Mr. Gonzalez would have been awkward and frustrating," he continued, snapping closed a pocket on his vest. "If Mr. Gonzalez was suspended so that his legs hung downward, tilting the body to try and drain all of the blood through one leg would have been difficult. And think of the blood remaining in the other leg that our killer was most likely unable to recover. Poor planning, very poor. We know the buried man was killed *after* Mr. Gonzalez, and his wounds show more efficiency in terms of gathering blood. He was strangled and a small hole drilled in the top of his head, meaning less loss of blood through an open wound, and good drainage. Our killer also progresses to using the arms, making an effective vertical slash up the radial arteries. And then there's Officer Garrett."

"But with the exception of having his balls cut off," Mitch said, "Garrett's wounds were just like the buried man's, right?"

"Yes, although I believe removal of the testicles was simply theatrical, designed to send a message to someone." He cut his eyes at Cass. "You perhaps, my dear, given your exchange with Officer Petchard the previous evening. An improvement on efficiency is that we're fairly certain Officer Garrett was alive when the hole was drilled in his head. Additionally, the killer used a larger drill bit."

Grey massaged his earlobe. "He wanted Garrett's heart to do the work of pushing blood from the body for as long as possible."

"Yes. And I believe he waited until Garrett was dead to cut the forearms, ensuring that no blood was lost through arterial spray."

"That's cold," Mitch breathed, glancing at Porky as the younger man shivered.

"But effective," Bernie commented. "As I said, this is all speculation on my part. But the timeline of the deaths and the improving efficiency of blood drainage lead me to believe this is an accurate hypothesis."

"Bernie," Cass said, "you may have something with all this. Blackie Cochran described the person she saw at Chad Garrett's murder scene as a devil made of light. Goober said the same thing about whoever started the fire at the hot house Saturday night. And Deacon Cronus talked about Humberto Gonzalez being terrified by a *diablo de luz* by the river bottom. Could all three of them have seen the same person?"

"You think Humberto Gonzalez saw something he shouldn't have? A murder or something?" Mitch asked.

"Or maybe just a ritual that The Church enacts. If they operate out of a deer camp, they likely have a campfire. If so, that would explain the motive for his death and link it to Garrett's and the buried man's."

"I hate to say it," Mitch said, "but is this a serial killer?"

Grey leaned into the counter next to Porky and tugged again at his earlobe. Bernie pulled a rolling stool from beneath a table and sat, twirling gently as he spoke. "Perhaps the term serial killer does fit. His behavior is escalating, but if he's killing to collect blood for a ceremony, then his activities may simply be opportunistic."

"Man Bernie, how can you be so… intellectual about all this?"

Bernie fidgeted with a flap on his safari vest, pondering the question. "It's not that I'm immune to the horror of what has happened to these men, Mitchell. I simply believe that I can best serve them in death by analyzing how they died in an attempt to help you find their killer."

"I wasn't criticizing," Mitch explained. "You've just got an ability to see bizarre little pieces and pull them together."

"Cheers," Bernie said as Grey chuckled. "There is one more thing I need to share with you."

"What's that?"

Porky handed Bernie two small sections of bone, each in a glass jar with evidence tags and chain of custody paperwork started. They rattled dully when he passed them to Kado. "Our buried man from Monday is a Mongoloid male, approximately thirty-five years of age. Although based only on my instincts, I believe DNA testing will confirm that he is Mr. Gonzalez's son."

CHAPTER 68

SHERIFF HOFFNER LOWERED HIMSELF into his chair, completely drained. Instinctively, he adjusted his blotter and straightened the phone to align with the edge of his desk. He'd been up most of the night, responding to complaints about reporters camped out on lawns. They started at Chad Garrett's house in Mole Hill, realized that nobody was home and moved to his parent's house. Garrett's father had the decency to call in and ask whether he was within his rights to shoot the news crews trampling his wife's flowers, and before Hoffner could get an officer to the house to hustle the press off, the elder Garrett had come out on the porch with a shot gun cradled across his chest. The news vans had cleared off posthaste, cameramen filming through open side doors as they sped away.

After leaving the Garrett family, they'd found the dead officer's wife, Charlene, at her mother's wood frame house. The reporters refused polite requests to leave the grieving widow alone, pulling lights from their vans and cracking open an ice chest full of beer as the evening wore on. The family tried to do the right thing, pulling down window shades and locking doors, ignoring the reporters and their crews. But when one pony tailed, tattooed, and very drunk cameraman had knocked on the door after midnight, belching his request to use the bathroom, Charlene wasn't so polite as to call the police. She started off by hurling a heavy glass paperweight at the unfortunate cameraman, whose forehead needed three stitches where she'd hit him. Still slightly dopey from another tranquilizer Dr. Ramasubramanian insisted she take before going to bed, she slid right past irritated and moved directly to pissed off when she looked beyond the bleeding cameraman to the troops settled on her mother's front lawn. She'd grabbed one of her brother's ancient hickory baseball bats and started down the front porch steps, fierce determination gleaming in her eyes and the porch light streaming through her flimsy nightgown, providing an appealing silhouette as she stormed the biggest man in the group. Thankfully, the neighbors had called the police department fifteen minutes earlier due to the general ruckus and Charlene was stopped in her tracks by one of Chad's colleagues from patrol, who grabbed the bat mid-swing and tossed the furious woman over his shoulder before carrying her up the porch steps and inside the house.

His partner cleared the press from the front lawn and provided directions to the nearest hospital for the battered cameraman. He also threatened the press with grievous bodily harm if a complaint was filed over the accuracy of Charlene's throwing arm or if any of the images filmed this evening ended up on television or in the papers. Unfortunately, it was a picture of that snarling officer and his comments, quoted with accuracy thanks to a live microphone, which ended up on the front page of the Alma paper this morning. Followed by a nice shot of Charlene's scantily clad bottom as the other officer had hoisted her over his shoulder.

A different contingent had shown up at Mayor David Wayne Rusted's home, looking for an interview. Hoffner had managed to get two patrol cars out quickly to drive them away. He'd heard on the scanner about an upset over on Whiskey Bend involving the press and a few of the locals. But that was somebody else's county and he had only wished more of the reporters were headed that way. He dug his fingers into his eye sockets, seeking to ease their burning. Lord, but if they didn't look like a bunch of illiterate rednecks over this whole thing.

In spite of being bruised and hung-over, the reporters had been back on the courthouse lawn first thing this morning, waiting for a statement. He needed something to tell them, anything, to avoid looking like an incompetent buffoon. If only Mitch would get his act together and find something useful –. Hoffner stopped mid-thought and steepled his fingers under his chin. If Mitch was so sure that this card Cass saw was an invitation, maybe he could do something to help. He couldn't give the press specifics, but just a taste. Maybe nudge the killer or killers, and score a few points with the press.

Sheriff Hoffner reached for his coffee and settled in to think through his press strategy as the phone buzzed. He reached for the handset, grimacing in anticipation. "Yes?"

"Mayor Rusted is calling," Elaine chirped. "Can I put him through?"

"Go on," he said, hearing the click of the transfer. "David Wayne, what can I do for you?"

"When are you gonna talk to these reporters, Bill? They keep ringing my office."

Sheriff Hoffner wondered whether it was wise to carry on with this idea without speaking to his detectives. He squirmed in his chair, letting the needs of his battered ego wrestle against the twinge in his gut that told him to hold off for now.

"Bill?" Mayor Rusted demanded, and Hoffner's ego won.

"Funny you should call just now. I've had some news from the detectives on the case and I'm ready to talk to the press about it. Just a teaser, of course. But this should keep them quiet for a while."

"You got a breakthrough?"

"I hate to do this to you, David Wayne, but you know I can't talk about the details. Let's just say that we've found a lead that could unlock the case pretty quick."

"What kind of lead?"

"Just something we've picked up in the last few hours, a connection we've made based on a piece of paper and a text from another case. There might even be a link between the two investigations. But that's really all I can say for now," Hoffner answered, allowing himself a small smile. He genuinely liked the amiable David Wayne Rusted, but he liked having an edge over the man even better. "I'm making an unscheduled appearance just now, to let the press know how serious we think this lead is. Should scare Chad Garrett's killer once he gets wind of it. Might force him into a mistake." Hoffner aligned the pen and pencil on his desk, the feeling of control calming his worn nerves. "You want to join me? It'd be good for both of us to be seen on this one."

Mayor Rusted drew in a sharp breath. "I'll be right there."

Hoffner pulled a snowy handkerchief from his pocket and wiped the handset before replacing it in the cradle, satisfied.

IN THE SOUTH WING of the courthouse, Mayor Rusted also pulled a handkerchief from his pocket, using it to mop the sickly sheen of sweat from his face as he opened a cell phone.

"Where are you?" he barked when the phone was answered.

"Mayor?" the old man asked, balancing his phone between his jaw and shoulder as he leaned in to look at the old tractor.

"Are you near a television?"

"I'm out in the barn. What's happening?"

"Hoffner's making a statement."

"What about?"

"Some new evidence they've just come across. He sounds serious, said it could unlock the whole case."

"What is it?"

"He wouldn't tell me," Mayor Rusted answered, voice nearing a whine. "But he mentioned a text they'd found in another case."

He wiped his hands with a red rag. "You think he's talking about Lenny Scarborough's book?"

"That's the only text they've picked up in the last few days, as far as I know." He drew a shaky breath. "But there's no link between The Church and Officer Garrett's death. I mean, whatever Hoffner thinks he's come up with, he's way off base with this."

The old man sucked his teeth, wondering what the sheriff thought was going on, and whether it was time to intervene. Technically, Mayor Rusted was right: Garrett's death had nothing to do with The Church. They would use his blood in the ceremony tonight, along with that from the two wetbacks, but it was only the Deacon who knew they were drawing closer and closer to the purity of Jesus' symbolism by moving from animal blood to human. And the Deacon didn't know with certainty where the blood had come from, even though he probably had suspicions.

"When's this press conference?" the old man grunted into the phone.

"Now. I'll stall him as long as I can."

CHAPTER 69

THE THREE OFFICERS GLANCED up as the squad room door swung open. Kado, Mitch and Cass headed for the coffee bar. "No luck on the phones," Truman informed them as Officer Greg Newton pushed his glasses up on his nose and leaned back from checking Truman's computer screen. Munk stretched his pudgy arms over the paperwork scattered across his desk.

"Nothing?" Kado asked, straddling a chair at a nearby desk.

"Nope. Probably one of those anonymous pay-as-you-go phones. But guess who the biggest purchasers of those types of phones are?"

Mitch looked up from the cup of coffee he was pouring and shrugged. "Who?"

"Alongside drug dealers, it's farmers and ranchers."

"How'd you figure that out?"

Munk looked up from his paperwork, exchanging a grin with Newton as Truman answered. The tips of his ears turned crimson as he cleared his throat. "Newton and I visited the phone shops. One of the girls out on the Loop was chatty. She said that men like Peavey and Craven come in and buy ten or fifteen cheap phones at a time."

"Why?" Cass asked, stirring her coffee.

"They told her it's for their crew bosses. They seem to be working several crews at one time, especially when the cows are calving and again when it's time to get the hay in and the calves to sale. Said those guys can't seem to hold onto a phone, so they find the cheapest option out there. If a phone gets lost or broken, they haven't lost much money."

"You think there's some link with Garrett?"

Truman shrugged. "Not necessarily. Their explanations make sense. And if it's Peavey and Craven buying phones, both of them are ranchers, so that makes it less suspicious."

Mitch grunted. "Can we get any records from that phone shop, about which phones each of them bought and the calls made from them?"

"Not without a warrant for the specific phone number."

"All right. Officer Newton, you ready to get back out on patrol?"

"Yes, sir," he answered, turning a smiling face toward Truman. "Thanks for letting me help. It was more interesting than riding around in a patrol car all day. And let me know if you decide to call that girl from the phone shop."

Truman blushed and waved Newton from the room.

Mitch watched him leave and glanced around the squad room, making sure they were alone. "Munk, Truman, I've got something else I need you to work on. If this card Cass saw turns out to be an invitation, and if she gets a look at it, how do we follow Salter to this Celebration, whenever it is?"

"Sir?" Truman asked.

"We can't use patrol cars. He knows everybody on the force, and most likely knows our cars. As bank president, he probably financed most of them," Mitch said. "How do we follow him without being noticed?"

"He lives near downtown, doesn't he?" Munk asked, shuffling papers together and closing his folder.

"In one of those big houses in Live Oak Park."

"Shouldn't be too hard, as long as he goes from home to work, or around town. Could be more difficult if he heads out of town."

"Jeez," sighed Truman, settling behind his computer. "It's not like we can stake him out down there, is it? Those rich folks will notice somebody hanging around."

"And we can't use just anybody from the force," Kado said. "If Chad Garrett was involved, it's possible that another officer could be."

"Let me work on it," Munk said. "I'll figure it out."

"If we find an invitation at the Salter house, we should follow Peavey, as well," Cass said quietly.

"Are you really worried about him?" Mitch asked.

She hesitated and glanced at Truman, who shrugged. "No. But his father's name was in *The Church of the True Believer*. The easiest way to be sure he isn't involved is to follow him on the night of the Celebration."

"All right. This could get complicated from a logistics perspective. I'll talk to the Sheriff about bringing in backup from Watuga County. That'll give us fresh faces and support if things get nasty during this Celebration."

"You think it might?" Truman asked.

"It could go either way. This Church may just meet out in the woods to grill steaks and shoot their mouths off. But it could be more sinister than that. If they're into something bad…" Mitch nodded. "It could get bad."

Truman drew a deep breath. "You're right."

"I'll bet The Sanctuary is somewhere down in the bottoms," Cass said.

"Why?"

"It has to be near the river. Angie told us about sandy mud, and so did Mrs. Shepherd. Then there are the pictures – the interior of that place looks pretty rough, and we think there's a rack of deer antlers in one of the shots. If it is a deer camp, it makes sense that it'd be down that way." Cass stood and moved to a map of Forney County on the wall, jabbing pins at specific locations. "We found Humberto Gonzalez's skeleton here last week, close to where the hot house burned," she said, pushing two red pins near Possum Creek. Drawing her finger along the map, she marked two more places. "Oscar Muckleroy found the buried man out near Logan's Quarters and Garrett was killed here, by Deuce's Flat."

"What about the courthouse?" Truman asked. "Where Garrett's body was found?"

Cass shook her head. "That was more for effect, to shock us. I don't think it has much connection to why someone has killed these three men and drained their blood."

"I agree," said Kado, standing and jabbing a yellow pin at the map. "That's where the Grove boys found Gonzalez's foot, in the fire pit."

Mitch leaned his chair back on two legs, hooking his thumbs in his belt loops. "If you draw lines connecting those four sites, there is an area," he said, pointing at the map, "near Deuce's Flat that might be a good choice."

"There are a few deer camps down there," Truman volunteered. "Don't know who owns them, but we could take a ride out there today to see what's going on."

"I don't think that's a good idea," Cass said.

"Why?" Mitch asked.

She leaned into the wall next to the map, eyeing it from the side. "If we're going to figure out what this is all about, and who's involved, we need to catch them out there, together. If we start checking out deer camps today, we may scare them off."

A clatter from outside drew her attention, and the metal blinds rattled as Cass flipped them up to look out over the back parking lot. Reporters were hoisting equipment to their shoulders and rushing around the corner, toward the front of the courthouse. Fighting a surge of fear, she strode across the squad room to manually flip on the TV and find a station from Stanton. The courthouse came into view, its sandstone façade a brilliant white in the noontime sun. The Stanton news camera was situated directly in front of the steps, angling slightly up at the courthouse doors. A sweating reporter was jostled but continued to speak solemnly into a large red microphone as other news crews fought for position next to him.

"What is it?" Mitch demanded, stretching in his chair to peer around her at the screen as the others crowded in for a better view.

"He's about to give a statement," she said, paling, "and the banner along the bottom says that there's new evidence in Garrett's death." Cass moved back and they saw Sheriff Hoffner framed in the cool shadows of the courthouse portico, microphones stretched toward him. Mayor David Wayne Rusted stood behind and slightly beside the sheriff, his large frame halved by the television camera.

Elaine pushed through the squad room doors, her pretty heart-shaped face flushed from her dash through the courthouse. "Thank goodness you're watching," she said, slumping into a chair.

"What's he doing?" Kado asked, eyes curious as they focused on the screen.

Elaine shook her head, curls swinging. "He came strutting through the lobby like a rooster, crowing about new evidence."

"He's not gonna talk about that invitation, is he?" Munk gasped.

Mitch's chair screeched as he shoved back from his desk, standing as Hoffner began to speak. Truman found the remote and inched the volume up.

"– a brief statement," Hoffner began, "about the investigation into Officer Chad Garrett's death." In contrast to the exhaustion he must feel, he stood upright, his posture erect and chin lifted. His flat gaze rested on the forensic tents still covering the war memorial before flicking across the crowd of reporters squinting up at him. "We've come across a new piece of evidence this morning, indicating that Officer Garrett was the target of what we believe to be a religious cult based in the area." A collective gasp rose from the crowd, and he raised one hand to quiet them. "We're following up this lead now, and hope to have members of this cult rounded up and in custody within the next few days."

Across the county, the old man settled into his recliner and squinted at the television, wondering what Bill Hoffner was up to. His wife bustled between his chair and the screen, fussing that he'd worn his work boots into the house, and he twisted to get a clear view of the press conference, shooing her out of his way.

Arms waved wildly as Hoffner pointed to the back of the crowd. "Jim Long, Sheriff, Alma News. Can you describe this evidence?"

"We've had officers out canvassing members of the public, asking if they saw Officer Garrett on Monday, helping us trace his movements," he answered, shifting his weight to one leg. "Through those efforts, we have an eyewitness who observed Officer Garrett behaving in an unusual manner on Monday afternoon. We'll continue canvassing throughout the day, and would ask anyone to come forward if they have information they believe is relevant to the investigation."

"What behavior was observed?"

"I can't go into details at this time," Hoffner answered, avoiding the pretty reporter from Dallas as he took another question.

"Scott Evans, Shreveport Daily. How does this sighting lead you to conclude that a cult is operating in the area? What was Garrett doing?"

"All I can say at this time is that Officer Garrett was behaving in a manner inconsistent with his duties."

"That's vague, Sheriff. I mean, what was he doing? Was it illegal?"

"No, not illegal, just unusual for Chad Garrett."

"Was he a member of the cult you referred to?"

"We have no reason to believe that Officer Garrett belonged to the cult. To the contrary. He was an upstanding officer and a fine member of the community."

"But you said he was targeted by this cult. Was he killed in retribution for something? Was this a message?"

"No, no," Hoffner huffed. "We have no evidence to tell us that Officer Garrett's murder was in retribution for anything, or that there was any message intended."

"But if you believe he was targeted, you must know *why* he was killed, correct?"

"We have ideas on motive, yes, but it's too soon to share that information with you," he said, a childish feeling of superiority winging through his system.

"Do your ideas stem from the fact that Officer Garrett was crucified?" the woman reporter from Dallas shouted, golden hair glistening in the sun.

Hoffner recoiled from her question. They would've made all the connections they needed from yesterday to confirm Garrett's manner of death, and in spite of the casual way in which she asked the question, it was still shocking to hear the word spoken in public. It somehow demeaned the agony Chad Garrett must have suffered. "The manner of his death and the nature of his wounds helped us make the connection, yes."

"Oh no," Kado breathed in the squad room. "Does he know what he's doing?"

On the courthouse lawn, the reporter from Dallas continued shouting questions. "His death was ritualistic?"

Hoffner sighed patiently. "Ma'am, I can't comment on those details."

She nodded briskly, glancing at her notes. "If Officer Garrett's behavior on Monday afternoon was unusual, and you're sure he wasn't a member of this cult you've found in Forney County, then what's the link between Garrett and the cult?"

Hands clutched over his head, Mitch mouthed a quiet stream of obscenities as he paced the squad room, eyes fixed on the television.

Mayor Rusted frowned from his position behind Sheriff Hoffner's shoulder, genuinely confused. Sweat broke out on Hoffner's forehead and he resisted the urge to wipe it away. "Miss Jefferson, wasn't it?"

"Yes, Sheriff, MaryAnn Jefferson, Channel Seven News, Dallas. I'm sure the public is anxious to help you find Officer Garrett's killer. But to help them help you, could you clarify please, what this evidence is that tells you there's a," she checked her notes again, "religious cult based here in Forney County?"

Sheriff Hoffner blinked rapidly, his bowels contracting as he realized he'd painted himself into a corner. A very uncomfortable corner. And in a moment of panic driven by self-preservation, words flew from his mouth. "We have a text...," he began, his voice drowned out by shouted questions.

Mayor Rusted shifted his bulk slightly, eyes darting between Hoffner and the histrionic press contingent.

In the squad room, Kado's mouth fell open and Cass lowered her head into her hands. Across the county, the old man hooted with laughter, causing his wife to poke her head into the living room.

"What is it?" she asked.

"Just Bill Hoffner making an ass of himself," he cackled, reaching for his pipe. She frowned and he sighed in defeat, tucking the pipe into his pocket. Satisfied, she pulled her head back into the kitchen.

In front of the courthouse, Sheriff Hoffner held up both hands, demanding quiet. "We have a text that describes the rituals this group performs. My detectives are still working on determining what this text means and how it's used. The public should be alert for activity or behavior that is out of the ordinary."

"If you believe this cult 'targeted' Officer Garrett, is there a risk of harm to others?"

"No, no," Hoffner said, regaining his sense of control. "Nothing tells us that there's a risk to anyone else at this time."

"Is it possible that the Ku Klux Klan is still active in your county?"

The horde of reporters had gone silent on the courthouse lawn, heads swiveling to follow the stinging questions and evasive answers. They were usually aggressive in the way of starving dogs, but were on this occasion content to watch the drama unfolding between Jefferson and Hoffner. It made for good footage, even if they weren't the ones hurling the questions.

Sheriff Hoffner smiled, confident with his answer. "No, ma'am, the Klan hasn't been active around here for a long time."

"If it's not the Klan, are there Satanists in Forney County?" Jefferson asked, blonde head cocked to one side.

Hoffner narrowed his eyes, trying to appear intent and intelligent, rather than exhausted and irritated. He chuckled grimly into the microphones, falling back on his most comfortable defense when challenged – intellectual intimidation. "The First Amendment to our great Constitution guarantees religious freedom, Miss Jefferson, as I'm sure you remember. Therefore, I can't say absolutely that there are no Satanists in Forney County. But for the record, I do believe the majority of our residents are God-fearing Christians," he answered, pleased that he'd thought to toss that last sentence in. Should win him a few votes come the election next year.

"Thank you for that primer on the Bill of Rights, Sheriff. As I asked yesterday, how much comfort should the good people of Forney County take in your knowledge, given that a commercial marijuana grower was operating in your county; one of your officers has been targeted by a cult; an elderly woman is still missing; there are two other vicious murders which are currently unsolved; *and* you refuse to arrest a woman who has repeatedly confessed to killing her husband?"

A drop of sweat beaded on Hoffner's temple and ran along his cheek. *How did she find out about the hot house that burned?* He leaned forward into the clutch of microphones and spoke slowly. "And as I answered yesterday, investigations are ongoing. Additional information will be released in due course. In the meantime," he glared at MaryAnn Jefferson across the lawn, his nostrils flared, bushy brows contracted over his closely set eyes, "I'd appreciate support from the press as we work on Officer Garrett's case. That's all for now."

For the second time in two days, Hoffner found himself spinning on his heel and leaving the press conference in a hurry. Mayor Rusted nodded gently at the shouting reporters before turning to follow Sheriff Hoffner into the courthouse's cool lobby.

CHAPTER 70

THE SQUAD ROOM WAS unnaturally still as the camera panned away from the now empty courthouse steps back to Stanton's reporter. Truman broke the shocked silence as he thumbed the remote, turning the television off. "Why did he do that?"

"What an idiot," Elaine muttered, jumping up and rushing toward the lobby.

Mitch collapsed into a chair. His voice was grim and his face flushed. "We've got to move fast. Cass, I want you and Truman to go see that banker, Mr. Salter."

"Now?" Cass asked, frowning in confusion.

"If he's got anything related to The Church of the True Believer, he'll try and dispose of it after that press conference. If he didn't see what just happened," Mitch nodded at the dark television set and stretched his long legs out in front of him, "someone else in that little group will have, and they'll contact him. Find that card."

Cass motioned to Truman and they headed for the door.

"Munk," Mitch continued, "figure out how we keep an eye on Jed Salter. We need to be ready to follow him when he leaves for this Celebration, especially if it's tonight. Put somebody on it while Cass and Truman are with him. But," he added as Munk stood, "do it quietly and on a slim crew. I'll check on availability of backup from another county."

"How slim a crew?"

"Two officers, three? Who can we trust?"

Kado stood as Munk pushed open the squad room door. "Kado," Munk called over his shoulder. "Nice work on the pee and snot."

"Thanks," Kado answered, stifling a smile. He glanced at Mitch. "From a forensics perspective, can I do anything to help?"

"Yup," Mitch answered, eyes bright with anger. "If Cass can't find that invitation, we're back to square one. Our next shot is DNA. Get the reports from the site where Garrett was killed."

"No problem. You want to come see what I get?"

Mitch's lips flattened. "I'm gonna talk to Hoffner."

Chapter 71

THE OLD MAN PUSHED himself up from his recliner, pulling the phone from his pocket as he shuffled across the living room, heeding his wife's instructions about not leaving dirt on the carpet. She called that lunch would be ready in fifteen minutes, and he grunted an acknowledgement as he stepped into an afternoon blazing with sun. He lowered his glasses from their perch on his forehead and jabbed a speed dial button.

"Did you see the press conference?"

"Yes, I did," Jed Salter answered. "That Elliot woman was at the bank this morning, looking for me. The text. Is that Lenny Scarborough's book?"

"I imagine so."

"How much do they know?"

"Not much, from what I can gather. Newton reported that they've been looking at phone records all morning, trying to figure out where Chad Garrett's cell phone came from."

"They find anything?"

"No, but it wouldn't hurt for us to change phones around. And to be on the safe side, you need to get your things out of the house."

"Will they come here?"

"They've been to see Peavey and Mrs. Shepherd. You'll be next on the list because your granddaddy's name was in Lenny's book." The old man lit his pipe. "I'll send a courier around to collect your things and we'll have them for you tonight."

"Garrett's death is nothing to do with The Church. Even if they manage to link the text to one of us, they can't tie us to murder."

"No, no," the old man murmured. "But some of our activities could be misconstrued. You agree?"

Salter grunted. "This feels like it's getting out of hand. You think we should go ahead with the ceremony?"

"We need to close the Circle. That woman reporter did us a favor by introducing the Klan and devil worship into the mix." The old man chuckled into the phone. "That'll keep people busy for a while. And they won't look at us for either of those things."

"All right. I'll let you know if anything comes of their visit."

"You do that. Turn this phone off and leave it in the briefcase. I'll have someone bring you a new one."

CHAPTER 72

MITCH PAUSED OUTSIDE THE squad room door, resting in the station's abnormal quiet. Although open for business today, the residents of Forney County seemed content to limit their visits to the courthouse to standing on the edge of the lawn, eyeing the camera crews and reporters. He trod slowly toward Sheriff Hoffner's office, the surge of fury he'd felt during the press conference momentarily defused as he tried to think through Hoffner's motives. He'd never been close to the sheriff, had never known him to have any kind of relationship with his officers. Mitch believed he was fundamentally weak, driven by lack of confidence. He didn't know where the insecurities originated, but he'd known that at some point, the sheriff's craving for recognition would damage the department or even worse, an investigation. And in the course of a five-minute press conference, Hoffner had managed to do both. A flash of disgust curled his lip as he reached the sheriff's office, and he fought to bring his features and a fresh surge of anger-fueled adrenaline under control. Hands shaking, he knocked twice and entered the room.

Hoffner glanced up from the papers on his desk, holding up a hand as he lowered his head to finish reading. Mitch pulled the door closed behind him. The office was cool and all signs of the stress the sheriff had endured while facing the cameras had disappeared. He straightened the papers and placed them squarely on his blotter, smiling as he motioned Mitch to sit.

"What can I do for you?"

"What was that press conference about, sir?"

"I'm not sure what you mean," Hoffner replied, leaning back in his chair, resting the ankle of one leg on the knee of the other.

"Why didn't you talk to me before you went out there?"

Hoffner smiled, managing to look down his nose at the tall man sitting across his desk. "I think I'm smart enough to handle the press."

"Handle the press? Sir, you released information into the public domain that is critical to the investigation. Any member of this Church who was watching will know that we're on to them. You gave them too much, sir."

Hoffner waved his concerns away. "This was a diversion, Mitch. It's helped you."

"Helped me?"

"Of course. It gives people something to focus on, some gossip, a little titillation."

"Telling people we think there's a cult operating around here is more than gossip sir, it's the truth."

"Come on, Mitch," Hoffner scoffed, his tone genial as he plucked at the crease in his trousers. "Nobody's gonna believe there's a cult in Arcadia. It's just too fantastic."

"Nobody except the men in those pictures with Lenny Scarborough, raping that child. And you've just told them we believe there's a link between Lenny's Church of the True Believer and Chad Garrett's death," he said, voice straining with the effort of control.

"You're overreacting. We've made connections," Hoffner tapped his temple, "that they aren't aware of. I didn't mention the text by name, did I? I didn't mention that invitation Cass is going on about." He shook his head, pleased with himself. "This will catch them completely by surprise."

"And what about the department?" Mitch asked quietly.

"What do you mean?"

"What about how we look? Now that people think Garrett might've been involved in a cult, what does that say for the integrity of your force?"

Hoffner frowned. "I told those reporters that Garrett wasn't involved in this cult. And he wasn't, was he?"

"Given the evidence we have so far, we don't believe so. But sir, most of what we've come up with is speculation. We have no proof. Garrett could've been a member of this Church."

Hoffner's eyes narrowed and blood rushed to his cheeks. "I took you at your word, Mitch. You were sure he wasn't involved. Did I just lie to the press based on your screw up?"

Mitch snapped to the edge of the chair, body singing with anger, voice rigid. "*My* screw up? You just gave away the few leads we have in Garrett's death. A cult, a text, the fact that he *was* killed in a ritualized manner. And for what? What did you get in return? What did *we* get in return?"

"What do you mean?"

"You must've had a plan, right? You must've thought that by giving the press our best leads in Garrett's death that we'd learn something more valuable in return. What was it?"

"This'll drive them out, Mitch," Hoffner replied, dropping his foot to the floor and leaning earnestly forward, forearms on the desk. "They'll be nervous now. They know we're catching up with them."

"And after that press conference they just might cancel this Celebration of Illumination, and we'll have missed our chance to figure out who they are."

A vein bulged at Hoffner's temple. "What are you saying, Mitch?"

"You thought you could save face with the public, the *voting* public, by showing them how smart you really are, how *in control* you are." A snarl rippled Mitch's lip. "And as a result, you have jeopardized our investigation into Officer Garrett's death."

Hoffner paled, fury driving color from his face. "I am doing my best to cover for your incompetence, Detective, and that of your team. In spite of having photographs and his wife's statement, you failed to identify a single piece of evidence regarding Lenny Scarborough's sexual abuse of those girls, and if you'd known about this cult, Officer Garrett would still be alive and our solve rate wouldn't be falling through the floor!"

Stunned, Mitch collapsed back into his chair. "That's what this is about, isn't it?"

"What are you talking about?" Hoffner barked.

"I should've seen it," Mitch said slowly. "Our solve rate. That reporter from Dallas. She kicked you in the balls about what's going on in the county, unnoticed by the force. The marijuana operation. The unsolved murders. Poor old Mrs. Glenthorne who's gone missing. And you can't stand to be outsmarted, can you? This wasn't about helping the investigation, about creating a *diversion*, was it? This was about your bruised ego."

"Don't be stupid, Mitch," Sheriff Hoffner replied wearily, cradling his head in his hands. "My intent was to help you. To make your life easier."

Mitch stood, a mixture of revulsion and pity in his face. "Well, Sheriff, that may have been your intent, but you've created one massive mess for the rest of us to clean up."

Startled at the change in Mitch's voice, Hoffner looked up to see his office door click quietly closed.

CHAPTER 73

SCOTT TRUMAN GLANCED AT Cass as she turned into Live Oak Park. Her mouth was a thin line, her violet eyes stormy. She lifted a hand in greeting to the patrol car leaving the exclusive subdivision. The sun flashed briefly on the wire-rimmed glasses the man wore, leaving soulless blanks in place of his eyes. "Looks like Greg Newton's back out on patrol already."

"You all right?" Truman asked.

She recognized the concern in the young officer's voice and sighed, trying to relax. "I'm fine. Just incredibly pissed off."

"Will Mitch be okay?"

"About the press conference? Yeah, he'll get over it."

"Will he be too hard on Sheriff Hoffner?"

Cass searched for street names. Live Oak Park had grown up as a fashionable neighborhood in the booming twenties. In contrast to the large homes built by the *nouveaux riches* on Apple Tree Drive after the second World War, Live Oak Park belonged to Forney County's old money – families who owned the mineral rights to land drilled for oil and gas, those involved in the cotton industry in the late nineteenth century, and the local barons of the now defunct railroad industry. Houses were large and comfortable. Many had been remodeled but still carried the stamp of the era in which they were built – evidence of art nouveau and the emerging art deco eras could be seen in doors flanked by stained glass windows in organic designs or the geometric, almost austere sweep of a chimney above a tiled roof. Live Oak Park was remarkable in the richness of its architectural integrity and the unbroken chain of family ownership for most of the homes.

She slowed the truck as she glanced at an address scrawled on a napkin. "Mitch is pretty smart when it comes to politics. But he's got a temper. I've known him for a long time and this is as mad as I've seen him."

"How could the sheriff do that to us?" Truman asked, lifting his

301

sunglasses to check house numbers.

"The man amazes me, honestly." She shrugged, slowing to check a mailbox hidden behind a rose bush heavy with bloody blooms. "I'd like to believe that he's on our side. But after that press conference, my faith is shaken."

She parked on the street in front of the Salter family home, a stately red brick affair with a long concrete drive. Monkey grass sprang around the paving stone walkway. Three vehicles were parked in spaces to the side of the house, a gleaming black Cadillac, bright yellow Hummer and curiously, a battered pickup. "Smells like money," Cass said. "You ready for this?"

Truman nodded, hand poised to open the door. "How do you want to handle it?"

"Play it by ear. Keep your eyes open, watch his body language. Even though we're pretty sure Salter's part of The Church, we'd better go in softly, like we did with Mr. Peavey. Explain about Lenny's book and his granddaddy's name being in it. And most important, find that invitation."

He looked across the cab at her, sunglasses suspended over his forehead as he prepared to lower them into place. "This one scares me, Cass."

She checked her hair in the rearview mirror, tucking a loose strand into her French twist and pressing gently at the soft tissue under her eyes. "I know. It scares me, too."

───────────

TRUMAN JABBED AT THE doorbell and a soft tinkling of "Jesu, Joy of Man's Desiring" trickled through the foyer. A small shape darted into the wide hall, pausing to glance through a side window hung with leaded glass before opening the door. A tiny woman peered out at them, dark brown hair shot with becoming streaks of white, eyes widening at the sight of Truman's uniform.

"Can I help you?"

"Yes, ma'am," answered Cass as she and Truman offered IDs and made introductions. "We need to speak with Mr. Salter. Is he in?"

A startled noise flew from her throat and a pale hand fluttered to her neck, hiding the pulse throbbing wildly at its base. "I'm Mrs. Salter. Is something wrong?"

"Just a few questions, ma'am. Is Mr. Salter home?"

She glanced over her shoulder, into the cool interior. Truman's eyes, hidden behind his mirrored shades, were busy taking in the foyer's marble tiles and the plush carpet that climbed a sweeping staircase. "He is, but he's asked not to be disturbed."

"We won't take much of his time."

"Is this urgent? Can it wait?"

"No, ma'am, it can't."

Mrs. Salter shifted her weight from one foot to the other, indecision flickering across her face. After a moment's hesitation, she pulled the door open a fraction wider and stood to one side. They slipped through the crack and followed her through the large foyer, her low-heeled shoes clicking tightly on the marble. She led them through a formal sitting room and the adjoining dining room, past an open door revealing a game room cluttered with three lanky teenage boys playing video games, through a cavernous kitchen and across an enclosed courtyard. Mrs. Salter paused in front of a closed door, and Cass realized that the room ran the width of the house, stretching from the backyard to the front, affording its occupant a clear view of the drive. He knew they were here.

Mrs. Salter hesitated, fist raised. She glanced at Cass over her shoulder, a worried look that spoke volumes about her relationship with her husband, and rapped sharply.

"Come."

Mrs. Salter drew a deep breath and opened the door across a heavy sweep of creamy carpet, apologizing for the interruption as she introduced Cass and Truman. Mr. Salter rose from behind a wide desk scattered with papers bearing long columns of numbers. The office was darkly paneled and several lamps glowed on low tables scattered around the room. The walls bore photographs of the Salter family's development, from sepia colored shots in front of a very new courthouse, through black and white photos of chubby expressionless children in the twenties, to modern color shots of the current crop of Salters. Legend had it that the family's original capital came from the profits of bootlegging during Prohibition, when the current Salter's grandfather took a risk and broke from the family's sharecropper destiny. He wisely invested his exorbitant profits and built what would become the largest bank in Arcadia, and was instrumental in making and breaking the destinies of families and businesses in Forney County. The Salter who strode across the thick carpet to greet them had the lean body of a runner. He was smooth with power yet dressed casually in jeans and a polo shirt. In his early sixties, his bearing suggested assurance and demanded obedience. He asked his wife to bring coffee and closed the door behind her.

"Elliot," he stated as he crossed the room, taking in her red hair. "Abe Elliot's girl?"

"That's right."

"Your family is hard on my bank."

"Sir?" Cass asked, heat rising across her cheeks.

"They don't borrow much."

"Sir?"

Salter lifted a shoulder in a gentle shrug. "Occupational hazard. I tend to remember the finances of individual families. Yours doesn't borrow, which is admirable from a personal money management perspective, but bad for my profitability," he replied, a smile tugging at his lips. "And I doubt you're interested in my bottom line. How can I help you?" he asked, waving an elegant hand at two chairs as he sank back into the leather chair behind his desk.

"We're looking into a group called The Church of the True Believer," Cass began as Truman pulled out a small notebook and pen, glancing around the room. "Are you familiar with it?"

"I don't believe so," Salter answered, rearranging the papers into piles. He lifted a heavy pen and signed several documents, silvered head bent over the desk. A medal was draped casually over a framed photograph of Salter in running shorts, smiling widely. Through the French doors behind him, Cass caught the sparkle of a swimming pool. "Why?"

"You've heard about Lenny Scarborough's death?"

"Of course."

"We found some information at his house that links your grandfather to this church."

Salter lifted an eyebrow in her direction as he slid the papers into labeled folders and reached for a stack of mail, shuffling the envelopes together. Cass caught a flash of cream in the stack and fought to keep her eyes from fluttering toward it. "My grandfather? What information?"

"His name was in a book, similar to a Bible. It had Lenny Scarborough's signature in it, and your grandfather's. Did he belong to a group with some sort of religious affiliation?"

Mr. Salter frowned. "We've always had our membership with First Baptist here in town. Is that what you mean?"

"No, it's not. From what we gather, this group is somewhat secretive. Your grandfather would have had possession of this book, as Mr. Scarborough did. It's large and nicely illustrated. Does that sound familiar to you?"

"My grandfather's entire library is in this room. My father inherited it, added to it and I had it moved in here when we built the study," he answered, waving a hand at the dark bookcases lining the walls. Cass glanced quickly at the folders, trying to catch a glimpse of the card. "You're welcome to have a look at them."

"Thank you, sir," Truman murmured, standing to examine the shelves.

"Does the year 1928 mean anything to you, or would it have been important to your grandfather?" Cass asked.

"Not to me, and I don't know about my grandfather. It was the year before the stock market crashed, why?"

"That was the date written next to your father's name. We think that's when he took possession of the book. From what we can tell, he was the first owner."

"You said Lenny Scarborough's name was in it?"

"Yes."

"Any others?"

"I'm not at liberty to say."

"But there were more names," Salter stated, nudging the folders into a pile and scooting them toward the desk's edge, piling the mail on top.

Cass realized that he probably knew the answer anyway. "There were. You don't remember anything about your grandfather's involvement in this group?"

Salter pursed his lips, absently nodding his wife into the room when she entered with a coffee tray. She placed it in front of him and busied herself with cups and saucers. "No, but he died in 1947, the year I was born. I never knew him." He waited as she served them and left, pulling the door closed with a soft click. "This book that you say my grandfather's name was in, is that the text Sheriff Hoffner referred to on television just now? The one that links some cult to Officer Garrett's death?"

Cass blushed. "I – I'm not sure."

He appraised her from beneath half closed eyelids, blowing across his steaming coffee cup. "You're working on Garrett's murder?"

"Yes."

"Yet you don't know what evidence Sheriff Hoffner was referring to in his briefing just now?"

"I'm afraid I can't comment on the investigation," she replied, silently cursing Hoffner.

"You said the book from Lenny Scarborough's is religious in nature. Makes sense that it would be the text Hoffner talked about." He settled in his chair, china cup cradled between his elegant hands. With effort, Cass kept her gaze away from the pile of folders and mail, mind gnawing busily at the dilemma of how to get to that card. "From what I understand, Officer Garrett died horribly. I knew Lenny through the insurance business he invested in, and he simply wouldn't have been involved in any group that promoted violence. And although I didn't know my grandfather, I can't imagine that a Salter would be involved in anything unethical."

Cass realized that he had given her an opening. "I understand, and," she said, lowering her chin, "a thorough investigation will let us evaluate all the evidence before we draw any conclusions."

"You disagree with Sheriff Hoffner's statement about a cult and that it's somehow linked to this text?" Salter asked, leaning forward.

"I just hear what you're saying about Lenny Scarborough. How the idea of violence doesn't fit with the man. And we know how active your family has been in the community," Cass began slowly. She cut a glance at Truman, who was still examining book spines, and lowered her voice. "It's hard to imagine someone from your family, now or in the past, being involved in anything… untoward. We did wonder if this Church might be like the Masonic Lodge or the Lion's club."

Salter frowned.

"Friendship, fellowship, helping people. Except that the people in The Church want to remain anonymous." She paused. "Sometimes the department finds it necessary to provide incomplete information to the public, to help the investigation, if you know what I mean."

"I suppose I do," he agreed as Truman returned to his chair, reaching over the stack of folders and mail to place his empty coffee cup on the tray. Cass despaired at his coordination. "Did you find what you were looking for?"

"No, sir," Truman replied, closing his notebook and slipping it into the shirt pocket on his uniform. The door behind Salter's desk whooshed open, and a teenage boy in shorts and a t-shirt tumbled into the office, a broad grin splitting his handsome face.

"Hey Dad," he called, stooping to hug his father and stopping short when he realized there were visitors in the room. A blush colored his cheeks as his gaze fell on Cass and took in Truman's uniform. "Oops. Didn't realize there was anybody here."

Mr. Salter smiled, indulgence sweeping his lean features. "Brian," he said, motioning to the boy. "This is Detective Elliot and Officer Truman, from Sheriff Hoffner's police force. This is my son, Brian."

Cass stood and reached over Salter's desk, placing her cup on the coffee tray and stretching a hand out. She shook Brian's hand, pulled her arm back and lost her balance, bumping the stack of files and mail onto the floor. Mr. Salter jumped from his chair as papers fluttered through the air, and Cass scooted the cream colored card out of the pile of envelopes and toward Truman with the toe of her boot. He stared, wide-eyed at the small rectangle, and Cass nudged him when she squatted to help Salter gather his files.

"I'm so sorry," she gushed.

"Don't worry about it," Salter replied, gathering the papers together and plopping them onto his desk.

Cass smiled at Brian as he bent to help his father, and the young man blushed. His build was slight, his chin dotted with adolescent acne. He tried desperately not to let Cass see him staring at the neck of her gaping blouse. "I'm normally not so clumsy," she said, flashing her violet eyes in his direction.

"It's all right," he said, voice breaking. "Come to arrest my dad?"

"No, I don't think he's going to jail any time soon," Cass replied, recognizing him as the boy who was with Mayor Rusted's son on Sunday, eager to talk to the Grove twins about their adventures in the fire pit. "We just needed to speak with your dad for a few more minutes."

"Cool," he replied, eyeing the gun riding on Cass's hip as he took the stack of mail and folders Truman had collected. "Sorry I barged in. Let me know when you're done Dad, okay?"

"What did you need?" Mr. Salter asked, sorting the papers and mail into piles again.

"I can't find the bag for tonight," Brian answered.

Salter's features remained in the exact position they'd occupied immediately before Brian spoke, yet Cass sensed a shift in his awareness. "It's been taken care of," he answered, careful to keep his voice light and his eyes fixed on his paperwork. "Just pack whatever clothes you'll need for one night."

"You're going out tonight?" Cass asked, cool adrenaline sliding through her veins.

"Yeah," Brian answered, blushing. "We're going camping. It's my first trip."

"Just the two of you? Not your sister?"

"No, this is guy stuff."

"Well, it's a good time of year for it. Not too hot yet. Hope you'll make it to school tomorrow," she chided.

"It should be okay," he replied, reaching for the door, "we'll be back early tomorrow morning."

"Where do you go?"

"Huh?"

"Camping. Where do you go?"

"Some friends from church have a cabin that we borrow," Mr. Salter replied, glancing at his son. "Get your clothes ready. I'll come help you in a minute."

"Okay," Brian answered. "Thanks."

"Nice young man," Cass smiled as he pulled the door closed. She glanced quickly at Truman. His face was expressionless.

"He is very special. Does well at school, is outgoing," Salter sighed. "My second son. He was a late baby. Unplanned." He smiled sadly. "We thought of calling him Isaac, for the son born late to Sarah and Abraham. You know the story, from Genesis?"

"Yes, sir, I do. Abraham had an older son, by Sarah's maid, didn't he?"

"Ishmael," he answered, eyes flicking toward an older photo of his family, with two sons present. "We lost our first son, Nathaniel, several years ago. It's a tragedy when a child precedes his parents, at any age. But," he added, "I'm lucky to have Brian and my daughter."

"Yes, sir, you are." Cass rose from her chair. "We'll be going now."

"I'm sorry I couldn't be more help," Salter said, lifting a heavy legal style briefcase to his desk before standing to slide the folders inside and close the flaps. Cass caught her breath and fought to contain the desire to snatch the case from the desk and dig inside, and sensed Truman tensing beside her. Salter was oblivious to their reaction. "You'll contact me if there's anything I can do?"

Cass tore her eyes from the briefcase and forced a smile as Salter crossed the room. "Yes, we will. Enjoy your camping trip tonight."

"Pardon?" he asked, hand suspended as he reached for the doorknob.

"With Brian. Enjoy your night in the cabin."

"Of course," he smiled, holding the door open. "I'm sure we'll have a fine time."

CHAPTER 74

TOM KADO DRUMMED HIS fingers on the desk, willing the fax machine to life. Elaine poked him as she spoke into her headset and he lifted his hands in defeat, leaving her alcove to stalk the courthouse lobby. Bernie Winterbottom leaned on the tall counter, waiting for Elaine to hang up, watching Kado pace.

"Your DNA results are due in?" he asked.

Kado dug both hands into his dark, wavy hair, stopping in front of the courthouse doors. "From the crucifixion site. The lab wouldn't use email." He peered through the narrow windows, shaking his head at the crowd hunched over laptops and shouting into cell phones. "Did you catch Sheriff Hoffner's latest press conference?"

"Was it an improvement on yesterday's?"

"Hardly," Kado snorted, returning to stand next to Bernie. "He released some information to the press that should've been kept confidential. I cannot understand that man. He's got an incredible group of people working for him, and he can't help but stick his foot in it and slow everybody down."

"May I make an observation?" Bernie asked cautiously.

"Sure."

Bernie glanced around the lobby and leaned closer, lowering his voice. "My comments come from my limited observations of him and the comments I've heard concerning his behavior. Although I'm not an expert, he strikes me as someone with a personality disorder. Perhaps narcissistic psychopathy. He functions at quite a high level, but is incredibly preoccupied with how he is perceived. From what I've observed, any type of challenge or rejection to his authority is particularly offensive to him."

"Wow," Kado breathed, "that sums it up. I hadn't thought about Hoffner in terms of his psychology, but what you described is exactly right. What can we do with him?"

"Unless he seeks help, there is little anyone can do for him, from what I understand."

"So we're stuck with him, like this?"

Bernie nodded. "Until he's voted out, should that happen. In the meantime, if he truly is a narcissistic psychopath, you might do some research to find out if coping strategies exist to help you and your colleagues work with him."

Kado jumped as the fax machine whirred. "Thanks Bernie. I'll think about what you said. Gotta run." He darted into Elaine's alcove, grabbed several sheets of paper from the tray and ran through the double doors.

MITCH STOPPED JUST INSIDE the door to the evidence room, watching Kado pace the length of the cord that tethered him to his desk phone. One hand was in his dark hair; his gray eyes were stormy and his face flushed.

"What you've described, what the results show, isn't possible. Tell me again," he said through clenched teeth, leaning down to fiddle with his computer's mouse and wake the screen, "how you processed the samples."

Mitch shut the door and leaned against a cabinet.

"And there's nothing left? You can't run it again?" He exhaled and closed his eyes as he listened. "Fine. Email it all."

Gently, he replaced the phone's receiver and collapsed in his desk chair, cradling his head in his hands. "This isn't possible."

"No hits?" Mitch asked.

"No hits. They identified four different DNA donors from the leather pieces. All male. One donor is consistent with the DNA collected from the urine and phlegm."

"It's not unusual that none of them would be in the system. That's just the way it goes. So what's the problem?"

"We got clean samples on three of the donors. The lab is saying that the samples for the fourth donor, the guy who gave us the pee and snot, were corrupted."

"All the samples?"

"Yes."

"If they got good samples for three guys from the leather pieces, how could the sample for the fourth guy, taken from the same leather, be corrupted?"

"Hallelujah," Kado said, throwing his hands up. "Somebody else gets it."

"The lab guys don't?"

"The lab guys refuse to get anything that might show fault with their procedures."

Mitch scratched his chin. "What kind of corruption are they talking about?"

"This is what drives me mad, and lets me know the lab screwed up," he said, jumping from the chair and passing a piece of paper to Mitch. "The corruption is the same in each sample. Exactly the same. See?"

"I see squiggles. What does it mean?"

"It's the DNA profile for the fourth man. They overlaid results from the snot, pee and leather to show they're exactly the same."

"And?"

Kado thrust his hands back into his wavy hair and started pacing again. "The lab says they don't even handle animal DNA. I kept asking what other samples they'd been working with, how this could've happened, but nobody will admit to cross contamination. They think I contaminated the samples at the scene. But how could I?"

"Animal?"

"It's just not possible," Kado said, coming to a stop in front of his computer. He swiveled the monitor so Mitch could see the photograph on the screen.

"German Shepherd?"

"Canis lupus."

"What's that?"

"The gray wolf, Mitch. The lab report shows DNA contributed by a human male and a gray wolf. There are no gray wolves in Texas. Not anymore. There is no way I could've contaminated the phlegm and urine samples. And if one DNA sample on the leather is contaminated, they all must be." He puffed his cheeks out and exhaled. "But it doesn't matter about contamination. Not really."

"Why?"

"That report doesn't show separate wolf and human contributors. It's one sample."

Mitch leaned into a counter, his eyes clouded as he handed the DNA report back to Kado. "So, what are you saying?"

"I know. It's not possible."

"What is possible?"

"Either I screwed up, or the lab screwed up."

"So what now?"

"I go explain to Sheriff Hoffner," Kado said, gently placing the report on his desk, "that the DNA is worthless. It's down to Cass and that invitation to help us find the men who killed Chad Garrett and raped those girls."

CHAPTER 75

TRUMAN HELD HIS TONGUE until Cass left Live Oak Park, heading away from downtown. Then he twisted in his seat to face her. "I saw it."

"The invitation?" She glanced at him, startled at his frown. "And?" she prodded, holding her breath.

"It's tonight."

Cass pulled to a stop at a red light, air whooshing from her lungs. "You're sure?"

"Checked it twice before putting it back in the pile of mail."

"You didn't bring it with you?"

"I didn't know if I should take it. He might look for it before tonight. If he couldn't find it, well, I thought might realize that we had it. Besides, we didn't have the right to take it, did we?"

"No, you're right. We didn't. All right," she said, flipping on her blinker and changing lanes as she pulled away from the light. "Tonight doesn't give us much time."

"Where are you going?"

"Food. It's after two o'clock. I'm starving."

He laughed. "You sound like Mitch. Do you think Salter knows we saw the invitation?"

Cass pushed her sunglasses up on her nose and shook her head. "He doesn't have a clue how much we know, does he?"

Truman's eyes danced above his mirrored sunglasses. "No, and when you started talking about the Masonic Lodge and Lion's Club –"

"You heard that?"

"Oh yeah. Making him think you don't agree with Hoffner that The Church might be a cult. That was good."

Cass dipped her head in acknowledgement of the compliment. "What about the daughter?"

"You think she might be the one in the photographs?"

"Maybe. But what do *you* think?"

Truman was silent for a moment. "She's about the right age, maybe twelve or thirteen. Thin, from her photographs."

"And the son?"

"You think they start 'em that young?"

"This morning, Rose said that the older son, Nathaniel, died on a camping trip."

"I remember when that happened. You hadn't moved back yet. Nobody reported anything funny about his death. It sounded like the kid had a heart defect nobody knew about and just fell over one day."

"The camping reference just made me wonder. If membership in The Church passes from father to son, maybe Salter was training Nathanial, and has moved on to Brian."

"Man," Truman said, "this stuff kinda freaks me out."

"Me too," she agreed, turning onto Arcadia's main thoroughfare. "Call Mitch. Tell him about the invitation. Find out where he is and what he wants for lunch."

"TONIGHT?" SHERIFF HOFFNER DEMANDED, hoary brows contracted in a frown. "Why tonight?"

Mitch shrugged. "Maybe they need to replace Lenny Scarborough as quickly as possible."

"You're going to tail him?"

"Yes, sir. Munk is looking at the roster now, trying to figure out who we can use. Also, I want to keep an eye on Mr. Peavey tonight."

"I thought you ruled him out of this."

"As best we could. But it's safer to have somebody watch him, just in case. We're struggling to find the right men, though."

"What's the problem?"

"We can't ask them to lift their shirts and show us their chests, can we?"

"Good point," Sheriff Hoffner grunted, pinching the bridge of his nose and releasing a long sigh. "I can't believe it's come to this."

"We don't have a choice, Sheriff. I don't like the thought of following these men any more than you do."

"I know you don't, Mitch. And since Kado screwed up the DNA samples, I suppose the invitation is our only lead. He came highly recommended," Hoffner mused, shaking his head. "I would've thought keeping samples clean would be easy. What else?"

Mitch winced inwardly at Hoffner's comments. He'd heard the tongue-lashing the sheriff had given Kado, but Mitch wasn't sure the forensics man was to blame for the DNA problem. "We'll also call printers in the area and find out who had the invitation printed. That should give us a lead as well."

"Good. Anything else?"

"I need approval to contact Watuga and ask for backup for the tail tonight."

Hoffner burst into a bout of deep-throated laughter. Mitch watched him, wondering what had gotten into the man. The Sheriff had been under immense stress for the last two days, but his usual reaction to difficult situations was to turtle in on himself, not to indulge in fits of thigh-slapping hysteria. Slowly, Hoffner regained control and wiped his eyes and nose with a snowy handkerchief. "Thanks, Detective. I needed that," he said through a few chuckles.

"Sir?"

"That was a joke, wasn't it?"

"No, sir. We need help tailing Jed Salter and watching Peavey. I also want backup in case something bad goes down at The Sanctuary tonight."

The Sheriff leaned forward in his chair, placing his forearms on the desk and clasping his hands together. "Let me be absolutely clear, Detective. You will contact no one outside this department about your activities tonight."

"Is *that* a joke, sir?"

"It most certainly is not. You're running this operation based solely on speculation. These men most likely have nothing to do with those photographs from Lenny Scarborough's house or with Chad Garrett's death. I won't have you bringing outside forces into this mess." He studied Mitch for a moment. "If 'something bad' goes down tonight, Detective, it's on your head. Are we clear?"

"Yes, sir," Mitch replied, no hesitation in his voice. Somehow, he had known the Sheriff would find a way to disengage from this whole investigation. Hoffner needed powerful, wealthy men like Salter and Peavey to finance and influence his election campaigns. He would do his best to distance himself from any situation that might tarnish his reputation.

Hoffner raised a white, bristling eyebrow. "Anything else?"

"It would help us if you can keep this away from the press."

Sheriff Hoffner's expression froze. "And it would help me if you keep the shit storm around your little folly tonight to a minimum, Detective. Understood?"

CHAPTER 76

"OH MAN," TRUMAN GASPED, closing his eyes and shouldering his way out of the autopsy room.

Porky looked up from the steel scales where a pair of blackened lungs rested. His purple scrubs were smeared with a dark substance. "His first time?"

"Yup," Grey replied, lifting a slippery section of intestines free from an abdominal cavity, pale gloves covered in blood. "Guess seeing a smoker's lungs is a rough initiation."

"Yeah," Cass agreed, feeling her stomach turn over. "I'll go wait with Truman."

"Save us some lunch, would you?" Grey called.

"Change your scrubs," she answered, pulling the door closed behind them.

ERNIE MUNK PULLED MINNIE'S chair into Grey's office, pushing it between Cass and Truman. He reached for a bun and looked over the food spread across the desk. "Pass the chopped beef."

"Who's watching Jed Salter's house?" Mitch asked, scooting the tub toward Munk.

"Two of the new patrol officers. Young ones. This is their first surveillance, and they're scared to death they'll screw it up," he chuckled, drizzling barbeque sauce onto his sandwich.

"How do you know they're okay?"

"I found them in the locker room, coming out of the shower. I'm not a pervert or anything, I just happened to be there while they were getting dressed. No scars on their chests."

"Where'd you put them?"

"In Live Oak Park, tossing a Frisbee with a dog. They have a clear view of Salter's driveway. I told them to call whenever a car pulls in or out."

"Are they just watching, or will they follow?" Mitch asked, reaching for the barbeque sauce.

"Follow. I want one of them behind whoever leaves, until we call them off. The road they're on exits the park near Salter's road. As long as they see a car pulling out of the drive, they'll be able to pick it up on the main road."

"Once we tag Jed Salter and know he's headed to this ceremony, how do we keep tabs on him without being noticed?"

"That's where I'm stuck," Munk answered around a mouthful of barbeque. "I'm not comfortable getting anyone else from the force involved. There are five of us, plus the two patrol boys. That should do."

"Good plan, but Cass can't follow him."

"Why not?" she demanded, potato salad dropping from her fork.

"Come on. All that red hair, your lily white skin?" Mitch shook his head. "You glow in the dark. There's no way you can follow him at night without being noticed, even if we change your truck. And as for the rest of us," he glanced around the table, "with the exception of the red hair, we're in the same boat."

"What about the officers from Watuga County?" Munk asked.

"Hoffner shot me down. I think he doesn't want to risk being embarrassed in front of another county if nothing comes of following Salter and Peavey tonight."

Munk heaved a disgusted sigh. "Great. And he's got no problem leaving his own officers hanging with no backup."

"Are you really that surprised?" Cass asked quietly.

When Munk answered, his voice was thoughtful. "No. I'm not." He looked at Mitch. "You think we need somebody with dark skin to tail Salter?"

"And ideally, somebody who's not on the force."

Cass hesitated, a smile playing at her lips. "What about Jerome?"

"Blackie's ex-con cousin, Jerome?" Mitch asked.

"Why not? He's black, and in spite of gettin' cleaned up, he still *looks* like an ex-con. I think he'd be happy to help us, and more importantly, he can keep his mouth shut. In the right car he's invisible. Menacing maybe, but nobody'll notice a black man driving out near the river bottom, if that's where The Sanctuary is."

"Can we trust him?"

"There weren't any black men in those photographs."

"Good point."

"What about cars?"

Munk wiped a smear of barbeque sauce from his chin. "I'll figure something out."

Grey and Porky emerged from the autopsy room, both in fresh scrubs. Truman blinked but kept chewing as Grey shuffled autopsy photographs into the file he carried and slid it into a box, scooting it into a corner. Chairs scraped across the floor and bodies shifted as the two men settled down and reached for food.

"Is this from Red's?" Grey asked as Porky moaned. The medical examiner cocked an eyebrow at the younger man.

"Sorry boss, but for white folks, they sure know how to do barbeque."

Cass frowned. "Speaking of white folks, where's Bernie?"

Grey took a long drink of tea and then burped quietly. "We ran out of bodies," he explained. "Bernie met Elaine yesterday, and I think he was stopping by the courthouse to see her. He's hooked. She's taking him to a local revival tonight. Give him a taste of the Southern church experience."

"Is she that interested in him?"

"I'm not sure. Bernie's always been something of a ladies' man. I've never understood it," he said, scraping the last of the potato salad from its container, "but he's never lacked for female companionship."

"As long as he doesn't break Elaine's heart, we'll be just fine. That girl's been through enough, what with a dead husband and four boys to raise," Mitch said.

"I wonder...," Cass said. She turned to Grey. "Which church is Elaine taking Bernie to?"

"I think it's the Church of the Nazarene, the one that's out in App Community."

"Truman, did Mr. Peavey say what church he goes to?"

The young officer slipped his notebook from a hip pocket and checked. "No. But that's the only revival going on in the county."

Cass gave him a quizzical look. "How do you know that?"

"My mom plays piano at our church and fills in for other churches, so she knows which church is doing what. She'll be playing at that revival in App Community tonight. Their regular pianist is out sick."

"What are you thinking?" Mitch asked Cass.

"I think it'll be easy to rule Peavey out. He told us that Mrs. Peavey was at their church getting ready for a revival meeting tonight. Truman, do you remember?"

The young officer checked his notebook again. "He said it starts at six o'clock and probably won't end until after midnight."

"What do you suggest?" Mitch asked.

"That we ask Elaine and Bernie to keep an eye on Mr. Peavey. If he leaves, they can make their excuses, call one of us and follow him until we can pick him up."

Mitch ate a forkful of beans and chewed thoughtfully. "Elaine can handle it, and be discreet. Do you think Bernie's up for this?" he asked Grey.

The medical examiner raised a dark eyebrow. "Our only trouble will be keeping Bernie from wearing a deerstalker and smoking his pipe."

Cass laughed. "He doesn't own a deerstalker, does he?"

Grey nodded. "And a calabash pipe with a meerschaum bowl. He loves the whole Sherlock Holmes thing. Ask him to show you his magnifying glass sometime."

"Okay," Mitch said. "I'll call Elaine and see if she's willing. And," he said, checking his watch, "we'd better find Jerome if we want his help tonight."

Cass caught his eye and glanced across the desk at Porky, who was happily gnawing on a chicken leg. Mitch nodded. Munk caught the exchange and smiled his agreement.

Mitch cleared his throat. "Porky?"

The thin man raised his dark eyes, chewing steadily. He motioned to Truman to pass the cole slaw and scooped a creamy spoonful onto his plate. "Yeah?"

"You working tonight?"

"Depends who dies."

Mitch blinked. "Of course. We need your help with something."

"Sure."

"It's not your normal thing, cutting up bodies and stuff. We expect these guys to hold a ceremony tonight."

"What do you want me to do?"

"We're not exactly sure where this ceremony will take place, but we think it's got to be in the river bottoms somewhere. We need a few people to follow Salter, and to change off following him. But he knows most of us on the force, and...," Mitch hesitated.

"He won't recognize a black dude, right?" Porky asked matter-of-factly.

"Er, yeah."

"Okay," he nodded. "But I drive a swish car, man. He might know it. You got an old beater I can borrow?"

"You're cool with this?"

Porky grinned, white teeth bright in his dark face. "Might as well put this beautiful black skin to use. Besides, my granny and aunties will be *proud* when I tell 'em I helped catch the men that killed Officer Garrett. That's a month of Sundays full of cornbread and turnip greens."

Mitch exhaled, and then grinned. "Munk will take care of cars and explain how tailing Salter will work, about communications and everything, okay?"

"Yeah, no problem."

Cass snapped the lid on her iced tea as Mitch continued. "Cass and Truman, good work today at Mr. Salter's house. If you hadn't seen that invitation, we'd still be treading water." Truman grinned at the praise. "Now it's back to the grunt work. You any good at getting radios into cars, quick?"

CHAPTER 77

DEACON CRONUS PUTTERED AROUND his garden shed, carefully folding his robe and placing it in the briefcase. He checked the wooden tools he needed for this evening, satisfied that they were clean enough to eat from. Blood was seeping through the bandage on his dimpled hand, and while he was grateful to know the knife was sharp enough to provide a clean cut, he was irritated at his own clumsiness.

He clucked as he worked, small unintelligible noises designed as much to help him focus as to provide comfort. In spite of the importance of his role, he always experienced a twinge of nerves before a meeting. And tonight was special. The last Celebration of Illumination had taken place in 1988, when Lenny Scarborough drew the lot that elevated him to the Circle of Light. The Celebration was an emotional event, sadness over the loss of a member mingled with the hope that came from the initiation of a new member and the drama of the ascension ceremony. Tonight would be no different. Lenny would be mourned, Petchard initiated and Warner promoted, closing the Circle. And from then, their work could continue. God was indeed good.

Deacon Cronus drew a stool up to his workbench and traced a finger over his copy of *The Church of the True Believer.* He would study, and then begin the complicated, roundabout process of arriving at The Sanctuary. All this subterfuge seemed a waste of time. The Sanctuary had never been violated in the past, but he would follow the old man's instructions to the letter, as would the others. He lowered his head and prayed before opening the text.

CHAPTER 78

CASS STARED AT THE colorful painting in *The Church of the True Believer*, eyes unseeing. Thoughts fluttered and crashed in her head, and she wondered if any of the illustrations in the book depicted a scene they would find tonight. She jumped as Mitch placed a cup of coffee on a phone book open on her desk. "Thanks," she murmured, blinking to clear her vision.

He settled in a chair opposite hers and put his boots up on the desk, frowning at her look of confusion. "What's up?"

"I don't know," Cass answered slowly, examining her thoughts. "I just... I guess I'm a little tired."

Truman slumped into the room and poured a cup of coffee. His uniform was filthy and the sweet smell of gasoline puffed into the air as he collapsed in a chair. Mitch grinned. "What happened to you?"

"Munk found the cars for tonight," he said, wiping an arm across his sweaty forehead. "From a junk yard. We had them towed out to your house and got them running and full of gas. Got radios in them, but it ain't pretty. Darla sure is nice – she made cookies for us." He took a sip of coffee, grimacing as the hot brew mixed with the dirt on his lips. "Did you call Jerome?"

"Yup. He's gone home to change into some dark clothes."

"Porky's done the same. Even said he was going to take off all his jewelry – that should take a while."

"Why's he doing that?" Cass asked.

"He said something about moonlight glinting on his ear cuffs," he shrugged. "I think he's pumped to be involved." Truman eyed *The Church of the True Believer*. "Anything in that book that'll tell us what they're going to do tonight?"

Cass turned the book around to face him. "Have a look if you want. I keep thinking about the girls in the pictures from Lenny Scarborough's place."

"Why?"

"I figure they'll be there. One kid, maybe I could understand how they could fall for all the attention that this group must lavish on them. But two or more? There's just no way a group of girls would allow themselves to be molested, is there? They'd have to be extremely vulnerable. Who would have access to more than one girl in that situation? Who would they trust?"

"With more than one kid involved, I'd imagine that somehow these men have made them feel special," Truman said. "Like being part of this group makes them unique, lets them belong."

Mitch looked thoughtful. "You remember John Lee Grifford? He got sent down for abusing his son a few years ago. When I talked to the boy about what happened, he kept defending his father. Saying how he and his dad had a special relationship. But when you saw how they lived." Mitch cleared his throat. "Man, it was disgusting. That man treated his dogs better than he did his wife and kid. She knew about the abuse, but didn't call the police because he beat her."

"Could this be something like that?" Truman asked.

Cass lifted one shoulder in a shrug. "It makes sense they would target kids who are in a bad situation." She glanced down at her desk and stopped speaking as her glance fell on the ad for the First Baptist Church in the local phone book. A list of the church's staff and their job titles was partially covered by her coffee mug, and she lifted it to get a better look. "I totally missed it," she breathed. "Jed Salter goes to church there. He was borrowing a cabin from a church friend for his camping trip tonight."

Truman had followed Cass's eyes as she examined the page in the phone book and now he gasped, blood draining from his dirty face. "Oh man."

"What is it?" Mitch demanded.

Cass froze as the horror of her thoughts crystallized. Truman snatched the phone book from her and leaned over the desk, motioning Mitch closer as he whispered, "Do you know what the Deacon's job is?"

"No, why?"

"It might have changed, but last time I heard…," Truman smoothed the phone book open and ran his finger down the list of clergy. "Yeah, Deacon Cronus is still the Youth Minister."

CHAPTER 79

THE OLD MAN PUT the truck in park and puffed contentedly as the lean man left his crew and ambled the short distance to meet him. He wore stained leather chaps over his jeans and a battered cowboy hat, hand-me-downs from one of the previous bosses. Hitch swept the hat from his head and slapped it at his chaps, dust billowing with each movement, before leaning an arm against the pickup's open window.

"You must have friends at the DNA lab."

Hitch grimaced, the movement drawing the lines in his narrow, weathered face deeper. "What was it?"

"You take a piss out there?"

"Shit."

The old man roared with laughter. "You took a shit, too?"

"No." Hitch sighed. "How did they find the site?"

"Some black whore saw you."

"How?"

The old man struck a match and sucked at his pipe, relighting it, wondering if the odd DNA explained the man's amber eyes, his lean features. The police department had dismissed the sample as corrupted, but the old man, he wasn't so sure. Evil, he knew, takes many incarnations. "No idea. She was doped up and it sounds like she was unconscious for most of it."

"I guess I'll be thanking you for your hospitality and moving on. You want me to take care of the whore before I go?"

"No. We'll deal with her later. I hate to lose you, son. You've been a help to me," the old man said, eyes watchful. "Keep your phone. Turn it on once a day, at nine thirty in the evening, Arcadia time. Leave it on for no more than five minutes. I may need you again."

"You sure that's a good idea?"

The old man grinned. "Not a lot of smarts in the po-lice department around here." He reached for the keys in the ignition. "Check the usual place. I've left a little something extra. Tide you over."

Hitch nodded and the old man cranked the engine, letting the diesel settle into a steady growl. He patted the side of the truck and watched as the old man bumped across the rutted pasture and for the first time in his life, Hitch felt a sense of loss. Pulling the brim of his hat low, he strode quickly to Victor, the crew boss, passing along instructions. He pivoted and climbed into the battered truck the old man had let him use, mind already searching for his next destination. *Somewhere cooler*, he thought as he slipped the pickup into drive.

CHAPTER 80

CASS RAPPED ON THE door marked 'Pastor', softly at first and then with more urgency. A frowning Pastor Luke Knightman pulled open the door, face breaking into a smile before softening into curiosity when he spotted Mitch standing behind her, knuckles white as he snapped his phone shut.

"Hello," he said to Cass, pulling the door open and motioning them inside. "Nice to see you both. Any chance you're planning to join us at church tonight?"

"Not tonight," Cass replied, stepping past him into his office's cool interior. "And we need your help."

"No problem," he replied, settling behind his desk while Cass and Mitch stood. "What can I do for you?"

"Is Deacon Cronus in?" Mitch asked, voice flat.

"No, he's working from home today. Is something wrong?"

Cass flashed a look of warning at Mitch, who had steamed as they wove through side streets to get to the First Baptist Church unnoticed by the reporters. Her own stomach was in knots at the thought of the young people Deacon Cronus could access, and over her failure to follow her gut and look deeper into the man's life. Although the sun had fallen lower in the sky, leaving a dull umber smear in its wake, the air was still heavy with humidity. Both of them were sweating from their rush to try and find Deacon Cronus. "What does he do for the church?" she asked.

"He's our Youth Minister and handles most of our outreach programs. Why?"

"What age kids does he work with?"

"Anywhere from junior high through high school. Ages eleven or twelve through to eighteen or so."

"Has he ever been accused of inappropriate behavior?"

"David Cronus?" Pastor Luke sputtered, laughing. "I can't imagine it.

Most of these kids come from rough backgrounds. No father, mother on drugs, that kind of thing. He's like a father to them. Takes an interest in their schoolwork, helps them find jobs when they're old enough, counsels them about relationship problems. Makes sure they go to the doctor and dentist." He waved a hand, dismissing the question. "There's no way he'd do anything inappropriate."

"Do you know the kids he works with?"

"I've met a few, but most are in and out of the program quickly."

"Why?"

"Their parents are usually transient, following work. From what David has said, there are only a handful that come regularly."

"Are they white, black, Hispanic?"

"We get everything here. New kids join all the time."

"Does he take them on outings?" Mitch asked.

"Sure. Fishing, bowling, to the zoo or ball games."

"Boys and girls?"

"Both."

"And when he takes the kids out, does he take them all, or just a few?"

"I guess it depends," Pastor Luke replied, eyes narrowing.

"On what?"

"On the activity, how suitable it is for kids of various ages. Whether he's got enough support to take more than just a few kids at a time. Sometimes parents volunteer, or others from the church. He takes a group of the least fortunate kids out at least once a month, but sometimes they'll make a few trips. Why?"

"Did Deacon Cronus have anything planned for this evening?"

"He did, as a matter of fact."

"What was it?"

"Camping," Pastor Luke replied and dread uncurled along Cass's spine. "Something he pulled together quickly. Just a couple of the kids are going."

"How many?"

"Two, I believe."

"Boys or girls?"

Pastor Luke swallowed. "He didn't say."

"Was anyone else going with them?"

"The Salters, I believe. At least the father and son. Maybe another family. What is this about?"

Cass struggled to hide her frustration as the tumblers fell into place. She was now certain that both Salter and Cronus were involved with The Church of the True Believer. She glanced at Mitch and he nodded tightly. Cass lowered her voice. "This is confidential Pastor Luke, extremely confidential. Do you remember when Mitch told you we had photographic evidence of men engaged in homosexual acts and abusing children?"

He exploded. "You *can't* believe David Cronus is involved in –"

"It's short work to rule him out," Cass said, cutting him off. "But we need to know where he's going tonight, and which kids he's taking with him."

"I can't believe you're suggesting this," he answered in a low voice, face mottled with anger. "Deacon Cronus is a fine member of this community and a humble servant of the Lord. I have never seen him behave in a way that is anything other than respectful and caring to those children. I won't have you spreading malicious rumors about him."

Cass released a long sigh. "We have no intention of spreading rumors about him, which is why we came to the church first. He's not in his office, so we came straight to you. But Pastor Luke," she pleaded, leaning toward the desk, "we think something is going on tonight that will involve teenagers. Girls, specifically. We have to know whether Deacon Cronus is involved. If he's not, it's a simple matter to clear him and let him get on with his trip. But if he is involved…"

He collapsed into his chair. "I don't know what to say. If – if there are children involved, then yes, you have to find out what's going on. I just can't believe that David Cronus could be involved in anything like this."

"Who are the kids he's taking camping tonight?"

"I don't know. He gets parental or guardian approval, keeps all the relevant medical information and paperwork. Why don't you just go see him at home?"

Mitch held up his phone. "The call I was on when we got to your office? His wife says he's already gone."

CHAPTER 81

CASS DABBED THE STICK under her eyes again, checking her work in the bathroom mirror. She was dressed in river bottom patterned camouflage pants and a long sleeve black t-shirt, hair pulled into a tight knot, and now, her face was dark. Slipping her shoulder holster around her body, she lifted her chin, twisted the greasepaint stick and slicked it against the creamy expanse of her neck. In the dark, only the whites of her eyes would be visible.

She checked her appearance one more time and took a deep breath to quell the butterflies roiling in her stomach. Since Truman had seen the invitation at Jed Salter's house, her body had been alive with thoughts of what tonight would bring, and she'd caught the scent of a campfire at the most improbable of times.

Anticipation, she'd told herself.

Dread, her little voice had replied.

Cass stepped into the hall and moved quietly toward the kitchen. Darla jumped when she caught the dark reflection in the window over the sink.

"Good Lord woman, you look like Rambo," she giggled, drying the last of the dishes. "The boys are out in the barn, checking the radios in those dreadful cars. You want anything else to eat?"

Cass shook her head, settling down at the kitchen table to slide nine-millimeter rounds into extra magazines. Zeus jammed his head against her thigh and his tail slapped happily on the floor as she scratched his ears. "No, I'm too nervous. But thanks for feeding all of us. That's above and beyond the call of duty."

"It's been kinda fun. Mitch had told me about Jerome and Porky, but it was good to meet them. That Jerome is so polite; you'd never know he's been in jail. Besides, it doesn't take long to fry chicken and mash potatoes." She wiped the counter and joined Cass at the table, her pretty face pulled into a worried frown. "How long will you have to wait?"

"Until it's good and dark. Maybe nine o'clock, nine thirty. Picking a day in the middle of the week is smart – not too many people will be out tonight."

Darla chewed on her thumbnail. "Cass, do you think it'll be dangerous?"

"They don't know we're coming, so we have that advantage." She watched the greyhound spin himself around and settled at her feet with a contented grunt. "But if it were me out there abusing kids, I'd be pretty jumpy if somebody showed up unexpectedly."

"You think you'll need that much ammunition?" Darla asked, eyeing the stack of magazines glinting on her kitchen table and watching as Cass checked a revolver before slipping it into her ankle holster.

"Better safe than sorry."

"I still don't understand why Sheriff Hoffner won't ask for backup from Watuga County. It doesn't make any sense. I understand why you can't have other officers from Forney County's police force with you, but why won't he even ask for three or four from Watuga?"

Cass placed her forearms on the table and laced her fingers together. "I think he's terrified of what we'll find out there."

"What do you mean?"

"Maybe we've got this all wrong, and we'll show up in the middle of some male-bonding ritual. Or, we've got it right and we'll find some pretty important people out in the woods doing bad things. Either way, Sheriff Hoffner loses: he's embarrassed in front of his supporters, or he looks even more stupid in front of the reporters for not knowing what's going on around here."

Darla gently worried at her lower lip. Tendrils of dark hair had slipped from her ponytail and curled around her shoulders. Her eyes were usually a clear brown, but tonight they were clouded with concern. "So, it's his ego?"

"That's just my nasty little guess." Cass sighed. "The budget probably won't take paying for extra officers. But, I think if I were in the sheriff's shoes, I'd either be fully behind what we're doing tonight and ask for support, or I'd call the whole thing off."

"Well, I feel better knowing that you're watching Mitch's back, and he has yours." Darla stood and fiddled with the coffee pot. "I'll take some out to the garage now, and fill up a thermos or two for tonight. You ready?"

———

CASS LISTENED TO JEROME and Porky take instructions from Truman on how to use the communications equipment. Both men were dressed in dark trousers. Jerome wore a black t-shirt and Porky a dark red silk shirt. All the jewelry was gone from his ears, nose and eyebrows, but as he asked questions, Cass caught the flash of a stud in his tongue and suppressed a smile. The boy couldn't help but style.

"All right?" Truman finished and both men nodded, taking car keys and heading toward their respective vehicles.

Porky raised an eyebrow at Cass's blackened face. "No offence, but you look better as a white girl."

Mitch held up a hand to stop them as he finished a conversation and snapped his phone shut. "You clear on what you're to do tonight?"

"Yes, sir," Jerome replied, eyes firm in the artificial light. "Just follow, hang back as far as possible, don't lose him, and keep you informed about where he's going."

"Good. Don't use Salter's name over the air. We're on a remote channel, but you never know who's listening. If he leaves a marked road, you let us know and keep going. Don't slow as you drive past his turnoff. We'll have somebody behind you, out of sight, but once he turns off we'll take over."

Mitch waved them to their cars. The uncertain clatter of hastily repaired engines broke the still night as they left to take up their positions on opposite sides of downtown Arcadia. Mitch watched their taillights flare before they turned onto the main road in front of his house, and he released a long sigh. Darla leaned into him, nestling her head against his shoulder. "That was Kado," he said.

"How is he?" Cass asked.

"Not good," Mitch answered. "Angry because the sheriff refuses to consider that the lab could be at fault. Mad at the possibility that he could've contaminated the samples."

"But wolf DNA, Mitch. That's bizarre."

He shrugged. "The lab made a mistake."

"Well, he's our devil of light."

"What do you mean?"

"We know he's the man Blackie Cochran saw in the clearing with Chad Garrett. If he does the dirty work for The Church, then maybe he's the man Goober saw when the hot house fire started. He probably killed Humberto

Gonzalez and the mummified man."

"Why do you think that?"

"Blood was drained from Garrett, and we think from Gonzalez and the other man. Gonzalez told Deacon Cronus he was afraid of a *diablo de luz* and he wanted to be baptized for protection. Whatever Gonzalez saw related to this devil of light must've gotten him killed."

"Good Lord," Darla breathed, snuggling closer to her husband.

"Any luck with the stationary shops or printers?" Cass asked.

"Nope," Mitch answered. "Elaine called every shop for fifty miles in all directions. Nobody would admit to printing those cards. I talked to her a little while ago. She and Bernie are at the revival, and they've spotted Mr. and Mrs. Peavey. If the order of service for tonight sticks, Elaine estimates that Mr. Peavey will introduce the visiting preacher at around ten o'clock this evening."

"Let's just hope he stays at church." Cass held out the stick of greasepaint. "You'd better get ready."

"I hate this. Not knowing where they are, what they're up to. I hate doing this with no backup." He squeezed Darla and reached for the greasepaint, eyes worried. "You think this will work?"

"It better," Cass replied. "It's all we've got."

CHAPTER 82

THE HEAVY OLDSMOBILE LURCHED with the impact and slid to a stop in the gravel next to the road, Willie Nelson crooning from the radio. Evelyn Grove's knuckles were white as she gripped the steering wheel. The sun was gone now, the road cutting through Deuce's Flat a satiny ribbon in the early moonlight. Her headlights angled off into the forest straddling the road and danced across water in the distance. The bridge that cut over the Sabine River was just ahead. She snapped her headlights off, pulled her seatbelt free and rested her head on her trembling hands, a bubble of laughter gurgling from her chest. *Unbelievable*, she thought. *Matt and Mark were telling the truth.*

Drawing a shaky breath, she pushed open the door and eased behind the car to a shadowy hump lying motionless on the verge. She crept nearer, amazed at the size of the animal, watching for movement. "You poor thing," she whispered as it finally heaved a shuddering breath. Evelyn was the last to leave a school board meeting and had chosen to take a short-cut through the back roads. Even though she was halfway across the county from where her boys had hit their deer, she crouched for a closer look. "I hope you're not the same guy my boys hit. Talk about having a bad week."

Evelyn stood and placed a hand on the trunk to steady herself, wondering what to do. The twins had been able to put their deer in the back of the car, but she couldn't lift that animal by herself. She could just drive away, letting it wake up on its own, but that didn't feel right. And something told her that she was obligated to contact the game warden when an animal was injured. She moved along the car's passenger side to squint at the damaged fender. It didn't look too bad, certainly no worse than the Vega. She'd call Robert and have him call the game warden. And when she got home, she'd apologize to Matt and Mark and tell them they didn't have to pay for their dent after all. They'd file both the damaged Vega and Oldsmobile fenders against insurance. She looked again at the fender and realized that something else was wrong.

Evelyn took a step back from the car and let her eyes run over the long vehicle. The hood dipped slightly toward the verge, and as she moved closer, she realized that the front tire was flat. "You've got to be kidding," she breathed.

She trudged around the car and opened the driver's door, then pulled the handle that popped the trunk. Standing with her hands on her hips, she surveyed the trunk's contents: scattered schoolbooks and papers, two unopened cans of engine oil, a coil of nylon rope, and five sneakers. Size Sasquatch. Evelyn leaned down to start moving objects so she could get to the spare tire, but then remembered the white trousers she wore. She'd loved them the moment she saw them, and they fit perfectly off the rack. There was no way she was ruining a good pair of trousers over a flat tire. Besides, problems like this were the reason God had given her a strong husband and twin boys.

With a smile, she tugged the passenger door open and leaned inside to dig through the contents of her purse, scattered across the floor. Snagging her phone, she pushed a button and groaned in frustration at the empty screen.

"Damn it!" she hollered, voice bouncing inside the car as laughter again burbled in her chest, spilling over at the absurdity of her situation. How much leverage would her twins have, now that she was in the same situation they'd been in, but one worse since she had a flat tire? It wasn't smart to let two teenage boys get one up on a parent, that much she knew.

Never one to accept defeat while wearing a comfortable pair of shoes, Evelyn scraped her purse and its contents together, pulled the keys from the ignition and stepped out of the car. She locked the doors and stood quietly on the asphalt, enjoying the release of the sun's collected warmth as the road cooled. Suddenly she turned and unlocked the car, pulled two dollar bills from her wallet, and flattened them on the car seat. "For the cuss bucket," she whispered.

She relocked the car and with a great huff, slung her purse over her shoulder and marched toward Arcadia, white shoes and trousers flashing against the road's surface, pace slowing as she caught sight of a lone headlight weaving toward her. She was still on the far side of the bridge and trotted forward, waving her arms to make sure they saw her in time to stop.

But the motorcycle slowed and arced gracefully into the trees before reaching the bridge.

"Come on! Just one break tonight," she demanded of the wide, silent sky. "Just one!" She watched as a star shot across the heavens, directing her to town. "Fine," she muttered, hoisting her purse and trudging toward the spot where the single taillight had disappeared. "I'll do it myself."

CHAPTER 83

"I'VE GOT HIM," PORKY said, voice broken by static. "He's headed west out of downtown."

"Is he still in that old pickup?" Munk asked, adjusting the radio's volume.

"Yeah."

"Anybody with him?"

"Not that I could see."

"Good. I'll have Truman call the patrol boys and tell them to drop back. They're itching to pull him over because the pickup's plates aren't registered. Mitch, you getting this?"

"Affirmative."

The radio was silent for several minutes and Cass fidgeted in the seat beside Mitch. They were in his truck waiting at a spot on the south side of town, watching as the minimal evening traffic flowed past.

Porky spoke again. "He's turned into the shopping center and parked in front of the grocery store."

Mitch cast a glance at Cass. "What's he doing?"

"Supplies?"

Mitch thumbed the radio's microphone. "Is he going in?"

"Yes, to that little card shop in the corner. What should I do?"

"Park among a bunch of cars, but make sure you can see the card shop's front door. Jerome?"

"Yes, sir."

"Park away from where our friend is parked, then go in the shop and keep an eye on him, just in case he tries to go out the back. Browse, and don't approach him."

Munk's voice broke through the gentle hiss of static on the radio. "Truman and I are taking one turn through the parking lot. Jerome's inside." He paused. "Porky, I see your car. That's a good place to wait. Sit tight."

Mitch adjusted the radio's volume and shifted in the driver's seat to look at Cass. "Why a card shop?"

"Meeting a fellow freak? Buying 'you're special' cards for the other child molesters that'll be there tonight?"

Mitch's chuckle was cut short by the sound of Porky's voice over the radio. "Here he comes."

"Does he have anything with him?" Mitch asked.

"A plastic bag."

"Can you tell what's in it?"

"It's small. Like they give you when you buy a card. Looks flat and like it doesn't weigh much."

Mitch nodded at Cass. "Guess you were right about the cards."

"He's getting into his truck," Porky said. "Jerome's just coming out of the shop now. What do we do?"

"Start following again, but keep lagging behind. Munk?" Mitch asked. "Where are y'all?"

"We've headed south and are tucked into a dirt road off the Loop in case he comes this way."

"Stay put until we hear different."

Jerome's voice broke through the light static. "Porky's following him out of the parking lot. Looks like they're going west out of town. What should I do?"

"Fall in and keep Porky in sight. What happened in the card shop?"

"He just browsed for a couple of minutes and went to the register. I didn't see what he bought."

"No problem. Munk?"

"We're headed back to town," Munk said.

Cass's frown was barely visible in the dim dashboard lights. "West doesn't make sense. Not if The Sanctuary is in the river bottoms."

"You're right," Mitch answered. "He should be going east or south."

"Uh, Mitch?" Porky said.

"Go ahead, Porky."

"He's about a mile out of town and he's slowing down."

"Drive on by," Mitch instructed. "Let us know what you see in your rearview."

"He's turning around. Toward town. Jerome, are you still back there?"

"I am," he answered. "I see him turning around. You're about to crest a hill, is that right?"

"Yeah," Porky said.

"Is there anybody coming toward you on the other side of that hill?"

"Nope."

"Mitch?" Jerome asked. "Is it okay for Porky to turn around and come back to town? If there's nobody else on the road, we shouldn't lose him. I'll do the same if it's okay."

"No problem, but switch places. Jerome, you go first and Porky, you follow. He's probably checking his tail. Just hang back."

Jerome spoke again after a few minutes. "He's turning south on the Loop."

"I see him," Munk said. "And you, Jerome. That's a perfect distance. We'll wait for Porky to make the turn onto the Loop and then follow."

"Let us know when he crosses the rail road tracks," Mitch instructed.

The radio was silent for several minutes before Jerome spoke again. "He's just crossed the tracks. Hang on a minute. He's exiting the Loop. Yeah, he's going south. Should I keep following?"

"Switch again. Jerome, you pull into the gas station like you're going to fill up. Porky, you take the lead in following our friend. Jerome, after Porky passes the station, you fall back in again. We're just pulling up to the light at the Loop. We'll follow you, and Munk and Truman will follow us. Clear?" Mitch asked.

A round of affirmative answers sputtered across the radio. It spat soft static while the cars moved into position.

"Mitch?" Porky asked. "Did you see the car between me and him? You want me to catch up with him?"

"Just hang back," Mitch instructed. "Let's see where he goes. Me and Cass are falling in behind Jerome. We're about three cars back, no more than a mile."

"– turning!" Porky cried. "Can you see him?"

"Is that FM 323?" Mitch asked.

"Yeah, it is."

"Good work Porky, drop him and keep going. Circle around to my house if you have time. Darla's got brownies in the oven and some fancy

340

coffee brewing."

"Grey told me I was on call tonight. Sugar and caffeine are just what I need."

Mitch chuckled. "Is he expecting new bodies in the morgue?"

"He's a cautious man. Just make sure it's not one of yours now, y'all hear?"

"Amen. See you later, Porky. Jerome, it's your turn."

"Yes, sir. I'll turn in after him."

"Give him some space, but keep your eyes on his taillights."

"Where are you gonna be?"

"We're passing 323 now, but we'll do a u-turn and follow you. I'll cut the lights before we make the turn, so don't worry if you can't see us. If you need anything, pick up the radio." Mitch watched in his rearview mirror as Jerome turned smoothly off the highway. "Munk?"

"I saw him."

"Drive past and do a u-turn behind us, then follow us in."

"Roger. You think it's wise to cut your lights?"

"Why?" Mitch asked, slowing down as he neared an opening in the highway median. He waited for several approaching cars to pass, and then swung through a u-turn and headed north.

"He might not be the last in."

Mitch glanced at Cass. "He's got a point."

"No lights," she said, white teeth flashing against her darkened face. "Don't give 'em a chance."

"All right," he answered, thumbing the radio mike. "Munk, we'll be dark. Give us a good thirty seconds before turning in, but keep your headlights on."

"Roger."

Mitch glanced at Cass's troubled face as he turned onto 323 and doused his headlights. "What?"

"Where did Jed Salter leave his kid, Brian? They were coming camping together."

"Maybe he changed his mind about bringing the kid, or the boy got sick or something. Either way, it's better that he's not out here."

"How's Sheriff Hoffner?"

"Unhappy with the whole thing."

"Is he monitoring us?"

He nodded. "I told him we'd use a quiet channel, hope nobody picks us up."

"You ready for this?"

"I can't even begin to imagine what they'll be into out there, can you?"

"No, but I'm prepared to see anything. Men and men, men and girls. Whatever."

"I hope they're just dancing around a bonfire, maybe biting the heads off of chickens. I can handle something like that. But the other…" A shiver ran through his body. "I don't know."

Jerome's voice broke through the steady hum of static. "Munk? Mitch?"

"Go ahead," Munk said.

"He's turning in before the Sabine River."

"Where Blackie's clearing is, south side of the road?" Mitch asked.

"Before that, and on the north side. I'm just passing now." Jerome's voice paused and static filled the silence. "I don't see any tail lights in there, but that's where he went. It's barely a dirt trail. Anything else I can do?"

"Nope. Go back to my house and drop off your car. If you've got time, have a brownie or two."

"I just might do that." After a moment, the radio clicked again through the static. "Y'all? There's another car out here."

"Where?"

"Parked on the other side of the bridge, headed toward town. Nobody in it. What do you want me to do?"

"Keep going. See you at the house later, all right?"

"Yes, sir. Over and out," he chuckled into the mike, a throaty sound. "I always wanted to say that."

"Munk?" Mitch asked, watching Jerome's taillights disappear down the dark road. "You there?"

"Yup. I caught it all. What are you going to do?"

"Drive by, spot the place where he turned off, and go check out this car."

"Truman says there's a county road just ahead, maybe three quarters of a mile before we hit the bridge. We'll park and wait to hear from you."

Mitch rolled down the dark road, eyes following the verge, looking for a break in the tree line. Cass leaned toward the dash, twisting to see past him into the night. "There." She pointed at a smudge of sandy road that vanished between dense brush. "See it?"

He maintained his speed, watching the odometer until they reached the bridge. He lifted the radio's mike. "Munk? The turnoff is on the north side of the road, three-tenths of a mile before the Sabine River. We'll pass the car shortly. Got that?"

"Yup."

Moonlight glittered on the silvery Sabine River. The bridge rose slightly and blocked their view until they reached the middle, where only yesterday Cass and Truman had dangled their legs over its side. No lights were visible along the eastern riverbank. "Car's on the north side," Mitch grunted. "Get the plates and type them in." He was silent as they approached the car and slowed as she wrote the number down. Stretching up from the driver's seat, he peered down into the vehicle. "Big Oldsmobile. I didn't see anybody in the car. But," he squinted at the moonlit road, "it's got a flat. Find anything?"

Cass typed quickly on the portable computer under Mitch's dash. "It's Evelyn Grove's car. Isn't she Munk's sister?"

"They live out this way?"

She shrugged, reaching for the radio and explaining the situation to Munk.

"A big gray Olds?" he asked.

"It could be gray."

"All right," he sighed into the radio. "Somebody must've come to pick her up. There's no way she'd change a flat tire. I'll make some calls and make sure she got home okay."

Mitch continued over a small hill before pulling to a stop on the side of the quiet road. Since they had turned off the main highway, they'd seen only Salter's vehicle plus the chase cars, and now Evelyn Grove's. Headlights still off, he checked his rearview mirror and swung the truck in a wide u-turn, heading back toward the bridge.

"What now?" Cass asked.

"Check out the western side of the river as we clear the bridge. They've got to have some light this time of night."

She lowered the window and the gentle hiss of tires on asphalt and then concrete drowned out the radio's static. A spring breeze caught the open window, carrying with it a quiet snicking as the truck passed over seams in the bridge. She squinted at the dark line of trees nudging against the river. "Nothing specific," she said in a low voice, pointing through the open window, "but there's a glow back where Salter turned in."

The tires found asphalt again and Mitch cut sharply into the woods, pulling onto the narrow trail Blackie had taken them down Tuesday. Wispy pine branches slithered along the truck's side and Cass raised the window. Mitch rolled to a stop after about twenty feet and cut the engine.

"What if we've got it wrong?" she asked, eyes digging into the dark forest, fingers linked in a tight knot.

"What do you mean?"

"What if those pictures are nothing to do with this cult? What if they really are just a bunch of men who get together for some pseudo-Christian rituals every now and again? What if there are no kids?"

Mitch twisted in his seat to face her, one arm crooked over the steering wheel, blackened face drawn in the moonlight. "Why are you having doubts now?"

"Every bit of it is circumstantial. We don't have one shred of evidence linking anyone to The Church, or to those photographs." She dug her fingers into her hair, scraping it tighter into its clasp at her neck. "This could be an almighty shit storm."

Mitch chuckled, teeth flashing in the dark.

"What?"

"You sounded like Sheriff Hoffner just then." He looked through the truck's back window, toward the main road. "You're right. We have nothing absolute about those photographs, or about Garrett's death. But this is the only lead we've got. We'll take a peek at what they're up to. If it's nothing more than a bunch of middle aged dudes greasing themselves up and dancing around a fire, we'll just back out, okay?"

Cass nodded and Mitch picked up the mike.

"Munk?"

"He's on the phone," Truman replied. "What's up?"

"We're parked across the road from the turn in, pulled back on Blackie's trail. We'll walk down the path that our friend took and see what's going on."

"What do you want us to do?"

"Cross the bridge and pull in behind Evelyn Grove's car, headlights only. It won't look strange if a patrol car is checking out an abandoned vehicle. Hang there until we call." Mitch paused. "Has Munk found his sister?"

"Not yet. He's trying his nephews' cell phones now."

"We'll use your cell as the primary point of contact for now."

"Roger. Cell reception is —"

"Mitch," a sharp voice barked through the radio.

"Sheriff? You've followed everything?"

"All of it."

"What did you need?"

"I can't find Mayor Rusted."

"Sir?" Mitch asked, gripping the steering wheel in frustration.

"I'm getting ready to talk to the press and I can't find him."

Mitch lowered his head to the steering wheel as Cass's eyes snapped wide. "I'm not sure that's a good idea right now, sir."

"I don't have a choice. The networks are here – FOX, CNN, ABC, CBS. All of them. Mayor Rusted wouldn't miss a chance like this."

"I can't help you, sir. I don't know where he is."

"You might find him before too long," Sheriff Hoffner said, voice faint through the static. "His wife said he was out at a meeting tonight. When I pressed her on what meeting, where it was, she started to cry." He sighed into the radio. "Good Lord, I'm afraid he might be part of all this."

CHAPTER 84

ANTICIPATION CRACKLED THROUGH CASS'S nerves and her senses responded with a jump in perception. To her sensitive ears, the night roared with the rustle of unseen creatures snuffling through the undergrowth and the tremble of soft wings across the sky. They had chosen their location wisely, this Church. After leaving the farm-to-market road, the dirt track doglegged sharply and bumped away from the river. Massive evergreen shrubs sagged against a path barely wide enough for a pickup and blocked further view of a vehicle from the road. Anyone turning in would sense only abandon, and the narrow trail was gouged deeply enough from the wash of rainwater to discourage further investigation at the risk of shocks and suspension. Cass and Mitch crept through the thin moonlight, testing with their feet to find the gullies and bumps, inching around jagged cuts in the earth's surface when a crack was too wide to step across, slinking along either side of the trail like shadowy wraiths.

Weapons drawn, they stole a quarter of a mile into the woods, the path angling subtly away from the river. The trail remained tightly wrapped in dense foliage and it was only as the noises from the night creatures faded and the faint scent of a wood fire met them that they realized they were nearing a camp. Mitch motioned for Cass to stop and he dropped into a crouch, inching toward a dim glow pulsing beyond the next twist in the track. Heart pounding in her ears, she strained to see his dark figure moving along the edge of the trail, and caught the faint movement of his hand as he waved her forward. Cass darted from one heavy bush to the next, avoiding the few puddles of moonlight streaming through the canopy overhead, joining him to peer around the thick hedge.

She took a deep breath and eased her head forward. Beyond the final corner, the track emptied into a wide clearing. A fire danced to one side of the large, roughly circular space, its light wavering against a wooden structure whose front porch stretched out toward the flames. A picnic table covered with white butcher paper squatted between the cabin and the fire pit, and aged logs were stacked neatly beneath one of the cabin's dark windows. Several sealed buckets stood near large trees ringing the clearing; fishing rods leaned against another whose heavy limbs were draped with ropes and a crude pulley system. A weathered plank, the words 'The Sanctuary' burned into its surface, was nailed to a tree. She pulled her head back behind the hedge and cast a worried glance at Mitch. He motioned her along the path, and they stood face to face, whispering. Cass could smell Darla's coffee on his breath.

"Did you see the sign?" she asked.

Mitch nodded.

"Where are they?"

"Must be inside the cabin."

"And their cars?"

"Tire tracks run through the clearing. There's a break on the other side. They must pull straight through and walk back."

Anticipation rose hot in her throat. "What now?"

"Let's get a look in the cabin. You take this side; I'll circle around the other. Stay low, take quick glances through the windows. If you can't see in, move on to the next. Keep off the front porch. The wood may creak. Meet me back here in three."

They crept forward again and Mitch eased around the bushes, checking the clearing. He motioned to Cass and both scurried forward, Mitch disappearing behind the cabin. The campfire flickered in a sudden breeze, tossing her shadow large against the building. She knelt quickly and shuffled beneath the rearmost window, gun at her cheek as she raised her head. A heavy blanket completely covered the opening and a blunted thunking came through the glass. Someone was inside. Her palms prickled with sweat.

She dropped and, shoulder gently scraping the wall's ancient, dried cladding, hurried to the next window. It too was covered, no light seeping from the edges, and all was silent. Easing forward, she reached the porch to peer around its side when the front door banged open, a rectangle of amber light spilling across the clearing's dirt floor. The sound of heavy footsteps echoed on the raised wood. Cass froze, adrenaline searing her veins, sweat slicking her body. The door clicked closed, the light was wiped away, and voices drifted into the clearing. From her position at the side of the building, she caught only fragments of frantic whispers.

"…woman… us?"

"…Deacon…deal with…"

"The sanctity… cleanse…"

A match scratched in the night and a sweet scent drifted into the clearing. Cass lifted her nose to the air and struggled to name its source.

"…carry…cannot hesitate…Circle tonight."

"…no choice, the wicked…purge…The Sanctuary."

"Focus … must continue…will… -stand?"

The voices were familiar, but in their hushed tones, Cass couldn't place them. The door creaked open and footsteps faded inside. She counted to ten and eased her head around the corner to find the porch empty. Releasing a slow breath, she started to pull her head back behind the wall when her eye caught a flash of white nestled against one of the posts supporting the porch's roof. A tennis shoe.

Startled, she pulled her head around the corner, pressing flat against the rough wood, thinking through the options. The shoe was a smaller size, maybe a woman's or a child's. Her mind leapt to the empty car across the bridge and her heart raced. She checked her watch and scuttled along the cabin, across the clearing and down the path. Mitch jerked her to him, nose to nose.

"What happened?"

"I think Evelyn Grove is in the house," she answered, panting. "There's a tennis shoe on the front porch. Would fit a woman or a kid. Two men came outside, arguing but in low voices." She caught her breath. "They mentioned a woman and needing to deal with something. One of them was panicking, the other reassuring him."

"Who were they?"

Cass shook her head. "Their voices were too soft. I couldn't see through the windows, but I heard a bumping noise at the back of the cabin. You?"

"Some scraping sounds from inside, like chairs being moved around. The side windows were covered. The back of the building has one door, no windows, and a generator."

"What now?"

Mitch's eyes roved the track for signs of movement. "We need to talk to Munk, see if he's found Evelyn yet. If she's in that cabin and missing a shoe, we've got problems."

"We can't leave these guys Mitch, not until we know what they're up to."

He frowned down at her. "I don't want either of us to be alone out here."

"Look, you go back along the trail and call Munk when you're far enough away that your voice and the light from the phone won't carry. I'll keep an eye on them."

"I'm not comfortable leaving you out here, Cass."

She pulled back and looked into his face, dragging her sleeve across her sweaty forehead, scraping greasepaint away and exposing a swath of creamy skin. Her eyes blazed. "You don't think I can handle it?"

"Cass," he breathed, rolling his eyes. "I know you can handle it, but these men could be dangerous. What do I tell Jack, or your dad, if something happens to you?"

"What would I tell Darla if it were you?" she hissed, watching Mitch shake his head in defeat. "Right now, I'm not your best friend's sister. I'm your partner. This is what I've trained for. I'll wait inside the bushes by that last bend until you're back, just watching."

"No heroics?"

"Not unless someone's gonna get hurt."

"All right," he agreed. "Smear some of that greasepaint on your forehead. I'll be back as quick as I can."

———————

CASS INCHED BETWEEN TWO bushes, pushing deeper into the shadows at the edge of the clearing. Resting her back against a heavy pine tree, she caught sight of a glossy vine trailing across the ground and uttered a silent prayer that it wasn't poison ivy. From this position, the back of the cabin was obscured, but she had a clear view of the front door, the picnic table and the campfire.

The building and clearing were still, quiet. While she waited for movement, she wondered at Mitch's reaction to the thought that she might be hurt. He and Jack had been friends since childhood and Mitch had always been around the house. And even after Jack went to prison, Mitch would stop by to check on the family in general, and Cass in particular. Their contact became less frequent when he joined the police force, met Darla and got married, and they lost touch altogether while Cass was away at Texas A&M. She'd contacted him when she decided to join the force, and as a uniformed officer she pestered him constantly for assignments that would help her reach her goal of becoming a detective. At the young age of twenty-five she had been promoted and partnered with Mitch. Since then, he had continued as her mentor and the bond they had forged through Jack when both were younger was reformed.

His concern wasn't sexual, Cass knew that. She had grown up surrounded by six older brothers and recognized the protective instinct of a brother for a sister that Mitch felt for her. While she loved him for it, she sometimes wondered if she would ever be free of the many men in her life, to stand on her own two feet. She'd fought for every scrap of food when she was growing up, against a hungry horde of growing boys who swept across groceries like locusts, leaving nothing in their wake. But in spite of the constant sibling jostling, she had always had someone to take her troubles to, someone to help with her problems. Secretly she feared that all the support and encouragement made her soft, and that fear had driven a single-minded desire to prove herself since she'd been a child.

Cass sucked in a sharp breath and fingered her gun as the door swept open and a stately procession garbed in crimson robes and matching hoods marched toward her hiding place. Unseen eyes stared from the depths of two holes punched in each soft hood, and solemn lips murmured a chant against a third opening. Her eyes followed the line of each hood up to its tall point, and although their color was of blood instead of a pure white, thoughts of the Klan skittered through her mind. As each figure approached, she studied its build and movements, trying desperately to recognize Salter, Deacon Cronus or the mayor. Flowing robes swirled around bare ankles as the line drew near the bushes and then coiled away, turning their backs on her and circling the clearing. Tiny puffs of dust rose in clouds with each footstep. She counted twelve figures, eleven in dark robes and one massive form in white. He lifted his arms and the robe's sleeves slide back along his forearms, revealing a white bandage wrapped around one hand. The procession filed silently into place around the fire pit.

"Brethren," a low voice began. Cass stretched her chin forward, straining to hear. "We are gathered on this solemn occasion in a spirit of joy, grateful to welcome a new member to our midst. And tonight, we have the rare honor of raising one among you to the Circle of Illumination."

———————

MITCH REACHED THE MAIN road, flipped his phone open again and immediately sprinted toward the river. He had no signal. *Unbelievable.* He raced through the quiet night, invisible thanks to his dark clothes and the greasepaint, eyes alert for new cars and ears straining to hear anything that would signal a change back at the cabin.

He'd been serious when he told Cass that he didn't doubt her ability to handle the situation. But this was volatile, uncertain. Mitch had to remind himself that although she might look fragile, Cass could more than take care of herself. But all of them were strung out from Lenny Scarborough's death on Sunday and Garrett's... well, Garrett's crucifixion yesterday. What was happening to his quiet little county?

Mitch spotted Evelyn Grove's car and quickened his pace, ignoring the stitch screaming in his side. He needed to know about Evelyn and get back to Cass.

CHAPTER 85

A MURMUR SWEPT THROUGH the group and the speaker raised his bandaged hand for silence. Cass leaned forward into the prickly bushes, straining to hear and again counting to see if she'd missed the thirteenth member of The Church. There were only twelve present. The figure in white spoke, voice trembling in the small clearing.

"Through the ages, Satan has adapted his role as deceiver to suit the circumstances and pursue his evil purposes. From taking the shape of a serpent in the Garden of Eden to tempt the weak woman and engaging in diabolical mimicry to distort the sanctity of our Lord's sacrifice, to vile demonic possession of hapless men and creating the modern scourges of drugs and crime, Satan is the master of fraud. And now," he continued, passion building, "we find ourselves trapped in a political system determined to sacrifice the rights of God fearing men to those of pale and dubious character. Men who would take what is ours, earned through sweat and honest labor, are now given comfort and succor by the law. The very institution designed to guarantee the freedom of those who abide within it has now been twisted by Satan to protect his wicked minions." A buzz of agreement rose from around the fire and he thundered on. "Our society has grown weak, failing to punish those who do harm, who seek to unbalance this proud nation formed under God. Our judges and politicians are frightened to do what is right, *because it is difficult*. Those who whine and moan about the human rights of criminals raise the wicked above the innocent, glorify crime above honesty and integrity. Make no mistake, the hands of our fine law enforcement officers are tied by the laws they swore to uphold." His voice dropped as he gazed around the fire. "Therefore, Brethren, unnoticed and unrecognized, it is our great glory to serve the Lord by delivering swift justice against Satan's despicable attacks."

The voice. Cass's mind reeled, struggling to make a connection. Her brain slammed together the sound and the body, picturing Deacon

Cronus's corpulent frame beneath the white robe, and she fought to remain still. From the way he spoke, he was the leader of this, this what? Group of vigilantes? She hadn't picked that up from reading *The Church of the True Believer.* Turning her wrist to check the time, she wondered if Mitch had made it back and was watching. So far, nothing illegal had happened and she had no choice but to stay put.

"Tonight," Deacon Cronus continued, "we reaffirm our commitment to the fight. As when we pledged to follow the holy orders, we will renew our commitment to The Church and each other, washed in the sacred blood of the lamb, purified by the innocents." He scanned the eleven men in maroon colored robes surrounding him. "Stoke the flames and bring forth the initiate."

The circle expanded from the campfire and two men stepped away – a burly figure moved to the woodpile and a slightly hunched form toward the porch. The fire leapt at the new logs laid atop it and the clearing grew brighter. At a creak from the front door, Cass peeled her eyes from the group who were forming a pathway from the cabin to the picnic table. Two men stepped onto the porch, the hunched figure pulling gently on the arm of another man. Cass caught a glimpse of him as he was led across the porch and between the two lines of robed men. His pale form was naked save for a white cloth wrapped around his hips and a bandage on his thigh.

A murmuring arose as he passed between the men, and several reached out a hand to touch him. He seemed jumpy, head bobbing as he edged toward the picnic table, and he hesitated before stepping fully into the fire's glow, hands fluttering at his hips. Cass's mouth dropped open in disbelief as Officer Hugo Petchard, pasty flesh spattered golden in the flames, tugged uncomfortably at his loincloth.

———————

SHE BLINKED, WATCHING AS his eyes darted around the clearing before he drew a deep breath and scrambled onto the picnic table, laying flat on the butcher paper, his belly as white as a frog's and legs a startling pink where new skin was repairing his burns. One man stepped forward, wrapping heavy ropes across Petchard's puny chest, hips and lower legs, careful to avoid his burns and checking occasionally to make sure the bindings were secure but not too tight. Petchard strained to lift his head, an anxious smile twitching at his lips as he watched the other man work. After a final examination of the ropes, the man joined the others in a semi-circle between the table and the cabin, their heads bowed.

Deacon Cronus stood at the foot of the picnic table, hands tucked into the billowy sleeves of his white robe. "It is a rare honor and grave responsibility to join The Church the True Believer. Members are carefully screened and selected, their worthiness tested before they are permitted to unite with one of the most sacred collectives in the history of man. Our accountability is to God and God alone. We are warriors; linked by our beliefs and by our desire to cleanse the world of Satan and his minions." He lowered his head to gaze at Petchard. "You, among men, have been chosen and tested. Your responsibilities have been explained to you and you have exercised free will in coming to join with us tonight. As a reminder of Jesus' sacrifice for us, you will bear the mark of the centurion's sword, where it pierced his side. In the tradition of Abraham and his son Isaac, as a reflection of their absolute faith in God to provide, tonight we participate in the ritual slaughter of the innocent."

At this, Petchard tried to sit up. "Hang on a minute. Ritual slaughter?"

"We await the sweet scent of the burnt offering –"

His eyes flew wide. "*Burnt* offering?"

"– from this specimen, perfected through our Lord's grace," Deacon Cronus continued, ignoring Petchard's protests.

In spite of the bizarre scene, Cass had to stifle a snort at the thought of Petchard as a perfect specimen of anything. She lowered a hand by inches to rub a calf muscle that was threatening to cramp the longer she leaned forward into the bush. Deacon Cronus pulled his hands from the wide sleeves of his white robe. An object was visible in his bandaged hand, and Cass's heart thrummed at the flash of firelight on metal.

Flicking her eyes at the dark path behind her, she wondered where Mitch was. This was moving too fast.

———

HE PAUSED AS HE reached the patrol car, rocking forward to brace his hands on his knees as he sucked in air.

"Why didn't you call?" Munk asked.

Mitch held up his phone. "No signal," he gasped.

Truman nodded. "I tried to tell you that cell coverage is spotty out here, but the sheriff cut me off. Where's Cass?"

Mitch hooked a thumb over his shoulder, swallowing. "We found them. They're in a cabin back in the woods. I left her there to come call you. Have you found Evelyn?"

Munk shook his head, face grim. "Car's locked and her purse is gone, but there are two dollar bills on the driver's seat. She left a school board meeting over an hour ago. Robert hasn't heard from her and neither have the twins."

Mitch nodded. "They might have her. Let's go."

CHAPTER 86

"THROUGH THE SPEARING OF the initiate, we are each reminded of the pain Jesus endured as he gave himself for us." Deacon Cronus moved the object from one hand to the other, and a long knife glinted in the firelight.

Petchard twisted as far as his restraints allowed, eyes probing the hooded figures, voice pleading for someone to untie him. A few shifted uncomfortably, but no one responded to his cries. His eyes shot to the robed figure beside him, imploring. "Newton, this ain't funny. I know you said there'd be some strange stuff going on tonight, but this is too weird for me. I don't want to get cut, man. Let me loose."

Newton? Cass gasped and screwed her eyes shut as the cramp hit her calf. She pressed her lips together to quell a moan and dug her fingers into the tight flesh. Her eyes snapped open at the sound of a shrill yelp, and she caught the flash of the blade as Cronus passed it to another robed figure. The man raised a finger to push glasses hidden beneath his hood up on his nose, then raised the knife over his head in a double-handed grip, his maroon robe slithering along his strong arms to puddle around his bare shoulders.

"No way, man! Come on, Greg," Petchard whined, fear raising his voice nearly an octave as he struggled. "Don't do this. You don't have to do this. Come on, man! I thought we were friends."

"We are," came a clear voice from inside the hood. "This is the best offer of friendship I can give you, Petchard." He raised his arms higher, the long blade flashing with the motion, its smooth surface reflecting the fire.

Officer Greg Newton? The question and its attendant horror barely registered as Cass shoved through the prickly bush and into the clearing, gun pointed at the figure with the knife, hobbling on her good leg and dragging the heavy, cramping leg behind her.

"Drop the knife, Newton," she ordered as his arm began a swift

356

downward arc toward Petchard. Figures whipped around at the sound of her voice, robes swirling, and a scream split the clearing. Time froze. Vision unnaturally clear, Cass followed the sweep of the knife as it fell toward Petchard's chest. Unconsciously, she registered that Newton had no intention of stopping. She drew a breath as images flashed through her brain past the searing, twisting pain in her leg – Newton guarding Angie's hospital room; working with Truman on Garrett's cell phone; leaving the neighborhood where Salter lived right before Cass and Truman arrived. Petchard was a pain in the ass, no doubt, but this was her sworn duty, to protect and defend, even against others who had taken the same vow. For a single heartbeat she hesitated, then released the breath and squeezed the trigger twice.

The gunshots boomed in the space enclosed by the trees. Twin dots pierced his chest and Newton flew back from the table, arms wide, scarlet robe billowing. The knife arced from his hand, hilt over point, glimmering as it caught the firelight before disappearing into the woods. He landed on his back with a thud, a rush of air knocked from his lungs, hood fluttering over a pair of glasses and settling to reveal a creamy chin and neck. Petchard's eyes followed Newton's fall and he struggled fiercely against his bindings, tiny sobs slipping from his mouth. Ears buzzing, Cass lurched forward, gun raised, praying that there was more than one Greg Newton in Forney County.

A voice rang out, calm, authoritative. "Jericho."

At the single word, as one, they dashed from the fire. The clearing swirled with crimson but was oddly silent except for Petchard's whimpering. Deacon Cronus stood motionless at the foot of the picnic table until another body crashed into his, jolting him from his stunned paralysis. He stumbled to one side, raising his white robe to reveal thick ankles and chubby calves as he stepped over Newton's body and trundled toward a break in the clearing. The distant sound of engines roaring to life penetrated through the trees.

"Police, Deacon Cronus. Stop right there," Cass demanded. He lifted a hand to his head, as if to check that his hood was still in place, and quickened his rolling gate.

She called again, ordering him to stop, but he only stretched his hands forward, reaching for a nearby tree. Cass drew another breath, her fingertips tingling, and for the third time in a matter of seconds, she fired.

CHAPTER 87

THE FIRST TWO SHOTS echoed off the patrol car's closed windows and adrenaline surged as Munk skid the car to a stop in the mouth of the dirt track. Three doors flew open and the men flattened themselves along each side of the narrow path, crouching in shadows as they moved forward, balancing the need for speed with the uncertainty of the track's bumps and gullies. Weapon drawn and eyes probing the night, Mitch's mind raced with the possibilities the gunshot brought and he shut the thoughts down, forcing his brain to be still even as his ears were filled with the harsh sounds of his own breath. He caught movement about twenty feet ahead of him, Munk's and Truman's dark bodies barely discernable as they pressed against the overgrown shrubs. In moments they were at the track's first dogleg and angling away from the Sabine River. Truman cursed gently as he jumped over a gouge in the path, regaining his balance and squatting again into a crouch.

A third shot boomed through the night and Mitch's heart leapt to his mouth. The three men broke into a run. Munk stumbled and fell to his knees before pushing himself upright and moving to the middle of the path. Riding the fresh wave of adrenaline, Mitch pushed his long limbs to move faster, heedless of the rough path beneath him, when suddenly his right foot failed to find purchase and he tumbled forward. A blinding light seared his vision as his leg snapped. He tried to scream but air whooshed from his mouth as his chest slammed into the side of the gully. Pain and nausea engulfed him as he choked, and darkness circled in to envelope him.

CHAPTER 88

BARK FLEW AND CRONUS jerked to a crouching halt, white robes falling to cover his ankles. Slowly, he raised his hands.

Two robed figures darted toward the cabin, one racing around its side and the other fumbling with a key at the front door. They met at the corner of the porch and Cass's eyes leapt at the movement. In that instant of contact, she caught the glimmer of an eye beneath the hood and then they were gone, melting into the trees, their maroon robes disappearing into the smooth depths of the forest. In a sudden rush, flames gobbled at the cabin's ancient wood, spilling bright light and dark smoke into the clearing. A scream cut the air as Munk and Truman stumbled from the heavy bushes lining the dirt track. Panting, Munk paused as a second terrified wail broke through the cabin's walls.

"Evelyn!" he roared, storming the cabin. He twisted the door's handle and stepped back when it didn't move. He slammed his shoulder into the front door. Truman rushed behind him, hurling his slight body with Munk's second blow. The door popped from its hinges with an almighty crack and black smoke billowed through the opening, driving the two men back, coughing against the fumes. An anguished cry tore from Munk's throat and he charged through the swirling cloud.

"Wait!" Truman called, running after him.

Cass gasped as two slim figures staggered from the cabin, clutching their throats as they sucked in fresh air, each wearing a sheet fashioned toga-style around them, and a blindfold. Truman tumbled down the porch steps, tangled between the bodies. He scrambled to his feet, ripped their blindfolds off and stopped, staring at the dazed girls. Neither was the Salter child. They were younger than Cass had expected, perhaps eleven or twelve, and Cass felt and mirrored Truman's shock.

A scream sounded from inside the cabin and the back door shrieked as it split open. Truman ran around the side of the building to see a smoke-blackened Munk stumbling through the open door, his sister, still tied to a chair, clutched in his arms. A white sheet was twisted around his ankles and they collapsed on the soft soil, gasping for air.

"Cass," Munk croaked, eyes streaming, and Truman darted toward the clearing to see her advancing on a large figure in a white robe, her arms locked, gun raised. A motorcycle engine whined through the fire's steady roar and the girls huddled close to one another, frightened eyes locked onto Cass.

"Let me cuff him," Truman called, stepping closer, eyes darting to Petchard's terrified, sniveling form on the picnic table and the scarlet-robed figure motionless on the ground. He glanced at her face, startled at the fury in her grease painted features. "Let me cuff him," he repeated, holding a hand out and gently touching her arm.

She nodded tightly, lowering her weapon. Stepping forward, she tugged the hood from his head. Deacon Cronus lowered his face toward the ground and shuddered. "Use the picnic table," she ordered, reaching down to massage her calf muscle, "then come with me."

Truman wrapped the Deacon's arms around one of the supports linking the seat and the table, cuffing his hands together. He scowled at Petchard, slick with sweat and fear. "I knew you were an idiot, but I can't believe you're involved in this."

"She shot Newton, man," Petchard whined. "She's crazy. Untie me before she shoots me. Let me up," he pleaded.

Truman slid a hunting knife from a sheath at his ankle and quickly sliced through the top rope binding Petchard's chest, his waist and his ankles, leaving the man to unwind himself. He glanced at the burning building and saw Munk's stout shape dragging his sister, still tied in her chair, away from danger.

"Watch him," he called to Munk as he drew his weapon and followed Cass toward a small break in the tree line where she turned to look at the terrified girls.

"Stay here," she ordered, face softening at the sight of the tears streaking their sooty faces. "Get away from the cabin. But stay here."

Wide eyed, they edged away from the burning building but stopped before reaching the picnic table, watching the half naked man struggling against the thick ropes.

"Where's Mitch?" she asked Truman, voice quiet beneath the fire's crackle.

"I don't know," he whispered, glancing into the clearing. "We were on that dirt track when we heard the third shot, and started running. He was behind us."

She frowned as she wondered what could've happened to him. Maybe he had followed the men into the woods when they ran. "I think they've all gone now," she whispered, crouching and creeping forward. "But we need to be sure."

He hesitated. "Was that Greg Newton?"

"I –," she cut her eyes at him then looked back out into the woods. "I don't know. I'll fill you in later. Let's go."

———————

THEY MOVED SLOWLY DOWN another tiny dirt track, the sound of the forest gradually muting the fire popping in the background. An armadillo shuffled out of the undergrowth, grunting softly, pausing as the two humans passed by before continuing his foraging. Cass stopped, twisting her head to one side. A mockingbird called and then – there it was – a low moan floated across the heavy air. She pointed right, and they followed the sound through the woods toward the murky smell of the river bank, hands stretched forward to feel for branches as dead brush and pine needles snapped underfoot. The moaning stopped for several seconds then resumed and they adjusted their path, angling closer to the river.

"Help me," a strangled voice called out. "Please."

Truman pointed straight ahead and they separated, moving in a wide arc to circle in on two sides. Cass finally spotted a hump folded in a pool of dappled moonlight. "Police. Who's there?" she called.

"I'm stuck," a voice coughed. "Please help me."

She moved forward and saw Truman's dark shape coming toward her. They met near the strange lump, finding the form of a man splayed in an awkward position. A small pool of liquid spread from beneath his robe, pulsing gently as it caught the moonlight. An old fence was strung in both directions, five strands of barbed wire, broken in places but still clinging to rotting fence posts. The man was wrapped in the rusted wire, arms spread out to his sides, neck twisted at an odd angle, legs scissored together. Patches of pale skin were luminous through the ripped fabric of his dark robe.

"Please," he repeated, his familiar voice trembling. "I'm bleeding."

Cass stepped forward and peeled the hood from his face, anger and frustration flooding her brain at the sight of Jed Salter's contorted features. Truman knelt beside the bank president and began probing gently, wincing as the other man moaned. He slipped a flashlight from his belt, running the beam along the twisted body before shaking his head up at Cass. "I don't know how to get him undone."

She squatted beside Truman, talking as her fingers fluttered across the four-pointed barbs, trying to find a way to work him free. "Where's your son?"

"He's dead," Salter stated flatly, voice a whisper.

"Brian?" Cass coughed.

"No," he sighed, frowning. "Nathaniel. My oldest."

"Where is Brian?"

His eyes found her face. "I made him stay at home tonight."

She breathed a silent sigh of relief that Brian was unharmed, her anger growing at what had happened to Evelyn Grove and the two girls. "You called off his camping trip?" she asked, sarcasm deep in her voice.

He shut his eyes briefly. "Yes."

"Why?" she demanded.

"It... wasn't time for him."

Truman worked at freeing the older man as Cass continued. "What were you doing out here, Mr. Salter?"

"It's not what you think – we've never hurt anyone." He tried to turn his head and gasped with the effort. "My leg. Please."

Truman slipped his knife from its sheath and sliced through the robe's delicate fabric. Thin trails of blood ran along Salter's naked, muscled body from the barbs embedded in his flesh. Cass quickly checked his back and arms, gently moving the shredded fabric to see how seriously he was injured and spotting the customary scar on his right side. Truman followed the wire's path between Salter's legs and raised slick, darkened fingers for Cass to see, his voice low. "The flow down his leg is steady. He's pierced something."

"Where?" she asked, surprised to feel indifference slide around her chest in the face of Salter's pain.

Truman worked his fingers along the twisted wire, calculating the distance between barbs. "Between his thighs. Maybe an artery?" He rocked back on his heels, pulling his belt loose from his dark trousers. "It's pretty high, but from the way his legs are pressed together, I can't tell how bad it is. Give me your belt." He poked the belt's smooth, flat end between Salter's legs, flinching as the older man groaned. Tightening it into a makeshift tourniquet around the right thigh, he reached for her belt. "Do you have a signal?"

She pulled her phone from its holster and flipped it open. "Nothing. You?"

"In my pocket," he said, thrusting a hip at her as he tightened the second belt around Salter's left thigh. She slid his phone out and shook her head. "Take these," Truman said, releasing the slippery tourniquets into her grasp.

Salter grimaced as she wrapped each belt around one of her hands, placing a foot on either side of his legs and leaning back to tug the belts tighter as the pulsing of blood into the small pool slowed.

"I'll find a signal and call an ambulance," Truman called as he trotted into the underbrush. A small explosion woofed through the forest and a bright glow arced toward the heavens, splashing light across the anguished, tangled man and the furious woman who held his life in her hands.

"Call Sparky," she shouted after the young officer. "We need the fire trucks."

CHAPTER 89

SHE WATCHED TRUMAN'S FLASHLIGHT bounce through the forest until the sounds of movement had faded. She stared at Salter, his face pale in the moonlight, silver hair darkened with sweat. "Evelyn Grove. What happened?"

A garbled chuckle escaped him. "She found us. I don't know how, but she strolled into The Sanctuary like she owned the place, asking to borrow a phone. There were just two of us outside then, the rest were inside. But she'd seen our faces and the robes." He tried to shrug, gasping as the barbs bit deeper into a shoulder. "We had to get rid of her."

Hot anger slid up her spine. "Permanently? After your Celebration of Illumination?"

Salter's eyes widened. "You *did* know."

"Yes," she replied, adjusting her hold on the belts.

"How?"

"The invitation. We found one out at Lenny's, from 1988. I saw yours at the bank this morning, just a flash of it. I wasn't sure what I'd seen until later."

"You knocked the mail off my desk on purpose."

"Yes."

"Hoffner knew, didn't he, when he told the reporters there was a cult operating in the area."

"Things weren't so clear at that point. I don't know what he thought he was doing." She shifted her weight, moving to see Salter's face more clearly. "Now, you know how I found you tonight. Tell me a few things."

He moved his head gently. "I can't."

The anger at her spine uncoiled, twisting hot ropes around her stomach. Cass leaned forward and loosened her grip on the belts, only slightly, and saw the pool at Salter's feet surge again. "You will," she stated. "Evelyn Grove."

His eyes flashed to her face and he gasped. "You're an officer of the law. You can't."

A startling awareness pierced her mind, and in that moment she knew with certainty that Jed Salter would die tonight. The desire to kill flooded her body and the image of a contorted Richard Nixon flashed through her brain. "Try me," she growled. "Nobody out here but us girls. You've lost a lot of blood." She cocked her head to one side. "How tragic, and completely expected, that a man bleeds out when he's got barbed wire digging into an artery. And you so muscled from all those marathons," she continued, running her eyes along his naked body, "not a lick of fat on you to protect that artery."

"Tighten them," he commanded, anger strengthening his voice.

"Gosh Mr. Salter, the belts are slippery. Hard to hold on to," she answered, voice flat. "Talk."

"She would've disappeared," he gasped. Cass tightened the belts and his face relaxed. "In the river perhaps, or maybe just buried if we didn't want the body to be found."

"What about the girls?"

"What about them?"

"Who are they?"

He grimaced. "I don't know their names. Cronus brings them. Training, he calls it."

"Are they always the same girls?"

He shrugged, a short movement against the wire. "Sometimes. They're never hurt. In fact, they're proud to be our acolytes."

"Acolytes," she repeated, anger twisting more tightly.

"They serve, assist. Nothing more. They're blindfolded when our hoods are off, or if we're engaged in one of the more sacred rituals, like tonight." He drew a shallow breath. "They help with the sacrament and keep the fire burning, that type of thing."

"Are they the girls in Lenny's photos?"

"What photos?"

"Come on," she snorted.

Salter searched her face. "Photos of what?"

"Men having sex with men." She watched his Adam's apple bounce in his throat. "Men abusing girls."

"My God," he murmured, sagging deeper against the wire. "Children."

Cass snarled, hands trembling as she slacked the belts. "You think He's listening? You think He cares about a group of child molesters? Molesting in His name?"

His eyes flew wide, beseeching. "I had no idea. You must believe me. I – I suspected." He struggled with the words. "It wasn't supposed to be like that. They wanted to help. Their innocence, that's what we needed."

"Innocence?" she asked, incredulous. "They'll never get that back. Don't bother protesting *your* innocence. We'll know exactly how sick you are when we compare your body to those in the photographs. Scars and moles don't lie, do they?"

"You won't find me in them," he insisted with a soft moan. "I can't believe it's gone this far."

"*What* has gone this far?"

"This isn't how it should be. The Church has experienced a –," he briefly attempted to move his arms, stopping quickly with the pain, "– a schism over the last two decades. Some of us believed it needed to return to its roots. Others thought it wasn't progressive enough."

"What are you talking about?"

"Tighten the belts," he begged. "Please."

Cass obliged, grasping the slippery leather more firmly and ignoring his gasp of pain. "What roots?"

"We were formed to fight corruption, back in the twenties. The world was in turmoil, morals declining, people forgetting their place; women, blacks, immigrants, all overreaching." He struggled to draw a breath, slowly expanding his chest against the barbs. "Satan was at the heart of the uproar – the lord of chaos and the master of deception. He's used the liberal movement in this country to weaken us all, to make us soft. We're no longer capable of punishing transgressions in a manner to ensure repentance and the seeking of forgiveness. We refuse to recognize evil and accept any excuse to justify horrible crimes. Our weakness allows the liberals to bleed for the perpetrators, then coddle the wicked in prisons with better food, clothing and amenities than their victims have." He drew another slow breath. "And when they're released back into society? They're better equipped for more evil, greater destruction. Ironic, some would say. Exactly what we deserve for our failure to deal with the root of the problem, that's what we believe. Is it any wonder the world is going to hell?"

Her mind flashed to her brother Jack, and the sparse life he enjoyed in the state penitentiary at Huntsville. 'Coddle' and 'amenities' were two words she couldn't attach to his experience.

"The Church's mission was simple," Salter continued. "Pure. We sought to right those wrongs that the law increasingly wouldn't touch."

"Vigilante justice?"

He inclined his head. "Our means were more financial than physical. We were never that harsh. We never had to be. The first Klan revival occurred at about the right time to deliver physical justice."

"The Church's initial focus was to maintain the status quo through non-violent means?"

"Aptly put," he sighed.

"And now?"

"The Klan has disappeared, hasn't it?"

"And The Church has filled the void? I haven't noticed any lynchings or crosses burning on lawns."

Salter's bloodless lips curled in a slight smile. "Our members are a little more sophisticated than that. We've hung on to the economic sabotage and," he grimaced, "some of our members are more accepting of violent means than others."

An incident that occurred several weeks previously flashed through her mind. Toby Waller, a local deadbeat with a history of petty violence, had stormed into the courthouse shouting about conspiracies and waving his shotgun. Elaine slapped the panic button and dropped behind her counter while Waller was taken into custody. It turned out that he had lost his job with a local oil company, and subsequently, he'd lost his family home, located on a prime piece of real estate near downtown. The bailiffs had come around with an eviction order and physically removed him from the house. The property sold immediately. The house was razed and within a week, construction for an automobile dealership had started on the site. Funnily enough, the same man ran the oil company and the car company. Waller was found a few weeks later, hanging from a tree that remained in his old front yard, now providing shade for the dealership's planned showroom. Suicide, people said, but Grey's autopsy was inconclusive and the case remained open.

"Toby Waller?" she asked.

Salter lowered his chin. "He was a stupid man."

"Toby was no Einstein, I'll give you that, but stupidity is a poor reason to steal the man's home."

"He would have been well compensated for that land, but he refused to see reason. When he continued to refuse, against even higher offers," Salter sighed, "steps were taken to ensure the land would become available for sale."

"How?"

"He lost his job, correct?"

Cass nodded.

"He wouldn't have found another, and he had little money in the bank. Eventually, the house and land would've come up for sale due to non-payment of taxes."

"That's... that's got to be illegal."

He chuckled grimly. "All perfectly within the law, I assure you. How do you think most of the landowners in this county have accumulated their property over the years? Purchasing real estate for the price of unpaid back taxes can be quite profitable."

"But someone caused Toby to lose his job, so the taxes would be unpaid. That's unethical, at a minimum."

His shoulder twitched. "Progress."

"How can you consider that progress?"

His lips twisted in a superior smile. "Do you have any idea how many jobs will be created thanks to the car dealership that's being built? How many God-fearing men will be able to support their families?"

"And how much money will the dealership make for its owner?"

Again, he attempted to shrug, grimacing with the effort.

Cass spoke softly. "It wasn't suicide, was it?"

Salter's eyes slid closed, the sneer sliding from his lips. "I objected."

Cass's heart hardened. "If you disagreed, why have you stayed?"

"Membership is for life. There is no leaving."

"Not true. Mr. Shepherd walked away."

"Shepherd," Salter said quietly, "knew things. I don't have that same luxury."

"Why not?"

"It's complicated."

"It's Nathaniel, isn't it?"

He recoiled as if she had slapped him.

"Your son died during the initiation ritual, didn't he?" Cass continued, speculating based on Rose's comments that morning. "He had a heart condition, something you didn't know about, and the shock of seeing his father raising a knife to kill him was too much."

"You don't understand."

"No," she replied, "I don't. I don't understand how you could expose your child to something like this…," a snarl curled her lip, "this cult. I don't understand how you could tie your son to a table and have him believe that you'll kill him unless God intervenes. You literally scared him to death. That's sick, Mr. Salter. They aren't responsible for Nathaniel's death. You are."

"Yes, I am," he moaned. "And they won't let me forget it. I cannot leave The Church. They won't allow it."

"Then let me help you, Mr. Salter. Help me destroy them, as they destroyed Nathaniel, as they're destroying you."

"I can't."

"Really?" She loosened the belts and ached from the surge of warm blood into her stiff fingers. "I was serious earlier when I said you've lost a lot of blood. You don't have much more to lose. What does it matter now?"

"Yes, Detective. I'll die out here, whether you have the rage inside you to kill me or not. That barb is deep in my thigh. They can't take me off the wire without disturbing it, and once it's moved it'll be difficult to stop the blood." He sighed as Cass pulled herself forward, tightening the belts again. "You were right about the running. I have overdone it. I've struggled with the activities of The Church, suffered over them, and running was an escape."

"Why didn't you report them?"

"They would've killed me," he stated flatly, tired eyes searching her face. "And my family couldn't have survived a second tragic death."

"How could they kill you and get away with it, Mr. Salter? You're the president of Arcadia's biggest bank. We might not worry too much over

Toby Waller, but we'd pull out all the stops to investigate your murder," she sneered.

"Investigate the men who ordered the killing of your associate, Chad Garrett?" He slowly drew another breath. "Men who can murder a police officer are too powerful for you. And you have nothing on Garrett's death, or Toby's, for that matter. And you'd never tie either to us."

"I've got your confession now, Salter. We'll find the evidence we need."

"Even if you did – and believe me, you won't – you wouldn't be able to tie it to us. It wouldn't be allowed."

A surge of fury at her helplessness flashed white through her brain. She loosened the belts again. "Too many important people, right? Who are they?"

"What?"

"We know there're thirteen of you, including your new initiate, Petchard. I've seen Deacon Cronus. Lenny Scarborough is dead, so is Greg Newton," she continued, watching as Salter's eyes fluttered closed. She checked the dark liquid pulsing into a wider pool. "Who else?"

"Tighten the belts," he gasped.

"Why should I, you sick pervert?"

"Please," he sighed. "You have no idea how much we do for you."

"For me?" she barked, jerking the belts tight, shoulders quivering from the strain.

"Yes," he gasped. "The police force, and justice in general."

"What are you talking about?"

"The hot house that burned this weekend?"

"What about it?"

"Your forensics man got no useable prints off the pots, am I right?"

Cass nodded.

"Tell him to slice open the bags of potting soil. He'll find cocaine stuffed inside them. An especially large shipment, hence our timing for the fire." She gasped as Salter grimaced. "What has Forney County been having a problem with lately? It started over in Elysian Fields, not too long ago. Your Officer Truman did some good work undercover over there, but it wasn't enough." His eyes fluttered closed and slowly reopened. Blood loss was making him weak. "Drugs. Cocaine, in particular. What better way to transport sealed bags of coke than tucked inside huge bags of potting soil?

It's just a shame the fire didn't purify the entire place. But the entrepreneur who started that operation has received a very clear message and will be moving on."

"How do you know all this?"

His brief chuckle collapsed into a sputter as he moved, barbs digging deeper into his torn flesh. "We have our ways."

"*If* this is true, why didn't you notify the police?"

"What would you have done, Detective? We couldn't have given you probable cause to search without sacrificing our sources. You didn't even know someone was growing marijuana commercially in Forney County. How could you have stopped him?"

"We have *our* ways, Mr. Salter. We could've followed him, observed him."

"And how many more kids would've been caught up in a toke or 'just a little sniff' while you tried to follow him? How many lives would be wasted?"

"So you and your Church helped us out?"

Salter's lips drew away from his teeth, his mouth a black slash across his pale face. "You'll dismantle that hot house, burn the marijuana and destroy the cocaine. Pretty good bang for our buck, don't you agree?"

"You justify all *that*," Cass lifted her chin toward the clearing, "that religious mumbo-jumbo and abusing kids, in the name of vigilante justice?"

"*Divine* justice, Detective. The kind our liberal country can no longer stomach dishing out. We should put that old hanging tree in front of the courthouse back to the use for which God intended it – swift and certain justice."

"What if you get it wrong?" she demanded.

"What do you mean?"

"What if one of your little projects targets an innocent man?"

Salter's eyes softened into a mix of pity and regret. "It has."

A tickle of apprehension swept through her body. "Who?"

"I can't betray them, even when they're wrong."

"Who? *Who* was innocent?" Through the trees, Cass heard the wail of a siren and fought to find the right words before help arrived. "Tell me who the other members are. You're right, you're dying. I'd love to let go of these belts and watch you die. Your sins are –," she choked, wondering how to measure sin. "You *let* them abuse those girls. You're a monster, the same as they are. Meet your God in peace, Mr. Salter. They can't hurt you now. Help me stop them," she pled.

His eyelids fluttered and again he attempted a smile. "You're a good kid. Your brother doesn't deserve what happened to him," he said softly, drawing a long breath as Cass froze, stunned at his words. When his lungs had reached full capacity, he tensed. "Tell my wife and children that I love them," he whispered before sweeping his eyes heavenward and wrenching his body against the wire, throwing Cass off balance. Stiff from her vigil, the belts slipped from her hands and she tumbled to the ground, sliding through the pool of blood.

"NO!" she wailed, finding her feet and lurching at the body, struggling to tug the belts tight again. "Was it Jack? Did you do this to Jack? Oh God, please no," she moaned as Jed Salter's body released its last breath and sagged into the twisted barbed wire. Truman crashed through the undergrowth, followed by two paramedics carrying heavy cases. All three were sweating heavily.

"Help me!" Cass cried, clutching at the belts with shaking hands.

They lunged at the body, a waft of wintergreen chewing tobacco following in the still air. Truman pulled her away as the paramedics checked for a pulse and probed at Salter's wounds. She strained against the firm arm wrapped around her waist, her hands in claws, fingers too stiff to move. Randall Mahaffey turned, white uniform shirt glowing in the moonlight, and shook his head once, hands still by his sides.

Her eyes slid closed and she covered her face with bloody, clenched hands. "Oh my God," she breathed, collapsing against Truman's slight frame, "I killed him."

CHAPTER 90

SHE FOLLOWED TRUMAN BACK through the forest leaving the paramedics to wait with the body for Grey to arrive and pronounce Salter dead. She was trembling, numb from pulling the belts tight, from listening to Salter, from fear for Jack. Her mind snapped to her absent partner.

"Have you seen Mitch?" she asked.

"We all started to run down that bumpy path when we heard the first shot. Looks like he stepped in one of the deeper gullies and broke his leg." Truman shook his head. "Somehow, he got back to the cruiser and called in for back up and ambulances. They found him passed out over the front seat. Guess the pain got him. Randall said they took him away in an ambulance."

The clearing was in turmoil when they reached its edge and Cass hung back, amazed at the damage. Flames leapt from the burning cabin as a firefighter struggled to drag a hose from the dark path leading to the road. He flipped a valve and water spewed forth in a white surge, forcing him to lean forward against the flow. Steam billowed upward, adding dampness to the biting smell of burning petrol and dried wood that permeated the air. Three officers stood at the mouth of the dirt trail, backs to the clearing, arms outstretched to hold back members of the press struggling to get clear shots of the action and shoving microphones forward. Sheriff Hoffner stalked the small space, lips in a tight, bloodless line. His eyes followed Kado's every move.

Kado darted through the scene, taking photographs and measurements, trying to preserve as much evidence as possible. Munk worked with him, collecting labeled bags, pouring casting mix and sticking flags into the ground. His potbellied form was scorched from his dash into the cabin to save Evelyn, most of his wispy brown hair now singed black. His eyes were grim. Cass wondered if his anger sprung from the kidnapping of his sister, or from putting faces to the abused girls. Munk's life was an agony of regret

374

over his own child, and Cass knew his heart was torn every time a child was hurt.

Greg Newton's body lay where it had fallen, the hood now completely removed from his face. Surprisingly, his glasses were still in place. Cass's stomach flipped at the physical confirmation of what she had done. Deacon Cronus remained hunched, still handcuffed to the table, head bowed in an attitude of supplication. Grey and Porky flitted between the two, and it was only when her stunned mind recognized what this meant that Cass squatted in the shadows to examine the Deacon's crouching form more closely.

"My God," she whispered, taking in the arterial spray across the butcher paper on the picnic table and the pool of blood soaking the Deacon's white robe and the dirt beneath his body. "What happened?"

"I don't know," Truman whispered. "When I came back to call for an ambulance, Munk was putting Petchard, those two girls and Evelyn Grove in a patrol car." He hesitated. "Cass, back there in the woods? You were yelling at Salter, asking if he did something to Jack. Who is Jack?"

"It's – I was probably wrong," she answered, glancing at his young face.

"Is Jack, isn't he your brother?" Truman asked, his words tumbling over one another. "The one in prison?"

She sighed. "He's my oldest brother. I just – I thought Salter… I don't know what I heard. The man was dying, maybe delirious." Cass drew a deep breath, fingering the badge in her pocket, wondering if she'd ever feel the weight of its authority and reassurance again. "Look, I'd better get out there and deal with whatever comes next. Hoffner will have to suspend me and he'll probably fire me for shooting Newton. You need to take Grey and Porky out to Salter." Truman nodded, his clouded hazel eyes making brief contact with hers. "Don't worry," she said, unsuccessfully attempting a smile as she stood. "It'll be fine."

They entered the clearing to a barrage of shouted questions and the blinding pop of camera flashes. Voices were silenced and all heads turned to watch as she strode, head high, directly to Sheriff Hoffner who waited with his legs spread, arms crossed, face severe.

"You injured?"

"No, sir."

He motioned for Kado as the chatter from the reporters again gained volume. The forensics man slipped a folded bed sheet into a paper bag and pulled another bag from his kit, holding it open as Cass placed her nine-millimeter inside before slipping the holster over her head and sliding it into a second bag. Kado's glance was scalding as he folded the bags closed, and she blinked in surprise. An image flashed through her mind, of Kado raising a tomahawk over his head, war-painted face fierce. Cass thought it was a likeness that wasn't far from the truth, given his intensity at the moment.

Hoffner shifted, drawing her eyes back to his. "Any other weapons?"

She squatted to lift the leg of her black trousers and remove the revolver from her ankle. "Three shots from the nine mil. Two at Newton, one at that tree," she told Kado, lifting her chin to point across the clearing. "The revolver hasn't been fired."

Cass dropped the revolver into an evidence bag and watched as Kado turned away without looking at her. Her heart dropped.

"Is this all your handiwork?" Hoffner asked, jerking his head toward the picnic table.

Acid crawled up her throat at his accusation and she swallowed it down. "Only Greg Newton, sir. Petchard's life was in danger and Newton didn't stop when I challenged him."

He grunted. "That's Jed Salter in the woods?"

"Yes sir," she answered, stomach churning with anger, her blackened face blank. "He's dead."

"What happened?"

"He was tangled in barbed wire and bleeding from his thigh. We couldn't tell which one was pierced, so Truman prepared two tourniquets, one from each of our belts. I tried to stop the blood flow until the paramedics could arrive. He bled out."

"Did you recognize anyone else out here?"

"No, sir. They were in hooded robes, like Newton."

He inclined his head away from the reporters. "You didn't see David Wayne?"

Cass again saw the procession flowing from the cabin toward her hiding place in the bushes, crimson swirling and hiding any distinguishing features. In her mind's eye, she could pick out several men fat enough to be Arcadia's Mayor Rusted. But there was no shortage of portly men in East Texas, and she had seen nothing to tell her that he was among the group gathered in the clearing tonight.

"I'm not positive, sir, but I didn't see anything indicating that he was here."

Hoffner's eyes flicked to the cluster of restless reporters and his nostrils flared. "You'll be debriefed tomorrow after we've had a chance to figure this mess out. In the meantime, you don't talk to the press or to anyone from the department, understood?" Cass nodded. "In line with department regulations, Elliot, you're suspended with pay until we've investigated Officer Newton's shooting."

"Yes, sir." With her chin high, she held out her badge. Slowly, he lifted it from her bloodied palm. Fatigue slid down her limbs, rendering them heavy, lifeless. "What happened to Mitch?"

His eyes touched hers, and then darted away to watch Truman point Grey into the woods. "I don't know. They took him to the hospital."

"He parked his truck across the road, back in some trees. Can I take it home?"

"Officer Truman," Hoffner called, running a hand across his weary face as Truman trotted across the clearing. "Use Mitch's truck to take Elliot home, then come back out here. You're not to discuss this evening with her, understood?"

"Yes, sir."

Hoffner glanced again at the reporters, arranging his features into a mask of authority. "What an almighty shit storm you've created, Elliot."

Something inside Cass snapped at Hoffner's assessment of blame. She leaned toward him, the last exhausted slide of adrenaline cool through her veins as the words flew unchecked from her mouth. "Yes, sir. I created this. All of it. Just so I could kill a fellow officer and watch another man die."

Hoffner flushed. "I don't like your tone, Elliot."

"And I don't like yours, sir."

"Watch your mouth, Detective," he responded, gaze bouncing between a stone-faced Truman, the reporters, and Cass. "That temporary suspension can easily become permanent."

CHAPTER 91

THEY FOUGHT THEIR WAY through the crush of reporters, eyes lowered, hands shielding their faces from the dazzling lights of news cameras. Uniformed officers cleared a path along the dirt track and helped them inch Mitch's truck past the tangle of news vans, emergency vehicles, wires and hoses snaking across the county road. Truman's eyes were wide and he drove in silence as Cass rolled down the windows, exchanging the scent of blood and smoke for fresh air. She turned on the radio and flipped through the local stations, the sound of Clapton's "I Shot the Sheriff" causing her to chuckle grimly. She pushed another button and found KOIL.

"...ing you breaking news from outside Arcadia. A shootout in the style of the Wild West erupted near Deuce's Flat this evening, followed by an explosion that demolished a deer camp near the Sabine River." Cass turned to look at Truman, frowning. He shrugged. "This reporter followed a dusty, bumpy trail into the depths of the Piney Forest to bring you, our faithful listeners, this story. Poised at the edge of a small clearing, I see a smoldering cabin and across the haze filled scene, the carnage of two bodies draped in white awaiting removal from the site. Wait, I see – yes, it is." The reporter drew a hissing breath. "Another shrouded body is being carried on a stretcher from the woods beyond the clearing. We have to break now for a message from our sponsor, but stay with us for more coverage of tonight's Slaughter near the Sabine. This is your faithful roving reporter, Wally Pugh –"

His voice faded as Cass jabbed the power button. "Carnage? Slaughter?" She wiped a filthy hand across her forehead. "Since when do we use shrouds?" She opened her eyes to see Truman pass the turnoff for Arcadia. "Where are you going?" she demanded.

He glanced across the cab, startled. "To your house."

Her mouth gaped. "We're going to the hospital, Truman. I need to see

Mitch. Turn around."

"Cass, Sheriff Hoffner told me to take you home."

"I heard him. And you will. But first, take me to the hospital."

Cocking an eyebrow, he slowed the truck. "Technically, as long as I take you home tonight, I suppose it's not disobeying an order."

"Technically, I think you're right."

———————

TRUMAN TURNED INTO THE hospital's parking lot as an ambulance roared past, lights swirling and siren screaming. A small car shot around the pickup to follow the ambulance, and Cass caught a glimpse of Darla's stricken face, tears glistening on her cheeks. Her heart stopped for a moment, fearful for Mitch for the first time.

She shot Truman a worried look. "I thought it was a broken leg," she said, lifting her chin toward the Emergency Room. "Why wouldn't they set it here?"

Eyes wide, he gunned the truck toward the circular drive, empty of all emergency vehicles. Cass leapt from the truck and hurried through the automatic doors as Truman was still skidding into a stop. She spotted a large man in dinosaur spotted scrubs slumped over a comic book at the Registration desk. A halo of mousy hair ringed a shining bald spot that danced in the fluorescent lights as she strode toward him. He didn't look up as she arrived at the desk, but pushed a clipboard toward her. "Fill in the front and back of the top form, sign the second and third, keep the fourth to read later and stick your driver's license and insurance card under the clip."

"I just need information," Cass said.

Still not raising his head, he pointed toward an alcove. "That desk. Someone will help you in a moment."

"Nobody's there," she said, frustration building in her chest as Truman hurried to join her, scowling.

"They'll be back in a minute," he replied.

"Hey," Truman barked, snapping his fingers. "We need information about Mitch Stone."

The attendant raised his head to reveal a blotchy face and a tag bearing the name 'John' pinned to his scrubs. His eyes widened at their greasepaint-blackened faces and dark clothes. "Are you family?"

"No," Cass replied. "I'm his partner. Was that him in the ambulance?"

"I'm sorry, I can't discuss patient details with anyone but family," he replied, catching sight of the blood on Cass and Truman, nostrils flaring at the scents of blood, smoke and sweat that wafted across the desk. He frowned. "Are you injured?"

"No," Truman replied, pulling his badge from a pocket and flashing it at the pudgy man. His young, handsome face was drawn into flat planes. "Forney County Police. Where are they taking Mitch Stone?"

"Sorry," he said. "I didn't realize. Were you out at the –"

Truman slammed a fist down on the desk, lips tight. "*Where* are they taking Mitch Stone?"

"Shreveport," John squeaked, pushing back into his chair.

"Why?"

"They've got better lung men over there."

Cass frowned. "I thought he broke his leg."

John nodded. "Damaged a lung, too."

"How bad is it?"

He shrugged. "Bad enough to transport him tonight."

CASS TURNED ON HER heel and strode back across the hospital's lobby, boots thunking loudly in the quiet, open space. Truman hurried behind her, climbing into the driver's seat. She nailed him with her eyes.

"Shreveport. Let's go."

He shook his head. "We can't."

"Why not?"

"Orders, Cass. I have to take you home and get out to the camp."

She slipped her phone from a pocket and flipped it open, pushing a speed dial button. Five rings and she was directed to voice mail. Patiently, she tried again and again got voice mail.

"Who're you calling?" Truman asked, turning out of the hospital parking lot.

"Darla, but she's not picking up." She checked the road signs. "It's faster to take the back roads."

"Cass," he answered, voice firm. "I'm not taking you to Shreveport."

"Fine," she snapped. "I'll drive from home. Just hurry up."

"I'm sorry," he said, eyes fixed on the road, "but we have enough problems right now without disobeying an order."

"'We', Truman?"

"Yeah, Cass. 'We'. What do you think Kado was so pissed off about back there?"

"What do you mean?"

"Sheriff Hoffner *will* have a scapegoat, Cass. And chances are, it'll be you," he answered, watching as confusion clouded her face. "Whatever happened out there tonight, with Newton, with Salter, we know you did the right thing. For Hoffner, it won't matter."

"Kado's mad at me?"

"No, he's mad at the sheriff, because he knows what's coming and what it'll mean to you. He and Munk were working like demons to gather evidence for the debriefing tomorrow. The way Kado figures it, the more data he has, the better your chances in the investigation."

Cass closed her eyes, relief sliding through her body. Finally, she spoke. "Okay."

"I can take you home?"

"Yeah, take me home," she sighed, digging her fingers into her stinging eyes. "You're right about the scapegoat. I think I kind of pissed Hoffner off." ·

Truman chuckled. "You got balls, Cass. He didn't know what to say when you talked back to him."

"It probably wasn't the smartest thing I've done, but it felt good." She glanced in Truman's direction. "That was some performance at the hospital. I've never seen you mad."

He grinned. "That was good, wasn't it? My mom always said I was too nice. But I'm learning…"

CHAPTER 92

THEY'D BARELY TURNED INTO the driveway before the front door opened and three men charged down the rickety porch steps. She climbed from the cab and was engulfed by Bruce, and then by Harry and her father. The tight knot of bodies clung together for a few moments before Abe peeled away, telling the boys to let her get into the house and sit down.

"Who's this?" he asked, eyeing the young man behind the pickup's steering wheel.

"Officer Scott Truman, Daddy," Cass answered from the circle of Bruce's arms. "He was on the stakeout tonight."

Abe reached through the open window and shook Truman's hand. "Thanks for bringing her home. Can you stay for a bite of supper?"

"No, sir. I have to get back." His eyes flicked toward Cass as he slipped the truck into reverse. "Take care of her. She's had a rough night."

Cass wearily followed Bruce to the kitchen, slumping in a chair at the table. Harry took a platter heaped with sliced roast beef and pepper jack cheese from the fridge, along with jars of condiments, and piled them all on the table, faithfully evoking the Elliot clan's ritual of using food as a balm for all troubles. As Bruce pulled down glasses for milk, he examined his sister's blackened face. "Darla called. They're taking Mitch to Shreveport and she'll call when they know more. You're not to come to the hospital for some reason to do with Hoffner. They said on TV that shots were fired. What happened?"

"I, um," she hedged, mind flashing over the events in the clearing and with Jed Salter. Cass searched her emotions, finding no regret lurking beneath her exhaustion. She had taken Greg Newton's life and could easily believe that her actions had led to Salter's death. She expected to feel sad, guilty, angry – anything other than the tired relief that comes with the completion of a difficult task. Was something wrong with her, with this inability to feel remorse? She drew a deep breath, eyes fixed on a jar of

French mustard. "I had to shoot someone."

Abe closed his eyes and reached a hand across the table for hers.

"Dead?" Harry asked.

"Yes."

"What happened?" Bruce repeated, bringing milk to the table.

Cass put her fingers to her temples and rubbed, wondering how to describe what she'd done. She opened her eyes to see worried glances darting between her brothers and father. "I'm fine. Just tired. It happened fast. Maybe it always does." She stopped to draw a breath and reach for a knife and two slices of bread. "Someone was in harm's way, I shouted a warning to the perp, he didn't comply and I believe he intended to use deadly force, so I fired to stop him. Horseradish?"

Harry reached to open the fridge, pulling gingerly on the duct-taped handle. "How do you feel?"

She lifted a shoulder. "Just numb."

"Did you save the guy?" Bruce asked, smearing mustard on a hefty pile of roast beef.

"Who?"

"The one in harm's way."

Petchard's terrified face entered her mind, and she nodded, wondering briefly if he would consider himself saved.

"Anybody else hurt?"

"Unfortunately, yes. I'm sure it'll be in the papers tomorrow. Evelyn Grove and a couple of teenage girls are a little charred, and Officer Greg Newton, Deacon David Cronus and Jed Salter are dead." She took a giant bite from her sandwich, nose and eyes tingling as the horseradish zinged.

"The banker?" Harry asked, mouth agape.

She nodded, strength returning as she ate.

"Is he the one you shot?" Bruce asked.

"She shot a man in defense of another," Abe scolded as Bruce dipped his head. "That's not something an officer does lightly. It's not for gawking over."

"Sorry, Cass," he mumbled, fingering his sandwich.

"It's okay," she replied. "I can't be too specific yet, but no, I didn't shoot Salter." *I didn't do much to keep him alive, but he didn't die from a bullet*, she thought. "We'll be debriefed tomorrow, and there'll be an investigation into the shooting. Until then, I'm off the force."

"Hoffner *fired* you? For doing your job?" Harry scowled, sandwich suspended between his mouth and the table, heavy dollop of ketchup splattering his plate.

"Suspended with pay, just until the investigation is done," Cass said with more conviction than she felt. "It's standard when a weapon's discharged."

Abe rose from the table and stood behind his only daughter, hands on her shoulders. He leaned down to kiss her head, smoothing her hair with one hand, and she caught his worried reflection in the darkened kitchen window. "I'm glad you're home safe and sound. Maybe with this time off, you can think about whether you want to stick with the force."

She froze, stiffening under her father's touch. "Why would I leave?"

"This is dangerous stuff, Cass. What would've happened if you hadn't acted in time, or if that man had come after you?"

She swiveled in her chair and looked up into her father's face. "But this is what I've trained for. It's what I want to do."

He cradled her face in his hands, thumbs gently wiping at the greasepaint on her cheeks. "Just a suggestion. That's all." He glanced at the clock on the oven. "Don't keep her up too late, you two. She's had a long day."

The door swung quietly closed behind him, and Cass frowned down at her plate. "I don't want to quit the force and I don't think I'll have to. The shooting was clean. And what we were trying to do tonight," she shook her head in frustration, "it's not done."

"What do you mean?" Harry asked.

"We didn't get all the members of the cult. Other than Cronus, Salter and Newton, we didn't get any."

"What happens next?"

"It'll depend on how much forensic evidence Kado finds in the cabin and the surrounding woods." She finished the last bite of her sandwich and drained her milk glass. "I'm going to bed. If anybody wants a shower, you'd better go first."

"Why?" Bruce asked.

"All this greasepaint has to come off. That could take a while, and all the hot water."

CHAPTER 93

Thursday

CASS JOGGED THROUGH THE woods, her pace a steady beat against the soft forest floor. Her breath came in a deep, regular rhythm, filling her lungs with clean night air, clearing her head of the pain and confusion from the previous night. She leaned easily into the awkward bough that hung over the path, swinging her legs up and over and back into their smooth cadence. The path bent to the left and as Cass followed its curve, a warm glow flickered from a break in the trees. Thunder cracked and lightning flared across the sky. Her heart began to pound from dread rather than exertion, and the sweat streaking her body ran cold.

She crept toward the sputtering light, her stomach in knots. Reaching the edge of the tree line she breathed deeply, inhaling a sweet scent, familiar but unidentifiable, and inched her face forward through a bush heavy with waxy leaves. The remnants of The Church of the True Believer circled a campfire, hooded heads bowed. Their scarlet robes were torn and dirty, and bloody scratches left trails on their arms, legs and feet from their dash through the woods. A low chanting filled the clearing as one member lifted a bloodied knife in his hands; an offering to the heavens. He pushed the hood from his head and Cass gasped at the sight of Richard Nixon's contorted face tilted toward the sky. Quickly, another figure stepped away from the group and untied a rope from a thick tree trunk, and Cass raised her eyes to see a cross dangling from a heavy branch. A man, naked save for a cloth at his hips, was fixed to its surface. His back was to her, but she heard an agonized groan as the cross was lowered with halting jerks.

As it fell, Nixon caught hold of the rough wood and pulled the cross toward him, twisting it. Her brain roared with pain and incomprehension as Jack's face came into view. Rage coursed through her veins at the wounds to his hands and feet, the crown of thorns pressing into his skull, the blood coursing down his body. The knife glinted as Nixon slashed at Jack's exposed side and her nostrils filled with the smell of burning cherry tobacco. Déjà vu swept over her and Cass called out as she reached for her nine-millimeter, shrieking in horror as she clutched at an empty holster. Suddenly, something hard covered her mouth and one hand was bound in immoveable iron bands. Struggling and twisting, she swung with her free hand until she connected with flesh and a voice hissing her name penetrated her dream.

She woke with a start to find Bruce beside her, one hand clamped around both of hers, the other holding his jaw. "What are you doing?" she choked, yanking to free her hands and surprised to feel moisture on her cheeks. "Let me go. What's *wrong* with you?"

"Shhh," he whispered. "You were having a nightmare. Something about Jack. And Richard Nixon?"

Cass swiped at the hot tears with her shoulder. "It was nothing."

"It was something. What were you dreaming?"

"Just mixed up stuff about last night. Let go," she urged, trying to tug her hands free.

"Be quiet," he answered, turning to look at her open bedroom door.

"Why are we whispering?"

"Be still." His voice was firm.

"What's wrong?" she whispered.

Bruce released her hands and stood, gingerly poking his chin. "You pack a pretty mean punch for a girl."

Cass swung her legs off the bed and rubbed her eyes. "What time is it?"

"Five o'clock."

"Jeez, Bruce," she moaned, preparing to crawl back under the covers.

"Get dressed without the lights."

"For goodness sake. What's up with you?"

He took her by the hand and pulled her upright. "Come look out my window."

She huffed along into his room, breathing in the soft smells of his sleep, peering through the tiny gap he permitted when he pulled the curtain back. A shadowy figure marched to and fro in front of the Elliot house, the silhouette of a long-barrel gun barely visible in the darkness.

"Who's that?" she asked, shivering.

"Herman the German."

"What in the world is he doing in our front yard with that... what is it? A rifle?"

"Twelve gauge. Look down the driveway."

Cass followed the sweep of the narrow drive until her eyes found a clutch of vehicles parked along the roadside. A van door slid open and an interior light flared to gleam on a carefully coiffed blonde head. "Oh no," she groaned. "Reporters?"

"Yep. I called Herman and asked if he'd come over and hold the fort, keep them away from the house. He brought ol' Barky with him –"

"Who?"

"That's what he calls the shotgun."

Cass shook her head in disbelief. "Did they wake you up?"

He let the curtain drift back into place. "No. Tom Kado called. He and Scott Truman are on their way. They need to talk to you."

"About what?"

"Don't know. He just called and asked if there was a back way to the house. I told them to cut through the woods. I've turned off the security light so they can come in through the kitchen." He squinted at his alarm clock. "They should be here pretty quick. Put on something warm. A thunderstorm is almost here and it's brought the Easter snap with it. I'll start the coffee."

CHAPTER 94

SHE STEPPED INTO THE kitchen, dim with only the light from the stove's vent hood. The air was pregnant with the expectation of the coming storm. Kado and Truman sat hunched at the table, hands clutching coffee mugs. The low light etched the lines of weariness on their faces deeper; the small room smelled of exhaustion, sweat and the faint coppery scent of dried blood. From the filth covering their bodies, she knew they'd spent the night out at the deer camp. Truman's face was still smeared with greasepaint. Kado's eyes quickly traced Cass's form in sweatpants and a long sleeve t-shirt before flicking to Bruce. Her heart skipped a beat when she saw no anger in Kado's glance, and she swallowed the relief down, trying not to care that he wasn't mad at her.

"Thanks," he said.

"No problem," Bruce answered, handing Cass a mug as he pushed past her toward the living room. "There's another pot on. Cream and sugar are on the table."

Truman scooted a chair out for her with a boot, and she sat warily, taking in their haggard faces. "What's up?"

They exchanged glances and Truman cleared his throat. "Kado thought we ought to get prepared for the de-briefing this morning."

"That's not exactly in line with procedure, is it?"

"We've got a fight on our hands," Kado answered slowly.

"What do you mean?"

"You know none of this when it comes to the debrief, right?"

"Right."

"Petchard's saying your shot at Newton wasn't clean."

"*What?!*" She shoved back from the table. "He was tied up and squealing like a girl, and Newton was about to slice him with a big ol' honkin' knife." She thrust her chin out, scowling. "I should've let Newton stick him, that little wimp —"

"Calm down. It gets better," Kado interrupted, waiting until Cass settled back at the table. Her mouth was set in a grim line, nostrils flared. "Petchard was babbling when Sheriff Hoffner showed up. He told Hoffner that he was working undercover with Newton, that this whole ritual was part of the induction process, that he knew Newton wouldn't really hurt him. Basically, he's saying that you overreacted."

Her jaw dropped and she felt gut-punched. "You have got to be kidding."

"Nope."

"Why didn't we know about this undercover operation?"

"Petchard said Mitch had authorized both him and Newton to work on the case."

"Did he know that Mitch was injured?"

Kado nodded, a smile threatening his lips.

"He's betting that Mitch is hurt bad enough that he won't remember authorizing Petchard and Newton to work under cover." She shook her head. "He's smarting over all this sexual harassment crap, and sacrificing me. It's my word against his."

"Let the evidence speak for you, Cass."

"What evidence? Nobody's left as a witness," she snorted. "Nobody that'll come forward, anyway. Just the ammunition Hoffner needs."

"Seen the news or the papers?"

"Oh Lord," she breathed, dropping her head into her hands. "How bad is it?"

"Pretty grim. They got a lot of footage out at the cabin and haven't censored much of it." He pulled a stack of newspapers from the countertop. Cass Elliot's grainy form, her hair wild, face dark with greasepaint, hand stretched flat toward Sheriff Hoffner, was prominent on the front page of each. The headlines varied from 'Brave Officer Suspended' to 'Cult Carnage Officer Fired', and in spite of herself, she chuckled. Kado slipped the Forney Cater out of the stack and flattened it on the table. Cass was again prominent on the front page, standing tall in front of Sheriff Hoffner, chin elevated and arm outstretched. The camera's flash glinted on the badge in her palm. A massive headline read 'Hero Cop Stops Deadly Cult'. The by-line was Wally Pugh. Smaller headlines below the fold cried out 'Officer Slain', 'Prominent Banker Dies' and 'Deacon's

Cult Goes up in Flames – Arcadia another Waco'.

"Wally's graduated from radio to print?"

"Obadiah Graham owns KOIL and the Forney Cater," Truman told her.

"Arcadia's answer to Rupert Murdoch," she said absently. "Hoffner'll just use all this against me."

"He can't fire you," Truman stated as she scanned Wally's article and then opened the paper to find additional photos of the damage to the cabin and the three body bags.

Cass snorted. "Why not?"

"The Forney Cater's behind you."

"So what?"

"So, what's in the Cater is what Obadiah Graham and all of Forney County believes, Cass. And that's what'll drive Hoffner's next move with you. If the public thinks you did right – *we* did right – then that's what Hoffner will think."

"I wish it were that simple," she said.

"The Forney Cater's coverage is a big part of how Hoffner will view this whole thing." Kado stretched and checked his watch. "But it also means that he'll be hell bent for leather to find something to hang one of us on, and that's why we want to get the facts straight before the debrief."

Cass nodded slowly. "How is everybody?"

"Munk is completely bald now. All his hair was singed off. He really looks like a monk," he said, whisper of a grin touching his lips.

"You two on friendlier terms?"

Kado hesitated. "Time will tell. But for now, yeah. We're fine."

"How's Evelyn?"

"Some blisters, a little adhesive burn."

"Jed Salter said she saw two of them without their hoods when she stumbled into the clearing. Who did she see?"

"No winners there. It was Newton and Cronus. The rest were in the cabin and pulled their hoods on before they took her inside."

She chuckled grimly. "Figures. What about the girls?"

Truman shrugged. "We still don't have their names. Dr. Rambo kept them overnight. He thinks they're about twelve years old and from what he could tell, he didn't think they were molested –"

"Thank goodness," Cass breathed.

"– last night."

"Oh."

"Nobody's reported them missing. We'll know more today. He sedated them pretty heavily, said they were in shock. And," he continued, "these girls weren't in Lenny Scarborough's photos."

"Are you sure?"

"Yes. We were looking for moles and birthmarks. Neither of these girls have them in the right places."

"That ties. Salter told me the girls are never the same." She drew a deep breath. "I kept trying to reach Darla last night but couldn't get through. How's Mitch?"

Kado flashed a glance at Truman, eyes blazing in a stab of lightning that penetrated the dark kitchen. "Darla called Hoffner a couple of times last night and he's not saying much. He's told her not to talk to any of us."

"Why on earth doesn't he want us to know what's happening?"

"It's either a control thing," Truman began, drawing a deep breath, "or Mitch is hurt so badly he doesn't want us to get distracted worrying about him."

"What a stupid man. Doesn't Hoffner know that he's pushing us farther away from wanting to help him? We'd be better off knowing what's going on."

Kado shrugged. "Truman said they took Mitch to Shreveport to treat a damaged lung. That doesn't sound good."

"No," she answered, "it doesn't."

Truman rubbed his fists into his eyes. "Munk said his sister was so worked up about Hoffner's behavior that she took off for Shreveport after they looked her over at the county hospital. Darla's not supposed to talk to anyone from the force, so Evelyn Grove will take care of communications. We'll hear back from her this morning, I imagine."

"Any leads on who owns The Sanctuary?"

"One of the volunteer fire-fighters works as a loan officer at Salter's bank," Truman answered.

"Let me guess," Cass said. "Foreclosure."

"Yup. He's not sure when, or who owned it, but the property has been on the bank's books for years. Since before he started working there. He'll go through the files tomorrow and see what he can find out for us."

Kado shifted his position and reached for the percolator on the stove, taking in the copper pipe taped to the oven door. He refrained from comment while he poured. "You ready?"

She nodded. "What do you need?"

He pulled a crumpled, soot-smeared sketch of the clearing from his pocket and flattened it on top of the Forney Cater as Cass quickly talked them through The Church's activities – the procession from the cabin, the gathering around the campfire and Petchard's near-death experience on the picnic table. Kado stopped her after she told them about the gunshots. "Show me where you were."

She pointed to where she'd been hiding. "I was standing here when I fired twice at Newton. And about here," she continued, drawing her finger deeper into the clearing, "when I fired the warning shot at Deacon Cronus."

Kado made two light marks on the paper and examined it. "What happened when you shot Newton?"

"He flew backwards, arms stretched out at shoulder height. The knife came loose from his hand…"

"Which hand?" Kado interrupted.

Her eyes darted into the kitchen's shadows, imagining the scene. "Right."

"What did it look like?"

"A dagger. Maybe a hunting knife, but more elegant than that."

"And then?"

"It flipped into the woods behind him. I didn't stop to look for it."

Kado refolded the paper. "What happened next?"

"Petchard was still on the picnic table. People started running, Deacon Cronus, too. He stopped when I fired over his shoulder. The others disappeared into the woods. But…" She frowned, awareness dawning. "They were prepared for this."

"What do you mean?"

"Nobody panicked when I came out of the bushes. They all froze for just a moment, someone shouted 'Jericho', and then everybody broke and ran. Almost like it was choreographed. Petchard was howling, but there were no screams, nobody yelled. Nobody tripped and fell." She nodded slowly. "They were ready. Maybe not for us, but they were ready just in case."

"Jericho?" Truman asked. "Like the Jericho that Joshua marched around and the city fell?"

"The walls came tumbling down. And they did. The cabin burned. It must've been a code word for how to react."

Truman shivered. "That's spooky."

"Good planning," Kado said. "What next?"

"The fire started. Is there anything left?"

Kado shook his head. "The generator was gasoline. Looks like someone splashed fuel on the building and as dry as the wood was, it didn't take much for the fire to catch and then for the generator to explode. I found piles of ashes that must've been their books. Some of the inside pages are undamaged but none of the back covers are legible. There's a small metal thing that melted down. I'll try to figure out what it is later. Munk got tangled in a bed sheet while he was trying to find Evelyn and dragged it outside with him. I'll see if I can't pick up some DNA from that and the sheets the girls were wrapped in. Not much else survived the fire." He drew a deep breath as thunder sputtered. "We'll have search teams out this morning, going through the woods to see what we can find." His eyes flashed to the window over the sink at a flare of lightning. "But I'm not optimistic given the storms that are coming. Go on."

Cass's eyes were on Truman. "The cabin was burning and we followed the others through the woods."

"Cars were starting up," he said.

"And a motorcycle."

"Did you see them?" Kado asked.

"No," she sighed. "There was a track running across the clearing, past the cabin. They must've parked somewhere down there. Did you get anything from the tire tracks?"

"We have a few partials of treads and shoes. I'll run them against the databases, but there's not much to work with. I found the old pickup that Salter drove from his house to the clearing. We found a shopping bag with a birthday card in it. Looks like it was for his daughter."

"So that's what he bought. Poor child, to lose her father like this."

"We also found a motorcycle and another truck with bad plates. We had them towed to the impound lot last night. I'll dust for fingerprints today." He exhaled heavily. The flat planes of his face were lined with fatigue. "There were several buckets full of blood in the clearing."

"Human?"

"Yeah. I don't know whose yet."

"Dear God," she breathed, rocking forward to place her elbows on the table.

"I guess you and Bernie were right, when you thought they might be collecting the blood for some sort of ritual."

"Washed in the blood of the Lamb. Unbelievable."

"Disgusting," Kado said. "When you found Salter, he was already bleeding?"

Cass glanced at Truman. "Yes. Truman tied tourniquets around his legs and I held them until he got back with help, but I couldn't stop the bleeding."

"Grey said you bought him an extra ten minutes or so, Cass," Kado said quietly. "That barb ripped into the femoral artery and he would've bled out sooner or later." He watched her closely. "You told Truman that you'd killed Salter?"

She stood and moved to the sink and raised the window above it a few inches, then crossed her arms over her chest. The night was silent, the air lifeless and chill in anticipation of the coming storm. She thought back through her interrogation of Salter, the actions she had taken to force information from him – holding the power of life and death in her hands and using it to get what she needed. What she *wanted.* Wasn't that exactly what The Church did? She wasn't proud of how she had handled it, and yet the only thing she would change was to hold on tighter as Salter alluded to Jack's imprisonment.

Lightning flashed again, illuminating her mother's garden. She studied her reflection in the darkened window and knew that lying to Kado and Truman wasn't an option, not if she expected their trust. "Salter would've bled to death one way or another. But," she added, shivering as she turned to face them, "I didn't keep full pressure on the tourniquets all the time."

Truman frowned in confusion while Kado slowly nodded. "Did he talk?"

"Some."

"Anything useful?"

She considered Salter's words. "He said he didn't know about Lenny's photographs and swore he wasn't in them."

"Do you believe him?"

Truman cleared his throat. "Grey let me take photographs of the bodies, and I matched some of the men in Lenny Scarborough's shots to Cronus and Newton. Salter wasn't in any of them."

"You sure?" Cass asked.

"Yes."

"Then maybe he was telling the truth. He was genuinely shocked at the idea that the group was abusing kids. He had some suspicions, but that The Church was suffering a split. A schism, he called it. Some members wanted to be more radical, violent, in what they were trying to achieve, and some wanted to go back to their original ways, which focused more on economic intimidation."

"Did he name names?" Truman asked.

She shook her head. "He wouldn't give the other members up. And when I asked why he stayed with The Church if he disagreed with the things they were doing, he claimed they would kill him. And he said a few things that were interesting. Remember Toby Waller?"

"Yeah," Truman said while Kado frowned.

"Toby died not long before you came to Arcadia," Cass told him. She explained Waller's erratic behavior after he lost his job and his house. "Salter claimed that he didn't commit suicide – he was murdered."

"Why?" Truman asked. "Waller was a nobody."

"Economic reasons, Salter said. What's happened to his property?"

Truman's hazel eyes widened. "They're building a car dealership on it."

"They killed him so somebody could build where his house was?" Kado asked.

"To create jobs for Christian men. There's more," she continued, telling them what Salter had said about the hot house fire. "He claimed that they've scared off a serious dealer by burning his marijuana factory down. Did you find any bags of potting soil at the hot house?" she asked Kado.

"There were quite a few stacked in one corner. None of them burned."

"Did you open them?"

"No. Why?"

"Salter claims they contain bags of cocaine." Kado blinked as Cass looked at Truman. "Those problems you were investigating, working undercover in Elysian Fields?"

"Yeah?"

"He said that the 'entrepreneur' running the hot house was supplying all the coke in the area."

Truman's eyes narrowed to slits. "And so they're helping us by putting drug dealers out of business?"

"Salter said that actions like these are necessary because the police don't have enough power."

Kado grunted. "So who started the fire?"

"Goober's devil of light. The guy who seems to do all the heavy lifting for The Church."

"I really screwed up," Kado sighed. "If one guy has done all this burning and killing, we could've had him."

"What happens to that DNA report?" Cass asked.

"It stays on file, for what it's worth."

"So if we do find this guy, we can link him to Chad Garrett's death?"

Kado snorted. "Only if his DNA swab gets contaminated in exactly the same way."

"Good point." She drew a deep breath. "What happened to Deacon Cronus?"

Kado cleared his throat. "It's not clear. Munk said Petchard got untangled from his ropes and came to help with Evelyn about the time the generator exploded. Nobody was hurt, but they must've been stunned. By the time they were able to check on the Deacon and the girls," he shrugged, "Cronus's throat had been slit and the girls were huddled together by the campfire."

Cass frowned. "Did one of the kids kill him? Retribution?"

Kado glanced at Truman. "We're not sure yet."

"If they didn't do it, who did?"

"Maybe a member of the cult circled back and killed the Deacon to keep him quiet," Truman offered.

"What was he killed with?" Cass asked.

Kado bit his lip. "A sharp knife."

"The one Newton was going to use on Petchard?"

"We couldn't find a knife. Any knife." Kado glanced down at his drawing. "Given what you've told me, we'll search for Newton's, but I'm afraid it's gone."

"Good Lord. That knife is part of my defense. What a nightmare," Cass said, pressing her knuckles into her eyes. "And all in the name of God."

"All in the name of power," Kado corrected her. He glanced at the window again. "I need to get back out to the site and organize the teams, then head to the station for the debrief."

"There's one more thing. I don't know if it matters, but the first time I snuck into the clearing, two men came out of the cabin and stood on the front porch. I didn't see them and I couldn't hear them clearly, but I think they were talking about Evelyn Grove and what to do with her."

"You didn't recognize either voice?"

Cass shook her head. "One of them was smoking. I didn't recognize the scent at first, but it was cherry pipe tobacco. Old man Peavey was smoking a pipe when we were with him in his barn, remember?"

"Yeah," Truman sighed. "But Elaine and Bernie stayed at that revival in App Community until almost one o'clock this morning when the thing ended. The Peavey's never left."

"That knocks him out of this group, then." She sipped her coffee. "Lucius Craven smokes one, too."

"How many men smoke pipes? Even if we could identify all of them, we can't ask them to raise their shirts to let us look for a scar on pipe-smoking evidence alone." Kado asked in frustration, and then answered his own question. "Too many. That's the way this entire case has been, one slim lead after another."

She hesitated. "I guess I should ask how Sheriff Hoffner's doing."

"About as good as a bear with a sore head. He's treading water, in serious danger of going under. That reporter from Dallas is ripping him apart because his officers were involved in a cult."

"If she's needling him, that can't be good for us."

"I wouldn't be so sure. With the exception of the knife, your details tie up with the evidence and we've played the forensics by the book. Petchard admitted that Newton had a knife raised over him, so you've got some corroboration there. The DA came out to The Sanctuary last night to have a look around. He said he'll clear it with Judge Shackleford, but now that he's seen what Lenny Scarborough was involved in, he doesn't plan to press charges against Angie." Kado yawned. "The press will love that story."

Truman checked his watch. "Should we go?"

As they pushed back from the table, Cass reached out and touched Kado's arm. "About Salter."

"You're wondering if it was torture, what you did?" Kado asked. She nodded once and he shrugged, eyes flat. "Who cares? He needed killin'." Cass blinked, and he turned to face her fully. "Think of The Church as a sick tree. Three branches were pruned tonight, and one of the newly emerging branches – Petchard – has been nipped off. That's a quarter of the sickness gone."

"But there's three quarters that's still growing."

"You can bet they'll be stunted for a while." His eyes softened. "Feel no remorse, Cass. And fear nothing from us. What you said goes no farther than your –," he glanced around the shabby room, "kitchen. Right Truman?"

"Absolutely."

Bruce pushed into the kitchen in a whoosh of the swinging door, cell phone pressed to his ear. A dressed and shaven Abe and a very rumpled Harry followed. Abe's face looked more worn than usual, and Cass wondered if her father had been tempted to open a bottle in worry over his daughter last night. Even when he was on the wagon, he kept booze in the house. Early on, his wife and older children had poured every bottle they found down the drain, but he simply bought more. Over time, they all realized that their efforts to keep him sober were a waste of money.

Cass studied him. Abe had been sober when she got home last night, and in spite of his appearance, was sober now. She turned her attention to Bruce, who put a finger to his lips. He listened, murmured a few words and snapped the phone shut.

"Who was that?" Cass asked as he slumped heavily into a chair.

"Evelyn Grove. Darla gave her my number."

"Mitch?"

He nodded as the others crowded around the table. "It's not good. His leg's in bad shape – he broke the tibula and fibula and the wound is dirty."

"Tibia," Kado corrected.

"Thanks," Bruce replied. "She said it's bad, but they can fix it. But his lung is another story."

"What do you mean?" Cass asked.

"They got him into surgery over in Shreveport, but he had trouble breathing. He... he died on the table."

"*What?*" Cass shrieked, fingers digging into his shoulder. Truman crumpled into a chair and Kado staggered into the countertop, his face pale. Abe reached for his daughter, pulling her to his side.

"And they got him back," Bruce hurried to explain as Harry sat next to him. "But things don't look good. Evelyn said he's still in surgery and they're working on him, but they don't know how much damage his brain suffered from lack of oxygen."

"Oh my God," Cass whispered, turning her face into her father's shoulder.

"What *exactly* did she say about his lung, Bruce?" Kado asked.

His brow knotted with thought. "Something about acute artery lactation."

"Acute atelectasis. It's when the lung collapses." Kado dug his fists into his eye sockets. "Truman, Mitch fell into a gully while he was running?"

He nodded.

"The impact could've caused his lung to collapse."

"How bad is that?" Abe asked.

"Not good, but it can be repaired."

"There was something else," Bruce said. "A concussion to the back of his head, softball size."

Kado frowned. "That doesn't make sense. If he stepped into a gully, he should've hit his forehead or chin."

"Somebody must've doubled back and clubbed him," Truman said.

"Softball-sized sounds like a good whack," Bruce said.

"A concussion can be mild or serious." Kado shrugged. "We'll just have to see."

"And the oxygen?" Cass asked quietly.

"Could be very bad. It all depends." He again looked at Truman. "We're not supposed to know any of this, right?"

"Right," Truman agreed.

"Then we get the word out, but nobody heard it from us." He pushed away from the countertop and looked at Bruce. "Let me know when you hear from Evelyn again, all right?"

"No problem. You remember how to find your truck?"

"Truman was an Eagle Scout. We'll be fine."

Bruce and Cass followed them down the steps into the cool night air, and watched as they slipped into the woods to a deep rumble of thunder. He reached out and pulled her to him. She shivered at the warmth and strength in his solid build. "It'll be all right."

"I don't know, Bruce. There's so much that can go wrong. Everything's changing."

He put his chin on top of her head and rocked her gently. "It always does. But Mitch has grit in his craw. He'll come through this just fine. And Hoffner? The man is an ass. *He* might not be fine, but the rest of y'all will."

"What's turned you into such an optimist?"

"It can't go any other way, can it? And then there's Kado."

"What about him?"

"You like him, don't you?"

"Shut up, Bruce," she sniffed, twisting to look up and seeing his lips pucker.

"Okay, but he seems decent enough. Come on," he said, hugging her briefly. "I'll make more coffee. You need to get dressed and into town, don't you?"

Lightning spiked jagged across the sky and Cass jumped at a sharp bark of thunder. "I guess so."

He led her back up the steps. Abe and a hastily dressed Harry stood at the stove, waiting for the percolator to sputter its last. "I know, Dad," Harry was explaining, "but the coffee is crap. You moaned about it all the time when Bobby was in the hospital. She'll need something decent."

"What are you doing?" Cass asked.

Abe held out an arm and she slipped underneath it, breathing in his comforting scent. "Harry's going to Shreveport to be with Darla. I'm going to pick up Mr. and Mrs. Payne to take them over. They need to be with their daughter."

The percolator emitted a wet burp and settled into a steady burble, and Harry filled the Thermos and two travel mugs. Cass glanced at the olive green phone on the kitchen wall. "Should we call Jack and tell him about Mitch?" she asked in a quiet voice.

"I already have," Abe said, releasing her and taking a mug from Harry. "He's worried to death about both of you. I'll call him again after I've been to Shreveport. I've also called the rest of your brothers. Didn't want them to wake up and find their sister on television, wondering what in the world was going on." He squeezed her hand. "Do you want a ride into town?"

Cass shook her head. "Bruce will take me."

"I called the police station. They're sending two patrol cars out here to either run the press off or clear a path so we can get out."

"Isn't Herman the German still out there?" Bruce asked.

Abe chuckled. "Even Herman's no match for that blonde from Dallas."

CHAPTER 95

CASS RAISED A HAND to shield her eyes from the blinding light. Bruce cursed and slowed to a crawl, glaring through the water sheeted windshield at the swarm of reporters pressing against the truck. The rain had started as they closed the doors on Bruce's pickup at home, a punishing thrum of fat drops that drove the reporters back into their vans and created a clear path for the patrol cars to lead them out of the driveway. A lone van had followed from the house, sticking close down the winding country roads and along the nearly deserted highway. The storm intensified near Arcadia's downtown, streaks of lightning illuminating the heavy courthouse trees thrashing in the wind, thunder bellowing in the close confines of the square.

Bruce pulled into the parking lot behind the building, the news van nosing against his bumper. A new round of lights flipped on and misshapen figures emerged from the wall of water – men and their cameras covered with slick rain gear and drenched reporters huddling under umbrellas that flipped inside-out with the wind, their microphones bravely thrust toward Cass's window.

She had been full of turmoil on the ride to the courthouse, her mind racing through a jumbled mix of dreams, events at The Sanctuary, and snatches of the conversation with Kado and Truman. Over and over she replayed her shots at Greg Newton, the scene with Jed Salter, and the sight of Deacon Cronus drenched in his own blood. Alternate scenarios fought for dominance in her brain, and a series of "what if" questions threatened her belief that her actions were legitimate. She battled thoughts of Mitch as dead or permanently injured. It simply wasn't possible that he wouldn't walk back into the squad room, blue eyes twinkling and looking for a donut. And then it struck her that maybe *she* was the one who wouldn't be in the squad room. Her already queasy stomach lurched.

Another light pierced the truck's cab, searching for her. She drew a deep breath and reached for the door's handle.

"Cass."

She turned to look at Bruce, seeing for the first time his bloodshot eyes and slumped posture.

"What Dad said last night... we're all okay with it."

"About quitting?"

He nodded and she stared at the windshield wipers as they threw sheets of water over the waiting reporters. Her heart was heavy with uncertainty – for herself, for Mitch, for Kado and Truman who had violated procedure to help her. The wiper's rhythmic pull was enticing. Just to stay in the warmth of the truck, to hide in its mechanical womb, was tempting. What was the point in fighting Hoffner? Why not just quit? She caught sight of her worried face reflected in the windshield, and realized how stupid she was for focusing on the negative. She'd overcome worse than this. Everything could go wrong, but everything could go right. And Richard Nixon was still out there. She needed the access a detective's role provided to find him. A weary smile touched her lips.

"I may get fired over this, Bruce, for reasons that have nothing to do with me. But I've never known an Elliot who quit."

He flashed a lopsided grin. "Then we're behind you. Don't worry about what happens next. You really are a hero."

"No, I'm not. None of us are. There's too much that isn't finished for any of us to be heroes." She reached for his hand and squeezed. "Finish those plans for Momma's kitchen."

"What?"

"This morning is just the debrief. I'm still suspended until they clear the shooting. And there's not much I can do for Mitch or Darla until he's out of the hospital. Until then," she shrugged, fingering the door's handle again, "there's nothing like power tools to help a girl keep things in perspective."

He reached across the cab and hugged her. Cass pulled the hood of her rain slicker over her head and pushed the door open against a throng of microphones and shouted questions. She glanced back into the cab at Bruce, then turned and disappeared into the noisy crowd.

CHAPTER 96

THE BOX OF DONUTS Harry dropped made a smacking sound when it hit floor. He'd stopped at an ancient bakery in Shreveport, unable to fight the Elliot instinct to feed in times of trouble and believing that sugar and a little grease were just what Darla and Evelyn needed after their long night. Driving through the heavy rain, he finally located the Emergency Room entrance to Shreveport's biggest hospital, parked and dashed shivering through the downpour. The perky woman at the Information Desk had pointed him down a long hall, turn right at the end and knock on the fifth door on the left. Harry had dutifully trudged down the hall, soggy donut box balanced on one hand, Thermos clutched in the other.

He rounded the corner to see Darla and Evelyn facing a doctor wrapped in bloodied scrubs. Stepping forward, the smile crossing Harry's lips died as Darla threw her hands over her face and sagged into Evelyn, crumpling them both against the wall. The sound of the donut box hitting the floor was lost behind his wet footsteps as Harry broke into a run.

CHAPTER 97

THE OLD MAN SAT patiently in a kitchen chair while his wife dabbed at the scratches on his face and arms with hydrogen peroxide. Her age-spotted hands shook slightly, and she scolded while she worked, fussing that he was far too old for night fishing. He murmured agreement and kept his eyes on the television in the living room, watching events unfold at The Sanctuary. He watched her eyes, too, searching for traces of disbelief in the story he had concocted to explain his injuries. Though her glance strayed to the television occasionally, and her fretting slowed while the newscaster spoke, her face remained impassive.

She finished her ministrations by dabbing antiseptic cream on his wounds, scooting him from the kitchen, and bringing him a fresh cup of coffee as he settled in his recliner. His eyes continued to scan the headlines scrolling across the bottom of the television screen, but his mind was engaged in damage control.

The events of last night, and those to come, were truly the greatest threat The Church had ever encountered. The cabin was blazing, its contents destroyed. Including every copy of *The Church of the True Believer*, save two. Lenny Scarborough's was in the evidence room at the police station. The other, the old man's own, was with a trusted friend to use as a template for preparing a new volume to replace Lenny's. Tomorrow, he would call his friend and ask him to deliver twelve new copies, instead of one. The cost would be enormous, but the supply of funds to The Church was under no threat.

Three of their members were dead. It was clear that the young Detective, Cass Elliot, had shot and killed her fellow officer, Greg Newton. And Jed Salter had died out in the woods, tangled in barbed wire, in spite of the Elliot woman's alleged attempts to save him. Reports of her actions ranged from heroic to homicidal. The old man wondered briefly if Salter had lived long enough to reveal any of their secrets. Their names. But there was no need to dwell on that now. If Salter had betrayed them, they would all know soon enough. The police would come, but find no evidence. The sacred texts were gone, their phones discarded around the county, soiled robes burned or buried. Few suffered injuries as they fled The Sanctuary, and those were slight, easily explained as occurring during routine maintenance on a house, a lawn or a farm.

The two acolytes had survived, but they posed no threat to The Church. Blindfolded, they had seen no faces during their time at the cabin. Hugo Petchard was no threat, either. An initiate was not allowed to meet the members of The Church, with the exception of his sponsor, until the initiation ritual was complete. That rule had been established decades ago for an occasion such as this, and the old man was grateful for the foresight of his father and The Church's other founding members.

The old man's thoughts turned to Deacon David Cronus. Reports were still unclear about who had caused his death. He was found handcuffed to The Sanctuary's picnic table, his neck sliced open with what was presumed to be a sharp knife. But no weapon had yet been found. The acolytes were too young for such a violent act. Hugo Petchard was essentially a coward, a fact the old man wished he had recognized before suggesting his initiation to The Brethren. That left the other members of The Church. It was possible that one of their number had circled back and tied off the loose end of the Deacon's mouth. And although he was certain that Deacon Cronus had been The Light of this generation, God was provident. If Deacon Cronus was dead, it must be the Lord's will that The Light be extinguished. The old man had no doubt that its flame would be rekindled in the very near future.

Satisfied that he and The Brethren who remained could deal with the immediate circumstances, he focused on the future. The men would discreetly regroup after a short period of time, receiving new phones and sharing ideas. There was much to accomplish. They would find a new location for The Sanctuary and start construction on another cabin. New members would be sought, and the Circle of Light would begin circumspect inquiries into possible candidates for The Light. The old man briefly considered contacting Hitch, requesting that he resume his role as collector of the sacred blood for their rituals. But that too, could wait.

For now, they all needed rest and a period of restoration. The old man muted the television and pushed back in his recliner. His rumbling snores filled the living room in a matter of moments.

HITCH WHISTLED AS HE walked, a familiar tune that brought to mind a dark-eyed singer whose death in the early 'seventies was still the subject of much speculation. A backpack rested over one shoulder and a comforting wad of cash bulged in his hip pocket. The old man had been generous, and that was a favor he wouldn't forget. The rising sun warmed the right side of his face as he headed north along the quiet country road, but a chilly breeze was building from the southwest. He'd be walking in cold rain before long.

A grizzled old trucker had picked him up outside of Arcadia late Wednesday afternoon and they made Arkansas before evening. Hitch had bedded down in a derelict barn, surrounded by the earthy scent of the cattle and goats that had once called the place home. He rose early to shower and eat at a truck stop on the outskirts of Little Rock, fascinated by the news coverage coming out of Arcadia. Something about cults and a fire; dead bank presidents, preachers and police officers; buckets of blood. Images of a beautiful woman, her face blackened but hair flaming in the light of a blazing building, were played again and again and he longed to hear the commentary about her.

Hitch resisted the urge to laugh when photographs of the dead flashed across the television screen. The old man wasn't there. He settled back in the greasy booth and contemplated staying for a while, catching the full story and sipping more coffee, but instinct drove him on.

He traveled without fear of the future, for evil always finds a home. Somewhere out there was another man with needs only someone like Hitch could meet. They'd find each other and the cycle would begin again. His time in Arcadia had confirmed the perfection of his role in this world, and all thoughts of living a clean life had been wiped from his mind. He remembered the cell phone zipped into his backpack and knew it would remain silent for many nights to come.

Stopping suddenly on the shoulder of the road, Hitch threw his head back and laughed. His brain had just latched onto the words to the tune he was humming, a song by The Doors about lighting fires. *How appropriate*, he thought. Chuckling, he straightened himself and thrust his thumb out at a pickup hurtling down the lane. It screeched to a stop about fifty paces in front of him and Hitch trotted to the open window. The woman in the driver's seat looked old enough to have survived the War of Northern Aggression. And the sour expression on her withered face told him that she *still* wasn't happy with the outcome.

"Headed west," she told him. "Any use to you?"

Hitch nodded and she motioned him into the pickup's rusty bed. He settled with his back against the cab, using a stained rope to soften the bite of the hard ruts against his bony rear end. A grin spread across his face as the truck picked up speed, wind slashing at his eyes and jostling his hat. The woman quickly took a left, true to her word, heading west. The morning sun caught Hitch across the face, filling his strange amber eyes with a fiery light, drawing crimson sparks from their depths. He clamped a hand onto his hat and drifted off to the smooth flow of the road. His dreams encircled the beautiful woman whose hair blazed with firelight, and his soul stirred with its first yearnings for Arcadia.

THE END

ACKNOWLEDGEMENTS

I could not have written and published this novel without the help of many people. My husband, Martyn Popey, always believed that I had it in me, and it is in large part due to his faith, constant support and yes, multiple readings of early drafts, that *The Devil of Light* is now out in the big wide world. (I suppose some credit is due to the amount of tea he brewed for me, as well. PG Tips is surely a stronger company thanks to our caffeine consumption.)

To my early readers, Mom, Terry, Tracy, Jackie and Jacque, thanks for your input, support and, most importantly, your desire to know what happens next to Cass, Mitch and the other good folks of Forney County – your interest has kept me afloat and is driving me forward into book two.

Carolyn, your thoughts were invaluable and have made this a much smoother read.

Jerry, thanks for all your advice about the medical stuff. Your answers to my poorly worded questions were very clear. So, although I'd love to lay the blame for errors at your feet, o brother of mine, I guess I'll have to take full credit for them. Never thought you'd hear that, did you?

Andrea, thanks so much for taking the time to offer your thoughts on how to improve *The Devil of Light*. They truly made a difference to the final draft.

And to those of you who plunked down your hard-earned cash to purchase a copy of *The Devil of Light*, you have my sincere gratitude. Stepping into a book by an unknown author is risky, isn't it? You've either found a new world that absorbs you and leaves you satisfied and wanting more, or you walk away feeling disappointed and perhaps a bit cheated. I hope this book has delivered a few hours of enjoyment and that you're looking forward to the next installment in the Forney County series. I sure am.

You can read the story behind the story on this blog post:

Genesis of a Novel: A Dirty Old Man

which can be found by browsing:

GaeLynnWoods.Blogspot.com

Gae-Lynn Woods
    June 2011

Please take a quick peek at the second Cass Elliot crime novel, AVENGERS OF BLOOD...

AVENGERS OF BLOOD

A CASS ELLIOT CRIME NOVEL

Prologue

IT WAS A BEAUTIFUL night for a killing. One of those gorgeous Southern evenings that occur only occasionally as summer draws near; cool and clear, nearly devoid of humidity. Overhead, the stars sparkled in a vast expanse of velvety sky, their shimmering brightness dimmed only by the whisper-thin gauze of smoke that hung in the nearly motionless air.

Despite the smell of terror and charred flesh, the clearing retained the cheery, slightly crazed atmosphere of a traveling carnival. The crowd had at first been pensive, watchful, but once the killing was done a sense of relief swept through the watchers. Women gossiped and tittered, drinking soda pop from bottles dotted with condensation. Children played chase through the forest of legs and took turns reenacting the murders they'd witnessed only moments earlier. Men smoked pipes and cigarettes, talking in low voices and tapping dried mud from their tired work boots.

The sheeted men nearest the fires took off their hoods and their damp faces gleamed in the flames. People pulled back to give the photographer room and a bright burst stung the night. At last the crowd drifted away, women calling children and fussing at their husbands to hurry home. A few engines cranked in the still air, but most left on foot.

The men in sheets lingered until the last of the crowd was gone and then congratulated themselves on how quickly justice could be served. A rustling startled them and one man took long strides to the side of the clearing and parted two azalea bushes bearing papery violet blooms. A filthy figure gazed up at him, face tear-streaked and snotty, a broken pencil and tattered paper clutched in one grimy hand.

It took a moment, but at last he recognized the child. He leaned over and snatched the paper, calling to his companions. They towered over the tiny body, muttering to one another and turning the drawing to the firelight to see crude representations of the horror they had wrought. At last one of them lifted a foot clad in a pointy-toed cowboy boot and nudged the child toward the road.

"Get on home, now," he said. "And don't you ever talk about what you seen. You understand? Don't draw no more pictures, neither." The child looked up at him with dark eyes that pierced his soul. He blustered on. "What happened here tonight can just as easily happen to you. Easier, even. 'Cause there ain't nobody to look out for you now."

He watched as the child scurried away. Once out of reach, it turned and looked back at them with a burning gaze, searching their faces. He lifted his foot again and the child fled, swallowed quickly by the night. The laughter of the others was at first hesitant, as if they too had felt the intensity of the child's hate. But the sound swelled and gained confidence and at last he joined in, hoping to obscure the vague uneasiness settling in his gut.

CHAPTER 1

Wednesday

CASS ELLIOT GROWLED AS she strained against a crowbar wedged between the wall and a stubborn two-by-four. "I hate these things."

"Easy now," Bruce coaxed, leaning around her to slide a piece of half-inch plywood between the crowbar and the wall. "You'll dent the sheetrock."

"I'll dent *your* sheetrock," she huffed, giving another mighty heave. The cabinet shrieked as three-inch nails screeched from their stud beds. She dropped the crowbar in the cabinet cavity, turned the volume down on the police scanner, and swiped Bruce's freshly opened soda from the table. Sucking a long gulp, she eyed his broad frame, dark features, and – she frowned – clean clothes. "Where're you going, my favorite brother?"

"I didn't know I was your favorite."

"You're my favorite when you're helping me rip out the kitchen." She watched as Bruce added a newspaper clipping to a collection beneath a magnet on the refrigerator. "I wish you'd stop that."

"Let me be famous vicariously." The clippings from the Forney Cater – featuring photographs of Cass, her partner Mitch Stone, or the smoldering remains of a cabin in the Sabine River bottoms – fluttered as Bruce tugged gingerly on the refrigerator's duct-taped handle. He grabbed another soda.

"I just wish it was over. Where're you going?"

"School."

"You don't teach on Wednesday night."

"Some of the students need time in the shop to finish their final projects. I told them I'd open up today."

"Those aren't teaching clothes, Bruce. Those are date clothes."

"I might have a little something planned for later on. And speaking of dates, Sam McGee called while you were hauling trash to the dump."

She winced.

414

"Come on, Cass. He's nice enough. The McGee's are a good family. The two of you would make pretty babies."

"What is it with men?" she asked, raking loose strands of hair, darkened by sweat to the deep red of a merlot, into her ponytail. "I went out with him once and declined every time he's asked since. Surely he's got the message by now."

Bruce lifted an eyebrow. "You gave him hope. He'll think it's possible that you'll say yes again."

"How do I get rid of him? Nicely?"

"It'll take mean. You can do it. I've got the scars to prove it."

"And every one of them was well deserved."

"Or you could start dating somebody else. That's a good way to get the message across."

"Yeah, and there are so many options in Arcadia."

"Tom Kado's one."

Cass groaned. "Don't start."

"The man has a thing for you." He cocked his head to one side. "But, it might be a conflict of interest if you went out with him, right? Since you both work for the police department?"

Do I work for the department anymore? she wondered. "Haven't thought about it," Cass lied. "Besides, his wife died about a year ago. He's in no shape for a relationship."

"Everybody grieves differently," Bruce said. "I don't know why you don't go out more –," he held up a strong hand when Cass tried to interrupt. "And that's your business. But if you're looking for a decent guy, I think Tom Kado might be one."

"Message received. Where's Harry?"

"Upstairs. The almost-ex-wife called and there's an emergency with a client." Her shoulders slumped and Bruce shrugged. "Daddy's not due back from this morning's delivery until tonight, so you get the crowbar and sledgehammer all to yourself. Paradise, if you ask me." Bruce knelt to examine the hole in the kitchen floor revealed when Cass removed the cabinet under the sink. He stuck his hand between the jagged edges and pulled out bits of a mouse nest. "I always wondered why it was so drafty when I was washing dishes."

"I said I'd help." Cass wiped the day's sweat from her brow with a forearm. "I didn't think I'd have to do the whole thing myself."

"It's good experience. Fixing the roof and leveling the porch was hard work. But tearing out a kitchen? That's plain fun. Hey," he continued, plucking his keys from the table, "when you get that one out, start on the cabinet in the corner. Might as well get it all done today."

Cass watched him stride across the tired linoleum floor, boots crunching over the grit and rubble strewn across its surface. The screen door banged shut behind him. Silence, followed by the cranking of a pickup's engine, filled the late afternoon air.

"Fine," she muttered, turning the scanner's volume back up and reaching for the crowbar. "I'll do it myself. But you're not my favorite anymore."

CHAPTER 2

GOOBER JERKED THE RED riding mower's steering wheel and managed to avoid an armadillo trundling across the county road. Scowling, he stomped on the little mower's gas pedal, urging the machine to move faster. Sunset wasn't for another two and a half hours, but the narrow lanes between his small trailer and The Whitehead Store were already crowded with shadow from the massive trees flanking the road. In Goober's world, darkness in any form was bad. Goblins lurked in the dusty gloom beneath the bed; vampires needed the night; and zombies, who could function during the day, vastly preferred terrorizing simple villagers while hiding beneath a cloak of darkness. Goober was a sudden expert on all things monster because, in a moment of insomnia driven weakness, he had flipped on the horror channel last night and watched, trembling, until the wee hours when he fell asleep on his sofa.

The mower's engine whined with the strain, but Goober pulled the tip of his baseball cap down over his forehead and kept his foot on the pedal. He briefly wondered how much gasoline was left in the little machine but pushed the thought away; he'd leave her on the side of the road if he had to. This trip to the store wasn't just for fun. Goober was out of snacks. Although he ate a fairly healthy diet, today's craving for salt and crunch would not be denied. Hence the venture out along Forney County's small, eerie roads in spite of the sun's continuing decline.

Goober rounded Church Bend and looked up to see the wink of a tail light in the distance. A thrill of fear raced through him and he patted the pocket in his overalls where he tucked his folding money. He extracted a battered Timex and saw that it read five twenty-nine – this was cutting it too close. The Whitehead Store closed at five-thirty on the dot. He lifted his heavy work boot and stomped on the accelerator again.

A squirrel dashed onto the road, flicked its tail at the red machine, and darted safely to the other side. So intent was he on reaching the store,

Goober hardly noticed. At last, the gas station's concrete apron came into view and Goober screeched to a stop at the pumps. He jumped from the mower and charged across the tiny parking lot, relief in his veins: the 'open' sign still hung in the door. He pushed inside with a greeting on his lips and reaching for the Frito display when he skidded across the sparkling linoleum. Startled, he looked down see to a trail of amber liquid on the floor. The smell of gas reached his nose and his ire rose. Most people were considerate enough not to trail gasoline when they came inside to pay. Goober always wiped his feet and if he made a mess, he knew good and well how to clean it up.

He looked for Mr. Whitehead and spotted a puff of smoke floating through the open stockroom door in the back of the shop. Goober gazed at that black abyss and in a move that would later surprise himself and everyone else, he squashed the ripple of terror threatening his legs and ran toward that open door instead of away from it.

A FIGURE IN DARK clothes stepped inside and watched the man in overalls dart to the back of the shop. He took in the neat rows of shelves and gleaming refrigeration units. There was no sign of disturbance, no indication that anything sinister had happened here. *Odd*, he thought. *If there was no one to murder, why would the three of them come here?*

He moved to the counter, avoiding the gleaming streak of liquid on the otherwise pristine floor. Again, nothing was out of place. A yellowed newspaper clipping taped beside a crucifix on the wall caught his attention. He leaned closer and read a short story about the store's grand opening in 1979. When his eyes rose to a picture of the ribbon-cutting, an icy wave of shock froze him in place. The unsmiling face staring from the photograph took him back almost twenty-five years, to his father's death when he was nine years old. *His father's death.* It couldn't be true.

He hurried around the counter to study the clipping more closely. The thick shock of dark hair, the chiseled features that were so similar to his own. There was no mistaking the man who held a pair of scissors over an uncut ribbon. He was a ghost, burned to a crisp in 1978. But he wasn't dead. He wasn't dead at all. In fact, he'd given up his life and his only child, for what? To open a gas station in some mosquito-infested backwater in

Texas?

The events of his life and their meaning re-ordered themselves in his mind, and an immense sense of loss and betrayal sliced through him. Tears stung his eyes and he drew a deep breath, tasting a foul smoke. He turned then, gaze coming to rest on the open stockroom door.

———————

A LAYER OF TRANSLUCENT smoke greeted Goober as he dashed into the ransacked stockroom. The sight of toppled shelves and a smear of some dark substance across the floor brought him up short. A creak drew his glance to the murky light filtering through the outside door. He went up on his tiptoes and sidled around the mishmash of food and broken containers. A rancid, stinging smell made his eyes water and a faint popping grew louder as he crossed the stockroom. Goober's empty stomach turned and he pulled a yellow kerchief from his overalls, covered his mouth and nose, and stepped out to a small courtyard.

A concrete patio was open to the evening sky and surrounded by a tall wood fence. The small area was a study in contrasts. The north side was orderly and somewhat peaceful. A hand truck rested against the wall beside neat stacks of wood pallets and flattened cardboard boxes. Garden implements and leggy ladders hung in tidy rows from pegs, and a green water hose was wrapped around a reel. A metal gas can squatted beside a weed trimmer leaning against the wall.

The rest of the area was chaos.

A wheelbarrow lay on its side against the southern portion of the fence, alongside a toppled step ladder. Closer to the middle of the courtyard, a misshapen pile of red plastic smoldered. A sycamore tree grew in one corner, its smooth-barked trunk rising gracefully from a patch of scraggly dirt. Goober whimpered as his vision expanded to take in the scene. Only seven feet or so from the ground, the tree's lowest limb sprung outward at a nearly ninety-degree angle, and from it dangled a zombie, blackened and blazing. Tongues of orange flame danced in a mouth stretched wide in a silent scream and nibbled at the rope around the zombie's neck. The concrete beneath him was scorched and heat rose in shimmering waves from its surface.

Goober danced in a tight circle and fought the savage urge to flee as a debate raged through his brain. Everybody knew that zombies were dangerous. They lived on human flesh. But zombies were undead, which meant that they were alive until they were dead. Goober hated to see any living thing hurt, and if this zombie was alive, it didn't deserve to burn even though he knew he'd have to kill it eventually. He wasn't sure he could save a zombie that was already on fire, but – in another surprising move – he decided to try.

He felt for the spigot, never taking his gaze from the zombie as it swayed ever so slightly on its noose. Goober yanked the hose from its reel and flinched away from the steam that rose when the sputtering stream hit the burning body. Suddenly, the rope around its neck snapped and the zombie hit the ground with a smacking thud. It lay motionless for a moment, then stirred.

Goober released a blood-curdling shriek before dropping the hose and charging into the stockroom. He slammed the door shut and stood trembling, heart in his throat, listening as the zombie staggered to its feet. Goober took a running leap over the gooey mess on the floor and sprinted into the store, where he dove behind the counter and grabbed the phone.

With shaking fingers, he pecked out 911. "Police? This is Goober. We got a burnin' zombie on the loose in The Whitehead Store. Bring the machetes. We gotta cut his head off."

THE MAN RECOILED AT the shrill scream and hid between two rows of shelves. He watched dispassionately as the overall-clad man darted behind the counter and started babbling about zombies. The door to the stockroom was still open and he slipped through it, taking in the toppled shelving and burst food containers. The rancid, smoky scent was stronger here and he sidestepped the mess on the floor to make his way to the outside door. Gently pulling it open, his eyes narrowed as he peered through a small crack and then opened the door more fully.

It seemed the murderous little trio did have a purpose in coming to this remote store.

He inched closer to the form smoldering on the concrete, gaze latching on to a sooty gold ring with a red stone fixed to its dome and then roving the figure more carefully. An unscorched tuft of thick white hair was still attached to the scalp. Although the face was blackened and stretched, its basic structure was still evident: broad forehead, defined cheekbones, angular jaw. Unbidden, his mind recreated the muscular detail that once covered those features.

The scarlet edges of rage crowded his vision and he sucked in a stinking breath, fighting back a scream. Everything he'd believed, all the circumstances of his life – it was a lie. Panic thrummed through his veins and he physically forced himself to study the smoking body, memorizing the horrifying tableau and dipping deep into the well of hate in his soul. His spirit quieted then and the despair morphed inside him, settling into a molten and searing ball of fury.

Without a backward glance, he retreated through the courtyard gate and melted into the woods, dabbing at the sweat beading his upper lip. He trotted at a slow but steady pace toward his car and brought his breathing and thoughts under control.

Until today, he had considered the murderous little cabal his silent partners. Granted, he had no idea why some of the same names had landed on both their kill lists, but between them and the work they had completed so far, the world was a far better place. Since learning their identities several months ago, he had traced them to this slice of redneck paradise and watched, moving with caution to learn the rhythms of their lives. But he hadn't stalked silently; instead, he had poked and prodded into their personal lives to see how fragile they were. If they were made of the right stuff, perhaps he would've approached them, wormed his way into their inner circle. He wanted to understand their motivations and discover who else they had marked for termination. The trio was careful, and that he appreciated. They must've known about this victim for some time, because they hadn't visited this little store since he'd been tracking them.

But any semblance of camaraderie he felt for this odd group of executioners vanished at the sight of their latest victim. In its place sprang the germ of revenge – they had bested him, understanding his own life even better than he had. And from their knowledge, they had taken his father from him. Again.

A hope he hadn't known existed, extinguished before it could form. They were now the enemy.

His mind focused on his new prey with an eerie intensity. He would extract payment from each of them for what they had cost him. Payment in full.

You can find *AVENGERS OF BLOOD* on Amazon.

www.ingramcontent.com/pod-product-compliance
Lightning Source LLC
Chambersburg PA
CBHW020503260626
47156CB00006B/1843